THE VANISHING TRACK

THE
VANISHING
TRACK

A Cole Blackwater Mystery

Stephen Legault

TouchWood
Editions

TouchWood Editions
touchwoodeditions.com

LIBRARY AND ARCHIVES CANADA CATALOGUING IN PUBLICATION
Legault, Stephen, 1971–
The vanishing track / Stephen Legault.

(A Cole Blackwater mystery)
Issued also in electronic formats.
ISBN 978-1-927129-03-6

I. Title. II. Series: Legault, Stephen, 1971– . Cole Blackwater mystery.

PS8623.E46633V36 2012   C813'.6   C2011-907336-6

Editor: Frances Thorsen
Proofreader: Lenore Hietkamp
Design: Pete Kohut
Cover image: Noah Strycker, istockphoto.com
Back cover image: kslyesmith, stck.xchng
Author photo: Dan Anthon

We gratefully acknowledge the financial support for our publishing activities from the Government of Canada through the Canada Book Fund, Canada Council for the Arts, and the province of British Columbia through the British Columbia Arts Council and the Book Publishing Tax Credit.

MIX
Paper from
responsible sources
FSC® C103214

The interior pages of this book have been printed on 100% post-consumer recycled paper, processed chlorine free, and printed with vegetable-based inks.

1 2 3 4 5 16 15 14 13 12

For Jenn
For Rio Bergen and Silas Morgan
For Josh
For the vanished

The Vanishing Track is a work of fiction. While the Downtown Eastside in Vancouver, British Columbia, is a real place, many of the specific localities in this book are fictional, as are the characters and events. Any resemblance to actual places or people or real events is coincidental.

ONE

KILLING THE FIRST ONE HAD not been hard. The *arrangements*—as he had come to think of them—hadn't been particularly onerous. Having to *wait* to kill the first one had been the hard part. Sean Livingstone had never had to wait for anything in his life. Now it was getting to be too easy, too boring. And this was only his third.

The light turned green and Sean crossed Main Street, heading east along Pender toward the row of ramshackle apartments, boarding homes, Chinese laundries, and low-rent hotels. The tumbledown neighborhood seemed to be listing to one side, away from the glistening West End and away from the center of power in Canada's gateway to the Pacific: the City of Vancouver. The boarded-up buildings and garbage-strewn empty lots housed the drunks and crackheads. The area was once known as Skid Row; now it was called the Downtown Eastside.

Sean shouldered his way through the throng of pedestrians, keeping pace with the man in the heavy overcoat in front of him. The street was busy—three o'clock on a Friday afternoon—and that thrilled Sean. He felt a rush of adrenalin as he followed Overcoat Man, trailing just ten feet behind him. If he increased his pace just a little, he could reach out and touch him. Overcoat Man pushed a shopping cart that wobbled with a rickety wheel, clearing a swath between the frenzied shoppers crowding the open-air fruit stands and meat markets in harried Chinatown.

Sean could see that the cart was overflowing with the man's possessions, which were wrapped in a tattered blue plastic tarp and bundled with frayed twine. The cart pitched to the left and Overcoat Man maneuvered awkwardly to prevent the cart from careening into the street. The constant chatter of Chinese voices and the din of traffic pulsed in Sean's ears. The air was electric with the current of life around him.

Sean was attracted to these colliding worlds. All the circumstances of his short life had brought him to this place and this point in history. Sean knew he was there for a singular purpose.

The street grew increasingly crowded, and Sean had to work to keep Overcoat Man in sight. This was more like it, he thought. This was what he needed: a challenge. Sean shouldered his way through a knot of men and women clustered around a fruit stand. He kept just behind Overcoat Man, who reeked like a barn in desperate need of mucking out. Overcoat Man stopped at the corner. Sean stopped, too, and examined the produce in a vendor's stall. Sean shifted his gaze back and forth between Overcoat Man, waiting for the light, and the stall's clerk. A man stepped from the back of a large white panel truck, the carcass of a pig on his shoulder, and passed between Sean and the clerk. Sean slipped an apple and a pear into the pocket of his soiled leather jacket.

The light turned green and Overcoat Man lurched to get his cart moving forward and began to cross the street. Sean felt a brief wave of adrenaline pass through him, and began to follow again.

When Overcoat Man made the other side of the street, he bumped his cart onto the sidewalk, the wheels threatening to wobble off entirely, and turned north. He passed in front of the First Baptist Church, where a line of men and women along the church wall huddled on tattered pieces of cardboard and rotten blankets. Sean had to stay focused. He could only make his special arrangements for one person at a time, and he could only attend to one a week. He pulled the apple from his pocket and took a bite, hanging back now as the street became quieter, watching Overcoat Man push his unsteady cart northward.

The man was heading for Oppenheimer Park, the epicenter of the Downtown Eastside. It was easy for Sean to blend in there: to observe and not be seen. Overcoat Man would have to head back toward Ground Zero before Sean could act, before he could fulfill his *purpose*. Oppenheimer was simply far too public, though the thought of making his arrangements in the open sent a shiver up Sean's spine. Overcoat Man ambled along. Sean had learned over the last month to slow his pace when he was following one of his subjects. When you've got nowhere to go, and no place to be, you're never in much of a hurry to get anywhere. The work he was doing in the Downtown Eastside was having an impact on Sean; he could see the changes.

The first time had been Umbrella Man. The vagrant carried a bag full of umbrellas. During the day Umbrella Man sat on a corner, spread his umbrellas out, and sold them for a dollar. Sean had seen him leave

Ground Zero one morning, his bag of umbrellas over his shoulder, heading west on Hastings for the downtown core. Sean had followed him that day simply for curiosity's sake. He needed to know what the people who lived at Ground Zero did during the day, if his plan was going to work.

At one point during the time Sean was following him, Umbrella Man had appeared lost in a haze of bewilderment, so Sean had shoved him and said, "Get a move on." The man had tripped, his bag of umbrellas falling to the sidewalk. Sean had kept walking, ignoring the cursing of the old man and the scornful gaze of the young woman who actually stopped to help Umbrella Man collect his wares. It had taken the rest of the day for Umbrella Man to make his way back to Ground Zero. While Umbrella Man sat on Burrard Street selling his goods, Sean sat across the street and revised his plans. When Sean had panhandled enough money, he bought a coffee and a bagel in a coffee shop on Davie, then hurried back, his blood racing with anticipation, only to find that Umbrella Man was gone.

Sean desperately searched the streets and found Umbrella Man had moved a block away and was sitting with his back to a building, spreading out his wares again. Sean walked past him, making eye contact. Umbrella Man didn't recognize him. Sean didn't let him out of his sight for the rest of the day.

Over the course of several days, Sean learned Umbrella Man's routine. On rainy days, and after rush hour was over, he would stagger to his feet and make his way northward six blocks to the Burrard Street SkyTrain station. Unless there were transit police in the station, the tramp wouldn't buy a ticket. Sean didn't purchase a ticket, either; he wanted to mimic the old man's routine as closely as possible so his arrangements would be genuine.

Umbrella Man would board the outbound train and ride it all the way on its ponderous loop through New Westminster and Burnaby. He would roam from car to car and pick up umbrellas that passengers had left behind. From time to time he'd get off the train and comb the stations, too. He was an entrepreneur. Sean admired the man for it.

Umbrella Man had been his first.

Overcoat Man walked into the park and sat down beneath recently planted cherry trees. The park was busy with the life of the Downtown Eastside community. Near the row of trees half a dozen men played baseball on a ball diamond using a cracked wooden bat. A man in a wheelchair was the catcher. Behind the ball diamond a cluster of black and Latino men wearing hooded sweatshirts stood on the dusty median next to Dunlevy Avenue.

Sean passed within a few feet of Overcoat Man and made for the new public washrooms and community center that backed onto Jackson. Overcoat Man sat for a few minutes, then lay down in the shade and fell asleep. Sean took off his backpack and sat on a picnic table in front of the community center and watched impatiently. He had to make the arrangements with Overcoat Man during the day, or the effect wouldn't be the same. Sean looked at this watch. It was four o'clock. The day was wasting away. Overcoat Man slept. The baseball game wrapped up. Behind the backstop the group of men milled about. A woman in a red dress squatted on the ground and peed. Several people came and went, buying and selling crack and heroin, the packets and cash passing between hands in swift, practiced motions.

Sean lay down on the table. How long had it been since he had taken an afternoon nap? Fifteen years? He closed his eyes to recall the moment in time when that experience of childhood had vanished.

SUNLIGHT THROUGH THE bedroom window. The sound of birds.

Sean was in the home he had grown up in, on Vancouver's upscale south side. The family housekeeper, Adelaide, had come into his room to find him awake, the bedsheets propped up like a tent with one of his grandmother's ornate canes.

"Sean, you're supposed to be asleep."

"I'm not tired, Adelaide."

"You need to rest."

"I'm not tired."

Sean was driving his Hot Wheels cars in circles around the cane, creating fabulous chases and spectacular accident scenes. Adelaide pulled back the sheet. Sean tried to grab it from her hands but she snatched it away. "You're to be having a nap now, young man."

"I'm not tired!" he shouted.

"Be quiet," she said sharply. "Do you want to wake your mother?"

Sean turned his attention back to his cars.

Adelaide looked at him, her hands on her wide hips. "What am I going to do with you?"

"Go away," he said, not looking up.

"What kind of way is that to talk to your elder?" Sean ignored her. "Your mother is sleeping. She was up all night. You should be sleeping too."

"I'm not tired!" he shouted, his face flushed. Adelaide squatted down next to his bed and grabbed him by the shoulders. "Let go!" he shouted.

"Be quiet, Sean. Be quiet. Your mother isn't well. Please . . ."

Sean wiggled free and ran from the room, into the wide hall that ran the length of the upstairs. Adelaide was close on his heels. She was a large woman, the shape of a pear. Sean headed for his mother's bedroom. He hit the door at a run and shouldered it open.

The room was dark, the curtains drawn. Sean smelled the familiar sweet aroma of his mother, an aroma that in later years he would recognize as sweat and liquor, but which as a child he only associated with her ethereal presence. He could hear her breathing from the massive four-poster canopy bed against the far wall. He stepped into the room, Adelaide behind him. She reached out to take his shoulder, but he slipped from her grasp. Adelaide stopped at the door, and Sean stepped up to the bed and looked at his mother.

He knew that last night she and his father went to a party. They had first come into his playroom to say goodnight. His father, a stout man with broad shoulders and short, prickly hair, had rustled Sean's shaggy mop. His father was wearing a tuxedo. His mother bent to give him a kiss. He could smell the mixture of flowers and alcohol on her. She kissed him softly on his cheek while his eyes stayed glued to the TV. She told him to be good for Adelaide.

Now his mother lay half under the covers, still clothed in last evening's ball gown. Her mascara had run down her face, making parallel black tracks across her cheeks. Her mouth was slightly agape, and Sean could see that a thin trickle of spittle had seeped from her lips onto her pillow. One arm seemed to reach out for him while the other was bent at an awkward angle. He stood next to her bed. He felt nothing at that moment. Not disgust, not sadness, not love. He knew he was *supposed* to feel something, an emotion *other* children might feel. Fear? Sean simply stood and watched his mother breathing heavily in the darkness of her bedroom. Adelaide was beside him now, her hands on his shoulders. He allowed himself to be guided from the room.

"What's wrong with her?" he asked when they were in the hall.

"She's just having a nap," said Adelaide. "So should you, young man."

"I'm not tired," said Sean, quietly.

Adelaide looked down at him. "Okay then, how about a snack?"

Sean nodded and Adelaide led him down the stairs, through the sitting room, and into the kitchen.

"Can I eat in here?"

Adelaide looked at him. "Sure," she said. "But it's our secret, okay?"

She moved about the kitchen, making a peanut butter and honey sandwich and pouring a glass of milk. She served him at the small table by the window that overlooked the side garden. Sean could see Jacob, their gardener, trimming the lawn. He took a bite of the sandwich and drank from the glass of milk. Adelaide sat across from him at the table and regarded him.

Sean looked around the kitchen. "I like eating in here."

"Well, you mustn't tell your mother or father."

"Is this where you and Jacob eat?"

"Sometimes."

"We eat in the dining room."

"I know, dear. Now eat up."

"I like eating in here better."

Adelaide took the plate and glass from him when he was finished and put them in the dishwasher. "Now, Sean," she said, "please go back to your room and play quietly while I prepare dinner. Would you do that for me? And please don't disturb your mother . . ."

Sean nodded and went back up the back stairs and down the long hall, past his mother's room. He had no desire to step back into that space, with its darkness and strange odor that prickled his nose. He went to his bedroom, where he set up his cars and created a huge accident.

SEAN OPENED HIS eyes and started awake, half rising from the picnic table. Overcoat Man was still lying beneath the tree. A wash of adrenaline pounded through his system. He settled back down, feeling his stomach rumble. He'd made some sacrifices in the pursuit of this recently discovered higher calling. Like regular meals and a clean bed.

Sean watched the park for another hour. A group of teenagers made their way onto the ball diamond. These weren't the crack dealers or dope pushers that Sean was accustomed to seeing at Oppenheimer, but a group of clean-cut kids—mostly boys, but a few girls—who had been playing baseball in the park for the last few weeks. Local kids who were part of a formal "reclaim the park" effort, spearheaded by the Business Council and the Vancouver Police. Two uniformed officers stepped from a cruiser across the street. They joined the game, gun belts and all.

It was nearly five o'clock when Overcoat Man woke and sat up under the cherry tree. His face widened in a yawn, then he wiped his nose on the arm of his greasy coat. Sean was about to stand and move closer when the door behind him opened and a young woman walked purposefully across the field to where Overcoat Man was resting. Sean had seen her before—she was a street nurse. She wore blue jeans and a sweatshirt that zipped up the front and a bright orange backpack. She hunched next to Overcoat Man.

Sean watched as the two of them talked. He stood and stretched, then walked back to the community center and leaned against the sun-warmed wall. The woman took out a small bundle from her pack and handed it to Overcoat Man. He looked at it as she spoke to him, slipping it into his tattered pocket. She put an arm on his shoulder and Overcoat Man smiled. She stood and walked to the far side of the park where she knelt by another man sleeping near the playground. Overcoat Man stood and arranged the contents of his cart. Time to get busy, Sean thought.

Umbrella Man had been the first. Dumpster Girl had been his second. She seemed to move through the streets around Ground Zero with satisfying regularity. Sean had seen her there often, and thought at first that she was a whore who used the place to turn tricks. But he never saw her with a john, so he decided that she must rent a room when she could, and sleep on the streets when she couldn't. He followed her one morning when she left Ground Zero early, making her way through the alley behind the landmark red-brick building, stopping to flip open the lids of dumpsters as she went.

She carried a dark brown duffle bag over one shoulder, into which she put various bits of rubbish as she went. Sean stood at the mouth of the alley and watched her, and when she had reached the far end, he quickly made his way through the wet, garbage-reeking gloom to emerge on the street at the far end. He saw her heading for the next alley across the street, and so he crossed through traffic, a taxi's horn blaring at him, and reached the other side in time to see her open the lid to another bin and disappear up to her chest inside. Dumpster Girl couldn't have been much older than he was, Sean guessed, but she looked twice his twenty-four years. She was scrawny, dressed in tight blue jeans and a baggy, blanket-lined jean jacket. Sean watched from the alley as she pulled herself from the dumpster carrying a keyboard, which she tucked into her bag.

With Umbrella Man, he had chosen to make his arrangements during the night when the peddler was sleeping. With Dumpster Girl, he wanted to make the arrangements when she was awake. It would be more challenging. People on the street were wary of one another at night. But Sean thought he had an ace in the hole with Dumpster Girl.

It took him three days before he could play that card. For three days he followed Dumpster Girl, learning her habits. Every morning around eleven she made her way to Carrall Street where she panhandled for spare change, and when she had enough, she would go into a small café and buy lunch. It seemed to Sean that it was the only meal she ate all day. On the third day of observation, he approached her just after she had settled in to panhandle.

"Hi," he said, crouching down beside her. "How's it going?"

"I'm just getting started," she said, jingling the change, holding a Styrofoam cup out to a passerby.

Sean smiled. "I mean in general. How are you keeping?"

"I'm pretty good," Dumpster Girl said.

"Good haul today?" he asked, nodding toward the bag.

"Why?"

Sean held up his hands in a defensive mode. "Just curious."

"You a cop?"

"Do I look like a cop?"

She looked him up and down. "Naw, too skinny for a cop. What do you want?"

"Just to be of help is all."

She regarded him coolly. He could see that one of her eyes didn't track with the other.

"You from the Community Advocacy group?"

"I'm new there. My name is Sean." He held out his hand.

She looked at it. His nails were dirty, and he had a cut on his thumb, but otherwise his hands were clean. She reached over and shook it. Her grip was strong, her hands dark with the stains of her trade.

"I'm Peaches." She smiled. "That's what they call me, anyway." She held the cup out to someone who dropped a nickel in it. "What do you want with me?"

"Look," he said, "I'm new, so you tell me."

She looked into her cup. Fifty-five cents so far. She jingled the coins. "You could buy me lunch."

Sean looked at her cup. "Yeah, you don't seem to be doing so well."

"You're cramping my style," she said.

They ate lunch at the front counter of the Esquire Grill, looking out onto Hastings Street. She had soup and a sandwich and coffee. Sean just ordered coffee.

"Tell me about yourself," he said.

She took a bite of her sandwich and began to talk, then paused and began again. "What do you want to know?"

"Anything. Where are you from?"

"Saskatchewan."

"Wow, you're a long way from home," said Sean, raising his eyebrows.

"Yeah. I've been on my own since I was sixteen."

"Run off?"

"Sorta. My mom was a drunk. Dad was never around. Better on the streets than at home. I tried Saskatoon for a year, but fuck was it cold there. I got enough for a bus ticket and came here."

"Can I ask you a personal question, Peaches?"

She shrugged her shoulders.

"Do you hook at all?"

She sipped her coffee. "I did a little," she said, looking around her. "You know, when I first got here. But I got beat up pretty good by my bastard pimp. I got into a shelter after that."

"Did he come after you?"

"Yeah, once. After I left. Threatened to kill me. But I got out of the area for a little while. Stayed over in the West End for a few months and he seemed to forget about me."

"You don't see him around no more?"

She shook her head as she finished her sandwich.

"So listen, Peaches. Where do you stay?"

"I got places," she said, eyeing him suspiciously.

"Inside?"

"Some."

"Like where?"

"I go to the women's shelter sometimes. But I hate that place. Fucking bitches always beating each other up over stupid shit. And I can't sleep 'cause of all the fucking noise, you know what I mean?" Sean nodded sympathetically. "I stay at some of the hotels when I got the money. I sell stuff I find. Good stuff. People throw it away, I find it, clean it up. I can get some good money for some of the shit I find."

"Really?"

"Oh yeah, like last week I got five bucks for a computer monitor. Still worked really good. And today I found a keyboard. I think I can get a couple bucks for that. I got a couple of places that leave things for me, too, you know, like food and clothing."

"People looking out for you. That's good," said Sean.

"Some. Most don't give a shit. They walk by all dressed nice, and I can tell they don't give a shit about me."

"It's like they look and don't even see a person . . ."

"That's it exactly," said Peaches, nodding, looking at him now with real interest.

"I know."

"How could you know?" she said, her smile fading.

"I know. I work now, you know, for the Community Advocacy group, but I've been on the street too," he said.

She nodded.

"So I'd like to check in on you from time to time, Peaches. Would that be okay?"

"Okay," she said.

"Where can I find you?"

"I'm usually in Carrall Street most days around lunch," she said.

"I want to look in at night too, Peaches. It's a dangerous time to be on the street. Where do you usually sleep?"

She looked at him and he could tell that she was deciding if he was trustworthy. Finally, she said, "There's an alley off Pender, just around the corner. There's a park there, with a fence. There's a spot not too many others go to."

"I know it," said Sean. "Behind the Lucky Strike."

"That's it. Look, don't tell anybody about it."

"I won't. It's our secret."

"Okay. Well," she said, standing up, "thanks for the food."

"No problem. It was my pleasure," he said with a broad smile.

"You're nice," she said. "You really seem to care. Thanks."

"I do care," he said, standing and extending his hand. She took it.

"See you around," she said, hauling her bag out the door.

"See you."

Then he went to the bathroom and washed his hands for two full minutes.

And he *had* seen her again, two nights later, when he came to make the arrangements.

"Peaches," he said into the darkness. He was squatted down in the alley, next to the small park adjacent to the Lucky Strike Hotel: Ground Zero.

"Peaches," he said again.

She woke slowly. She had her duffle bag next to her, and was sleeping on a large sheet of rain-darkened cardboard. She had several tattered woolen blankets over her, and a frayed piece of blue tarp for protection against the light rain that fell.

"Peaches, it's Sean."

"What time is it?"

"Three AM."

"What do you want?"

"I've come to check on you."

"I'm fine."

"It's my job, you remember?"

"I remember. Now let me sleep."

"I need you to wake up so I can ask you a few questions."

"Find me in the morning."

He reached out and nudged her.

"Hey, fuck off, okay?" she said drowsily.

He nudged her again, a little harder. She turned over, her eyes open. "What the fuck is wrong with you? The other one never does that."

"The street nurse?" he asked.

"Yeah. With the health people."

"I'm not a nurse, Peaches."

"What the fuck do you want that can't wait till morning?"

He reached into his backpack, rummaging for something, his face opaque, and said, "We need to make some arrangements to get you off the street, Peaches."

IT WAS A learning experience. Each day was a new lesson. How to move like them. How to abandon any sense of time, as they did. Sean Livingstone was growing.

Overcoat Man was on the move, heading south away from Oppenheimer Park. Sean felt in the pit of his stomach that now was the time. Sean followed him for ten minutes as Overcoat Man maneuvered through the Downtown Eastside. When Overcoat Man stopped to wait for the light, Sean quickened his pace a little to catch up with him. They were across the street from a park with a ball diamond with bleachers.

"Give you a hand?" he asked, stepping up beside him with a wide, affable smile.

"Don't need one," said Overcoat Man.

"I'm heading across anyway. Let me make sure you get all your stuff over in one piece."

"Don't touch my stuff," said Overcoat Man.

"I won't, friend. It's okay, I'm from the Community Advocacy Society."

"No you ain't."

"I'm new."

"I got a visit from the lady already. I don't need anything."

Traffic had thinned and Overcoat Man started to cross. Sean kept up with him. Several cars blew their horns at them and Sean just waved and smiled. "Made it," he said good-naturedly when they reached the far side. "Can I get you anything?"

"Got everything I need," said Overcoat Man, pushing his cart toward the gate for the park.

"You staying here tonight?"

"None of your business."

"I could bring you a blanket."

"Don't need one. Got a sleeping bag in here."

Sean felt his pulse quicken. This was harder than he had expected. "Okay, well," he finally said. "I guess I'll be seeing you."

Sean turned to go, then looked back to watch Overcoat Man make his way toward the set of bleachers that flanked the park's ball diamond. The park was vacant except for a man throwing a ball for a dog at the far side. After the man left with his dog, Overcoat Man set himself up under the bleachers, preparing for the possibility of rain. He looked as though he was eating something from a tin can. Sean walked directly up to him.

"I told you I don't need anything," he said when Sean approached.

"Look, friend," said Sean, hands wide at his sides. "I've been told to give you a hand. My boss at the Society will be pissed if I don't report back that I gave you the money for food that I was supposed to."

"Since when did the Community Society start handing out money?"

"We got a new donor. Money for meals." Sean hunched down in front of the man and slipped his backpack off. He could smell the sour stench of dog food in the enclosed space beneath the bleachers.

Overcoat Man seemed to pause in his hostility a moment, waiting to see what Sean would produce from inside his bag. "I got it right here," said Sean. He made a show of rummaging in his bag. He pulled on the white smock coat that he had liberated from a butcher shop, its arms and chest dotted with dark red splotches.

"What the fuck is that for?" the man asked. Sean didn't answer him.

From the bottom of the bag he drew a foot-and-a-half-long iron tool called a come-along. Often found at logging sites, the hand winch helped pry vehicles from the mud or trees from entanglement. This one wasn't functional, though; it was decorative. Nickel plated, it was hard and heavy. The hooks on both ends had been broken off, so that only the winch and handle remained. It weighed about nine pounds in Sean's hand.

"What the fuck you got there?" Overcoat Man said, pushing himself back, dropping the can of dog food.

Sean smiled, lifting the heavy tool, then swung it at Overcoat Man's head. The blow caught him on the left side of his face, crushing bone and splitting the skin between his left eye and his mouth. A wet spray of blood splattered across the underside of the bleachers. Sean struck the man again as he fell, connecting with the top of his skull. The gratification was akin to sexual release. Overcoat Man lay on his side, his eyes still open with the amazement of his final moment.

"We got to get you off the street, partner," said Sean, his hand still wrapped around the heavy tool.

TWO

COLE BLACKWATER COULD SMELL HORSES. He could smell the sticky sweet aroma of their bodies pressed together in the blackness of the stables beneath the barn. He could smell hay; for Cole that was the scent of green spring afternoons when the sun burnt down on the Porcupine Hills that surrounded his childhood home.

"Open your eyes, goddamnit," said a voice, shattering the nostalgic darkness. Cole shook his head, and beads of sweat sprayed from his face onto the canvas mat below his feet.

"Goddamnit, boy, when I say open your eyes, I mean it." The glove connected with Cole's nose and he felt his head snap backward, but he couldn't fall. He was suspended above the canvas mat, dangling there like meat on a hook.

"That's all you ever were to me, boy. That's all you'll ever be: a fucking punching bag. You are worthless." Cole braced himself for the next blow. It caught him in the chin and snapped his head back, a spray of blood coming from a cut that the strike reopened.

"Look at me, boy," and this time Cole opened his eyes. The sweat and blood stung them. He blinked to try and focus on the barn.

The shape of his father swayed before him. "You think you're *so* great. You're nothing but a worthless drunk who can't take care of his own daughter, who fucks up everything he touches!"

"Just like you," spat Cole.

"Why don't you just get it over with?" asked Henry Blackwater, pacing around Cole like a caged animal, his face shadowed in the faint light seeping through the boards of the barn. "Why don't you just do it?"

"You first," said Cole, clenching his teeth.

"Oh, I will. I will. But I'm taking you with me this time, son. You're coming with me." His father steadied Cole's swinging body. "Got to work on my combinations," the old man slurred. Cole closed his eyes.

Soon it would be over. He waited for the punches to stop, eyes pressed shut.

What happened next always surprised Cole. No matter how hard he tried to keep his eyes closed, he could not help but watch. His father took the shotgun leaning against the ropes of the boxing ring and turned it so the barrel was under his chin. Then he took up a branding iron and put the crook of it in the trigger guard.

Cole shouted, "Wait—!" But his father pulled the trigger.

It was the blast that always woke him.

Cole's eyes snapped open and he felt his body tremble, his hands gripping the damp sheets. It was five o'clock. His ears rang from the final deafening sound of his nightmare.

It was a Sunday. He knew from experience there would be no return to sleep, so he headed for the shower in the faint light of dawn. Sarah was asleep in her tiny room next to the kitchen. At ten years of age, she was all bright smiles and sunny days. He longed to keep it that way. Sarah had witnessed the collapse of her parents' marriage thanks to Cole's philandering ways. She was only four when Cole had been outed in the worst-kept secret in the nation's capital—his affair with Nancy Webber, the *Globe and Mail's* star parliamentary correspondent. When Jennifer Polson kicked him out of the house they had lived in together, it was almost a relief. Then she announced that she was leaving Ottawa to move to Vancouver, and was taking Sarah with her. Cole left Ottawa and drove west, following his daughter. He faltered in Alberta and visited the place he hadn't set foot on for nearly twenty years: the Blackwater Ranch, tucked into the Porcupine Hills, two hours south of Calgary. And there, bore witness to the vicious end of a man who was not just his father but his tormentor. His nightmares relived the incident.

That was four and a half years ago, thought Cole, standing in the shower, his left hand pressed against the wall, his right hand limp at his side, the hot water pulsing on the back of his neck. He thought he had buried that tragedy. But then, a year and a half ago, Cole had gone back to Alberta in a desperate attempt to help save the Cardinal Divide, and the unearthing began.

The water began to run cold, and Cole realized he'd drained the tank. He turned it off and stepped from the shower. He dressed quickly, then padded barefoot to the kitchen to brew the morning coffee.

Cole took up the weekend edition of the *Vancouver Sun*. His tiny

Eastside apartment offered one large living room–kitchen area that he had tastefully furnished with ware from the local thrift store. Pushing aside some files and books on his tattered couch, Cole sat down and leafed through the paper, sipping his coffee.

On page three he found a story by Nancy Webber with the headline, "City Hall and Homelessness." He flipped the page.

Nancy had moved to Vancouver from Edmonton in June. After the debacle in the Broughton Archipelago last spring, she had accepted a position as one of the paper's political reporters. She could pretty much write her own ticket, she had told Cole, after winning a National Newspaper Award for the series she produced on the murder of Mike Barnes in Oracle, Alberta. She had chosen Vancouver, she said, because it was a bigger market, and because it *wasn't* Edmonton, with its biting winters complete with freezing rain and ice fog. And though she hadn't said so, she had been none too subtle in letting it be known that her choice of Lotusland had more than a little to do with one Cole Blackwater.

Cole sipped his coffee. He didn't want to think about Nancy Webber that morning. Since she had moved to Vancouver late in the spring, Cole had seen her only infrequently. In July, several months after the tragedy in Port Lostcoast, Cole, Nancy, Denman, and Sarah had returned for a few days on Grace Ravenwing's boat, *Inlet Dancer*, celebrating the life of their lost friend and Grace's father, Archie.

The nightmares had begun in August, and Cole found that Nancy always seemed to be on his mind when he woke from them. He wanted to believe that this was simply because she was always on his mind, but he couldn't help but associate her role in the unearthing of his past with his reliving of it every few nights.

Nancy's professional life was now converging with his once again. Nancy had taken to the story of homelessness in Vancouver's Downtown Eastside like a feisty dog to a piece of meat. In the few months that she had been reporting on the politics of homelessness in Vancouver, many at City Hall had come to fear her, and advocates for the homeless to celebrate her. She could be just as hard on the advocates, though, pigeon-holing the more radical elements of the movement, such as the End Poverty Now Coalition, as zealots and anarchists.

Cole had been helping his best friend, Denman Scott, and his street-smart law firm, Priority Legal, figure out ways to leverage decision makers to solve the challenge of homelessness. It had been the first time in his four and a half years as a strategy consultant that Cole could actually donate some of his time. Despite setbacks in the spring, when he almost entirely ignored several high-paying clients due to his entanglement in the fish-farming problems in the Broughton Archipelago, Cole had steady work advising several of the city's growing ethically-based businesses. When Cole noticed that his friend was in need of some strategic advice on dealing with City Hall and the provincial Minister for Housing, Cole was glad to offer his professional assistance.

Cole stood and stretched, wincing. He pressed the ribs on the right side of his body, as if his fingertips could find and finish healing the cracks left by a gang of thugs who had jumped him in Port Lostcoast last spring and nearly beaten him to death. The cracked ribs had kept Cole out of the boxing ring since then. Boxing had been a good way to get back in shape, but being in the ring hadn't done much for Cole's temper. He thought about what Denman, an aikido master, had said to him after they had gotten back from Port Lostcoast.

THEY HAD BEEN sitting in Oppenheimer Park in late July of that year. They had just returned from the Broughton Archipelago.

"Why are we sitting here?" Cole had said, his back hunched, his eyes narrow, watching suspiciously as the derelicts moved about the park, pushing shopping carts. He eyed the wrapping from several syringes and wondered where the needles were.

"You want to help me with the homeless problem, right?" asked Denman, his legs crossed at the ankle, his brown hands folded together Buddha-style in his lap.

"Yeah, but . . ."

"But nothing," the lawyer said with conviction. "You can't help fight homelessness if you don't think of the problem from the perspective of these people here. Part of the reason why homelessness is so prevalent in our society is that we don't *see* these people," he said, motioning to the clusters of men and women around the park. "They are objects to us. Not living, breathing, loving human beings."

"You've been hanging around the Dalai Lama again, haven't you?" Cole quipped.

"Maybe," said Denman, looking at Cole sideways from under his flat cap. "But the truth of the matter is that everybody here has a story to tell. Every one of these people has a reason for being here, now, today. You wouldn't believe the stories I've heard."

"I bet some of them are even true." Cole started to laugh, then held his side.

Denman nodded. "Everybody has their own take on what reality is." He looked at his friend. "Speaking of reality, ribs still bugging you?"

"If you could call having a knife stuck into your side every time you laugh, breathe hard, or try to sleep on your side bugging . . ."

"I've got just the thing."

"You're not going to try and align my chakras again, are you?"

"I've given up on that," said Denman.

"What now, then?"

"Follow me."

The two men stood and walked across the park, heading for Cordova. They walked slowly, Cole moving stiffly.

"You had a doc look at that?"

"Oh yeah, but not much they can do for cracked ribs."

"You'd look good in a body cast."

Cole suppressed a laugh. "Wouldn't help," he said.

"Make you easier to wheel around. We could just put you on a dolly. What about a Chinese doctor?"

"Yeah, I thought about that."

"Thinking about it help much?"

"Look, Denny. I'm from Alberta, okay? We don't lie around with needles in us if we can at all avoid it."

"It would help."

"So would a good stiff drink."

"How's that working for you?"

"Not so good, Dr. Phil," said Cole.

They found their way to East Pender and walked west.

"Where are you taking me?" asked Cole.

"Live in the mystery, brother Blackwater."

They walked another two blocks and stopped. Cole found himself in front of a small area of worn grass. It was nearly noon, and the spring sun felt good after a week of rain. They stood on the edge of the green, which was little more than an empty lot surrounded by a chain-link fence. They regarded the ancient building that rose beyond it.

"Did I read in one of Nancy's articles that the Lucky Strike is on the chopping block?"

"You read right," replied Denman. "The Lucky Strike is where the fight over the future of single-room occupancy facilities, or SROs, in this city hits the road. There is a tug-of-war happening right now between the west side of the city and the east. The west has all the money, all the power, all the glitz and glamor and political and media savvy. The east has the drugs, the pimps and hookers, the poverty, and the homelessness."

"Sounds like a fair fight," said Cole.

"But the west side is running out of room. The east is starting to look pretty good to the developers. Someone wants to tear this hundred-year-old landmark down and build a twenty-five-story condo and shopping mall. So that," said Denman, pointing to the Lucky Strike building, "is where the fight will be won or lost."

Cole turned his head sideways as he looked at the building.

"Thanks for showing me this, Denny."

"No problem. There is talk of some low-income housing in it too," said Denman, "to be fair."

"So you're showing me this because . . . ?" asked Cole.

"Because it's not yet noon."

Cole flipped open his cell phone. "It is now," he said.

"Patience, grasshopper."

They stood at the edge of the park, and before long a small group of people had gathered, coming from all directions of Chinatown. In a few minutes twenty or so people were clustered at the center of the park. They formed loose rows and began to move together, as waves would on the sea. Their arms flowed like the wind that whisked over the water, their bodies gently turning and twisting, bowing and bending in rhythmic form.

"That's really something," said Cole.

"It's called tai chi."

"Looks a lot like dancing."

"Same idea. This is dancing with the flow of energy all around you."

"No disrespect, Denny, but why are you showing me this?"

"You can't box anymore. At least not right now, can you?"

"It's going to be at least six months."

"Time to exercise something else then," said Denman, reaching over and tapping Cole on the chest, above his heart.

THREE

JULIET ROSE WOKE ON MONDAY morning haunted by the same thoughts she had fallen asleep with. She stepped out of bed and padded from her bedroom to the bathroom she shared with Becky, her only roommate in the ancient Eastside home.

She had been so lucky to find this place, a gem in the Grandview Woods area of the city. Just off Commercial Drive—"the Drive," as Vancouverites called it—the home was among the oldest in the district. It had once belonged to a lumber baron, who, after Pearl Harbor, dug an air raid shelter beneath the home's basement. In the sixties, he converted the refuge into a nuclear fallout shelter. The new owner had closed the shelter off when he converted the home into suites. Juliet had never been down the long, narrow stairs that led from the home's tiny backyard to the shelter, two levels below the old Victorian house.

Juliet loved the old home not just for its character but because it was close enough that she could walk to work in the Downtown Eastside and still be just far enough away that she didn't have to bring her work home with her. She had one rule: no work at home. She almost always adhered to it. It was what allowed her to continue working for the last eight years without burning out. She went downstairs and as she measured coffee into the steel stovetop espresso maker, she had to admit that her work *had* followed her home, if not physically, this time, then at least emotionally.

She cut a bagel and slipped it into the toaster and found some dill cream cheese in the fridge that didn't appear to have gone off yet. The twin aromas of coffee brewing and the bagel toasting helped take her mind off the disturbing thoughts, but when she flipped on the radio to listen to the 7:00 AM news, she was brought back abruptly.

Vancouver Mayor Don West says there is no additional money for emergency shelter beds this fall, and that has advocates for the homeless up in arms. When asked to comment, Beatta Nowak of the Downtown Eastside Community Advocacy Society said, "What Mayor West and the provincial government don't understand is that we can spend money on opening more emergency shelter beds to ensure people have a safe, dry place to sleep, or we can spend thousands of dollars a day treating them for pneumonia after they fall ill while sleeping in doorways. It's a choice the city and the province have to make."

But Mayor West says that the City is doing all it can until council approves a broad-scale plan to address homelessness, poverty, and the deteriorating relationship between law enforcement and the homeless in the Downtown Eastside: "We've got to stop our piecemeal approach to these problems. You know, it's all one big problem, and that's why I'm working with other councilors to try and address this problem."

Juliet's bagel popped and she stared at it for a moment before she spread the cream cheese across it. She poured coffee and sat down, blowing the steam from the top of the mug.

Almost every single day Juliet thanked heaven that she worked for the Health Authority and not the City of Vancouver. Left to their own devices, the mayor and his hard-right-leaning council would study the problem, but very little would be accomplished.

But that didn't keep her awake. What did was her suspicion that two people she knew well had disappeared.

Bobbie had gone missing almost three weeks ago. Bobbie had well-defined habits, spending his nights in a single room in a low-rent hotel called the Lucky Strike. When he didn't have enough money to rent a room, Bobbie slept rough, choosing one of the area's parks to sleep in rather than doorways or alleys. Most mornings he headed west, into the downtown area or the West End, where he sold umbrellas that he found on the street or discovered abandoned on the SkyTrain. Juliet had known Bobbie for the better part of three years, and in that time, he had never been absent from his routine for more than a few days. Now she hadn't seen him in almost three weeks.

The second missing person was Peaches. Juliet had known Peaches since the woman's first week in the Downtown Eastside six and a half years ago. Peaches had shown up on one of the area's prowls, fresh off a Greyhound bus from Saskatchewan. Peaches started off on the wrong foot in Vancouver, falling in with a notoriously rough pimp, known as Johnnie "Hangover" because of his habit of beating the daylights out of his girls when he was hungover. When Juliet had met Peaches, she was black and blue and huddled under a blanket on a street corner across the street from the Carnegie Centre.

After only forty-eight hours in Vancouver, she'd been raped by a john, then beaten senseless by Hangover when she showed up without the money for the trick. Juliet had treated the cuts on her face, given her a giant box of condoms, and found her a room at the women's shelter. Over the next few months, there would be many encounters between Peaches and Juliet. More stitches, a pregnancy, HIV tests, searches for housing, calls to the police to file charges against Hangover, and calls to crack down on abusive johns. Peaches' second abortion in six months was the clincher, and Juliet was able to secure a bed for her at the Women's Hospital Detox Centre where Peaches was put on a thirty-day program.

Juliet had personally overseen Peaches' release from detox to ensure she didn't fall prey to a common problem among addicts: the post-detox rush. Dry and clean, addicts would emerge from detox and immediately seek out their drug of choice—crack, heroine, speed, or crystal meth—and dope up again. The rush of shooting up or smoking crack after having been clean for a month was often too powerful an urge to resist. That was the first time Juliet had broken the cardinal rule of street nursing: do not bring your work home with you. Her roommate at the time had been suspicious when Juliet told her that Peaches was her cousin. Peaches' stay lasted for three weeks, until Juliet found her a room at the Lucky Strike Hotel. Peaches had lived there, on and off, for more than six years now. Juliet saw Peaches nearly every day, but now the last time was two weeks ago.

Juliet contemplated the possibility that after six years of being clean, Peaches had succumbed to the ever-present temptation of a fix, and over-dosed. She had been searching for the young woman everywhere, to no avail.

She finished her breakfast and went back upstairs to dress for work. She pulled on faded jeans, long-sleeved shirt, and gray zippered sweatshirt. Eight years ago, when she had first taken the job as street nurse, she had dressed more like a nurse. She quickly learned that blending in with her clients' world was an important element in being able to approach them. Juliet donned her faded windbreaker and picked up her orange backpack, bought at the Army & Navy store on Hastings, and headed out the door.

The morning was bright but cool, September having settled into the Lower Mainland, eclipsing what had been one of the hottest summers on record. Since Peaches had gone missing, Juliet had been varying her route to work each morning, hoping to find her in a different part of town. It was nine o'clock before she reached the clinic at the Carnegie Centre. In daylight, the Carnegie Centre retained much of the magnificence it had possessed when it was built in 1903, when steel magnate Andrew Carnegie donated funds to build Vancouver's first public library. At the time, City Hall was located right next door, and the corner of Hastings and Main was the geographic center of the city. The area had been surrounded by multi-cultural neighborhoods: Little Japan to the north, Chinatown to the south, and to the east, rich ethnic blends of Italian, French, Spanish, and half a dozen other nationalities.

Now the Carnegie Centre was altogether a different place, Juliet thought, as she climbed the front steps and entered the historic building. For those unfamiliar with the face of Vancouver's Downtown Eastside, the hundreds of people milling around the Carnegie Centre each night could be intimidating, even frightening. Drug use, drug deals, and acts of violence in plain sight were not uncommon. But most of the people who found their way to the corner of Hastings and Main each night were there seeking community. The Carnegie Centre was often called the living room for the Downtown Eastside, and more than four hundred volunteers helped provide its services: a public reading room, weight room, art gallery, and kitchen serving three hot meals a day.

Juliet greeted people as she threaded her way to her tiny, cramped office at the back of the building. She poured a cup of coffee in the small staff lunchroom, then poked her head into the director's office.

"Morning, Debbie," she said. The director of the Centre was a woman in her late fifties who looked as though she was seventy. Once on the street herself, she had beaten an addiction to alcohol and cocaine twenty-five years ago, and begun a career in social work. Now she was back on the streets helping others get clean.

"Heyya, kiddo," said Debbie French, then coughed. "What's going on this morning?"

"I'm heading back to Oppenheimer for most of the day. There's a new batch of kids I've been seeing around. I need to make contact with them, get them into the clinic for an HIV test." Debbie was already looking back at her computer screen, her shoulders hunched forward, her gray hair falling in ribbons across her cheeks.

"And then I'm heading over to Priority Legal at lunch today. I've got a few questions from clients about their legal rights that I can't answer . . ."

Debbie turned her head from her computer and looked at Juliet.

Juliet continued, "So I thought I'd put them to Denman Scott and see if he could give me an answer."

"You know how City Hall feels about Priority Legal," said Debbie, sitting back in her chair and pulling her gray cardigan sweater across her chest.

"I do."

"Denman sure gets under the mayor's skin. And the chief constable's. And our local lad Andrews'."

"John Andrews needs a good swift kick in the butt," said Juliet, crossing her arms. "He's treating the Downtown Eastside like a rung in his own personal career ladder. He's heading for the chief constable's office, and District 2 is just another 'challenge' that he has to 'deal with' on his way to the top. Since he's taken over, harassment charges against the Vancouver Police Department have gone up twenty-five per cent in this neighborhood!"

Debbie had turned back and was tapping on her keyboard. Juliet figured it was time to hit the streets. "Anyway," she said, "I'll be there at lunch."

"Alright, hon. You be careful out there," Debbie said, without looking at Juliet.

"You too," said Juliet, smiling.

THE GEOGRAPHY OF a place fascinated Juliet, and as she ran down the steps to the corner of Hastings and Main, she felt relieved to be outside again. The western-most part of the Downtown Eastside was Gastown, historically the city's center of industry. According to the city's interpretation of its history, the turning point came for the area in 1958 when streetcars stopped running to the Carrall Street hub. The subsequent loss of pedestrian traffic, along with the rise in housing prices elsewhere that forced low-income people into the area, was the harbinger of doom for the Eastside.

The community had in many ways thrived with renewed diversity as the Strathcona, Oppenheimer, and Chinatown areas swelled with blue-collar workers looking for affordable accommodation. Post-war housing prices surged in newer, trendier parts of the city. To Juliet's way of thinking, though, three things led to the Downtown Eastside becoming the troubled neighborhood it was today: in the 1970s, the loss of funding for provincial psychiatric patients who were released into the community; in the 1980s, the rise of cocaine; and the crime spree that accompanied it.

Juliet reached the new Community Outreach Centre at Oppenheimer Park just before ten. Already the park was buzzing with activity. She spotted a few of the young people she was looking for sitting on the grass. They had never met her, but her reputation preceded her.

"You checking to see if we're junkies?" one of the young men asked. He was wearing a sweat-stained ball cap on his head covered by a dark brown hoodie.

Juliet crouched down so she was at eye level. "Just here to say hi," she replied, smiling.

She chatted with the kids for another five or ten minutes, assessing health and addictions, handing out condoms, and making sure they all knew about the safe injection site. By noon she had talked with about thirty people around Oppenheimer, and it was time to head to Priority Legal's office up the street. She walked to the two-story building with no street sign and nothing to indicate the goings-on inside. A man slept in the doorway of the office, his face pressed into his folded arms, his knees drawn up to his chest.

Juliet knelt down in front of him and quietly said, "It's Juliet. I'm a street nurse. I'm just checking to make sure you're okay."

The man lifted his head from his folded arms and opened his eyes.

"How you doing today?" Juliet asked.

TEN MINUTES LATER she and Denman Scott were walking west on Cordova.

"I met Ernie," she said.

"Yeah, he likes our place. Figured out that nobody's going to bug him in front of *our* building."

"He's HIV positive."

"I know. We've got him into treatment a couple of times. He's also schizophrenic. He's had a tough time remembering when he needs to be at the hospital, or even how to get there." Denman was wearing his trademark flat cap over his bald head, his tight, compact body in a jean jacket, his hands buried into the pockets of his brown canvas pants. He wore scuffed black Doc Martin dress shoes, and Juliet had to walk fast to keep up with him.

He continued, "We need more community-supported housing. We need about a thousand units of it. Maybe two thousand, to be on the safe side."

"The City is looking at a few places for that right now."

"The City," said Denman, turning to smile at Juliet, "is always *looking* . . ."

Juliet faced straight ahead as they crossed the street. "Don't get me wrong, Denny, I'm not an apologist for them. Remember, I work for the Health Authority. They do seem to be always *just* looking. There seems to be support from the public, though."

"Of course the public wants to solve it. That's because the yuppies living at Denman and Davie have junkies in their doorways now too. The problem is much bigger than the Downtown Eastside. It's spilling out of Skid Row and onto people's manicured front lawns. People are afraid to let their kids play in the parks because of needles, or they're worried about drug deals at the local shopping mall. It's the whole Lower Mainland."

Juliet asked, "Where are we going?"

"Place in Chinatown I know. Good noodles. You up for it?"

"I'm up for anything," but she didn't sound like it, and Denman looked at her.

They sat at a table near the back of the restaurant, Juliet the only white person in a noisy room filled with the lunchtime crowd. Denman liked the Chinatown atmosphere since it reminded him of his roots. Sipping green tea, they continued their conversation.

"I think the gentrification of the Downtown Eastside is making our problem the region's problem. Look at the number of low-rent hotels that we've lost in the last five years to condo projects. It's like . . ." Denman thought for a moment. "Five hundred rooms and counting. These places were dives. Real rat-infested fire traps, but they beat the street. We need to build three thousand housing units just to meet current demand."

Their lunches arrived: thick soba noodles and vegetables in a dark, steaming broth. They both picked up their chopsticks.

"That's just current demand," said Juliet, lifting noodles to her lips.

"The Eastside is going to look like a shorter version of the West End by the time Mayor West's first term is over," said Denman. "People on the streets, who find a temporary shelter in places like the Gaslight, the American, or the Cobalt hotels, will have nowhere to go. We're in for an epidemic." Denman pushed some noodles into his mouth and wiped his lips with a paper napkin. He took a sip of tea. "I'm sorry to be ranting at you," he said, looking down at his food. "It's just that we're getting pretty frustrated right now."

"It's okay," Juliet said, touching his hand. He looked up at her. "It's not a rant. It's just the facts."

"Just the facts, *Ma'am*," he quipped. He sat back in his chair, tea in hand. "You sounded worried on the phone, Juliet. Surely you didn't want to have lunch just to hear me fume."

"Does a girl need a reason?"

"No. But my guess is that there is one."

They finished their lunch and paid on their way out. "Let's walk," Juliet smiled. "I'll tell you about my . . . thing."

Chinatown was busy with afternoon shoppers, the sun warming the air so that Juliet took off her sweatshirt.

"What is it that's troubling you?" Denman asked.

"You're going to think I'm being silly. Hysterical."

"Try me."

"I really think it's nothing. It seems stupid now." Denman stopped. They stood on the corner of Keefer and Taylor. The SkyTrain rounded the bend from the Main Street station, groaning toward the Stadium stop, its wheels squealing. Traffic on the Dunsmuir span droned in their ears.

He looked up at the Lucky Strike Hotel.

"You know that one's on the block, too, eh?"

Juliet absently regarded the landmark hotel, its ashen façade dreary in the September sunlight. "Denman, I think something is happening to the people in this neighborhood. I think people are disappearing."

FOUR

SEAN LIVINGSTONE WAS VERY HUNGRY. It was Monday and he was standing in a line waiting to buy lunch with two dollars in his pocket. Lunch at the Carnegie Centre cost a buck seventy-five. Sean had learned that the line wasn't as long as the free soup kitchens around the city, and the food was much better. He was always hungry after eating the free food at the Salvation Army and the other shelters. One of the hookers who worked the low track had told him about the meals at the Carnegie, and he had started eating there when he could panhandle enough coin. The room was warm, and he couldn't escape the body odor rising from the man in front of him. Sean kept blowing his nose on paper napkins, trying to clear the stench. He felt a wave of revulsion surge through his body, and he looked for an exit, thinking that maybe he'd just step out onto the street to get some fresh air. His stomach rumbled and he decided to stick it out in the line.

Sean wondered how long it would take for him to smell as bad as the man standing next to him.

He looked down at his own feet and shuffled. *He* was different. He would never let himself fall *that* far. He was, after all, here by choice. He had a purpose. Sean still wore the brown dress shoes he had donned the day he had walked away from the downtown campus of the BC Community College. The shoes were scuffed and the damp had gotten into the seams of the loafers and begun to rot the stitching. One of the soles had pried loose and flapped awkwardly when he walked.

College wasn't a good fit for him, Sean had decided. The professors were complete idiots, who were either bored or incompetent, or both. It was beneath him to be stuck in a classroom with a bunch of retards who could hardly count or read or write, to be lectured at by someone he thought fit the age-old axiom that "those who can't do, teach."

"I'M SORRY, MR. Livingstone, would you repeat that?"

Sean sat in the middle of the class. His face was a study in calm control.

"Mr. Livingstone, I asked you to repeat that remark."

Sean looked around the class and grinned. He caught the eye of a brown-haired girl two seats in front of him. She smiled back.

"Mr. Livingstone . . ."

"I said," he interrupted loudly, and then lowered his voice, "I said, those who can't *do*, teach."

A few students snickered behind him. Sean breathed easily.

"What exactly do you mean by that, Mr. Livingstone?" Harry Banks had been at the college for eight years. He had taken early retirement from the provincial civil service where he had worked with small business start-ups, helping them get their feet under them. Now he taught a couple of classes in small business to first-year commerce students at the college.

Sean looked around, an affable smile on his face. "It's not that difficult a concept. People who can't make it in the real world end up in community colleges, teaching."

"That's an interesting theory, Mr. Livingstone. Thank you for sharing that pearl of wisdom with the class. Now, if we can return our attention to the subject at hand . . ."

"You shouldn't feel insulted, Harry," Sean cut him off.

"I don't," said Banks, looking at Sean from beside a computer that was running a PowerPoint presentation on small business start-up cycles.

"Good, because lots of people who have failed in their careers find meaning and value after they get put out to pasture." There were more snickers in the class, and Sean leaned back, relaxed in his chair.

"I think, Mr. Livingstone, you would do well to focus, for a change, on the lab work. In case it has escaped you, I'm at the head of this classroom, and you are a student." A red flush began to seep up from under the instructor's shirt collar as he spoke.

"Are you saying that you're better than me?"

"I'm reminding you that I am the one doing the teaching here. You are supposed to be doing the learning. If you don't like or respect those roles, you're welcome to leave."

"Are you saying that you're better than *us*?" asked Sean, gesturing to the class.

"I'm asking that you respect this classroom and keep your opinions about my credentials to yourself."

"If you think that somehow you're better than me, than the rest of us, I've got news for you . . ."

Banks interrupted.

"I've got news for *you*, young man," he said, standing up from his desk. "You are a constant disruption to this class. This isn't high school, Mr. Livingstone. This is college. You may not take it seriously, but I am gathering that your classmates do. If you don't respect me, I really don't care. At least respect them. If you can't, then get out!"

Banks stood with his fist clenched and pressed into the metal desk. Sean looked around the room, his charming smile still on his face. A few students still looked at him, grins on their faces. Others now looked away. The brunette was looking straight ahead. Sean felt fear wash through him and then it was gone.

He stood. A few students shuffled. He walked toward the front of the class, slowly closing the distance between himself and Banks. He still wore his bright smile. He felt nothing at all. He simply walked up to Banks, stopping only a foot in front of the teacher, and regarded him coolly.

"Mr. Livingstone, I suggest you leave and never return here . . ."

Sean smiled broadly, then quickly reached over, yanked the laptop computer from the desk and hurled it across the room. It smashed against the wall of the class next to the door, sending a shower of electronic debris across the first few rows of desks. A girl screamed. Several students gasped and ducked their heads.

Banks took two steps backward, his mouth agape. Sean looked at him coolly, smiling faintly. It only lasted a second but Sean had felt a red hot wave of excitement pass through him.

Sean turned and looked at his fellow students. Like sheep, he thought. Followers. Sean Livingstone was not a follower. He was a leader with big plans. He started to make for the door. A twenty-year-old student who had ducked for cover from the exploding computer rose from his desk and was about to block the door.

"Let him go . . ." Sean heard Banks say. The boy apparently thought to stop him, detain him until the authorities could be summoned. Be a hero. Sean kept walking. When the boy stepped in front of him, Sean drove his head into the boy's nose and heard the snap of cartilage. The boy buckled in front of him. The brunette screamed.

Sean stepped out of the room, blood from the boy's face on his forehead. He walked down the hall, then descended the front steps of the college and into the bright June day. He turned east on Pender Street. It was time to get to work.

Two days later he was arrested. He had been sitting on the steps of the Carnegie Centre when two uniformed police constables approached him.

"We're placing you under arrest. Please come with us," one of them said, touching his arm. Sean smiled, stood, and winking at one of the vagrants sitting next to him, allowed himself to be accompanied to a police van that rolled to a stop on Hastings Street.

Sean spent a night behind bars, was brought before the magistrate in the morning, assigned a public defender, and ordered to appear before the courts in two weeks' time. Then he made the now-familiar call to his father's office and spoke with the old man's secretary. The next day he was released with a promise to appear. His court date was delayed, and delayed again, and so he spent July living in a backpackers' hostel near Gastown. His money had started to run out in August, and Sean began a closer examination of his purpose by direct immersing himself into the plan. He had a pretty clear idea of what he had to do, but several important questions remained, such as where?

He walked the streets. He stopped for coffee at Macy's on Carrall, his feet aching. He drank two cups of sugary coffee and then hit the streets again, heading east on Pender. He found his way back to the steps of the Carnegie Centre, where he passed the afternoon watching the dope dealers and vagrants and miscreants and then, on a whim, walked west again. He thought he might see if there was a room at the backpackers' hostel again—he'd come into some money that morning—but before he reached it, he stopped dead in his tracks. It was like a lightbulb had gone on. He stood and stared up at a massive building, its familiar name having been bantered about his father's home for what seemed like ages.

He knew *what* his mission was. Now he knew *where* his mission would be carried out.

All that remained was *how* and *when*.

SEAN EVENTUALLY MADE a phone call.

"He won't see you," said Adelaide.

"But he's my father," said Sean. He was on a pay phone, the howl of rush-hour traffic in his ears.

"He's left very clear instructions," said Adelaide.

"I need to see him. I have to explain things to him," said Sean, looking across the street at two uniformed police officers busting up a drug deal.

"Sean, he won't see you."

"Can I come by and get a few things? I need some stuff for where I'm living now." Adelaide was silent. "Adelaide, please," he said, his voice slow and sad. His face betrayed no emotion.

Finally, she said, "Come by tomorrow morning. After your father has left for work."

"Is my mother there?"

"She's sick."

"Is it bad?"

"I don't know. She's in hospital again."

"Okay, thanks, Adelaide. I'll see you tomorrow."

The next day Sean rode the bus across the city to his parents' Kerrisdale home. It took him two hours, and he still had to walk a dozen blocks to reach the hundred-year-old stone house set far back from the road, protected by a high wall overgrown with ivy. He stepped through the gates and walked up the drive, around the back of the house, and to the kitchen door. It opened and he saw the familiar happy face and broad girth of Adelaide, who gave him a hug.

"Look at you, you're so skinny."

He smiled. "Student life," he lied.

"Well, sit down. I'll fix you a nice brunch."

Sean sat at the table by the window while Adelaide busied herself preparing him coffee, eggs, sausage, toast, and home-fried potatoes. He told her about his time at the college, and how he hoped to use it to springboard into a business program at Simon Fraser University.

"I think Simon Fraser has a better program than UBC," he said, accepting the cup of coffee she offered. "They don't have their heads up their butts. It's less snooty, you know? I'm going to apply in September.

For now, I'm just going to concentrate on learning what I can from these college types and get a job for the summer."

She turned to him with his plate of food. "Eat up."

"Thanks, this is great." He tucked into the food.

"I'm going to move out to Burnaby in the fall," he said. "Live on campus. Simon Fraser has a great view of the city, when it's not in the clouds." He shoveled eggs and sausage into his mouth.

"That's great, Sean. I'm proud of you."

"I wish my father was," he said, looking down.

"He's just upset right now."

"Did he tell you why?"

"Oh no, he doesn't discuss family matters with me."

"He's not happy with my marks. He's peeved that things didn't work out for me at UBC. You know how he is—'good enough for the old man, good enough for you, Sean.'" He mocked his father's voice, tucking in his chin and feigning a slight English accent.

"He just wants what's best for you."

"Well, I think he wants what's best for him, but he won't talk with me about it, so I guess we'll never know." Sean stood and cleared his plate away, and when he was done he gave Adelaide a hug.

"What was that for?"

"For being so kind to me. I really appreciate it."

Adelaide blushed. "It's no problem, Sean. You go ahead and get what you need from your room. I'll tidy up here and pack you a lunch."

"Thanks, Adelaide," he said, smiling broadly, and went into the hall to the main stairs. At the top of the stairs, he headed directly to his father's study. He knew exactly what he wanted. When he'd been a child, he had always admired it. The times when he'd been allowed to step into his father's study, the times when he had felt the white-hot wrath of his father's scorn, he had seen it high on a shelf, wedged between legal texts. He never dared ask his father about it.

At the door, he tried the knob. It was locked. He knelt down and felt under the edge of the carpet for the key. He let himself into the darkened study. The wood-paneled walls, the heavy mahogany desk, the rows of bookshelves, the club chairs, and the high-backed leather chair with brass fittings behind the desk gave the room an oppressive feeling. Sean flipped on the light switch, and the dim pot lights along the walls did nothing to alleviate the pall over the room. He closed the door behind him and walked directly to the bookshelf. The object of his desire was still there. He reached up. It was heavier than he imagined it would be. Nearly a foot and a half long, the nickel-plated come-along was mounted on a heavy piece of hardwood, complete with a metal plate and an engraving.

Sean read it aloud: "For Charles Stanley Livingstone, ESQ, for your meritorious service to the Forest Products Association of BC. Our thanks for breaking the log jam, and getting us out of the mud."

He smiled, put the come-along on the floor and stomped on it has hard as he could, snapping the tool from its wooden base. He scooped up the wood and hid it behind a set of legal texts on the shelf. He hefted the tool by its handle. It was perfect.

Next, Sean went to his parents' bedroom. It smelled close, like a room where someone had lain dying for many years. His mother was back in the hospital; Sean imaged that she was in the grips of a spell of raving lunacy once again. He went to her dressing room and opened her jewelry box. All of her most precious items were locked in a strong box, but he knew he could pawn a handful of these lesser items for enough money to allow him to sleep indoors for another month or two. He also found a wad of cash in his father's sock drawer. Next he went to Adelaide's room, where he quickly searched through her things, finding two pairs of earrings worth taking and a small white envelope of cash that was labeled "for Christmas gifts" in a drawer in her writing table. He slipped it all into his pocket. Finally, he went to his own room, grabbed a sweater and a jacket and a couple of pairs of socks and underwear, wrapped the come-along in them, and pushed everything into a blue backpack he hadn't used since high school. He stepped back into the hall and listened. The house was quiet.

He was about to head back downstairs when he felt the urge to use the toilet. He smiled, stepped to his father's study, went to the corner farthest from the door, unzipped his pants, and relieved himself on the heavy carpet. He re-zipped his trousers and locked the door behind himself.

Adelaide was waiting for him in the kitchen. When he entered, she looked up from cleaning the counter.

"I've prepared some lunch and dinner for you, Sean," she said.

"Wow, that's really great!" he said, finding the right inflection to seem genuine.

She handed him a large paper sack. "Did you get your things?"

"I did," he took the bag and put it into his backpack. "Look, I should get going. I don't want to have a run-in with the old man."

Adelaide stepped to him and embraced him warmly. He put his arms around her and studied the far wall of the kitchen, wondering what time the next bus would arrive.

What, *where*, and *how* had now been determined. All that remained was the *when*.

SEAN FINALLY REACHED the front of the queue at the Carnegie Centre kitchen. A large woman heaped rice, vegetables, and chicken onto his plate. He smiled, paying the dollar seventy-five to the cashier.

Sean looked around the crowded room for a place to sit and eat, but his stomach twisted with the thought of being cramped together with all these people. He took his food and found his way back outside, taking a place on the steps. He ate the meal, eyeing a ragged-looking man with a greasy ball cap who studied him intently. Still sitting, Sean finished and put his face down onto his folded arms, supported on his knees, and let himself drift. He must have fallen asleep, because he woke with a start.

"I'm sorry," said a young woman's voice.

He cleared his eyes and looked around. She was hunched down on the steps next to him. She was older than he was, maybe early thirties, and wore a plain gray hooded sweatshirt that zipped up the front, and had a bright orange backpack on her back. He had seen her just a few days ago when he had been following Overcoat Man. She had given the vagrant a package of first-aid supplies. Sean remembered that same package was now in *his* backpack.

"I'm sorry to have woken you," the woman said again. Sean focused on her, his flat eyes scanning her face. "My name is Juliet. I work for the Health Authority. I'm a nurse. I wanted to check in with you and make sure everything was alright."

Sean set his composure. "Thanks," he said, blinking the sleep from his eyes. "I'm okay. I just ate for the first time in a couple of days. I guess I drifted off."

"What's your name?"

"Sean."

"How long have you been on the street, Sean?"

Sean paused a moment to give the appearance of calculation. "I think about six months. Maybe a little longer."

"Are you from Vancouver?"

"No, Toronto."

"How did you come to be in Vancouver?"

"I came out to go to school, but my father cut me off when I didn't get all A's after my first term. I couldn't afford to go it on my own."

"How old are you, Sean?"

"Twenty-two."

Juliet regarded his face. She knew that living on the street aged people beyond their years. "Sean, can I ask you a few personal questions?"

"Sure, I guess."

"Do you use any drugs?"

"Oh no," he said. "Even if I could afford them, I wouldn't do that sort of thing. It really messes you up. I still really just want to get back into university. I was studying physics and chemistry. I want to be a scientist some day."

"I have an even more personal question, Sean. I hope you'll understand it's just my job. Have you had any unprotected sex while on the street?"

"What do you mean?" Sean asked, tilting his head innocently to one side.

"Have you had sex without a condom?"

Sean looked down at his hands. "No," he said.

"That's good, Sean. That's good."

"I'm not like *these* people," Sean said, looking back up at Juliet, his eyes meeting hers. "I'm not a vagrant. I'm not a bum. I come from a good family. It's just that my father was really hard on me as a kid. My mother died when I was little. I just want to get my feet back under me so I can go to school. I'm smart. I know I can do well," he said.

Juliet looked into Sean's eyes. In her years working on the street she had become adept at reading people's intent and their sincerity. Sean was hard to read. He seemed to be genuinely in distress, but she just couldn't see anything in his eyes. His voice, his words, his body language all cried out for help, but his eyes betrayed nothing.

"Can *you* help me?" he said, mimicking the emotion he had seen so many homeless people employ as they pleaded for assistance.

She regarded him. "I think I can, Sean."

With that sentence, Sean felt his purpose shift. Felt his purpose deepen and expand, giving new scope to his arrangements.

FIVE

ON TUESDAY MORNING DENMAN SCOTT woke at six, and as was his custom, went immediately to the small sunroom on the back of his Mount Pleasant home and meditated for half an hour. He sat in the lotus position on a low cushion centered on a bamboo mat, clearing his mind of thoughts. It had taken him ten years to reach the point where he could sit for thirty minutes each morning without fantasies or stories or to-do lists cluttering his mind.

When the tiny bell on his meditation timer chimed, he opened his eyes. He rose, stretched, then stepped from the sunroom into his kitchen to brew a strong cup of tea. As the kettle boiled, he retrieved the *Vancouver Sun* from the front stoop, and standing at the counter, opened it and read the headlines.

One caught his eye: "Violence Expected at Today's Anti-Poverty Protests." He ate his breakfast at the counter, the paper spread in front of him.

The Vancouver Police Department is warning anti-poverty activists not to use today's planned rally, to be held in the Downtown Eastside, to advance a radical and violent agenda. The VPD says it has received information that the End Poverty Now Coalition will use the event to further its own narrow aims, so the VPD will be posting additional officers along the route of the march. John Andrews, Division 2 Commander for the VPD, says: "We've learned that members of the End Poverty Now Coalition plan on turning today's event into some sort of venting exercise and that we should expect violence and hooliganism. That sort of behavior is not acceptable in the fair City of Vancouver."

The rally, originally organized by the Downtown Eastside Community Advocacy Society to highlight the plight of the homeless and those living in poverty, is to start at 1:00 PM at Pigeon Park, and will include a parade through some of the city's poorest neighborhoods. "The purpose of today's rally is to demonstrate to the people of the City of Vancouver first and foremost that the Downtown Eastside is a community in crisis," says Beatta Nowak, Executive Director of the Community Advocacy Society.

Advocates for the homeless say that the City of Vancouver must build up to two thousand units of community supported housing a year for the next three years in order to house all of the city's homeless.

Andrews says that the VPD is sympathetic to the needs of the homeless, but violence will not be tolerated. "The VPD will make a proportional response."

Nobody from the End Poverty Now Coalition could be reached for a comment.

Denman finished his breakfast and cleared his dishes away. He looked at the clock on the stove in the neat, orderly kitchen. It was just after seven. He took his jean jacket from the hall closet, put on a comfortable pair of leather shoes, donned his flat cap, and slinging his computer bag over his shoulder, headed out into the morning. He walked west to Main Street, then turned north along the rejuvenated main artery of the old city, heading toward downtown. Most mornings he would stop and catch the #3 somewhere along the way, but this morning he decided to walk the entire distance. He needed the time to contemplate the day ahead, and the complex challenges that he might face.

There were many. It seemed to him that John Andrews was *inviting* a confrontation with the End Poverty Now Coalition. In a little over six hours—Denman looked at his watch—little old ladies and mothers with kids in strollers and small businessmen would be gathering in Pigeon Park to hear a speech or two, sing a few protest songs, and march five or six blocks into the Downtown Eastside as a show of support for the work being done there to solve homelessness and end poverty.

It wasn't news to Denman that the more radical elements of the anti-poverty movement thought that peaceful marches did little to solve the problem. He had become a lawyer and started Priority because the mainstream groups working on homelessness had fallen into a trap of complacency. Denman used the law to address homelessness the way he applied aikido in a confrontation with a street thug: use as little force necessary to get the job done, and try to make sure nobody gets hurt.

The skyline of downtown Vancouver came into view. He considered his next challenge: what Juliet Rose had told him over lunch the previous day.

Juliet believed that people were disappearing from the Downtown Eastside. There hadn't been anything about it in the media, but if Juliet said that people were disappearing, then people were disappearing. For the last eight years, she had been one of a handful of people who knew just about everybody who made the streets of Vancouver their home. She had the best information around; the VPD often turned to her when they received a call from a family member claiming that someone had disappeared.

Juliet not only kept tabs on her flock, but she had a network of people she could check in with just by picking up the phone. Primary among those was the Welfare office; you want to find someone living on the street, thought Denman, find out where they are picking up their check. Juliet had told Denman that she knew of two people who were missing—two people whose routines she had known for months, if not years. Two people who, in the space of a few weeks, had suddenly stopped doing what habit and convenience had dictated they do for years.

Denman couldn't help but wonder if there would be more. He would have to raise the issue with the VPD. He thought about the man in charge. Divisional Commander Andrews was forty-five, and had risen quickly through the ranks of the police force. He had a reputation as a hard-ass, a "get the job done no matter what it takes" sort of man. That meant cracking skulls if need be. And for Andrews, that need seemed ever present. It was a doctrine that got passed down from the Divisional Commander's office to the beat cop on the street.

People were disappearing. And people were being harassed and assaulted by police. Denman's office had more than a dozen cases of complaints filed with the Police Commissioner against officers in the Downtown Eastside for harassment, wrongful arrest, and assault. Was it possible that an officer had gone too far? Had someone on the force taken John Andrews' "kick ass and take names" attitude *two* steps over the line?

As he made his way toward his office, the doomed façade of the Lucky Strike came into view. Denman now remembered his third interrelated challenge: Cole Blackwater.

THE LONG WALK meant that Denman reached his office later than usual, although still early enough to wake the three men who were sleeping on the front step. Denman offered them coffee and made a few calls to try and arrange rooms for them at one of the nearby SROs. One man needed to have a gash on his left hand attended to, so Denman called him a cab and phoned ahead to a nearby twenty-four-hour medical clinic.

That daily routine finished, he sat down in the tiny room that was his office, turned on his computer, and checked for messages on his phone. Today, Denman told himself, he would focus exclusively on the rally and on the disappearances. He scribbled a plan of action on a legal pad with a stubby pencil. He was about to pick up the phone to start making calls when it rang.

"Priority. Denman here."

"Denman, this is Trish Perry from the City calling."

"Good morning, Trish. You're up bright and early. How are things at City Hall this morning?"

"Pretty good."

"You're taking a bit of a chance calling me *this* morning of all mornings, aren't you?"

Her laugh was girlish. "I guess I am. I'm on my cell phone in the garden behind City Hall."

"Really?"

"No, not really. Well, I *am* on my cell phone. Until you and the mayor make nice, I've got to be careful. Look, I'm calling you with a heads-up. A courtesy call, really. Verbal brown envelope."

"What is it, Trish?"

"The Lucky Strike sale is going to close today." Denman was silent. "You there?"

"You know, it's funny. I must have had some kind of premonition about that. I just walked by it this morning on my way into the office."

"Yeah, well, the sale has been in the works for a month or so. It's closing today."

"Frank Ainsworth?"

"Yup."

"Evictions?"

"Afraid so."

"How long?"

"People will get forty-eight hours."

"You're kidding."

"It's better than two hours."

"Not by much, Trish."

"What do you want me to do, Denman? The new owner is exercising his right to evict and make renovations. Like I said, this is just a courtesy call."

"Okay. Well, thanks. I don't mean to be pissed at you. But this is going to hurt a lot of people. And the timing couldn't be worse."

"I know. I've already had Andrews on the phone this morning. He's calling out the riot squad."

"Good God." Denman put his bald head in his left hand, his right hand cradling the phone. "Okay, well, I've got to go. It's going to be a busy day."

WITHIN AN HOUR twenty people were assembled in Priority Legal's windowless boardroom.

Denman stood at the front of the room, a whiteboard behind him, dry-erase marker in his hand. "We'll coordinate the legal challenge," he said loudly over the three or four other conversations taking place around him. "Patrick Blade—" he acknowledged one of the lawyers in the room with a nod "—will be leading our response."

"I'm heading over to the Lucky Strike in about fifteen minutes to start collecting affidavits. If anybody wants to hop a ride, be out front in ten. There's going to be a lot of upset people," said Blade. "If the Advocacy Society can spare a few bodies, that would be helpful."

"I'll make a call," responded Beatta Nowak, her dress billowing around her voluminous body as she rose. "They'll likely meet you there."

"Does anybody here have access to the people at End Poverty Now?" asked Denman.

"I do," said a young woman at the back of the room.

"I'm sorry," said Denman, "We've not met. Lots of people coming and going this morning."

"I'm Francine Lanqois. I'm working at the Carnegie Centre as an out-reach worker."

"Francine, are you able to contact the Coalition and ask them if there is any way of dialing things down today? With this news breaking, I'm worried about the police response."

"I can try. They seem to keep their own counsel."

Denman smiled. "I'd be happy to talk with George Blunt if need be. I don't know if he's still the ringleader over there."

"He is and he isn't," said Francine. "Some of the younger members of the Coalition are trying to push him out. Not radical enough."

"Denman, I just got off with some of my people." Nowak shut her phone. "We'll have some folks meet Patrick over at the hotel in about twenty minutes. We'll coordinate the effort to find new housing from our office."

"Great." Denman looked down at his notes.

The room started to break up.

"Listen, folks," Denman called out over the chaos. "This is going to be a long day. Let's just remember that if it's a long day for us, it's going to be even longer for the residents of the Lucky Strike. Those people won't be able to go home for a hot shower and a cold beer after they've put their day in. So let's keep them in mind. My staff, if you want to take time this afternoon for the rally, that's cool. But if the Coalition shows up, your job is to document and steer clear. No doubt we're going to be getting calls about police brutality and what have you. Take your cameras and keep your eyes open."

People began to leave and Denman sat down. He heard his name and looked up, then smiled.

"Juliet." She was standing at the door.

"I heard the news on the radio. I thought I'd walk over and see how you were doing."

"I'm fine. *I've* got a place to sleep tonight."

"Can I buy you a coffee?"

Denman looked around him as the boardroom emptied.

"It's going to be a long day, Denny. Come on." She motioned with her head toward the door. "Hard to say no to a girl with an orange backpack."

IT WASN'T A Starbucks kind of neighborhood; wrong demographic. They sat in a small, brightly lit Chinese café and drank drip coffee from porcelain cups.

"This is our worst nightmare come true," she said.

"By tomorrow there are going to be hundreds of people on the street, frightened and desperate. Between now and then Beatta's people at the Community Advocacy Society should be able to find temporary housing for maybe fifty of them. Sixty if we're lucky. But you're right, it's a nightmare."

"I'm going to have to do a new round of night inventories next week," Juliet pointed out.

"No rest for the wicked."

"Yeah, but it's necessary with all the changes that are occurring. I need to keep track—"

"Of your flock?" grinned Denman.

"I was going to say, of my charges."

"Same thing."

"Up at midnight for breakfast, then walk, wake, and talk till 8:00 AM."

"One night's not going to do it."

"You're probably right. Want to come along for a night?"

"Is that your idea of a date?"

It was Juliet's turn to smile. "I'm an old-fashioned girl."

"We'll see. If I get any sleep between now and then, I'd love to."

"Invitation is always open."

They sipped their coffee, a calm pool around them in the storm of the day.

"I'm going to call Cole," said Denman.

"Good," said Juliet. "You know, I still haven't met the famous Cole Blackwater."

"I can't believe that!"

"It's true. But his reputation precedes him."

Denman smiled. "Cole is a professional pain in the ass, which if you're the mayor, or a developer, means trouble. A smart guy to have at the table when you're trying to figure out how to stop things. I think if you asked Cole, that's what he'd say. 'I stop things,'" Denman said in his best Cole Blackwater, southern Alberta drawl. Juliet laughed. Denman smiled at her.

She stopped. "What are you smiling at?"

"It's just that I love it when you laugh."

Her smile faded. "Let's just see if anybody is laughing tomorrow morning."

SIX

COLE STEPPED FROM THE SKYTRAIN at Stadium and made his way down Beatty Street toward the old *Vancouver Sun* building. He plodded toward Pender, his thoughts dark and distracted. His cell phone rang as he reached the steps of the Dominion Building, which housed the humble headquarters of Blackwater Strategies.

"Blackwater."

"It's Denman, Cole. How you doing this AM?"

"Hey, Denny. I'm good. How about you? I heard you on the radio this morning. Another one bites the dust."

"Yeah, it's a biggy."

"It's funny, you and I were just there the other day. Bad timing," said Cole. He sat down on the steps.

"Listen, Cole, I could use your help right now," said Denman.

"What do you need?"

"I've got a perfect storm on the horizon. I've got Captain Condo choosing today to close the sale on the Lucky Strike, a march this afternoon to highlight police brutality in the city, and the End Poverty Now Coalition ready to start burning tires in the street. All the elements of a disaster."

"I can't stop a riot, Denny."

"No, but you can spin it and help us figure out how to salvage the opinion of the mainstream voter in this city, after they see pictures of kids throwing rocks at riot police on their televisions later today."

"Okay, I'll check in with Mary and walk over to your office. Be about an hour."

"Cole, there's one more thing."

"What is it?"

"Well, I don't want to sound alarmist. Juliet Rose, you know the street nurse? She came to me the other day with a story that I think has a lot of credibility."

"What is it, Denny?"

"People are disappearing, Cole."

MARY PATTERSON HAD been in the office for two hours when Cole arrived at ten.

"Good morning, Mr. Sleepyhead,"

"Morning, Mary."

"You look like you were awake most of the night again."

"Up at four this morning."

Mary regarded him with a concerned smile. "You should see somebody about that. Take some pills. Get some sleep."

"I don't have any problem falling asleep." He took the carafe of coffee from its warmer and poured himself a cup, adding cream from a carton on the tidy table across from Mary's desk. "It's once I'm asleep that I have trouble. I wake up between three and five and can't fall back asleep."

"Can't stop thinking about work?"

"Something like that. Can you check out a group called the End Poverty Now Coalition for me, Mary?"

"Sure, Cole. Is this a new client file?"

"No. It's part of the pro bono work I'm doing for Denman. Somebody has a riot planned for later on today. The Coalition people are the likely ringleaders. Denman wants my help salvaging his campaign to stop the closures of SROs. It looks like the Lucky Strike is on the chopping block for today."

"Not so lucky." Mary turned to type something on her keyboard.

Cole went into his cluttered office and sat down in his chair, then got up again, pulling from his pockets his cell phone and keys, SkyTrain tickets, change, a crumpled wad of five-, ten-, and twenty-dollar bills, a stick of lip balm, two tiny hooks for hanging cups in a cupboard, a mini measuring tape, and a startling amount of lint. He dumped it all on his desk, adding to the pile of papers, books, magazines, and newspapers.

He needed to call Nancy. Her phone rang four times, and as he was preparing to leave a message, he heard the familiar voice.

"Nancy Webber."

"Hi, Nancy. It's Cole."

"To what do I owe this rare pleasure, Mr. Blackwater?"

"You're being polite this morning."

"It's only Tuesday. But Friday you'll just be 'Asshole' like everybody else."

"Story of my life."

"What's up?"

"Where are you right now?"

"I'm on my way to City Hall. They closed the Lucky Strike this morning. There's going to be a riot. I thought I'd get the mayor on record before all hell breaks loose."

"Sounds like a plan. Can you come and talk with Denman Scott afterward?"

"Sure. You know, since meeting him in Port Lostcoast in July, he and I have never actually sat down and talked about his work. Now that I'm on the City Hall file for the *Sun*, I should really talk with the mayor's public enemy number one," said Nancy.

"Is that really what the mayor's office calls him?"

"Not in so many words, but he is persona non grata around the City offices. I've got a memo one of the staffers leaked to me saying that nobody from the City is allowed to talk with anybody from Priority Legal unless one of the City's lawyers are present."

"Come over to the Lamplighter at noon."

"Another high society lunch with the venerable Cole Blackwater?"

"Man of the people."

"See you then, Cole."

He hung up without saying goodbye, his mind distracted. He dialed Denman on his cell.

"Denman here."

"Meet me at the Lamplighter at noon, okay?"

"Sure."

"We're going to sit down with Nancy."

"She's been writing good stuff."

"She's on her way to City Hall right now. We'll get a good story out of it."

"See you at noon."

NANCY WEBBER CAUGHT a cab in front of City Hall. She had been shut out. That didn't happen very often. In fact, in the year and a half since she had won a National Newspaper Award, it had *never* happened.

Now she wondered why. She had shown up at the mayor's office after calling his press liaisons that morning, requesting an interview, and being assured that she would get ten minutes with His Worship. But when she arrived, she was intercepted by a woman named Trish Perry, the deputy planning commissioner for the city.

"Ms. Webber?"

"Yes."

"I'm Trish Perry. Mayor West has been called away on an urgent matter. His office asked me to talk with you."

They shook hands. Nancy said, "You understand, Ms. Perry, that these things aren't interchangeable. If I had wanted to talk to a civil servant, I would have called one. I want to speak with the mayor."

"I understand. I was made the new spokesperson on housing this morning. Come, let's walk to my office. Or would you rather grab a coffee across the street?"

Nancy stood a moment considering her options. "Let's go to your office," she said. They walked through the corridors of City Hall and arrived at the planning department's section on the second floor.

When they were seated at a round table in Trish Perry's cramped office, Nancy opened her notebook. "What is the City's plan to address the needs of the two hundred and fifty people who will be homeless as a result of closing the Lucky Strike?" asked Nancy.

"It's actually more like three hundred people," responded Perry. "Though it's single-room occupancy, some of the rooms have couples living in them. We're working with the Downtown Eastside Community Advocacy Society right now to find housing for those people."

"Where?"

"Various shelters around the city, and in some SROs that aren't at capacity."

"How many of those three hundred people will have roofs over their heads tomorrow night?"

"We're aiming for one hundred per cent."

"Realistically?"

"We expect to get close."

Nancy thought of something Cole always said when he heard that refrain: "Close only counts in horseshoes and hand grenades." She didn't think it appropriate to repeat.

"And those you don't find space for?"

"I don't think anybody believes we can find a bed for every single person who is displaced by this closure. No doubt some folks are going to end up on the street. Understand that the City is doing everything it can to attend to their needs. The Lucky Strike Hotel is a mess. It hasn't had a renovation in twenty-five years. The inspector found over fifty violations of code. Wiring that's been eaten by rats. Half the doors in the place don't close. There are only a handful of fire exit signs. Hallways don't have lighting."

"Advocates say they have been asking the City to order the SROs to clean up their act for a decade, and the City has been purposefully dragging its feet."

"I don't know about that. We've known that the SROs need work. Some of them are a hundred years old. And none of them make much of a profit for their owners; otherwise they wouldn't be selling them, right? There is only so much the City can do."

"You can enforce fire codes."

"Sure we can. We walk in the door, make our inspection, give the owner fifteen days notice to fix up the place, and then they turn around and sell it."

"You can fix it up yourselves. You have that authority. Bill the owner for your work."

Perry smiled. "In some situations we do. We spent two months fixing up the Liberty Hotel just last spring. Forty-five rooms. Some sixty people living there, including a Chinese man who was one hundred years old. A centenarian. Can you believe that? He'd been in that room for a decade. Hadn't left. Meals on Wheels brought him three squares a day. Did his laundry in the sink, watched *The Price Is Right*. Crazy. We spent two hundred and fifty thousand dollars getting the place up to code. The owner sold the week after we'd finished. Sold it for $1.2 mil. Now lives in the Bahamas. We're suing for our costs. The new owner plans to knock it down and build a hundred-unit condominium. Units will sell for half a mil to start."

Nancy was making notes.

"My point is, Ms. Webber, that this is a complex problem. The City can only do so much. We can't force owners to provide social housing if they want to sell condos."

"But you can, can't you? You can enact bylaws? You can create housing regulations? There are dozens already on the books . . ."

"The mayor has been exploring these options with council."

"According to your critics, the mayor has been stalling. 'Dragging his feet,' I think is the quote I got the other day."

"Council is divided on the issue."

"Down party lines. The mayor's party has the balance of power. They could push regulations through that addressed this issue."

"Like I said, it's a complex issue, Ms. Webber. The mayor is building support on council, and with other stakeholders, in an effort to address this issue. In the next couple of weeks you should see some dramatic movement."

Nancy flipped a page in her notebook. "What about Councilor Chow's motion to put a moratorium on SRO conversions from low-income housing to condominiums?"

"That doesn't sit well with many council members."

"Why not?"

"The mayor favors more of a free-market approach to the situation."

"Chow is a member of the mayor's own party."

"Like I said, they are exploring all of the options."

"Any comment on today's planned demonstration?" Nancy changed the subject.

Perry blinked at her. "What's to comment on?"

"The rally is to protest what many feel is a police force that is abusive toward homeless people, prostitutes, and street people in general."

"That's really a matter for the chief constable or for the divisional commanders."

"John Andrews."

"Or one of the other commanders."

"The trouble is concentrated in the same area as where the SROs are shutting down."

"You'd have to take that up with Commander Andrews."

"Well, the mayor is head of the police commission, which is why I had hoped to talk with him today."

Perry shrugged. "You have me instead. Mayor West got tied up in something."

"You don't find it strange that there are more than double the number of complaints against the police in Division 2 for excessive force as there are in any other part of the city?"

"I think you'd find that the number of crimes committed in the Eastside is also more than double."

"Are you saying that the Eastside is experiencing a crime wave?"

"I'm only saying that the Downtown Eastside is a complex area to police, just as it is a complex area in which to solve the problems of homelessness, addiction, and health care. My area of expertise is planning, not policing."

Nancy sat back in her chair. "Will the mayor be commenting after today's rally?"

"I expect so," said Trish, visibly lightening. "He'll be there."

NANCY WATCHED THE industrial section of Main Street whir past.

"Would you take me across Pender and down Carrall Street, please?" she asked. "And drive by the Lucky Strike?" The cabbie nodded. Nancy checked her watch. She had time to kill. When the cab made the turn onto Pender, she said, "Just drop me in front." She handed the cabbie the fare and took the receipt.

Nancy was a block from the Lucky Strike, but even from that distance, she could hear the crowd. The morning was cool and gray and the air seemed to be charged with anticipation. She walked along the side of the road, stepping over piles of wind-blown garbage to reach the cracked sidewalk in front of the stalwart building. Though the homelessness rally was scheduled for one o'clock at nearby Pigeon Park, Nancy got the distinct impression that there had been a change of plans.

At least a hundred people were gathered in front of the hotel. Heaps of personal belongings littered the sidewalk and spilled onto the street. She saw lamps missing their bulbs, urine-stained mattresses, dressers missing drawers, dozens of duct-taped and dilapidated chairs, boxes of clothing held together with twine, and piles of shoes and clothing of every description. As Nancy drew closer she began to pick out individual faces in the crowd: an elderly Chinese man sitting on the curb holding a fish bowl in which a small carp swam lazily in circles; an enormous black woman standing next to the building, staring up at its brick façade and screaming at the top of her lungs while those around her gave her a wide birth; a man cooking his lunch on a small stove like the ones backpackers use.

Angry and confused voices could be heard among the sobbing and wailing.

There were already two TV crews on site. Bright halogen lights from one camera shone on the wrinkled and worn face of a man still dressed in his stained pyjamas. As Nancy walked by, she caught the interviewer's question.

"How does it feel to have lost your home?"

She slowed to hear the man's reply. "It don't feel too damn good. How do you think it feels?"

Nancy walked up the front steps of the building. Posted on the door were bright yellow signs—the eviction notice. As she was reading it, the double wooden front doors swung open, nearly catching her in the chin.

A woman cradling a box of clothing in her arms stopped and said, "Oh goodness, so sorry. Didn't clip you, did I?"

Nancy managed a smile and replied, "Nope. Everything's intact."

She was about the step inside when the woman said, "Shouldn't go in there."

"Just taking a look around," said Nancy. The woman sized her up. "My name is Nancy Webber. I'm with the *Sun*."

The expression on the woman's face changed completely. She shifted the box into one arm and held out her hand. "Beatta Nowak, Downtown Eastside Community Advocacy Society. We've talked on the phone once or twice."

Nancy shook the extended palm. "Nice to meet you face to face."

"Let me deliver this box, and I'll give you a quick tour." Nowak stepped to the curb and put the box down next to the growing mountain of personal belongings.

"Come on," she said, taking Nancy by the arm as she might a toddler who had strayed.

Nancy allowed herself to be led inside the building.

"This was the lobby," said Beatta. Nancy saw a twenty-foot-long check-in counter, with old-fashioned key boxes behind the desk and thick Plexiglas separating the clientele from the hotel staff. Half a dozen cracked and faded vinyl club chairs were scattered randomly throughout the dingy room. It smelled of cigarette smoke and cooked food. The carpet was so worn that plywood could be clearly seen along the most commonly traveled path. The ceiling soared above them, crafted from ornately tooled tin. Two decorative chandeliers hung down on heavy black chains, but they no longer cast illumination. Instead, floor lamps of various design were scattered here and there, throwing a sickly yellow light around the room.

"We'll take the stairs," said Beatta. "The elevator is unreliable on a normal day. Today . . ." She shook her head and frowned. "Not a good idea."

They walked up a flight of stairs, Beatta breathing hard and holding the hand rail. "Let's look in on some of the guests," wheezed Beatta. They stopped and knocked on an open door. Beatta took a breath, then called out in a singsong voice, "It's Beatta from the Advocacy Society!"

"What's that?" said an older woman, looking around the door.

"It's Beatta," she repeated, "from the Advocacy Society."

"You come to help me with my things?"

"We've got people coming this afternoon," Beatta smiled.

"I could use a hand with that dresser," the old woman said, pointing a crooked finger at a bright purple dresser that was pasted with children's stickers.

"We'll have someone here soon to help."

"What's that?" The old woman was stuffing a few knick-knacks into a shopping bag.

Beatta smiled at Nancy. "This is Nancy. She's a reporter."

Nancy stepped into the twelve by twelve room. Along one wall was a slouching bed that nearly touched the floor. The linoleum was worn and peeling. No curtains adorned the single window, but a flowery sheet over the opening kept out the light.

"There's a common bathroom on this floor, where about thirty or so people wait in line for the toilet or the shower," said Beatta.

"We'll have someone come by later," yelled Beatta as they left.

The old woman didn't turn.

"That's one of the cleaner rooms. The old girl takes care of the place," said Beatta, walking down the hall, Nancy following behind. The corridor was dark and smelled thickly of fried food, grease, marijuana, and urine.

Beatta stopped at another door that was ajar. The noise of a television blared from within the room.

Beatta knocked loudly and raised her voice over the sound. "It's Beatta from the Advocacy Society!" She pushed the door open, which hung on the frame by a single, rusting hinge. She looked into the room, Nancy right behind her.

"Hi, it's Beatta," she said to the thirty-something man lying on his bed. The room was smaller than the last one, not quite ten by ten. The mattress was bare of linen, yellowed and stained with what looked like spots of blood. The man was dressed in faded blue jeans and a dark hooded sweatshirt with the right sleeve rolled up to his biceps. There was no sign of a hot plate. Two needles lay on the floor beside a small black and white television with a clothes hanger for an aerial. The young man looked up at them, glassy-eyed.

"Don't step inside," said Beatta, looking back at Nancy.

Then she turned to the young man, "You okay?"

The man seemed to be looking right through her, his eyes thick and colorless. He nodded.

"Can I get you help?"

The man shook his head.

"Did you shoot twice?" Beatta looked at the syringes on the floor. The young man held up a single finger.

"Okay, I'll be back to check on you in a few minutes."

The young man turned back to the television.

"Prime candidate for an OD," said Beatta, as they moved down the hall.

They looked in on half a dozen other hotel guests on that floor and then climbed up to the second. The stairwell was dark and wet and reeked of cigarette smoke. Residents pushed past them, the contents of their lives crammed into boxes and bags. One man bumped down the stairs with a shopping cart.

On the third floor Beatta knocked on a door and said to Nancy, "This gentleman has been here for twenty years. He's got throat cancer. He's a hoarder. OCD," she said, knocking again and announcing herself. A wall of debris could be seen through the crack in the door. The stench emanating from the room was putrid.

"Where does he sleep?" asked Nancy.

"There's a bed in there, somewhere."

Nancy looked at her watch. "Beatta, I have to go. I'm meeting Denman Scott for lunch."

Beatta turned. "Okay, dear. Will you be covering the rally?"

"I will."

"Good, then maybe we can talk after that. Need me to show you out?"

"I'll find my way."

"YOU'RE LATE," GRUMBLED Cole as Nancy walked into the pub. He looked at the bleak expression on her face. She was flushed from her rapid walk to the Lamplighter. Cole and Denman were sitting at a table near the windows.

"Nice to see you too, shithead," Nancy managed a half-hearted grin. Denman rose and Nancy gave him a kiss on the cheek. "Hi, Denman," she said.

"Nice to see you again, Nancy."

"Can you believe it's been over two months since we were in Lostcoast and we haven't had lunch yet?" Nancy opened a menu. "What's good here?"

Cole sipped his beer. "It's standard pub fare. Roll it in flour and bread-crumbs and throw it in the fryer."

Nancy looked at Denman, "What's up with Mr. Grumpy here?"

Denman smiled and shrugged. Since they had arrived at the Lamplighter, Denman had watched as Cole's buoyancy of that morning descended into a dark funk. They ordered and Cole asked for another beer.

"I want to get over to the rally for one o'clock. It's only a few blocks, but we should talk business now," said Denman.

Cole looked down at his beer. "I think the two of you need to discuss what's going on around here," he said, looking behind him, as if he was peering beyond the walls of the pub. "Denman, why don't you tell Nancy what you told me this morning?"

They spent the better part of an hour discussing the general situation in the Downtown Eastside, focusing on the closure of the Lucky Strike Hotel. Nancy colored the conversation with her observations of the hotel itself.

Their food arrived. While Denman and Nancy talked, Cole found himself bewildered at how hard it was to be in the same room with Nancy. For the last two months she had been on his mind almost constantly. After their lives had become re-entangled in Oracle, Alberta, because of the bloody Mike Barnes affair, she had been haunting his thoughts. Cole chalked that up to their troubled history and the affair in Ottawa: the lie, the dismissal, the exodus, the heartache. She had as much as admitted she still loved Cole, and he knew he still loved her. But instead of feeling good, he felt an icy fear. And it wasn't just Cole's run-of-the-mill fear of commitment. It was much, much darker than that.

Sitting at the table with her, Cole felt that dark fear taking hold. The last time they had spoken at any length was in July in Port Lostcoast, in the Broughton Archipelago. Watching her now, he could vividly recall that exchange.

"WITH EVERYTHING THAT has gone on over the last few months, I'd almost forgotten how beautiful it is here," Nancy said, looking east toward the Coast Range and the narrow waters of Knight Inlet. It had been three months since they had scrambled to solve the mystery of the disappearance of Archie Ravenwing. Now they were standing together on the bluff near Archie's house. Maybe they were finally at the conclusion of a desperate and deeply troubling time for both of them.

Cole still had his doubts about what motivated Nancy. She clearly wasn't sure about why she became involved in the Ravenwing affair, and Cole's personal nightmare. Was she there as a friend or as a journalist? Cole could not forget how she had chased down the story of his father's suicide, even going to the family ranch and questioning his mother and brother while he was in Port Lostcoast investigating Ravenwing's disappearance.

He knew she had harbored a suspicion that Cole had pulled the trigger of the shotgun himself; revenge for years of physical abuse that Cole had suffered at the old man's hands.

"Listen," said Nancy, which is what she always said when she was about to broach a difficult subject.

"Don't," Cole said.

"Cole, I'm sorry."

"Just don't. It's okay. You're right."

"I am?"

"Don't let it go to your head. It doesn't happen very often."

Nancy punched him in the arm. "What am I right about?"

"That I'm rotten at talking about these things . . . About my father."

"You can't keep it bottled up inside."

"I know that."

"It's eating you alive. All your friends can see it."

"Denman says he's got something that's going to help."

"What is it?"

"He won't tell me. Says I have to trust him."

"That sounds interesting. Can I watch?"

"As long as it doesn't involve needles, crystals, or someone purging my body of all its worldly desires, you can."

"Can I write about it? I've got to make a good impression on the people of Vancouver."

He shot her a look and she laughed.

"Thank you," he said, turning toward her, strands of his hair lifting in the breeze.

"For what?"

"For *not* writing about it."

She looked at him a moment, her dark eyes meeting his. "You're welcome."

He looked away, toward the harbor. "I thought you were just in it for the story."

"I wasn't sure myself what I was in it for."

"And now?"

"Now I'm sure," she said.

"DOES THAT SOUND about right?" asked Denman, bringing Cole back to the present and making him aware of the silence.

"What?"

"Does that sound about right?" asked Denman again, smiling.

"I'm sorry, I didn't catch that last bit."

"Denman is speculating about the connection between the timing of the closure of the Lucky Strike and these disappearances that Juliet Rose told him about," said Nancy.

"Do you think there might be a connection?" asked Denman.

"Anything is possible." Cole looked at Denman.

"What the hell is wrong with you, Blackwater?" demanded Nancy.

"Nothing," he said defensively.

"'*Anything is possible*,'" she mocked. "What the hell kind of mush-ball line is that?"

"I'm sorry, I didn't realize we were on the record here," he said, his voice rising sharply. "Let me see if I can come up with something sensational enough for you. How about, 'I have no doubt that the City of Vancouver is snatching the homeless from the streets and dumping them in Burrard Inlet to make way for ritzy high-rise condos.' Or how about, 'I won't rest until every one of the vanished have been found!'"

Several people in the pub stopped talking and were looking at him. Nancy and Denman were silent.

"Cole . . ." said Nancy.

"No, I'm sorry," he stood up. "My work here is done. The two of you are talking. I'm through with this shit."

He stood up abruptly, knocking the table and spilling his beer. He dug a twenty-dollar bill from his pocket, receipts and lint cascading onto the floor, and threw the money on the table.

"I'm going to a rally," he barked, and made for the door, leaving Denman and Nancy bewildered.

SEVEN

IT WAS LIKE CHRISTMAS MORNING. The dregs of society spilled out onto the sidewalk as the news of the closure of the Lucky Strike Hotel spread, and Sean Livingstone stood on the corner watching. He leaned against a wire fence, selecting and dismissing over and over again candidates for his special arrangements. There were so many to choose from that he felt like the proverbial kid in the candy store. He straightened up and made his way to the front of the hotel. He sat down on the steps just as television reporters approached several of the newly homeless. The familiar woman from the community group ushered a woman who was also likely a reporter through the front doors.

A scrawny woman in an oversized hooded parka meandering through the crowd caught his eye. She was casually picking up things from the piles of belongings and stuffing them into her coat. It's your lucky day, he thought. Lady Luck is on my side, too.

He stood up and dusted the dirt from his jeans, adjusted his backpack, and set off to follow her. She wove her way in and out of the crowd, and at the street corner, turned west on Hastings, heading toward a row of pawn shops near Cambie. She went inside the first one. Sean stopped two doors up and waited for her to emerge. It was twenty minutes before Lady Luck came out, and when she did she turned and threw something back into the shop. Sean watched as the owner came to the door and threw whatever it was back at her, hitting her in the shoulder. She screamed obscenities at him, and the man told her to stay the fuck out of his shop or he'd call the police.

Sean leaned against the wall of an adjacent pawn broker and watched the entertainment. Passersby gave Lady Luck a wide berth, and when she started walking again, she went east, right past Sean. Her face was crooked and twisted with rage. She walked with a slight limp and wore her heavy parka open, exposing a thin frame in dirty loose-fitting clothes. Sean felt a moment of elation as he thought of his arrangements. Lady Luck posed a challenge he would meet willingly.

She circled back past the Lucky Strike for another pass at the accumulated detritus of people's lives. She got in a fight with the large black woman when she tried to steal a small portable radio, and got punched by a man when she was caught looking over his things. The police arrived as the crowd grew, and Lady Luck fell in with the throng being corralled toward Pigeon Park by youths in black shirts who were from the End Poverty Now Coalition.

Sean was caught at the back of the crowd. The street was filling up with people, and it was getting harder to keep his eyes on Lady Luck's parka. Cars honked their horns, and somewhere close by someone was yelling into a bullhorn. Sean noticed groups of ten and twenty police officers scattered about as he threaded his way through the crowd, pushing people with his shoulder when they crushed in around him, voices blaring in his ears. He felt as if they were tearing at his backpack, so he slipped it from his shoulders and let it dangle from his left hand.

He spotted Lady Luck disappearing into an alley. I bet she's going to shoot up, thought Sean, and he forced his way through. A café entrance straddled the corner, so he put his pack down in the doorway and stepped into the alley. He scanned it for Lady Luck. She wasn't there. The excitement made him need to pee. He unzipped his fly and pissed on the trash cans and the heaps of garbage piled next to them. He was just finishing when he heard a voice say, "Zip it up, son, and come with us."

"I'M SORRY THIS took so long, Sean," said the lawyer, sitting down across from him in the small interview room. "We had quite the night last night. I hope that your one night in jail wasn't too difficult. I'm Denman Scott. I work for an organization called Priority Legal Society. We work with people in the Downtown Eastside to ensure that their rights under the law are respected, and we advocate for the homeless and other people often overlooked by the criminal justice system. I'll be your lawyer during the proceedings for your recent arrest."

Sean was seated across from Denman, a cup of coffee in a Styrofoam cup before him. He no longer had his coat and was disheveled. He had a bruise on his left cheek.

"How did you get that bruise?"

"Cop hit me," said Sean.

"During the arrest or after?"

"After, in the back of the wagon."

"Did you do anything to provoke it?"

"Nothing. I was shackled. I couldn't do anything. I was just sitting there."

"Have you ever been arrested before?"

Sean didn't hesitate. "No. I mean, I've been in trouble here and there. Nothing serious. I've had some bad luck, that's all."

"What happened yesterday, from your perspective?"

Sean looked at Denman for a split second, then down at his hands. "I was on my way to the rally." He noticed his hands were dirty, his fingernails broken. He put them under the table. "I wanted to be a part of the cause, you know? You know, do my part," he looked up, and saw Denman nodding and making notes.

"I come from a life of privilege. I hate the way this city has turned its back on the poor. So I wanted to go to the rally, add my voice. Do my part. I guess I had too much coffee in the morning. And there aren't any bathrooms around. I couldn't hold it any longer so I slipped into the alley there near the park and took a leak. Then there's this cop behind me with his baton out and he tells me that I'm under arrest and before I can say anything he cracks me in the side of the head with the baton."

Denman made some notes. "You said that you were assaulted in the paddy wagon."

"That's right."

"And just now you said the arresting officer hit you in the alley."

Sean looked into Denman's eyes, his own flat and unreadable. "That's right. Both times."

"So you were assaulted twice, once at the alley by the arresting officer, and again in the wagon after you had been shackled."

"That's right."

"Okay," said Denman, rubbing a hand over his bald head.

"Can you help me?"

"I think so," said Denman. "I'll have to talk with the arresting officer about your charges. These are serious accusations, Sean, but if what you're saying is true—"

"Of course it's true!" Sean said loudly.

Denman stopped. "I'm not questioning your word, Sean. I'm just saying, if we can make this case in court, it could help us out with our complaint against the VPD about excessive force."

"You think I could help that way?"

"We'll see. But I think so. Sean, can I ask you a question?"

"Sure."

"It's personal."

"Okay."

"Are you on the street now?"

Sean looked down at his hands. "My parents are dead. They were killed in a car accident a few years ago. There's a big fight about their estate. They were worth millions. The whole family is trying to get their greedy hands on the money."

"And somehow you got cut out?"

"I'm the only child; you'd think that I'd be in line for some of it. I don't want it all; just enough to get a good start in life."

"So you're living on the street?"

"I was living in the Lucky Strike Hotel for the last few months, but . . ."

"But it's been closed down," said Denman.

"Yeah, it really sucks. I don't know where I'm going to go."

"I'll have my office look into a temporary shelter."

"Those places scare me. Too many drugs. And crazies. They steal your shoes at night. They do things. Bad things."

"We'll see what we can do. The Crown will likely release you on a Promise to Appear. That doesn't require a cash deposit. It does mean you have to show up for a court hearing. Can you do that?"

Sean nodded. "I've got important work to do," he said. "I'm volunteering to help with the homeless problem. I really want to get back to work."

"THE KID WENT berserk when we tried to put him in the wagon," said Staff Sergeant Paddy O'Connor. They were sitting in an interview room a few doors down from where Denman had interviewed Sean Livingstone.

"He says that the arresting officer hit him with his baton in the alley before he was even in the wagon," said Denman.

The staff sergeant shook his head. "Not the way I read it," he said, holding the arrest report in his hand. "Look, Denman, I know things are pretty tense right now. The arresting officer was Jim Meyers, a good man. Solid. Saskatchewan farm boy from way back. Twenty years on the force here in Vancouver. He's not one of the hotshots looking for collars. He's just doing his job. Says the kid was taking a leak in the alley and when he tells him to zip it and come with him, the kid gives him some lip. Meyers escorts him to the wagon and tells the kid to sit down and the kid spits at him. Can you believe that?"

Denman didn't respond.

"Meyers tells the kid that he's out of chances. He tells the kid that the Crown could charge him for assault for that and the kid says go ahead, he'll sue for false arrest. That's when Meyers says that nobody is under arrest, *yet*. At this point the kid isn't listening, and tries to push past Meyers. Meyers uses his baton to slip a hold on the boy and work him into the wagon that way, and the kid goes crazy, flailing and kicking. Did more harm to himself than to my officer, thank God."

"How did he get the bruise, Paddy?"

"Probably when he was flailing around in the wagon."

Denman looked at the police officer.

"Look, Denman, I shouldn't even be talking with you about this. You know what Andrews has said. Personally, I think your heart's in the right place, but I think you got a beef with coppers and that's clouding your judgment a little. Everybody should just sit down over a pint and sort this thing out. You got to believe me, the kid was the one who went crazy. Not Meyers. He's a straight cop."

"Thanks for the perspective, Paddy," Denman said, rising.

"You're going to represent him?"

"Yeah. I'm going to talk with the Crown, see if we can't cut the kid a break. And I appreciate your time, Paddy. Thanks," Denman said, reaching across the table to shake the staff sergeant's meaty hand.

IT TOOK SEAN a few hours to get his stuff back after Denman secured his release. First he had to wait to have his jacket delivered to him at the police station. Then he went to the mouth of Trounce Alley and asked about his backpack at the café where he had dumped it.

"Yeah, we found a pack."

"Can I have it back?"

The proprietor was a skinny man with a handlebar mustache. "What's your name?"

"Sean."

"Sean what?"

"Livingstone."

"Why you got a funny nickel-plated tool in the bag?"

"It's called a come-along. They use them for pulling trucks out of the dirt. It was my father's. He was a logger. He's sick. I had it nickel-plated and was going to have it mounted. But the fucking cops busted me at the rally."

The man looked at him. "And what's with the butcher's coat?"

Sean looked at the man narrowly. "I'm an artist. I use it to paint."

The café owner silently regarded him.

"Can I get my stuff, please?" Or I'll burn your fucking place to the ground, you prick, he wanted to say, but decided to smile innocently instead.

"Sure."

It took Sean two whole days to find Lady Luck again. Forty-eight hours lost because of the pigs. The last of the tenants of the Lucky Strike Hotel had been cleared from the building. That's when the End Poverty Now Coalition had shown up in force and occupied the whole second floor. Sean had seen them storming the place while he walked by. The obligatory TV crews waited, their hungry cameras eager for the action to unfold, as it inevitably would.

Sean checked all the pawn shops. He even asked after her here and there, pretending to have been ripped off by her, and trying to track down his goods. It was no use. He was growing frustrated.

On the afternoon of the second day out of jail, he found himself on the steps of the Carnegie Centre.

"Hi, Sean," he heard a voice beside him say. He turned his flat eyes to the smiling face of Juliet Rose.

"Oh, hi." He affected a pleased-to-see-you tone.

"Haven't seen you for a while. I was getting worried."

"I got arrested. I went to the rally and got busted. Cops beat me up," said Sean, pointing to the fading bruise on his cheek and the torn jacket.

"I'm so sorry to hear that."

"Got a lawyer though. A good one."

"I'm glad. You sound like you need representation. Have you eaten today?"

"No. Not yesterday either."

"Can you come in for something hot?" Juliet nodded toward the Carnegie Centre.

"I'm waiting for someone," said Sean. "I can't miss her. She's got something of mine. But I lost her when they arrested me."

"Maybe I know her?"

"Naw, she's not from around here."

"Okay," said Juliet, slipping her bag form her shoulders. "I've got some granola bars here," she said, unzipping the orange pack and handed Sean two bars. "Sean, where are you staying?"

"Nowhere," he said, looking down at his feet. "I mean, I was at the Lucky Strike. But it's closed. The protesters are there now."

"I know."

"I got nowhere to stay."

"Come see me tomorrow at lunch. I'm doing a Saturday clinic at the Centre. I'll see if we can't find you a place."

"That would be really great," said Sean. "I know I can get back on my feet if someone would just give me a chance."

"Sometimes that's all it takes," said Juliet.

HE FOUND LADY Luck half an hour later. She was panhandling outside a pawn shop. He watched her go down an alley, buy a hit of smack from a dealer, and sit down to inject the drugs behind a dumpster.

Sean walked right up to her and hunched down as she was rolling up her sleeve.

"Waddaya want?" she said.

"I'm Sean," he said, slipping off his pack. Lady Luck eyed him. She had her sleeve rolled up and was tying off her arm with a length of rubber surgical hose.

"You a pig?"

"Nope, I'm a street nurse."

"You don't look like one." Lady Luck looked at his hands, which were now stained and dark.

"I like to blend in," he smiled, but hid his hands behind his pack. He was aware that his hygiene was slipping the more time he spent sleeping rough.

"I don't need nothing," she said, taking a needle from her pocket and holding it in her teeth. She used a lighter to heat up a blackened spoon in which the smack sat.

"Why don't we get you to InSite?"

"Too many fucking pigs."

"They won't bother you."

"I've got a sheet," she said, the drugs boiling.

She drew the plunger back and the hot smack flowed like lava into the syringe. She held the syringe in her mouth again while she pressed her arm for a vein. Her arms were bruised and purple from so much abuse. Several of the veins in her left arm were hard and black.

"I want to help you. What's your name?"

Lady Luck laughed.

"I'll just call you Lady Luck then," said Sean, reaching into his pack.

She inserted the needle into a vein and pressed the syringe down, her eyes rolling back as the juice coursed into her system and caused her adrenal glands to react immediately. Sean first pulled his stained coat on and then took the come-along from his backpack. Her eyes began to glaze and her mouth dropped open.

EIGHT

IT HAD BEEN THE LONGEST week of Denman Scott's life. Since he had left his house on Tuesday morning, when the Lucky Strike had closed, he'd only seen his bed for a few hours. Now it was Friday, and there was little he wanted to do more than slip between his sheets and sleep for the entire weekend. Instead, he stepped off the bus at Cambie Street and made his way toward the Cambie Hotel, last known location of one Cole Blackwater.

He had received a call from Martin Middlemarch about forty-five minutes earlier, as he was finishing the paperwork on the last of his newly acquired clients from the Lucky Strike Hotel, and what the media was now calling the Lucky Strike Riot. In all, Priority Legal had taken on fifty-three new cases in the course of thirty-six hours. He had spent twelve hours at police headquarters, interviewing people arrested in the frenzy that had erupted when the riot police showed up and mask-wearing anarchists started throwing balloons filled with red paint.

Martin had called him from the Cambie Hotel to say that Cole was in the bar, drunk, and looking for a fight. "Normally, I'd let him fight it out," said Martin above the racket all around him. "But with his ribs, he's liable to get hurt. You're the only one he'll listen too, Denny."

He could hear the pub from a block away. Twenty or so young men and woman were huddled by the door, smoking. The gas-fired heaters warmed the outdoor patio where people packed tables and music blared from speakers. Denman smiled as he threaded his way between the revellers and into the bar. Cole, Martin, and Dusty Stevens were at their favorite table toward the back of the pub.

"Hey Denny!" Cole stood and lunged for his friend. He tripped on the bench and nearly fell, but Denman caught him by the arms and returned the accidental embrace. "Denman Scott, you old bugger. How are you?" Cole pounded Denman on the back.

"I'm good, Cole, good. A little tired."

"I have the perfect antidote for that," Cole said, grabbing Denman by the shoulders and looking earnestly into his eyes. "Sleep. Let's sit before some of these frat boys think we're queers and try to beat us up!" Cole lurched toward the table and jostled the bottles on it.

"How are *you*, Cole?" Denman asked.

"Never better. Top shelf," he slurred. "Right next to the peanut butter," and he laughed.

"You've just been drinking tonight, right? Nothing else?"

Cole looked at Denman through bleary eyes. "Whaddaya mean?"

"No meds?"

"Nothing. Just some brews with the boys."

"Just asking," said Denman. Cole was usually a quiet, brooding drunk, so his effervescence surprised Denman.

"It's all good," said Cole, dragging out his words. "It's aaaaaaall good." He splashed beer from the pitcher on the table and into his pint glass. He raised the glass above his head.

"To Denny Scott," he yelled, "my best friend. Man of the people. A hero for our times!" He stood and clashed glasses with Dusty, who was drinking a pint, and Martin, who hoisted a half-empty glass of cranberry juice. Then Cole swung his arm around to the cabal of college students.

"Raise a glass to my friend, Denman Scott!" he shouted over the din of the room at the dozen or so men and woman at the table.

A few of them raised a glass in Cole's direction, but still not satisfied, Cole hollered, "Raise a glass, you pre-pubescent punks!" Cole's voice had slipped from jocular to edgy in a heartbeat. A few of the men at the table looked in Cole's direction, but none offered their glass. Denman put a hand on Cole's shoulder. "Come on, buddy. I'll drink to me . . ."

Cole shrugged off Denman's hand. He swung his glass toward the half-pint a boy at the next table was raising to his lips. The boy's glass flew from his hand, spraying beer over his friends, the glass rolling across the checkered tablecloth and crashing to the floor. A girl at the table screamed and the room grew still. The boy stood up, and Cole reached for him as if to embrace him. The angry young man shoved Cole away, a scowl on his face. Denman tried to get between the two, but the drunk and stumbling Cole was still quick with his hands, and he took a poke at the boy. He managed only to clip the boy's shoulder. The boy, more surprised than worried to be in a bar fight with a man twice his age and slobbering drunk, was slow to strike back. By the time the punch came, Denman was able to easily guide it harmlessly past Cole's astonished face, and Dusty quickly moved in front of Cole.

"Everybody cool down," Denman said, loud enough for Cole and the boy to hear him. He turned to the boy, his face open and friendly, but meaning business.

"Your fucking friend is wasted, man," the boy said. Several of the other young men at the table were standing now.

"You're right. He is. I'm taking him home before he gets hurt," Denman said.

Denman turned and helped Dusty manage Cole out of the Cambie.

"Call us a cab, would you?" said Denman to Martin.

Ten minutes later, Denman was sitting next to Cole in the back of a cab moving out of the downtown area, passing the Carnegie Centre. Cole was half asleep, and Denman watched the street scenes unfold. He thought about Juliet Rose and the people she knew were missing from the area. In the midst of the debacle over the Lucky Strike and the riot on the streets of the Downtown Eastside, she had come to him to report that another of her flock had failed to surface in over a week.

Three people now gone. Had they simply moved on? The only better place to be on the streets, and even then only if you didn't like the weather in Vancouver, was Victoria, across the Strait of Georgia on Vancouver Island. Vancouver had better social services, more shelter beds, and a community that wasn't so hostile to the homeless. If they had decided to head to Victoria, they would have had to take the bus, which meant money, always in short supply. Stashing away the bucks it cost to take the bus and ferry wasn't something that happened overnight. Juliet or one of her colleagues would have known if any of the locals were planning on making that move.

They had to be here still. Somewhere. If the unthinkable was true, if they were dead, where were their bodies?

Cole grumbled beside him.

"You're going to start the program on Sunday, my friend."

"What's that?" Cole's head bobbed up.

"You and me, we're going to start your training on Sunday."

"Can't. Ribs busted."

"Don't worry. It's not in the ring."

Cole seemed to drift off to sleep again.

"But it's going to make the ring look easy," murmured Denman.

OVER THE WEEKEND, the weather turned. Summer vanished inside of two short days. Saturday showed up with scattered clouds, and Sunday threatened rain. By Monday, the sky had closed in on the Lower Mainland, clouds bunched between the mountains and holding fast to the low alluvial plain where the city of a million people sprawled. By noon, the rain was falling in sheets across the Downtown Eastside.

Denman walked from his office to the headquarters of the Eastside detachment of the Vancouver Police Department. He wore his flat cap and a Gore-Tex coat and carried an umbrella.

As he approached the reception desk, he closed his umbrella and took off his cap. He stated his business and a uniformed staff sergeant he didn't recognize asked him to wait. Two minutes later a red-haired woman in a business suit came into the reception area carrying a cup of coffee and a thin file folder. She tucked the file folder under her arm as she approached Denman and held out her hand. She had a firm grip and held his hand a second while she said, "Marcia Lane. I'm the Missing Persons Task Force's team leader."

"Denman Scott. Priority Legal. Nice to meet you."

"Coffee?"

"Sure."

She led him down a set of stairs to a cafeteria. The room was mostly empty. Windows along the top of one wall let what little light the day provided into the room. Overhead, fluorescent bulbs cast their stark glow over the room, erasing shadows. Even under the glare, Marcia Lane was surprisingly beautiful. Her long red hair was tied back in a single ponytail, with a few errant strands artfully left to fall across her temples. Her cheeks were high, her skin soft and clear and alabaster under the glare of the lights. Her blue eyes were almost translucent.

"This isn't Starbucks," she laughed when she handed Denman a cup, "but it's not as bad as you might think. The one thing cops have a discerning taste for is coffee." She poured herself a cup and offered the pot to Denman. "Like a donut?" she asked, and when she saw the expression on Denman's face, laughed again.

They sat in a table close to the high windows, next to a fake palm tree, and sipped their coffee.

"It's turned pretty cruel outside," she said. "How is the City doing with emergency shelter space?"

"They managed to add another thirty-five spaces for use during the extreme weather protocol this winter, but we need to add a thousand spaces to meet demand. Trouble is, even those thirty-five spaces are designated *only* for extreme weather. So, for example," Denman turned his face toward the window, "tonight likely won't count."

Marcia raised an eyebrow. "Not cold enough . . . The solution seems simple. Build more community-supported housing."

"Simple to say, hard to do," Denman responded. "There's simply no political motivation. The mayor and council are elected for three-year terms. It takes longer than that to build these spaces, in the market we're in. And what council wants to be the one to say, 'We're going to spend a billion dollars to house people who in all likelihood will never pay a dime of taxes in their lives.'"

"I thought the argument went that if we could just get a roof over these people's heads, they would become contributing members of society."

"Some will. Some may land decent jobs in a few years and find themselves actually writing a check to the tax man on April 30. But most never will. You've got to understand," said Denman congenially, "that many of these people are sick. They are alcoholics or drug addicts, or suffer from a raft of mental illnesses. It's too much to hope that they will contribute to the country's tax rolls."

"I read somewhere it costs the city, the province, and the feds forty thousand dollars a year just to have a person on the streets," said Marcia.

"That's right. That was one of *our* reports." Denman smiled wryly. "People on the street use a disproportionate amount of the province's health care resources. People like Councilor Chow have a point. I think Chow exaggerates the nature of the problem sometimes, but I'll give him credit where it's due. He's even asked council to consider a ban on converting single-room occupancy hotels while the City addresses the housing crisis."

"Is that going to pass?"

"Not a hope," said Denman. He paused. "I was surprised you agreed to meet with me, and here."

"I'm not afraid of you," she smiled back.

"Good. I don't bite."

"But you sue and that's what's got everybody nervous." Denman shrugged. "And just between us girls," she said, leaning forward a fraction of an inch, "your poking around into excessive force has everybody on edge."

"You've got to understand—"

Marcia held a hand up. "You don't need to tell me, Denman. I'm not on the beat, if you'll pardon the pun. I'm just stating the obvious. But you didn't call this morning to talk about housing or about excessive force."

"No. It's about your task force."

Marcia smiled, inviting him to speak.

"Do you know Juliet Rose?"

"The street nurse. She helped us out a couple of years back with a missing person's case."

"She came to me the other day with concerns that people she knows are disappearing."

Marcia seemed to straighten in her chair. "How many?"

"Three so far. Two men and a woman."

"Over what period of time?"

"A month. Really over the span of September, so far."

"How does she know that they're not just in another part of town? Or maybe moved to Victoria or Kelowna?"

"She just does. She keeps tabs on people. She sees them every day. She knows their habits. If she says they are missing, I believe her."

"Don't take it the wrong way; I just have to ask."

"I know. Sorry."

"It's okay. You're used to people on the force giving you the gears," Marcia smiled. "Before I can open a file, I need more information."

"Okay. What do you need?"

"Who these people are; their last known address, if any; when they were last seen; and by whom. That's just to start."

"Maybe I should call Juliet—Ms. Rose. She will have a better handle on the details."

"Okay. You call, I'll get more coffee."

"You want to do this now?"

"Why not?"

Denman smiled. "I'm not used to getting immediate results from the VPD."

"Hi, I'm Marcia Lane," she said, holding out her hand in a mock introduction, and grinned.

THREE HOURS LATER Juliet and Denman stood under the marquee of the Vancouver Police Department headquarters while water poured down onto the sidewalk in front of them and cars splashed up waves from puddles as big as lakes.

"I need to get back," Juliet said. "This is the first storm of the season. The Carnegie Centre is a zoo. By tomorrow we're going to have a bunch of sick people."

"Can't buy you lunch? You know, debrief and all."

"Okay, but let's make it quick."

"I know just the place."

They ran through the rain and stepped into the door of a small noodle bar nearby. A small woman seated them silently, and they fell into conversation, oblivious to others around them. When the waiter came, they hadn't looked at the menu.

Denman ordered in Mandarin for both of them. The waiter nodded and left.

"Your Mandarin is pretty good."

Denman frowned. "No, not really. I'm rusty."

"Sometimes I forget it was a first language for you."

Their food came. "It's good," Juliet remarked. "What is it?"

Denman slurped noodles into his mouth. "It's called Priority Legal Special. I know the cook here. He surprises me."

"What did you think of Marcia Lane?"

"I wish every cop in Vancouver was more like her. Smart. Professional—"

"Beautiful."

"I hadn't noticed."

Juliet shot him a look.

"No, really. Talking with her was the best three hours I've ever spent with the VPD. Ever. It's almost too good to be true."

"I feel the same way. Like our concerns were taken seriously."

"I'll admit I'm troubled by some of what Lane was asking about."

"Like?" Juliet pushed some noodles into her mouth.

"Well, bodies. If people are disappearing, where are they ending up?"

"It took a decade to track down the missing women to the Pickton farm."

"I know. That's what worries me. The body count there was high. We can't wait for that to happen again. Do you think this could be drug related in any way?" asked Denman.

"I don't think so. Peaches was a user, not a dealer. The other two were clean. Both Bobbie and Jerry had never used, to the best of my knowledge."

"Maybe they saw something they shouldn't have, something more serious."

"Maybe. Or maybe it's got nothing to do with crime at all." She stopped. "I can't believe all three of these people decided to head to Saskatoon for the winter. Maybe they were in the wrong place at the wrong time."

"That's what Cole Blackwater thinks. He immediately said he thought that our three missing persons were linked to the development of the Downtown Eastside."

"Why is that so crazy?"

"It is and it isn't. This *is* Vancouver. *Canada*. It's not some despot-ruled country in Africa. I doubt that the government or some rich developer would knock off a bunch of street people to make way for development."

"Why not?"

"You really *are* sounding like Cole," Denman said. "First of all, *why?* It's not like a bunch of homeless people are going to somehow impede the development of a condominium. These people are invisible to City Hall, and to the development community. Why get rid of them? It doesn't make sense."

"Maybe they knew something or saw something."

"That's my theory, but about drugs, not development. People get killed over the drug trade all the time. People don't get killed to make way for condos."

"Where are we on this?"

Denman leaned forward. "I'd say we're further ahead than we were this morning. We've got someone at VPD who seems to be sympathetic to our concerns."

"There's still no official investigation."

"In time."

"I'm just not sure how much time we've got," said Juliet.

They hugged before putting on their still dripping jackets, and Juliet hurried into the downpour to walk the two blocks back to the Carnegie Centre.

Denman hadn't gone a block in the other direction when a man passed him and a second later he heard his name. Denman turned.

"I almost didn't recognize you under all that gear," said the man from beneath his own umbrella.

"Councilor Chow?"

"Hi, Denman." The man thrust out a small, powerful hand from his overcoat. Denman shook it. Ben Chow was in his sixties, but Denman knew that he kept in good shape, and still practiced tae kwon do twice a week.

"I was just talking about your motion before council to ban conversions of SROs."

"Oh yes, very good. Well, it's due for debate this Wednesday."

"You think it will pass?"

"Who can tell? The mayor is all over the map on this one."

"He was at the rally the other day. He seems to be waking up to our plight."

"You mean the riot? Well, that was a publicity stunt. It's the first time he's been to the Eastside in more than a year. I think he's afraid to walk around down here. Right now, I think the best policy is not to put too much pressure on him and my fellow councilors. They're smarting these days. The closure of the Lucky Strike and that business with the rally turning violent, and the pictures of all those people with their things all piled up? Not good for City Hall. Not good. They need a moment to collect themselves."

"People are getting wet, Councilor."

"I'm getting wet," said Chow.

"But you and I will sleep inside tonight."

"I know, Denman. But you've got to be patient with us. So much of this is out of our hands. This council has eighteen months left in its mandate. Then we'll have elections. His Worship isn't the most popular man inside our party, Denman. And this city is growing impatient with his sitting on the fence. It might be time for new ideas from someone who actually knows what the problems are."

"Are you thinking about running?"

"Maybe."

"Might be good to have solved some of these problems while on council to show a record of success."

"My record speaks for itself. But I know what you're saying. Believe me, Denman, there is a lot of work going on behind the scenes to tackle this problem. More than you'll ever know."

"Why not talk about it in the open? The people in this city want solutions. They would be willing to help."

"It's not about Joe Citizen. It's not about the average resident getting involved, writing letters. It's more complicated than that. It's about the power structure that underlies the official decision-making system here. You've got to lay off a while. We're working on something big."

JULIET ARRIVED BACK at the Carnegie Centre soaking wet. The building was packed with people drying themselves and their belongings. The stairway that gracefully, if not somewhat lopsidedly, circled up through the rotunda of the building was crowded with people sleeping or just sitting. Every inch of floor space was carpeted with dejected faces, a grim reminder that the long, wet, and cold winter had started. Juliet threaded her way through the throng to her tiny office. She hadn't taken her coat off when a volunteer knocked on her door.

"Hi, Andrea," she said.

"Sorry to bug you, Juliet, but I wonder if you could help me out with something."

"What is it?"

"Well, one of our regulars came in this morning, and he had a new coat on."

Juliet took hers off and hung it on a hook on the back of her door. "And?"

"Well, the thing is, it belonged to Veronica. It's the big, black parka she always wore. I asked him where he got it, thought maybe she traded it for something. He said he got it in a dumpster nearby. How many days has it been since you've seen V?"

Juliet closed her eyes. "It's been three, maybe four days. I saw her outside the Lucky Strike about two days after the demonstration. That would have been last Thursday."

"That's about when Jack says he found the coat. He says it was Friday night. Three days ago."

"Thanks, Andy."

"No trouble. You think everything is okay with her?"

"No," said Juliet, reaching for the phone. "No, I don't."

NINE

NANCY WEBBER'S MONDAY HAD STARTED off badly. Gray skies and the portent of rain. She hadn't factored so much gray and rain into the picture of herself on the West Coast.

"They call it the Wet Coast for a reason," mused Frank Pesh, her editor at the *Sun*. "I want to talk with you about how we should deal with the calls I've gotten from the mayor's office. They were pretty pissed with our coverage of the riot."

"To be expected. The City looked like a bunch of idiots."

"They said the mayor didn't get his chance to have his say."

"I went to his office on the morning of the rally, Frank. You and I discussed that before I went, and we talked about it before I filed."

"I know, Nancy, keep your shirt on."

"Did you straighten them out?"

"I tried to. They told me that they felt you went around the mayor's back on this."

"That's ridiculous," she said, shaking her head.

"That's City Hall."

"Trish Perry met me at the door of City Hall. I never got to the fourth floor. The only question I have is, was it a mistake or on purpose?"

"Better find out. They are willing to sit down again this morning."

She caught a cab from downtown across False Creek and up Cambie to 12th Avenue where City Hall rose above the streetscape.

Nancy waited for nearly half an hour in the mayor's anteroom, as City Hall staff buzzed in and out. A secretary offered her coffee every five minutes. Finally, the secretary said, "He'll see you now," and ushered Nancy into the spacious office.

Mayor Don West was slight of build and nearly bald. When he stood behind the mahogany desk that dominated one side of his wood-paneled chamber, Nancy guessed that he was no more than five foot eight.

"Ms. Webber, nice to meet you," he said when they shook hands. He gestured to a woman sitting in a chair next to the big desk. "This is Beatrice France," he said, "my press secretary." Nancy nodded in her direction.

"We had a bit of a mix-up last Tuesday," said His Worship. "My deputy planning commissioner seemed to think it was her turn to talk about the housing issue. We'll get that all sorted out today. So you must have some questions?" the mayor asked.

"Lots," she said. "How much time do we have?"

He looked at his assistant. "About twenty minutes," she said, looking at her watch.

"Let's get started then," said Nancy, flipping open her notebook. "What is your reaction to last Tuesday's rally?"

"The riot?"

"Call it what you like."

"I call it organized anarchy." He looked at his press secretary. "This city is trying to tackle a serious problem. A serious problem." He folded his hands on his desk and affected a solemn demeanor. "Groups like End Poverty Now showed up with masks and rocks and assaulted police officers and disrupted businesses—businesses supporting the very people these hoodlums are supposedly trying to help. It's nothing more than an excuse to get in a tussle, if you ask me. They're not serious about tackling poverty or homelessness."

"There are accusations that the police provoked the violence. That agents provocateurs were a part of the group that showed up when the rally crossed Main Street and started mixing things up."

"Those are baseless accusations."

"I have a number of sources, including one inside the police department, who say otherwise."

"Are they going to go on the record?"

"The police source won't. That person is afraid of getting fired."

The mayor shrugged. "So there you have it. Another anonymous source. Nobody takes that sort of thing seriously."

Nancy jotted a few notes and smiled. "So you dismiss the possibility of the police overreacting to the rally?"

"The fact of the matter is, the Coalition is a bunch of malcontents who aren't serious about solving homelessness or ending poverty. They are a bunch of kids with chips on their shoulders who would rather throw rocks than volunteer at the food bank or a soup kitchen. Frankly, I'm not interested in talking about them anymore."

"I gather you're not interested in talking about the occupation of the Lucky Strike, now in its third day?"

"Nope. That's a police matter."

"So when things turned violent, when the rally crossed Main Street and the police moved in and dispersed the crowd, were you still a part of the rally at that time?"

"I was."

"What went through your mind?"

The mayor was silent for a moment. He leaned back in his leather chair and pressed his fingers together. "Frankly, I thought it was pretty much what I had expected."

"But you went to the rally anyway?"

"I'm not going to be held hostage in my own city by a bunch of thugs."

"And what happened when the rocks started to fly?"

"My VPD escort asked that I leave."

"And you did?"

"Wouldn't you?"

"It's not a story about me, Your Worship."

"I attended the rally because I believe that homelessness and poverty are a problem this city needs to address. I thought that by marching with other folks in Vancouver, I could demonstrate leadership. That's what the mayor does, leads." He was smiling as he said it. From the way he delivered the line, Nancy knew that Beatrice France had written it for him.

"Tell me about Councilor Chow's proposed bylaw to put a freeze on SRO conversions."

"Ben Chow is a good councilor. He's a good member of his community. And a good party member. Ben's doing what he thinks is best for his constituency. I've got to look out for the whole city."

"Meaning what?"

"Meaning that I think there are better ways of addressing the housing shortage than putting restrictions on what private developers can or cannot do with their properties."

"So you're not going to support it?"

"It hasn't come before council yet."

"It's on the agenda for Wednesday. How will you advise your party to vote?"

He laughed. "You haven't been around Vancouver politics very long, have you, Ms. Webber? I might be the mayor, and the official head of the party, but councilors here tend to vote with their conscience. Maybe that's unheard of in Alberta, or Ottawa, but here in Vancouver, each councilor keeps his or her own, well, counsel."

Nancy let the quip slide. He had answered the question without realizing it.

"So what is *your* plan? You said that there was a better way. What is it?"

"There's a lot we can do. The City is making its biggest investment in shelter beds in more than thirty years. We continue to support InSite, the safe injection site, despite the hostility of the feds and the Americans. We're developing a housing strategy in conjunction with the private sector, non-governmental groups, and other levels of government. I'm set to make an announcement in the next few days, maybe a week, on the issue of homelessness. I think you and your colleagues in the press will find it a very bold, even daring, strategy."

Nancy made some notes. "Can you tell me more about it?"

"I'll be doing a press conference shortly, right, Beatrice?"

"That's right," she confirmed from the side of the room. "We'll have an advisory soon about the date."

"What else can you tell me?" asked Webber.

"This council, and my office, take the issue of homelessness very seriously. It's one of the most pressing problems we face today, not just here in Vancouver but across Canada."

"Will you be allocating additional funds?"

"I want to remind you that housing is a provincial matter, and that the province slashed funding for social housing over the last ten years by more than fifty per cent. I don't want to sound like I'm passing the buck, but that's a fact."

"Your Worship, I've heard reports that several homeless people in the Downtown Eastside have gone missing over the last month. Can you comment on that?"

He looked at Beatrice France, his face suddenly gray. "This is the first I've heard of this. Beatrice, do you know anything?"

"No, Mr. Mayor."

He turned back to Nancy and said, "My office will look into it and get back to you."

"The disappearances have been documented by people working with the homeless. Three so far. All street people well known to social service providers. Do you think that they are in any way related to one another?"

Beatrice France stood. "We really should wrap this up, Mr. Mayor. You have a meeting with administration." She tapped her watch. Nancy glanced at hers and saw that her twenty minutes had turned to twelve when she brought up the subject of missing people.

"Right you are, Beatrice," confirmed West, standing. "Tight timelines around here, you understand."

Nancy looked at Beatrice. "So can I expect you to get back to me on that?"

"As soon as we look into it, we'll call."

Nancy shook the mayor's hand, then Beatrice's. She gave her a business card and was escorted to the door. "Thanks for the opportunity," Nancy turned to leave.

"Any time," smiled Beatrice, but Nancy knew that wouldn't be the case.

THERE WAS A message waiting for her at the office.

"Hi, it's Beatrice France calling from the mayor's office. I've asked District 2 Commander John Andrews' office to contact you. They said that they haven't had any complaints outside of the ordinary registered about missing persons, but if you have information that might be useful to them, they'd be happy to talk. Thanks again for your interest in the story on homelessness. The mayor was happy to talk with you today."

That was that.

Nancy poked her head into Frank Pesh's office. She couldn't see him. "Frank?"

"Follow the sound of my voice," he said from behind stacks of paper.

"Can you tell me a bit more about Don West?"

"What do you want to know?" He moved into sight.

"Who's got their hooks into him?"

"Sit down, my child. That is a fascinating story."

"CAN WE HAVE lunch?" Nancy was on the phone with Cole Blackwater. Against her better judgment she had called him around eleven thirty, after spending an hour with her editor being illuminated about the troubling rise to power of Don West.

"Noon at the Water Street. It's a nice place, Cole. Try to act like a mature adult, okay?"

"Do you want me to call Denman?"

"After."

Cole arrived a few minutes before Nancy, got a table by the window, and ordered coffee. When she arrived, Cole said, "I'm sorry about the other day. I don't know what got into me."

"Cole, I think you need to get some help."

Cole looked down and bit his lip. "Denman had me out with him on Sunday. We did tai chi and aikido. Ate miso soup. Meditated. Drank some rancid root tea. Sarah came too. I think she did better than me at the aikido thing. She'll be kicking my ass pretty soon, I think."

"That's great, Cole, but I think seeing a professional would help."

"Help with what? So I'm having a tough go right now. I've been down before. I'll come around."

"Are you sleeping?"

"Yeah," he lied. "Just fine."

"You don't look it. Have you seen yourself in the mirror lately?"

"Every morning. Beautiful," he said, pushing his mouth into a smile. She smiled back.

"But really, I feel fine. A little frustrated that I can't fight right now. These ribs are taking their time healing."

"I don't think what you need is more time in the ring, Cole."

"Everybody knows what I need these days."

"Denman and I are just trying to help."

"Look," he said. "Did you call me to lecture me about the bags under my eyes and eating my spinach and seeing a shrink because of bad dreams, or was there something else?"

Nancy sat back in her chair. "There was something else," she said. "But one more thing before we change the subject."

"Go ahead."

"Cole, I moved to Vancouver for two reasons, and one of them wasn't the weather," she looked out at the pouring rain.

"A good reporting job?" offered Cole.

"That was one."

"And me?"

"See, you're not as stupid as you look."

Cole smiled. Their food came and each of them took a bite.

"I've been here for three months now. I have no idea what is going on in your head. I have no idea why I'm even bothering to talk with you about this."

Cole took another bite. "My charm and good looks?"

"Neither," she said, forking a spear of asparagus. "I'm telling you, Cole, you had better smarten up. Deal with your shit, and make peace with your ghosts."

Cole regarded her coolly over the plates of food. Her hair was pulled back and clasped in what looked to Cole like an oversized paperclip so that it stood up and flopped over. She wore a tight black shirt that plunged low in the front, revealing enough of the smooth curve of her breasts to raise Cole's heartbeat. Her face was tanned. That would fade with the West Coast winter, but her stunning beauty wouldn't.

"I need a little time," Cole managed.

"Take it. I want to help. Just let me in."

Cole took another bite. "So what was the other thing?"

"I interviewed the mayor this morning. His Worship has some good sound bites to explain the riot and his position on homelessness. Sounded like he was reading from cue cards handed to him by his press secretary."

"Not the brightest bulb, His Worship," said Cole.

"So here's the thing. I talked with Pesh after the interview. I got the distinct feeling that Monsieur Le Mayor was feeling beholden during our talk."

"To who?"

"Whom. To whom."

"Whatever. To whom, then?"

"Not sure. Business interests, certainly. But when I brought up the disappearances, his aide ended the meeting—practically slammed the door in my face. By the time I got back to my office, she'd already called and blown me off, saying that Andrews from Division 2 of the VPD would be handling it."

"Denman is over there right now."

"Really?"

"Yeah. Why?"

"Well, the mayor's office said that the VPD hadn't received a complaint yet."

"They have now."

"Okay, well, I guess I'll follow up with Andrews this afternoon."

"You want to talk with Marcia Lane," said Cole, "the team leader for the Missing Persons Task Force. The VPD set it up after the Pickton thing. Lots of flak from people over not taking missing person reports seriously enough in the Downtown Eastside. Good luck, because Andrews is a Nazi about the media."

"I'm a big girl. Do you think that Don West could be into something illegal? Pesh told me of rumors that organized crime had financed his first run for office five years ago. It was the nasty sort of stuff that an angry opposition pulls out in the dying days of a failing campaign. There was a photo of West with a man named Hoi Fu, a Korean Canadian, who at the time was responsible for much of the distribution of heroin in the Eastside. Fu also runs a bunch of legitimate businesses. It was one of those stupid 'shake hands with the Hells Angels' type of photos, his campaign managers said. They claimed ignorance. Thought Fu was just a nice business man running a laundromat and a noodle shop. Does any of this sound at all familiar to you?"

Cole shook his head. "I wasn't here yet. During *that* election campaign I was still in Ottawa."

"Pesh tells me that in the last two years Don West has been a spectacularly mediocre mayor and has kept his nose out of trouble."

"That's a great reputation to have as a civic leader."

Nancy laughed. "Just what I'd want my political epitaph to say. My point is that West, as head of the Police Board, has caused very little trouble for the narcotics business in this city. I don't know if that is any indication of guilt, but it's not saying much for his leadership."

"Heroin ain't what it used to be. Crack and meth are the thing. I don't know who is controlling that."

"Denman would know, wouldn't he?"

"Probably. So what's all this got to do with three missing homeless people?"

"I don't know. Maybe nothing. Maybe everything. There may be more to these three people than meets the eye."

"You think one of these people was actually a dealer? From what Denman told me, one of these guys sold umbrellas. You think that was his cover?" Cole was smiling despite himself.

"Don't be cute."

"I can't help it sometimes."

"Try," said Nancy, but she was smiling too. It was good to see Cole's sense of humor surface. "Maybe they were in the wrong place at the wrong time, and this guy Fu took them out. Maybe they were low-level street operatives in his organization, or used to be, and he was cleaning up loose ends."

"And you think that Don West knows something about this?"

"I think West is a mouthpiece. His cue card answers were *way* too pat to be heartfelt. The question is, who is he a mouthpiece for?"

"Might be time to find out," said Cole. He knew that in more ways than one, his work was just beginning.

TEN

BY TUESDAY MORNING SEAN LIVINGSTONE was as cold and wet as he'd ever been. For the last two nights he slept in an alley adjacent to the now closed, but still occupied, Lucky Strike Hotel. He had found a somewhat sheltered place, under the lip of a doorway that lead to the loading ramp of an import-export business. The previous evening, the wind had changed direction and the deluge had begun. His single wool blanket, scavenged after making arrangements with Umbrella Man, was so wet he could wring water from it, and it stank like an old dog. His clothes stuck to his clammy skin. He felt itchy, and his eyes were watering and he was dizzy with hunger.

He rose long before the sun and began to make his way toward the Carnegie Centre, which didn't open its doors until seven. He dragged his feet and looked down at the glistening pavement and dirty pools of water. He searched doggedly for distractions. He found one about two blocks from the Carnegie. Two men huddled beneath an overhang just inside an alley off Hastings Street. Like him, they were cold and wet and weary. Driven by an impulse, Sean strolled toward them.

"You fellas awake?" he asked, stepping into the alley.

One of the men looked up at him, bleary-eyed.

"I'm from the Community Advocacy group. My name is Sean."

"You ain't from no community group. You're as goddamned wet as we are."

"I've been out all night making sure folks are okay."

"Bull shit. Fuck off," the man muttered.

Sean grinned and took his dripping pack off his back. The spontaneity of what he was doing thrilled him. "I've got some food here for you."

"You've got jack shit," said the man, looking at him from under the soaking brim of a greasy ball cap.

"Let's try to be polite," said Sean, reaching into his pack.

That's when Ball Cap Man hit him. It wasn't a hard blow, but it caught Sean completely by surprise, and sent him sprawling onto his back in a puddle of water-soaked garbage.

Ball Cap Man nudged his friend, who woke up and blinked hard. Sean tried to get to his feet, his hands still entangled in his pack. Ball Cap Man stepped forward and kicked at Sean's face. Sean managed to pull the come-along from his bag in time to deflect most of Ball Cap Man's blow. The second man stood, his blanket falling as he too kicked at Sean, connecting with his ribs. Sean grimaced and swung the come-along low. Ball Cap Man howled in pain as the tool connected with his ankle and he went down.

"You motherfucker," he yelled, falling backward. "You broke my fucking ankle."

Sean swung the come-along again and narrowly missed the second man, who grabbed a garbage can from the doorway and threw it at Sean, hitting him in the torso and face.

As Sean pushed the trash can off, he saw both men disappear around the corner of the alley and out onto the street. He lay in the alley a moment, breathing hard, his back in the filthy puddle, his face turned to the sky, rain pelting down on him.

WHEN THE DOORS of the Carnegie Centre opened at seven, a hundred people waited to get inside out of the rain. They queued up for coffee and slices of bread with peanut butter for breakfast. They sat around the main hall and in the corridors talking quietly and drying out. The building smelled like a barn full of animals, thought Sean, but realized that he was very much a part of that stench now.

Sean got coffee and something to eat and found a quiet place near the reading room where he could think about the morning's events. He had to admit that taking on two men at a time had proven too much for him. But the thrill of simply deciding spontaneously to approach the men had been worth the beating he'd gotten. He felt his face and realized that there was still blood on his nose, and that his cheek was tender. There would be an opportunity to settle that score in time.

At half past eight he saw Juliet Rose come into the Centre, and he made his way toward her.

"Sean, my God, what happened to you?"

"I got mugged. Bastards beat me up. Took my money."

"Come with me," she said. He followed her toward the back where she had an office. It was quieter there, away from the hurly-burly of the main room. "Step in, Sean. Have a seat, and take off your jacket."

"I'm awfully wet," he said dolefully.

"We need to fix that cut on your face." Sean dropped his jacket on the floor. Juliet pulled on a pair of gloves, found some supplies in the cabinet, and laid them out on top of her desk.

"Let's get this cleaned up," she said, swabbing at the cut with an antiseptic pad. "Can you tell me what happened?"

"I was sleeping in an alley a few blocks away." Sean closed his eyes as she dabbed at the wound. He winced. "I woke up and these two guys were going through my pockets. When they saw I was awake, one of the guys hit me with a rock."

"Sean, I'm going to put a couple of stitches in, is that okay? I'm afraid that living rough means a better than average chance of infection in open wounds."

"Okay," he said weakly.

"I'll do my best not to hurt you," she said, preparing the suture materials. He closed his eyes while she stitched up the cut. He winced again, and felt a hot tear run down his face.

"All done. This will help the cut heal faster, and if you're lucky, there won't be a scar."

"Thanks," he said, touching the sutures with his fingertips.

"They will dissolve in a week. If they don't, come back and I'll pull them out."

"You said that you might be able to help me find a place to live. Can you still help me?"

"Yes," she said, packing away the medical supplies. "I can have a look around the city for shelter space." She smiled. "The thing is, there is a long waiting list for community-supported housing. For every room that comes open, there are ten people in line for it. And unfortunately for you, you don't fit the target demographic."

"What's that?"

"You aren't a user, you don't have kids, and you're a man."

"Three strikes," he said.

Juliet nodded. Sean looked out her window.

"When I was a kid," he said, "I wanted to be a doctor. I had this vision of myself helping people, the way you do." He turned and touched the stitches. "I thought that by becoming a doctor I could work in a place like this, you know, helping people with their problems. Maybe go to Africa or Central America and help people there. I did really well in school. I worked hard. I got into university. It was great. When my parents died everything went crazy."

Juliet thought back on her first meeting with Sean only a week ago. "Sean, when we met you told me that your father had cut you off."

Sean looked out the window again. "He did. He and my mother got themselves killed in a car accident. That's what I meant. They went and died and I got nothing."

"How long have you been living on the street, Sean?"

He looked up at the ceiling. "My folks died about a year ago." He shook his head. "I just want to get on with my life. Get my feet back under me. I feel like I'm slipping."

Juliet stood up. "Meet me back here at five this afternoon."

JULIET WAITED FOR Denman to answer his phone.

"Hi, Denny," Juliet said, sitting in her office after Sean had left.

"How are you? You sound pretty down."

"It's the rain."

"You suffering from SAD already?"

"No, it's not me. It's everybody else. It's only been raining and cold for two days and already things are starting to fray. And there's something else."

"What is it?"

"I think another person has gone missing."

"Jesus Christ."

"Yeah, a woman named Veronica. Someone came in yesterday wearing her parka. It was pretty distinctive. She wore it summer and winter."

"Could he have just found it? Or picked it up at the Sally Ann?"

"I know the guy who's wearing it. I've talked with him. He says he found it in a dumpster. And I've got a call in to Marcia Lane."

"What do you need help with?"

"Night count. I've got to check on my flock."

"How about tonight?"

"No, not tonight. I have to take care of something after work. Tomorrow?"

"Okay."

"Meet me at Macy's at midnight. We'll have breakfast."

"Sounds like a date."

"Yeah—you, me, and a sleeping city." She paused. "Denman, I'm getting scared."

He was silent a moment. Through the phone line, Juliet could hear his light breathing and pictured him with his eyes closed in his cubicle of an office.

"Me too," he said.

DENMAN SNATCHED THE phone from its cradle again and dialed the familiar number, then asked for Marcia Lane. He got her voice mail and left a message.

He stood and paced up and down the main hall of Priority Legal's office. His staff knew that when he was pacing, it was best to leave him alone.

He looked in on one of his staff lawyers. "How are things over at the Lucky Strike?" he asked.

Patrick Blade looked up from a stack of briefs. "This is the last of the affidavits that we'll file in the suit against the City."

"And what about the occupation?"

"I heard from the Community Advocacy Society that the police are getting antsy, arresting anybody who brings food. The Coalition is trying to find ways of getting food up to their people, but it's been about twelve hours."

"Has the City made a statement yet?"

"Nothing out of the mayor's office. We keep hearing rumors of some big announcement." Blade made quotation marks with his fingers when he said *big*.

"Thanks," said Denman. He grabbed his raincoat from a hook by the front door as he walked past the reception desk. "Dave, I'll be out for a bit."

He stepped onto the street and into the rain, adjusting his flat cap and pulling the collar of his coat up around his chin. Denman wondered, What did he know? Three—now four—people were missing from the Downtown Eastside. There seemed to be no pattern, at least not that he could see. Two men, middle-aged, both of whom had been on the street for some time. Not drug users, Juliet said. And one woman, a former prostitute and user, but who had cleaned herself up, thanks to the help of Juliet and others. And now Veronica, a kleptomaniac for certain, a serial thief, he recalled from the times he'd represented her. She was also a user and a small-time dealer. What was the connection between these four? If any?

What else? The Lucky Strike had closed. That brought to seven hundred and fifty the number of single-room-occupancy beds lost this year. That meant more than a thousand people displaced. And one man largely responsible for all those closures: Frank Ainsworth, "Captain Condo."

Was there any connection between the four missing people and the Lucky Strike? Denman would have to check with Juliet. They would have a chance to do that tomorrow night, when they went on a night count.

Now the End Poverty Now Coalition had occupied the Lucky Strike. Denman had little good to say about the Coalition. He didn't like their tactics. He had to admit, however, they were bringing the issue of homelessness and poverty in Vancouver to the public's eye. What else did he know?

Bloody well little. So far there had been no bodies. These people had just vanished.

He walked through the driving rain, the water beading on his cap and dripping down the back of his neck. He was soaked to the skin when he heard his cell phone ring deep in his pocket.

"Scott."

"Denny, it's Cole. Hey, look, I want to thank you for Sunday. I just loved getting my butt kicked by my ten-year-old daughter. That was great. Just what I needed."

"Happy to oblige."

"Well, thanks, really."

"We're just getting started. The rabbit hole goes all the way to the bottom, you know."

"Bottom of what?"

"You."

"Great."

"My phone is about to short circuit in the rain, Cole. Anything else up?"

"Yeah, in fact. I had lunch with Nancy yesterday."

"She's speaking with you. Progress."

"Right, funny. Well, she interviewed the mayor. Actually got past his flack at City Hall. She's got a theory."

"What?"

"Let's coffee up."

They met at three o'clock at Macy's, a twenty-four-hour breakfast joint that had quickly become a place where local business people, social service providers, panhandlers, and even beat cops could meet on neutral ground. When they had coffee in front of them at a small table by the window, Cole said, "Nancy thinks there might be a connection between Hoi Fu and Mayor West." The well-lit room contrasted with the darkness beyond the pane of glass.

Denman sipped his coffee. "Yeah, of course there is." Cole tilted his head to one side in question. "Hoi Fu gave Don West five thousand dollars under the table during his first run at the mayor's office five years ago. West lost, but not by much. He tried again in the next election and won."

"Is this public knowledge?"

"Depends on what you mean. Listen, Hoi Fu runs most of the crime scene down here. He's a big fish in a small pond. Don West needed to take votes on the east side of the city. Fu, for all of his illegal activity, actually owns a bunch of legitimate businesses—groceries, laundromats, a video chain, a bunch of restaurants, and some stuff that skirts the edge of legal, like a raft of Asian massage parlors. He's totally connected across the east side of the city, and even into the West End and Point Grey. If you want to get elected in Vancouver, you need to work the four quarters of the city, and Fu can deliver the east. He's got half the Asian community working for him in his legitimate businesses and half in his illegal operations."

"The VDP know about this?"

Denman shook his head. "You've been working with the environmentalists too long, Cole. You think everything is white collar, white bread, and white skin. Of course they know. And every now and again they bust some of his middlemen, just to make sure Fu doesn't get too cocky. But the guy covers his tracks pretty well."

"What about now? Is West in thick with Fu?"

"It's hard to say. But the mayor's office would have to officially seal itself off from such undertakings. It's okay to flirt when you're running, but it's another thing altogether to be sleeping with the enemy once you're in office. I just don't see how West could be officially connected."

Cole fiddled with his coffee cup. "Could Hoi Fu be behind these disappearances?"

"I don't see how."

"Well, what if these three folks saw something they weren't supposed to? Or maybe they were in the wrong place at the wrong time? Maybe they owed him money, or it was drug related."

"Slow down, Sherlock. First off, Hoi Fu isn't going to be lending cash to folks on the street. That's not him. Second, what might they have seen? A drug deal? Jesus, I saw three go down walking here to have coffee with you. And it's four, now."

"Four what?"

"Four missing people."

"Good God," said Cole, pressing a palm to his face.

"Yeah. Juliet is pretty upset. A woman named Veronica. User. Petty thief with a long sheet. Her coat showed up on another guy."

"We should brace him!"

"Juliet talked to him. She knows the guy."

"What? You let her talk with him alone?"

"She's a big girl."

"Denman, this guy could be dangerous. What if he's working for Fu? What if Fu has this guy taking out people who are in his way somehow? What if Fu finds out that Juliet is onto his button man?"

"Cole, slow down," Denman said again. "This isn't television. This is the real world. Take it easy."

Cole shook his head. "Now who's not living in reality? You're the one who just told me that Hoi Fu has a lot riding on this region. Lots of money, lots of power. Nancy said that when she brought up the disappearances, His Worship clammed up and his handler rushed her away, then called her fifteen minutes later telling her that one of the divisional commanders of the VPD would be handling matters related to any crimes. Seems like West has a lot to say on just about everything, but when this comes up, he shuts up. Now you're saying you don't think there is a connection?"

"I just don't see it, Cole."

"Open your eyes, Denman. It's starting to become pretty clear that the City, organized crime, and maybe the bloody condo developers for all I know, are working together to steamroll the Downtown Eastside. I think maybe our four friends got in the way somehow."

Denman sipped his coffee. "How are you sleeping?" he asked.

"What's that got to do with anything?" Cole asked angrily.

"Just wondering. I'm heading out tomorrow night with Juliet to do a street count. I wonder if you'd like to do a little night work together before she and I hit the bricks."

"Now you're talking my language, son," said Cole, grinning widely.

ELEVEN

"I'M HEADING HOME," SAID MARY from the door to Cole's office.

Cole looked at his watch. "I don't know Mary, it's only seven-thirty. Starting to slack off, aren't you?"

She smiled at him. "You need anything?"

"Nope. Thanks."

"You've got a call with Nexus Energy at 9:00 AM."

Nexus was one of Cole's most promising clients, and a living example of Cole's new philosophy on how to save the world. The alternative energy company had started with tidal power and were now moving into syn-gas and solar power in a big way. He knew that during the call in the morning the company's CEO would ask if he would consider representing them in a new multi-stakeholder alliance to develop climate change solutions.

Cole looked up at Mary. "I'll be here."

"Okay, goodnight."

"'Night," he said, turning back to the window. Night. It was almost time to hit the streets.

"SO WHAT EXACTLY are we looking for?" asked Cole, his baseball cap pulled tightly down over his forehead, his dark curls tucked up under the cap. Cole and Denman walked side by side through the rain. It fell with a steady pulse, one moment light and little more than mist, the next moment driving against the asphalt in violent bursts.

"No idea," said Denman, walking beside him, stepping around the larger puddles that spanned the sidewalks.

"You're kidding. We're just two guys out for a walk in the most dangerous part of the city on a stormy night, looking for trouble?"

"Something like that."

"Okay," said Cole, splashing through a puddle.

A few minutes later Denman drew a deep breath and said, "So *you* think there might be some connection between Hoi Fu and Don West. Between organized crime in the Downtown Eastside and City Hall. Only one way to find out."

"What's that?"

"Ask."

"Now you *are* kidding me."

In the darkness Cole could see Denman smile, and he knew that he wasn't kidding.

"So where are we going?"

"The Golden Dragon."

"The Asian restaurant?"

"Yup."

Cole was silent as they ran across Gore Street, the rain pounding down on their heads.

"Look, I'm happy to just go along for the ride, Denny, but if you want me to be of any help, you might want to tell me what you've got in mind."

"I don't really know, Cole. That's the honest truth. I really can't figure this whole mess out any better than you can. Do I think that the mayor and a crime boss are colluding to bump off homeless people? No. Do I think that Hoi Fu might somehow be involved on his own? Maybe. Does the mayor's office want to cover something up related to the disappearances? Maybe. Is there some kind of connection between all these people? Who knows? I really don't know anything right now, and it's frustrating as hell, so we just need to start poking around and see what turns up."

"I can go along with that," said Cole.

Denman smiled at his friend. "Good."

"I'm good at poking people," said Cole, raising his voice as the din around them increased.

"Don't I know it," Denman teased.

They turned toward the row of shops and restaurants next to the vacant lots on Prior Avenue. Instead of walking to the front door of the ancient building that now housed the Golden Dragon, Denman slipped through the slats in a wooden fence and made his way down the darkened alley between two buildings. Cole followed him, his heart rate increasing as they made their way through the shadows, sloshing through standing puddles that smelled like burnt sesame oil and garbage. Denman disappeared around the back of the building. Cole quickly followed. When

Cole caught up with Denman, his friend was standing in front of a door. The rear of the old brick structure was flanked by a tall wooden fence rimmed with rusty barbed wire, separating it from the busy street beyond. A heavy dumpster reeked of fish and rotting vegetables.

Denman knocked on the door.

"Seems kinda dramatic," said Cole, fighting the tightness in his throat.

The door opened a crack. A line of light spilled across the water in the alley.

"What is it?" Cole heard a voice from inside the doorway ask.

"Denman Scott to see Mr. Fu, if it pleases him."

The door closed.

"Friendly sorts."

"Cautious."

They waited in the darkness, the rain falling in sheets in the alley. After a minute Cole was about to speak again, when the door opened.

"Just you," the voice said.

Denman turned to Cole. "I'm a big boy."

"Ten minutes and I come in through the front door," said Cole.

Denman stepped through the portal of light and the door closed behind him.

DENMAN WAS NOT unaccustomed to the less than savory underworld of Vancouver's Asian crime scene. For the last ten years he had lived among the elements that made up the dark underbelly of the city, so when the door closed behind him, he wasn't surprised to be not too gently shoved against the wall and roughly frisked by a Korean man who must have outweighed him by a hundred pounds. A few feet away, a second man stood eyeing him coolly. The rough business of the search complete, Denman was allowed to turn around. He was in the kitchen of the Golden Dragon, where half a dozen Japanese, Chinese, and Korean cooks were filling orders. The room was a cacophony of kitchen sounds—pots and pans clanging, food sizzling in woks, waitresses yelling at cooks to hurry with their food. Flames leapt from the grills and the cooks wiped their faces with rags as they bantered among each another. The smell of Korean barbecue and Japanese noodles was thick in the air. Everything seemed to be coated in a thin sheen of sesame oil.

"Mr. Fu will see you upstairs," said the large man who had patted him down. "Follow me, please." The second man stayed by the back door.

They walked through the bustling kitchen and then mounted a set of stairs near the entrance to the dining room. "Right this way," the big man said, and they walked down a long hall. At the far end a man stood watch by a doorway, and when Denman approached with his escort, the man poked his head into the room and then nodded for Denman to enter.

The room he stepped into from the dark hall was well lit by ornate Asian lamps and smelled of jasmine incense. Hoi Fu was seated at a low table along the far wall. Three other men sat with him. They were eating a dinner of Korean barbecue, the pork and chicken roasting on a small cylindrical grill at the center of the table.

"Come in," Hoi Fu motioned to Denman. Denman slipped off his shoes, bowed, then came forward. A thick carpet covered the floor, and red and orange tapestries adorned the walls.

"Thank you for seeing me, Mr. Fu," Denman said, coming up to the table.

"Please, sit. Would you care to join us?" Fu was a short, compact man with a head of short black hair and a cleanly shaven face. Though in his sixties, he looked no older than forty. His skin was clear and free of wrinkles, save for the crow's feet around his eyes, which deepened when he spoke with his broad, friendly smile.

Denman sat and accepted a plate.

"These are men who run some of my businesses around town," said Fu. Denman nodded as Fu made introductions. "And Denman Scott runs Priority Legal on Hastings. He is one of our city's great citizens. He provides free legal assistance to those in need. The homeless, those in poverty, those abused by the system or by our over-zealous police force."

Denman smiled and turned his meat on the grill.

"Now, what is it that I can do for you? Have you come seeking a donation to your excellent cause?"

Denman's smile widened. "No, but thank you for thinking of it. Perhaps in the future. My business today is of a more troubling nature, Mr. Fu. I've come to ask for your assistance. It seems something is terribly wrong in our community. Four people have gone missing in the Downtown Eastside in the last month. All long-term street people. All well known by those providing social services."

"By that you are talking about Juliet Rose, the excellent street nurse."

"Her, and others," said Denman, holding Fu's eyes.

"You and she are developing a strong friendship," said Fu.

"We share a common cause."

"Indeed."

"I was hoping you might have some knowledge as to their whereabouts."

Fu took a mouthful of pork and chewed thoughtfully. "I know nothing of their whereabouts. I try to stay abreast of the rumors and gossip on the streets, if only just for the sport of it. But where these . . . men or women?"

"Two men and two women."

"Where these men and women have disappeared to, I do not know."

Denman dipped some pork into hot sauce. He nodded as he ate. "Mr. Fu, I have heard concerns that the City itself is cracking down on homeless people, making their lives uncomfortable. I've received an increasing number of complaints of excessive force. Prostitutes are being beaten. Homeless people roughed up. The rally that was to show support for the Downtown Eastside community last week turned violent. The police beat people and tear-gassed the crowd."

"Yes, I understand His Worship the Mayor had to be rushed from the scene," Fu smiled.

"Have you heard anything that would suggest that the City is cracking down in the Downtown Eastside to try to bully people out of the area to make way for condo development?"

Fu sat back against his cushions. "Surely you must know that if the City wants to build condominiums in the Eastside, all they have to do is support the developers' efforts to buy up the low-rent hotels and to fast-track development permits. It's really that simple. They don't need to beat up hookers to do that. Now, that being said, the VPD never needed an excuse to pick on the least privileged among us. As you might know, I have associates who make their living any way they are able, which sometimes skirts the strict legal parameters in our society, and I have come to understand that to do so one risks far more than arrest in our fair city. If you take my meaning."

Denman allowed a smile and a nod. "But you feel certain that this excessive force isn't in any way connected to the closure of places like the Astoria Grand or the Lucky Strike Hotel."

Denman felt it, though he couldn't see it. At the mention of the Lucky Strike, the energy changed in the room. It was for just a split second, but it caused the hair on the back of his neck to rise.

"I assure you, if there was any connection between the abuse our city's finest heap on the citizenry of our community and the redevelopment of low rent hotels, I would know. And I would gladly share that with you."

Denman took a last bite and then a sip of tea. "Mr. Fu, you have been a gracious host. I appreciate your time. With your permission, I will take my leave," he said, rising.

"Come back and see me about a donation to your excellent work, Denman. You are welcome here anytime."

Denman bowed gently to his host, retrieved his shoes, and made his way back down the dimly lit hall.

COLE STOOD IN the darkness, leaning against the wall beside the back door, the rain drumming down on his ball cap. A steady drip had formed along the brim of his hat and slid down his coat. He dug out his cell phone and checked the time. Denman had been gone for just two minutes and already he was growing antsy. He had been serious about the ten minutes. In eight more ticks he would be marching through the front door, and God help anybody who got between him and his best friend.

"Of course, I do that and I won't be able to piss in this city without looking over my shoulder," said Cole aloud, grinning.

In the near total darkness of the alley he took a few steps and bent his knees to loosen his legs. He scanned the space around him, trying to discern objects—the large metal trash bin, a few wooden crates, the leaning piles of empty cardboard boxes being soaked into a pulp. He stood up again and was about to take a few steps into the passage connecting the alley to the street when he heard distant voices.

Cole held his breath and listened. A foot splashed in the puddle of water spanning the main alley and a man cursed.

The voices grew louder. Cole felt an instinctive need to hide. He squeezed between the garbage bin and the tall wooden fence, crouching in a tiny space thick with the smell of fish and rotting vegetables and discarded cooking oil. Two men passed within ten feet of him and knocked on the same door Denman had just passed through. They talked in loud voices.

"Fucking rain."

"Never going to let up, it seems."

"Now until April."

"You're kidding me."

"You haven't been in Vancouver very long, have you?"

"I just got here in June. It's been sunny since. I thought I was living in Shangri-La."

"You're in for a rough fucking ride, buddy."

"Knock again. They must not have heard the first time."

Suddenly the door opened and the shaft of light spilled into the alley again. Cole could see the two men clearly. They were burly, dressed in long raincoats, the downpour driving against their crew cuts. White men, somewhere in their early thirties, Cole guessed, with square jaws and mustaches.

Cole could not see who answered the door, but the man closest to Cole said, "Pickup for the Lucky Strike Supper Club." The other man laughed.

The door closed and the alley turned dark again. A few moments later, it opened wide, and someone handed out large packages of food wrapped in plastic bags.

Cole was only ten feet away, trying to shrink farther into the small area behind the garbage bin. The light illuminated the alley well enough that if the men turned to look in his direction, he would be discovered. His heart raced as he crouched uncomfortably.

"Better not have forgotten the fried wontons," the man farthest from Cole said. "Andrews loves his fried wontons." Both men laughed and the door closed. They disappeared from the rain-soaked alley.

Cole stood up. The rain continued to drum down on his head but he didn't feel it.

Lucky Strike Supper Club. What were they talking about? Cole wondered.

He fished his cell phone from his pocket and checked the time. It had been twelve minutes since Denman disappeared. The pickup had distracted him, but now he was able to squeeze out from behind the dumpster. Time to go in with a blaze of glory. He pressed past the door and was about to round the corner when the door behind him opened again and he heard Denman say something in Mandarin. Cole stopped and turned. Denman emerged with a box of food in his hand.

"Like a fried wonton?" he asked Cole.

TWELVE

"I THINK WE NEED TO huddle the troops," said Cole, feeling the rain again after the adrenaline had subsided.

"Agreed."

"Let's call Nancy and Juliet in the morning and start putting our heads together."

"You said they called it the Lucky Strike Supper Club?"

"Yeah."

"Pretty strange, I'll grant you. But suspicious?"

"Come on, Denman. Who picks up eats from the back door of a crime-owned restaurant in the Downtown Eastside at eleven o'clock on a rainy night?"

"Okay, it's strange. I'll call Juliet and you call Nancy. Eleven tomorrow morning at Macy's?"

"I've got a nine o'clock, which Mary will kill me if I miss, so yeah, eleven is good."

Cole couldn't sleep, though. When he arrived home, he stood in the shower until the stench of fish and oil was washed from him. He'd gone to bed but lay awake staring at the ceiling. Finally, at two o'clock, he got up and poured three fingers of Irish whiskey into a glass with a little ice, just for show, and sat down to read. Instead of reading, though, his thoughts roamed freely over the night landscape, returning again and again to the conversation between the two muscle-heads in the alley.

Who were those guys? They seemed out of place in an alley in the Downtown Eastside. What was the Lucky Strike Supper Club? And who was this Andrews who liked his fried wontons?

His mind drifted from the events of that night to his thoughts from the moments just before the men appeared in the darkness. It was there that he found a more oppressive darkness, or rather, where the darkness found him. Cole lurched toward sleep preoccupied by the source of his diurnal nightmares.

Cole's phone rang, and instinctively he raised his fists in front of him, half rising from the armchair he was slumped in. A bolt of pain shot through him, his ribs aching from the awkward sleep and reflexive jarring. "Good God . . ." he mumbled, sitting back down and holding his arms across his ribs. He reached across the clutter on the table and fumbled for the phone. The portable receiver slipped from his hands and hit the floor and he bent too quickly to retrieve it and another spasm of pain pierced his chest. "Fuck," he finally spat, grabbing the phone from the floor and hitting the receive button.

"Blackwater," he barked.

"Cole, it's Mary."

"Oh, Mary. Hi, sorry. What time is it?"

"It's 8:00 AM."

"Right, God—the Nexus call."

"The cab will be outside your door at eight-thirty, Cole."

He rubbed his eyes. "Thank you, Mary."

"Don't mention it, Cole. Let's get your game on, okay?"

At ten to nine Mary greeted him at the door. "The Nexus file is on your desk," she said by way of greeting.

"Thank you, Mary. Where would I be without you?"

"In bed." She smiled.

"Don't I know it!"

"And out your best client," she added.

"Right," he said, entering his cave of an office to review the Nexus Energy file.

As he expected, during the telephone meeting he was invited to sit on the company's behalf on a new, pioneering energy and climate change association. Cole had felt a rush of pride. It had been almost five years since he decided to fly solo as a strategy consultant, and the invitation was a sign of his success. But his euphoria was short-lived. Late in the meeting, he learned that the association would be led by Brian Marriott. Brilliant, charming, and politically connected, Marriott had been the Ottawa lobbyist for the Petroleum Resources Group when Cole was the conservation director for the Canadian Conservation Association. In public they had been outwardly tolerant, but everybody in Ottawa knew the two men despised each other. Cole heard through the grapevine that Marriott had had a change of heart in the last couple of years. Marriott had read

The Weathermakers—a revolutionary look at the ecology and politics of climate change—while on vacation sometime back, and left the PRG when they refused to yield on the issue of global warming. Somehow Cole couldn't fathom Marriott leading a climate change association, especially one that Cole was now involved in.

Cole sighed. "Anybody but Brian Marriott," he said aloud after he put the phone down.

"What's that, Cole?" said Mary, her face appearing at the door.

"Brian Marriott."

"That name sounds familiar."

"I think I may have just screwed myself, Mary."

"And to think it's only eleven in the morning," she said in a chipper voice.

"Can you find out everything that Brian Marriott has been up to since I left Ottawa, Mary?"

"Sure."

"And look under the rocks."

"That good, eh?"

He arrived in the Downtown Eastside ten minutes late. Nancy, Denman, and a beautiful, plainly dressed woman sat together in the window of Macy's. He rushed in and offered his apologies.

"Up most of the night," he said by way of explanation.

Denman stood and said, "Cole Blackwater, Juliet Rose." The two shook hands.

"Finally, the infamous Cole Blackwater darkens my doorway," Juliet said with a smile.

"Finally," he responded, "I get to meet the saving grace of the Downtown Eastside. Does anybody else need a coffee?" He looked around, saw no takers, and went to the counter. He ordered a coffee and bought a sugary doughnut and sat back down.

"Let's get right to this," said Denman, and proceeded to fill the women in on the evening before.

"You did what?" Nancy exclaimed after hearing the story.

"Cole has this theory," said Denman. "He thinks that City Hall is somehow mixed up with organized crime on the Eastside and is knocking off homeless people to eliminate opposition to condo development."

Nancy shook her head. "You know, Cole, when I told you that I thought that maybe the missing people were connected with Fu, I didn't expect you and your sidekick to go kicking in doors looking for them."

"Actually," said Denman, "Cole was my sidekick . . ."

Juliet jumped in. "I think you're overlooking something important. None of these four people were involved in street-level crime. And none of them were operatives for Hoi Fu."

"How can you be sure?" asked Cole.

"I work with these people every day," she said. "I know them as well as anybody could. I know who the dealers are, the runners, the muscle. You have to believe me, these were four ordinary people."

"Ordinary?" asked Cole.

"As ordinary as you can be living on the street. Sure, they have their troubles. A week on the street and you would too. Mental illness and addictions. Peaches hooked for a while. Veronica was known to re-sell some smack. But they weren't mixed up with Fu. No way."

"Juliet knows what she's talking about, Cole," said Denman.

"No argument from me. I'm just trying to figure this all out," agreed Cole.

"You said they called it a Supper Club. Sounds like something that happens on a regular basis." Nancy pointed out.

"Sounds like," said Cole. "But at least one of the guys who were picking up food was a first-timer."

"Why do you say that?" asked Nancy.

"Just the way they were talking. It was like he'd never been out of the West End, you know what I mean?"

"Describe them again, would you?" asked Denman.

"Big dudes. Even with long raincoats on, I could tell. The one guy, the one farthest from me, was cruiser weight. Like one-eighty. The other guy was easily heavyweight. Two hundred easy. And not fat. Fit. Big dudes . . ."

"Don't mind Cole," said Nancy to Juliet. "He can't help but size everybody up as a potential opponent."

"Few too many shots to the head," said Denman, making a face. Juliet laughed.

"Ha ha," said Cole. "My point is these guys were big. And I could see they had short hair. Their hoods didn't cover their foreheads, and their hairlines were like brush cuts. And mustaches."

"They were cops," said Juliet.

"Come on, how do you know that?" asked Cole.

"Who the hell else wears a mustache and a crew cut?" asked Nancy.

"Fair point," said Cole.

"And that means the Andrews they mentioned, the one who likes his wontons fried, is John Andrews," said Denman.

"Division 2 Commander," said Nancy.

Cole sat back in his chair and fiddled with his empty coffee cup. "Okay, so if these guys were delivering food to a meeting hosted by Andrews and dealing with the Lucky Strike, what does that mean?"

"Maybe nothing," said Nancy.

"Or maybe it's a nightly strategy session to address the standoff," said Denman. "That would figure."

"Sure," added Juliet. "You know that the City and the cops are stewing over this occupation. It's a total mess."

"Ironic that the cops are getting takeout when they've stopped food from getting to the protesters," said Nancy, making a note.

"You can't write about this," said Cole.

"Really? You're not willing to go on the record?" she mocked. "'Overheard in Dark Alley, Fried Wonton Conspiracy Theory . . .'" Her hand inscribed the headline in the air in front of her.

"No, really."

"She knows, Cole," said Denman.

"I'm just making sure," said Cole.

"I learned my lesson, asshole," said Nancy.

Cole shook his head and looked down.

"People, please, not in front of the kids," Denman said, looking around.

"So what we have is the possibility of the cops and the City feasting while the protesters starve. Is that it?" asked Juliet.

"No, we've got *way* more," said Cole. "We've got these meatballs picking up chow from the back door of a restaurant owned by a crime boss."

"That doesn't necessarily mean anything," said Nancy.

"It doesn't mean nothing, either," spat Cole. "Look. I don't know why I'm the only one who sees this." He raised his voice. "We've got cops picking up grub from the back door of a place that is a front for organized crime in the city, delivering it to a meeting where the divisional commander is talking about the Lucky Strike. We think it's got to do with the occupation, and that the City is involved, but we don't know that for sure. Meanwhile, back at the ranch, we've got four of Juliet's flock gone missing, all in the last month. All this while the city gears up for a huge development push into the last real estate available for condo development in the city's core." He pounded his flat hand on the table, making the coffee mugs bounce. The other three stared at him.

"Cole, I swear to God, if you yell at me one more time I'm going to punch you," said Nancy.

Cole took a deep breath. "I'm sorry." He put his face in his hand a moment, then rubbed his eyes. "I'm sorry. I didn't get any sleep last night. I couldn't shut down."

"You need to deal with your shit," said Nancy. "We're your friends. We're here to help. But you need to do it without taking it out on us, okay?"

"Right," said Cole. "Got it."

"Juliet, what do we know about where these people were when they disappeared?" asked Nancy, her voice calm again.

"Well, the first man I noticed missing, a fellow named Bobbie, sold umbrellas in the West End but slept down here most nights. He had rooms in various places around the Downtown Eastside, including the Lucky Strike, from time to time. The second person, Peaches, was a regular at the women's shelter and at some of the SROs. She hung outside Macy's here most days. The third fellow, Jerry, was a real roamer, but I knew him from Oppenheimer Park.

"Veronica, well, she followed her nose." Juliet smiled. "She could smell a score from a mile away and a B and E opportunity even farther. She was a piece of work. Liked to wait for places to close and then move in and clean house."

Cole took his hand from his face and looked up. His face was white, but not from pressing his fingers against it. "What did you say?"

"I said she was a piece of work."

"No, after . . ."

"That she would wait for an SRO to close and then move in and swipe people's stuff."

Cole interrupted. "Denny, you still have that map of SROs?"

"Yeah, why?"

"Let's go. *Now.*"

He wouldn't let them walk. "I need to see something now, before it fades."

They hailed a cab on Pender and rode the five-dollar fare to Denman's office.

Three men outside the office of Priority Legal sat panhandling. Denman was about to stop, but Cole barked, "No Mother Teresa stuff right now! Come on."

Juliet looked at Denman and he straightened up. "I'll be back in a minute, fellas," he said, and followed Cole. He keyed in his security code and the four walked inside.

As soon as Denman entered, someone poked their head out from an office and said, "Marcia Lane has been calling for you."

"Okay, I'll call her back in a minute. If she calls again—"

"You're in a meeting," growled Cole as he continued down the hall.

"I'm in a meeting," smiled Denman. "Tell her I'll ring within the hour."

"Could be about the missing people," said Juliet.

"Likely is," said Denman. "She's not inviting me to the Policeman's Ball."

"I'll take you," said Nancy. "Apparently, I get tickets to cover it."

"That would be fun," said Denman.

Cole stopped in front of the boardroom. "Map?" he said.

"Right," said Denman, and went into his tiny office to retrieve a map tube. In the boardroom, he took out a laminated map of the Downtown Eastside and spread it across the table. The map was actually a series of aerial photos of the city, showing each building, park, street, and vacant lot in some detail. Street names were printed over the photos, and single-room occupancy hotels were shaded in three tones.

"What do the colors mean?" asked Nancy, her finger touching one.

"Green means intact. Yellow, on the block. Red, gone."

"Seems straightforward," she said.

"Tell us again what you said at Macy's," said Cole, looking at Juliet.

She repeated her knowledge of the four people who were missing. Cole took a dry-erase marker from the whiteboard and traced what they knew of the travels of each of the four, one at a time. Slowly the shapes covered much of the map, illustrating a "home range" for each man or woman. For some, the range left the map, and for others, like Veronica, it was very small.

"What do we know of the last known whereabouts of each of these people?" asked Cole, staring at the map.

"Nothing," said Juliet. "They're missing. No bodies."

"Not yet," breathed Nancy.

"Let's hope not *ever*," said Denman, but he knew it was a long shot.

"What about the last place *you* saw them?" asked Cole.

"The first man, I saw him on my last night count at Keefer and Taylor."

Cole made an X at the intersection.

"Peaches. At Macy's. I bought her lunch."

Cole made another X.

"The third man, at Carnegie."

An X on the old library.

"And Veronica, at the Lucky Strike, on eviction day."

A final X.

Cole grabbed some masking tape and hung the map on the large whiteboard, then stood back. They all stared at it. The four home ranges created ovals and oblongs that converged and overlapped at a central location. The X's formed a triangle, the bottom a straight line between the intersection of Keefer and Taylor and the Carnegie Centre at Main. The X where Veronica had been seen pillaging the recently evictees' possessions at the Lucky Strike marked the center of the bottom of the triangle, and Macy's Coffee Shop the tip.

They studied at the map and the overlapping circles around the landmark hotel.

"We need to know more about the relationship between these people and the Lucky Strike Hotel," said Cole.

"There's an easy way to find out at least one thing," said Juliet.

They looked at her.

"How?" asked Cole and Nancy in unison.

"Welfare," responded Juliet.

"What does Welfare have to do with this?" asked Cole.

Juliet picked up the phone at the end of the conference table, while Denman said, "Maybe a lot. If any of these people were staying at the Lucky Strike Hotel recently, or even in the past, there's a good chance that Welfare was footing the bill. In a lot of cases, when someone who is collecting welfare stays at an SRO like the Lucky Strike, they sign over their check to the place housing them. Welfare deposits it directly to the hotel. It usually covers most of the rent."

"Most? Are you saying that some of these shitholes actually charge more than what Welfare pays?" spat Cole.

Denman smiled. "Most do. Standard rent is four hundred and twenty-five dollars per month. Welfare pays three hundred and fifty dollars. Some of these places aren't half bad, Cole. It really depends on the owners."

Cole shook his head.

"The city inspectors are pretty good. They check these places out about once a year. But there's only so much they can do. At least in the SROs the desk clerk has to check on people once a day. It's the law. On the street, people can just slip through the cracks. Except for the street nurses and people from the various social service agencies, there's nobody looking in on them."

Juliet hung up the phone. They turned toward her. "I called Kerry at Welfare. She does her rounds making sure that the people the SROs say they are housing are actually there. I've tagged along a few times, looking into people's health. Anyway, I gave Kerry the list and she's going to run it against her records. She'll call back in a few minutes."

"It might not tell us everything," said Denman.

"Why's that?" asked Nancy.

"Some of these people have never been on welfare. Some have been kicked off because they don't want to go on the system. For some it's paranoia about being kept track of; others don't want anybody's help. There are a lot of rugged individualists on the streets of this city. For others, they get the boot. They don't show up for the programs intended to help them find work, or maybe they try to cheat the system. One way or another, not everybody at the bottom of the barrel is collecting."

The conversation continued in this vein for another five minutes. Then one of Priority Legal's staff leaned into the room and said, "Juliet, there's a call for you on three."

Juliet picked up the receiver. Cole, Denman, and Nancy watched her speaking. Cole stood up and paced with his hands behind his back.

Juliet was on the phone for a couple of minutes, making notes. She nodded her head a few times, then said, "Thanks again, Kerry. I owe you one." When she hung up the phone, she looked at her friends. "At one time or another, Welfare paid for a room at the Lucky Strike for all four of our people."

"Okay," said Cole, his arms folded across his chest. "Anybody still think that the Lucky Strike Supper Club is about the occupation?"

"HAS COLE SUFFERED any recent trauma?" asked Juliet when she and Denman were alone. The meeting had gone on another twenty minutes, with Cole refusing to listen to any other theory other than his own. Then Nancy, shaking her head, left for the *Vancouver Sun* building, and Cole followed shortly after.

Denman laughed. "Cole himself is a walking trauma."

"I'm serious, Denny."

"Me too. The man is a wrecking ball picking up speed. But recently, though? Four and a half years ago, Cole saw his father kill himself. The old man blew his own head off with a shotgun right in front of Cole."

"Oh my God." Juliet raised her hand to her mouth. Tears immediately welled in her eyes.

"His father was pretty rough on Cole. You know how Cole boxes, or used to, right? Well, I guess the old man used Cole as a punching bag through much of his adolescence and into his teens. By the time Cole was seventeen, he'd had enough and split. But the damage was done. He didn't see the old man for, like, sixteen years? Then when his life exploded in Ottawa . . ."

"What do you mean, exploded?"

"Holy shit, down the rabbit hole . . . Okay, this is really top secret. Cole was married, had a kid, Sarah, but was having an affair with Nancy."

"Webber? Nancy Webber?" Juliet jerked a thumb in the direction of the boardroom as if the reporter was still there.

"Yeah."

"Rabbit hole is right."

"Anyway, Cole and Nancy get to talking one night, and Cole, being at that time a little too focused on Cole Blackwater, tells Nancy the big lie. Something about National Defence and tanks and endangered species, or something like that—" Juliet made a face "—and Nancy ran the story."

"Really?"

"Yeah. It got past the *Globe and Mail*'s fact checkers and everything. It was enough to get Nancy fired. Cole also got his ass fired from his top job at the Canadian Conservation Alliance, and he decided to follow Jennifer Polson, his ex, and Sarah across Canada to Vancouver. Stops at the family ranch on the way. I guess Cole learned that his father had gotten rough once or twice with his mom after he had left the home place, and Cole flew into a rage. As I understand it, Cole was going to beat his father, maybe to death, but didn't get the chance. He walked into the barn to confront the old man, and blam. He sees his father blow his own head off." He stopped for a moment. "What I don't get is, why now?" he mused.

"What do you mean?"

"Why is he losing his marbles now? That was four and a half years ago. I mean, maybe there is a time delay on this stuff, but that seems a little long."

Juliet looked down at the floor. "Remember when you went up to Port Lostcoast last spring . . ."

"Well, summer, actually. We went up to spend a couple of days on Cole's boat before he signed it over."

"Who else was there?"

"Sarah, Nancy, and me."

"Nancy was there?"

"She was also there with Cole in the spring during the whole Archie Ravenwing episode."

"I think Cole is suffering from post-traumatic stress disorder. I think something happened in Port Lostcoast that triggered the release of that stress, and right now we're watching as your friend Cole Blackwater slowly implodes."

After more discussion, Denman and Juliet agreed that they would have to intervene somehow in Cole's downward spiral.

"Denny, it's serious. I know *you* believe me. People who have suffered PTSD can do crazy things. You need to get him in to a counselor for treatment."

"Cole isn't exactly the 'sit around and get in touch with his feelings' type."

"Seeing as how we're all now working on this missing person thing together, we better do something to keep Cole from going postal on us."

Denman took a deep breath and exhaled. "He's going back out tonight."

"You better go with him."

"I thought we were doing a night count?"

"Not tonight. This is more important. And the weather sucks for counting folks. Nobody wants to be bugged in the pouring rain. Plus," she said, "I have a guest."

"Who? I'm insanely jealous."

"Really? I didn't know you cared . . ."

"Then you're as blind as Cole," Denman said, faking a pout.

She smiled and touched his hand. "No need to be jealous," she said. "Just an old friend who stopped by from out of town. Be gone in a few days."

"Better be." Denman smiled and put his hand on Juliet's. "Or I'll have to come by and throw the bum out myself."

She smiled back. "Denny, I don't want to sound dramatic, but Cole needs your help. You need to watch him. He saw his father kill himself. Something happened in Port Lostcoast; whatever it is was some sort of trigger. It wouldn't be out of the question for Cole to consider taking his own life."

THIRTEEN

IT WAS LUCKY THAT SEAN had met Ben. For the better part of a year, they were like two peas in a pod.

"What are you doing?" Sean asked, finding Ben hunched over something near the edge of the school property.

"None of your fucking business. Piss off," said Ben, not turning to see whom he was talking to.

"Someone is coming, that's all."

"I said . . ." He looked up and saw a woman making her way across the field. "Fuck. Okay, come here."

Sean stepped forward. He trusted Ben. There was something in Ben's eyes—pale dark pools—that reflected his own and made him recognize a kindred spirit at once.

"Take this," said Ben, handing him a sharp stick that had something sticky on the end. "Dig here, quick."

Sean took the stick and began to dig in the dirt near the fence. Ben jammed something furry under the wire mesh.

The school's vice principal stood beside them. "What are you boys doing?" she asked.

"Hey," said Ben. "Well, I was walking home for lunch and I noticed this squirrel caught under the fence. Me and my friend here decided to try and save him, but I think it's too late."

"Oh my," said the vice principal, bending to see. "You've got yourselves quite a mess there, boys. Lots of germs on those things. Better visit the washroom before heading back to class."

"Yes, ma'am," said Ben. Sean nodded. "We'll just make sure he's in a place where he won't attract other animals, ma'am."

"Leave it alone," said the vice principal, her face a little twisted. "I'll call a caretaker. You two head inside. Class is about to start." She turned and walked away.

Ben looked at Sean. Sean regarded him with awe.

"Want to see how to pull the legs off one of these fuckers while it's still alive?" Ben asked.

BEN AND SEAN were inseparable that summer.

"It's nice that you've found a friend," his mother said at dinner one night late in August. She had been home from the hospital for almost two months and was feeling better. It was one of the longest stretches that Sean had seen her in recent memory. "What's his name?"

"Ben Doer," said Sean, poking at his roast potatoes.

"He lives in this area?" asked his mother.

"Yeah, in Kits."

"What sort of things do you do together?" asked his mother, her face bright, but her eyes a little clouded.

"I don't know. Hang out. Play video games. That sort of thing."

"Staying out of trouble, I hope," said his father. He was reading a law journal while forking baked salmon into his mouth.

Sean looked at his food. "Hey, Mom, can Ben stay over on the weekend?"

"I don't see why not, Sean."

"We've got that party at Ted's place," said Sean's father. "Senator Simmons is in town and wants to talk urban renewal. Ted's putting on a thing."

"Well, that's fine. Adelaide will be here."

His father grunted without looking up.

"Great, thanks, Mom," said Sean, jumping up and kissing his mother on the forehead. She smiled.

When Sean had left the room she seemed to slump in her chair. "Darling, would you mind drawing the curtains a little? I'm feeling a little sensitive right now."

BY THE WEEKEND, the upswing in her mood had entirely subsided, and Martha Livingstone slipped into depression once again. Adelaide attended to her in her bedroom. Charles dressed in his own room, stopping in on his way out of the house.

"Are you sure you'll be okay?" he asked Adelaide, straightening the tie on his tuxedo.

"I'll be fine. How much trouble can a couple of boys be?"

"I was thinking about Mrs. Livingstone, actually," he said, studying himself in the mirror.

"Oh, this is no trouble," she said, taking a tray of food from the bedside.

"Good, then." He left the room.

"THIS IS BORING," said Ben. They were sitting in Sean's room playing a video game.

"I've got an idea," said Sean. "Come on."

Ben followed Sean into the hall. Sean stopped in front of his father's study. He found the key under the rug by the door and let them both in. He stepped to the cabinet where his father kept the port and sherry and tried to open it, but his father had locked it.

"He doesn't usually . . ." said Sean.

"Must not trust us."

Sean smiled and went to the desk and found a heavy letter opener. "This should do the trick." He jammed the letter opener between the doors of the mahogany cabinet. The wood around the lock splintered, popping open.

"Fucking A," said Ben. He grabbed a bottle of cognac.

"That's a good one. I heard my dad bragging that it was worth two hundred and fifty bucks."

"Better be good," said Ben, popping the cork out and taking a hard pull.

Sean took a bottle of port and did the same.

"Come on," said Ben, "let's get out of here before that maid of yours comes along and ruins everything."

They grabbed their coats and headed out into the night. The streets of Kerrisdale were quiet. They walked the sidewalks, drinking the expensive liqueur, laughing and talking loudly.

"Let's steal a car," said Ben.

"Do you know how?"

"Sure. It's really fucking easy. You won't believe it."

"Show me," said Sean, taking a hit from the bottle of port.

"First, you got to find one that you like. Nothing too expensive or it might have an alarm, but no beaters either."

They walked for a block and Sean said, "That one."

"Yeah, that's perfect." It was a newer model Ford Mustang parked on the street in front of a house. Ben took out something that looked like a long shoehorn; it was a slim jim.

"Where'd you get that?"

"Stole it from a tow truck."

Sean beamed. "That's excellent."

In a minute Ben had the Mustang open and they climbed inside.

"Now," said Ben, handing Sean his bottle of cognac, "we'll just see what we can do here." He reached under the steering column and wrenched a sheet of plastic a few times, snapping it. He threw it into the back seat. "The key is to not electrocute yourself while you're doing this." He proceeded to give play-by-play instructions to Sean on how to hotwire a car.

They got the Mustang started and in a few minutes were racing down toward Granville Street.

"Now we need some fucking girls," yelled Ben over the blare of the stereo.

Sean guzzled from his bottle and beamed.

HE DID FOUR months in Juvie. Ben did eighteen months. Sean sold him out but not before facing his father. The man sat behind the mahogany desk in his study and regarded him as he might an unfavorable stain on the floor. "I'm not even going to ask what you were thinking," his father finally said. Sean regarded him blankly. "You weren't. You couldn't have been."

Sean looked around the room. His eyes fell on the wooden display holding the nickel-plated come-along.

"You know, I did some crazy things when I was young," his father said. "Drank. Fooled around with girls. But stealing a car? Breaking into my liquor cabinet? Picking up a hooker! Sean, you didn't seem to *care* if you got caught . . ."

Sean studied the shape of the come-along. In that moment, Sean imagined what it might be like to hold that in his hand and club something with it. A dog, or a cat.

"Sean, listen to me when I am talking to you!" His father was suddenly caught in a rage. He smashed his hand on his desk, knocking a crystal tumbler to the floor. Sean continued to stare indifferently at the come-along.

"Your friend Ben is going to go to jail for a good, long time, do you understand me?" he roared. "A long time. Your only hope is to cop a plea and tell the prosecutor it was all Ben's idea." He took a breath and stood up and walked toward Sean. "Don't you care what happens to you?"

Sean pried his eyes from the come-along and looked at his father quizzically. "What do you mean?"

"Haven't you been listening? You're going to jail, Sean. Jail. Maybe for as much as a year. Don't you care about what this will do to your mother? To me?"

"To your career, you mean," Sean sneered.

His father hit him. It was open handed, but Charles Livingstone was a big man, and Sean was small, and he flew from the chair and landed on the ground like a sack of laundry.

"I've spent my whole career trying to earn money to provide for you and your mother. As far as I'm concerned, you can rot in that jail. Don't come looking to me for any help, you little pissant. Now get out of my sight. But if you leave this house before you are sentenced tomorrow afternoon, I'll have every cop and private dick in this town hunting your ass."

Sean got up, feeling the sting on his cheek and the side of his head. His left ear was ringing. But he didn't look at his father. Instead, he let his gaze drift coolly past his father's heaving shoulders to the come-along. He now had a plan. It might take some time, but he had a plan.

ON TUESDAY JULIET managed to get free from work shortly after five. It had been the kind of day she dreaded, and which was blessedly rare. She had spent most of it at the Centre. By the time five o'clock came around, she was exhausted. Then she remembered Sean. She drew a breath as she stuffed her things in the orange backpack. A commitment is a commitment. She left the Carnegie Centre through the side door to the alley and made her way through the rain to the front of the building. Already there were fifty or more people crowded there. She went to the steps where she had asked Sean to meet her. He wasn't there. She almost felt relieved.

Then she remembered the flicker of optimism in him—what Juliet always hoped to see. It took her more than an hour to find him. When she did, he acted as if nothing had happened. "Oh, hey!" he said.

"Sean, you were going to meet me an hour ago at the Carnegie Centre," she said, hunching down beside him where he was panhandling. His dirty ball cap on the sidewalk held a few coins.

"Oh God, I'm sorry, Juliet. I'm so sorry. I completely forgot." His face was blank.

"It's okay. Come on, let's get going. It's a bit of a walk, and I've had a really long day."

"Okay, yeah, let's get going. Do you want to get a cab? I'll pay."

"No, that's okay, Sean."

"I've got a little money." He smiled.

"The walk is good for me."

In the half hour it took to walk home, Sean didn't stop talking for more than a few minutes.

"My plan is to get my PHD in biochemistry. I want to be part of the team that finds a cure for cancer. I just know I've got what it takes to do it," he said, his hands moving before him in exaggerated enthusiasm. "Once I get that done, I'm going to dedicate myself to serving people on the street. You know, working with them to end hunger and poverty and homelessness. I think that would be a good way to use my gifts."

Juliet walked along beside him, her fatigue somehow alleviated as Sean talked about all the good he hoped to do for the world. She wanted to believe in his energetic youthfulness. By the time they got home, Juliet felt refreshed.

"Wow, what a great place!" said Sean.

"It *is* nice," Juliet admitted.

"You're so lucky to have found something like this that you can afford. This city sucks when it comes to affordable housing."

"It's great. I have a roommate, though . . ."

"Oh, yeah?"

"Look, I think we need a good story."

"I totally agree," said Sean, looking upwards. "Leave this to me," he said. "You got any siblings?"

"Yeah, a younger sister and an older brother."

"Tell me about your sister," he said.

AFTER A LONG, hot shower Sean prepared dinner. "My mother was a great cook," he explained, slicing scallions into a frying pan, then mushrooms. "I always watched her when she was in the kitchen."

Juliet had just finished her shower and her hair was still damp. She had on fresh clothes. The kitchen was warm and inviting. Sean moved around it easily. She had given him a pair of jeans and a Simon Fraser University sweatshirt after he had cleaned up.

Sean added shrimp to the sizzling concoction on the stove. "I even did a stint as a sous-chef in a restaurant once. I don't have any papers, but I was so good they just hired me on the spot and put me on the line. I didn't get along with the head chef though. I quit after a week. Working in a restaurant kitchen is really not my thing."

Juliet sat at the table and watched Sean move around the kitchen, steaming rice and preparing a salad. She made a note to call a local catering company that specialized in employing the hard-to-hire and ask if they had any work for Sean. Juliet knew she was taking a risk, bringing Sean in like this. She had taken the risk before and it had always paid off. The one time she had given in to caution had led to a friend's fatal overdose. Working on the streets, Juliet knew she couldn't save everyone; but she could save some, and that had led her to risk opening up her home from time to time.

"I was once asked to work in a kitchen at a convention center here in town," said Sean. "Somebody had heard about my stint at the restaurant and called me up and asked me to come and work during a big international convention, but I had to say no. Too stressful. Who needs it?"

"Why haven't you pursued a career in cooking?" she asked after a bit of salad.

Sean looked up at her from his meal. "Most chefs are complete jerks," he said, putting a fork full of shrimp and mushrooms in his mouth. "They just yell at you all day. I don't need that. I think what I'd really like is to open my own restaurant some day, you know, that way I get to control what's going on. I get to be the boss."

"You sound like you've got big plans. Science. Social services. Cooking. A restaurant. Wow, you've got big dreams. Maybe this is the break you've been looking for."

"Yeah, maybe," he said.

After dinner Juliet showed him around the rest of the house. "This place is *so* cool," said Sean, admiring the old woodwork, high ceilings, and stained glass in the living room.

"This will be your bed," said Juliet, pointing to a futon couch. "I hope it's going to be okay."

"It will be great," said Sean with a wide, appreciative smile.

They ducked their heads under a low door and descended a set of open stairs into the basement. Juliet pulled a cord and a bare bulb illuminated the large open room. She showed him where the laundry was.

"There's a back door to the basement that we always keep locked," she said, showing him the deadbolted door.

He looked out the dusty window and over the small, hedge-enclosed yard. Near the back door he saw an opening in the lawn ringed with stout concrete walls. "What's that?" he asked, pointing to the set of stairs that descended into the darkened alcove.

"That's the bomb shelter," said Juliet, smiling.

"No kidding!" said Sean. "Can we check it out?"

"I've never been in. The man who owns the place said it's empty and put a padlock on it to keep people out. He tells me there's still electricity down there, but nothing else. It's a relic from World War Two when the first owner of this place was worried about the Japanese bombing Vancouver. I think he was a little crazy," Juliet explained.

"Oh, I don't know. It sounds pretty sane to me. My grandfather served in the war," said Sean, still looking out the window at the descending stairs. "He was in a Japanese prisoner-of-war camp for almost five years. They tortured him," he said casually.

AT BREAKFAST ON Wednesday morning Juliet introduced Sean to her roommate, Becky. "He's a friend of the family, I suppose," she said as Sean shook hands firmly.

"Nice to meet you," he said with a smile. "Juliet is so nice to let me stay here for a few days while I get back on my feet. My parents just died and I'm still in shock, I suppose you might say."

"I'm so sorry," said Becky, looking from Sean to Juliet.

Juliet nodded solemnly. "Well, I've got to go. Things at work are just crazy these days."

"More so than usual?" asked Becky.

"You might say that," said Juliet.

"Be careful," Becky said. "I worry about you."

"Thanks, B. Don't worry. I know how to look out for myself."

"What time are you coming home?" asked Sean. "I'll have dinner ready."

THAT AFTERNOON SEAN found a hardware store. The bolt cutters and new padlock were a simple snatch.

FOURTEEN

"WHAT DO YOU THINK THE odds are that they get takeout from the same place twice?" It was Wednesday night and Cole stood outside the Anglican church and peered up the block toward the Golden Dragon. Through the rain the streetlights cast a dim glow, and the street below was like the oily back of a slow-moving snake. Cole had his cell phone pressed to his ear.

"I'd say pretty good," Denman replied. He sat slumped in a car he had borrowed from the Vancouver Car Share Co-op for the night, a green Toyota Prius.

"I still think one of us should have hid by the back door," said Cole over the drone of the rain. "No way of missing them then."

"True, but if we hide there we run the risk of getting caught trying to follow them out of the alley. This way we've got the bases covered. If they are on foot, easy for you to follow. If they are driving, I can trail them."

"Okay. Well, let's wait and see what happens." Cole paced back and forth in front of the church. "Thanks for being here, Denny."

"Wouldn't want you to have all the fun."

"While you're having fun in the nice hybrid, I'm freezing my ass off in the rain."

"Well, the fact that you brought a car back to the Co-op a week late and missing its spare tire might have something to do with why I'm sitting in the Prius right now and you're freezing in the rain."

"The spare tire was there. It was the original that was missing. It was a logging road."

"It was a hiking trail."

"It looked like a logging road. Anyway, thanks for being here."

"Cole, I got *you* into this."

"We're all in this together now, Denny."

Cole closed his phone and held it in his hand. He pulled the collar of his coat up. It was a cool night and the rain was soaking right through his worn Gore-Tex shell. It was hard to believe the rain would ever end.

Cole wore a black watch cap on his head over his messy curls for warmth and fingerless gloves on his hands to allow operation of his cell phone. He leaned against the wall and waited. He sent Denman a few short text messages to practice. Kids seemed to be able to do this in their sleep, but it took him some getting used to the rhythm of the numeric alphabet.

After an hour, his cell phone buzzed. He flipped it open to read the message. "Showtime." Cole looked up and saw a new Chevrolet Impala parked in front of the restaurant. Two men got out. He watched until the men disappeared into the alley next to the Golden Dragon, then crossed the street, his feet splashing through the running water. They had agreed if there was time he would join Denman in the car.

He reached the Prius just as the two men slipped out of the alley and returned to their Impala, each carrying a takeout bag. A third man joined them, getting into the driver's seat. Their car did a U-turn in the street and came within twenty feet of the Prius.

"You ever followed anybody before?" asked Cole, dripping wet. He yanked on his seatbelt.

"Nope."

"You know what you're doing?"

"Nope, you?"

Cole shook his head. Denman started the engine and pulled out into traffic, a few cars back from the Impala. The car turned right on Gore Street, where the Dunsmuir viaduct began, and Denman followed. He was now right behind them. His head lights illuminated the back of the occupants' heads.

"Not so close," said Cole.

"Trying," said Denman, easing off.

"Try to make it look like you're just out for a drive."

"How do I do that?"

"I don't know," said Cole. "Drive casual."

The Impala drove north and then turned right. The traffic thickened and Denman managed to keep a car or two between them. Cole was pretty sure that the two pickup men were the same guys he had seen the previous night, but he had to admit that when you've seen one two-hundred-pound cop, you've seen them all.

"Where are these guys going?" asked Denman.

"Turning again," pointed Cole.

"I think they're on to us," said Denman.

"No way. We're just one of hundreds of cars out here."

"Making all the same turns."

The Impala stopped at the lights. The Prius was two cars back. Cole and Denman watched silently as their quarry idled. When the light turned green the Impala drove ahead and then, without signaling, stopped at the corner of Abbott Street in front of Tinseltown, a sprawling shopping center that featured a massive cinema complex. The two back doors opened and the pickup men got out.

"Great, now what?" muttered Cole, unhooking his seatbelt.

"Cole . . ."

Cole already had the door open. The Prius rolled to its silent stop. Cole was out before Denman could finish saying, "I'll park." Denman watched as he splashed across the street after the two men.

The two men crossed the sidewalk, deserted in the driving rain, and went into the Tinseltown mall. Cole dashed after them, holding his sore ribs. The mall was quiet on a Tuesday night. Cole watched as they mounted an escalator to the second level, the cavernous space making them easy to see, and Cole easy to spot following them. He drew a deep breath as they stepped off the escalator. He ran a few steps and reached the top of the moving stairs as they walked through the concourse toward the food court.

"Forgot the chopsticks, boys?" Cole muttered. His cell phone buzzed and he flipped it open while he walked.

"Where r u?" was the message. He awkwardly keyed in "Fdcrt," then looked up to see the two men moving past the court toward the row of shops beyond.

"If they get in the elevator, I'm hooped," muttered Cole. He felt his pulse quickening, felt the surge of adrenaline course though his veins. Suddenly Denman was beside him. They said nothing. They walked slowly, keeping the men in sight, who were now heading toward an escalator at the opposite end of the mall. The men took the escalator to the main floor again.

"They're hitting the street," said Denman.

"Hope they don't have a car waiting."

The two men exited onto Abbott Street and walked south.

"I can see the Lucky Strike from here," said Cole, looking east as he and Denman left the mall. The hotel's darkened bulk loomed above the city around it.

"What are they doing?" asked Denman. One of the men gave the other a brown bag of Golden Dragon food to carry.

"Don't know."

"We're made."

"Come *on* . . ."

"Just watch," said Denman. When the two men reached the corner of Abbott and Taylor, one of them dashed across the road toward the Foodmart and the SkyTrain stop at Stadium. The other headed east toward the Lucky Strike.

Denman stopped and grabbed Cole by the shoulder. "They're onto us, Cole."

"So what!" Cole said angrily.

"It's too dangerous."

"This is the only shot we get. Maybe they are onto us, maybe not. But this is it. There won't be another chance to find out who is dining at the Lucky Strike Supper Club."

One of the men reached the corner by the grocery store.

"I'll go east," said Cole, and slipping from Denman's grasp, moved toward the Lucky Strike.

"Don't do anything stupid. And keep in touch," Denman said, and ran across the street toward the Foodmart.

Cole clutched his cell phone in his hand and followed the other two-hundred-pound delivery boy from a couple hundred feet back. Here the sidewalk was nearly empty, so his prey was easy to watch, just as Cole's presence was easy to detect. Any farther back and he ran the risk of losing his man.

The bag carrier turned north again, passing behind the darkened behemoth of the Lucky Strike. On the corner two uniformed officers sat reading in the lighted cab of a squad car, part of the effort to keep the protesters starved.

Instead of stopping, the man slipped his cell phone out of his pocket and put it to his ear. Distance and the rain, now driving in sheets, eliminated any chance Cole might overhear the conversation. He watched the meatball snap the phone shut and put it back in his pocket.

The delivery man reached the end of the block, then stood motionless at the corner. Cole quickly slipped into a doorwell, but the man never looked back.

"What are you doing?" Cole grumbled. "Your fried wontons are getting very, very cold."

After a couple of minutes, Cole saw the man reach for his phone again, and this time Cole doubted he said a word before he snapped the phone shut and dashed across the street, a few horns blaring.

"Here we go," said Cole, quickly following. There was a greengrocer fronting the street. The man swung open an unmarked door next to it and vanished up a set of stairs. Cole quickly texted the address to Denman. He was less than a block from the Carnegie Centre, and within sight of the Lucky Strike.

He scanned the building. It was a dreary, four-story building put up in the 1940s with tan brick and white trim. A discount shoe store and the grocer occupied the street level. Cole guessed that the inside housed offices, maybe fronts for organized crime.

Cole stood in the doorway across the street a moment. He knew damn well that he couldn't just run up the stairs after the delivery man. The likelihood of being caught there and questioned about his presence was much too high. What could he say? Instead, he stepped back into the shadow of the doorway and assumed the panhandler position, tucking his knees to his chest and folding his arms across them, watching the door. He waited.

Where was Denman?

Sitting with his face to his knees, his eyes peeled for any action at the door, Cole felt a growing restlessness and sense of urgency. He sat motionless for another minute, then two, feeling the cold from the concrete penetrate his butt and move into his spine. Across the street the door flew open. Cole pressed his face closer to his knees, his eyes mere slits, and watched as the big man he had been tailing made his way down the street toward Tinseltown, then across the street and around the corner without looking back.

Once the man was out of sight Cole jumped to his feet and crossed Pender. He grabbed the metal door handle and the door swung open. He was surprised to find the door unlocked. He quickly took his cell phone from his pocket and texted Denman, "Gng in."

The stairs rose up from street level in darkness. He took a deep breath to quiet his heart and listened. Nothing. Just the drone of traffic on Pender, the hiss of tires on wet pavement. He mounted the steps. Halfway to the top he stopped and listened. Another step and he kicked a can in the blackness. It clanked down the steps. Cole froze, but he heard nothing else. He took three more steps into the blackness. He still faced an eerie silence, but now a familiar scent came to him: Korean barbecue.

Cole reached the top of the stairs. He now stood at one end of a long hallway that disappeared into the darkness. Many doors lined the hall, but none seemed to emit any light. He smelled the odor of stale cigarettes, takeout food, and something else, something strangely out of place.

He started down the hall, looking at the doors, some of which had small signs announcing the businesses that occupied them: Double A Accounting. Frank's Home Heating. Dominion Music. In the darkness it was hard to make out the names on some of the offices. Cole took out his cell phone and flipped it open to read the signs by the dim blue light of its display screen. The silence was broken when his cell phone buzzed with an incoming message. He dropped it to the floor where it snapped shut.

"Mother—" Cole muttered under his breath, cutting off his curse. He dropped to his knees and patted the greasy carpet, feeling for the phone. He grabbed it and read the message from Denman.

"Cming."

He snapped it shut and made his way farther into the silent darkness.

He almost tripped over the package. Sitting on the floor next to a door without a sign was the parcel of takeout food. He bent down and touched it. It was cool and the paper bag was damp. He looked both ways down the hall. He was alone. There was no light coming from under the door. He tested the doorknob. It was locked.

"What is going on here?" he asked himself. He tried the knob again. "If this isn't an invitation, I don't know what is."

He stepped back and quickly kicked the door. The frame splintered and the door wobbled open. Cole put his shoulder to it and pushed it the rest of the way open. He flinched with the pain that burned in his chest.

Cole stopped and listened. The room he had entered was dark and quiet. He felt for the light switch and flicked it on.

DENMAN FOLLOWED HIS quarry up the steps to the SkyTrain station at Stadium. The man quickly turned and headed down to the platform. Denman paused at the ticket dispenser. Even though he had a pass, he needed a moment to think. It was quiet on the SkyTrain at this time of night. He would be conspicuous. His only other option was to give up on this tail and rejoin Cole.

He decided to stick with his man for the time being, just to play this out. He pretended to buy a ticket and walked down the steps to the platform. The man with the delivery was waiting for an eastbound train. Half a dozen others stood around on the platform, reading newspapers or listening to iPods.

Eastbound: the next stop was Main Street, just a few blocks from where this whole charade had started. And then Commercial Drive, a good half-hour walk from where Denman had left Cole.

He heard the whistling of the train approaching from the underground tunnel. A gust of air preceded the train's arrival. The squeal of brakes grew louder and the train appeared. Four or five people got off, and those waiting, including the delivery man and Denman, boarded the train. The delivery man took a seat, setting his package down next to him and making himself comfortable as if for a long ride. Denman stood by the doors, holding onto one of the overhead bars. The train pulled out of the station and a moment later he could see the Lucky Strike Hotel whiz past.

Denman hazarded a glance at his quarry. The man was looking straight at him. Denman let his gaze scan past the man and to the other passengers. Denman's cell buzzed and he pulled it from his pocket and flipped it open. The message from Cole read, "82 Pender."

Denman looked back up and was certain the delivery man was grinning at him.

He felt the train slow as it took the sharp corner at Quebec Street, then speed up again as it raced toward the Main Street stop.

Grinning at him.

Cole was about six blocks away now.

Grinning. When the train stopped Denman swung through the rear doors onto the platform. From the corner of his eye he saw the delivery man rise, leaving the food on the seat, and make for the train's front doors. About to dash for the stairs, Denman knew that the delivery man would step in front of him in a split second. As he drew adjacent to the front doors, Denman jumped high above the brick platform and with his right leg kicked sideways, connecting with the big man's chest. The delivery man's face froze in shock as the blow knocked the wind out of him and he stumbled backward into the train car.

Denman came down on both feet, upright, and directly in front of the open door; the delivery man crashed into the front doors on the opposite side of the car. He caught his breath and charged. Denman stood his ground, and when his attacker was just about to collide with him, quickly stepped to the side and drove his forearm up into the man's chin, his arm bent and his open hand reaching skyward. He then quickly reversed direction and drove his hand down toward the train station platform. The man crumpled to the ground.

Denman heard the sound signaling the doors about to close and quickly pulled the man back on board. Then he deftly stepped backward and escaped the closing doors. In another second the SkyTrain was speeding to the next stop. The whole confrontation had lasted less than thirty seconds.

Denman raced down the stairs out of the station and ran toward Cole's address.

The man on the train had been a decoy.

But a decoy for what?

COLE STOOD UNDER the glare of the fluorescent tube lights, the smell of Korean food heavy in the air. Two folding tables, pushed together in the middle of the room, were surrounded by six chairs. The tattered venetian blinds on the windows were closed. Cole quickly pulled the tangled cord to hoist them open. They raised no dust. He looked out toward the Dr. Sun Yat-Sen Classical Chinese Garden, then west at the darkened outline of the Lucky Strike. He turned back to the room, and noted a chalkboard mounted on one wall, nothing written on it, and no chalk. A small garbage pail sat by the door. As Cole surveyed the empty space, he smelled expensive cologne and the delicate scent of roses over the oily fragrance of the food. He studied the floor, and in addition to his own wet prints he could see the outline of other wet shoes and boots. Based on their shape, he guessed that they had been made by both men and women.

People had been in this room. And had just left.

DENMAN HAD HIS phone in his hand, managing to key in a message as he ran. He hit send and then put the phone back in his pocket.

He could see the Lucky Strike Hotel to his left. Suddenly the darkened shape of the building was illuminated from outside. Spotlights around the base of the building blazed brightly. Two dozen police cars and vans roared to a near simultaneous stop in front of the building. Christ, he thought, the shit is going down *right now*. He slowed a moment, but then decided it wasn't his concern. His concern was Cole Blackwater.

COLE HESITATED, THINKING about the man he had followed. He had used his cell phone twice, once when Cole and Denman split up, and again when he turned onto Taylor Street.

He had tipped off the Lucky Strike Supper Club, hadn't he? Dinner is not being served, Cole imagined him saying. I've been made.

What was the second call? Coast is clear. But Cole had been out front by then. Back door.

Suddenly the night outside the window lit up like day, and Cole could see the Lucky Strike pop out of the darkness into sudden clarity. Now what? he thought. But he didn't stop to look. Instead, he bolted from the room and ran down the darkened hall toward the far end. There must be a second exit. He found the stairs and started down, as if into a darkened pool. He reached the bottom and felt for a crash bar. He pushed his way through and found himself in the alley that ran parallel to Pender, forty feet from its exit onto Columbia Street.

He had time to draw one quick breath of the damp night air.

The blow caught him behind the ear. He felt a hollow ring and then pain shot through his skull and down his neck. He fell to his hands and knees in a slick puddle of water.

He heard a man laugh.

Not the ribs, he thought, not the ribs.

ADRENALINE POURED INTO Denman's system, but he channeled it, making it work for him, giving his feet wings. He found a break in the traffic and dashed across the street, horns blaring, a car skidding to a halt in front of him, an angry voice. More sirens. Popping. Shouts.

He reached 82 Pender. Denman wrenched the door open, the stairwell inside lit by a faint light at the top. He took the stairs three at a time, then ran down the hall, where an open door spilled light into the corridor and illuminated a takeout package on the floor. Denman slowed and skidded through the doorway. The room was empty.

COLE CRAWLED FORWARD, his mouth open. He spat. From his position he could see two sets of feet behind him. Not the ribs, he thought. He felt the heat of blood on his temple, leaking toward his eyes.

He tried to crawl across the alley to where a garbage dumpster loomed. One set of legs moved behind him, closing the distance in a few strides. Cole ducked his head to protect himself from the anticipated blow, and a heavy object caught him on the shoulder, knocking him into the trash surrounding the dumpster. Cole struck out with his left leg and felt it connect with his attacker's shin. He had been aiming for the knee, hoping to break it. The blow turned the man sideways and gave Cole a second to grab the dumpster and pull himself up.

His vision was blurred, but at least he could see his assailants now. One man had a piece of lead pipe in his hand. He wore a balaclava over his face. The second man had on a dark hooded sweatshirt under a tattered raincoat. He wore a bandana over his mouth. He had a knife in his hands, the short blade pointing down, the way you would hold it if you wanted to stab a man.

Cole straightened up and tried to clear his vision, but the forms of his assailants moved in and out of focus. The man with the pipe swung for Cole's head, but Cole blocked the swing. The pipe missed his face by two inches. Stepping forward, Cole drove his right fist into the man's nose, breaking it. A jet of blood hit Cole in the face. The attacker staggered back into the wall, his left hand holding his nose, his right still clinging to the pipe.

The second man came forward with the knife held low and deadly, and flashed it back and forth toward Cole's gut. Cole wore layers of clothing that would protect him from some of the force of the knife, but not all. He kept his back to the wall. The man lunged when Cole feigned a slump. Cole side-stepped and drove his fist into the man's temple, momentarily disorienting the attacker. Cole tripped backward and found himself against the dumpster again, a telephone pole between him and the distant street.

His attackers both pressed forward.

Sirens sounded in the distance. The man with the broken nose swung his pipe at Cole's head, but Cole let his legs go out from under him and the pipe grazed his cap, knocking it off his head and leaving a spray of rainwater hanging in the air. The pipe clanged angrily against the garbage bin. Leaning forward on his knees, Cole drove his right fist into the man's groin. The man's legs buckled, and suddenly he was kneeling in front of Cole in the rain-soaked alley. Cole drove his forehead into the man's face, colliding with the man's broken nose. The man let out a blood-curdling scream. Then Cole felt a boot connect with his back and he went numb from the pain. He felt himself sink into the bloody embrace of the man holding the pipe, only just aware of the knife-wielding man behind him. Cole closed his eyes; all of his will to fight seeped into the bloody alley. The knifeman grabbed him by the hair. Cole's only thought was of Sarah.

WHERE THE FUCK was Cole?

As Denman scanned the room, the sound of a scream reached him from somewhere outside. He ran to the other end of the hall and down the stairs. The momentum of his body carried him through the door and into the alley. Cole was slumped over a man's body, blood on his shadowed face, and another man held him by the hair, a knife to Cole's throat.

Denman was on him in a second. He grabbed the hand holding Cole and flipped the man over his hip and face down onto the ground, catching the man's blade safely in his other hand. Denman pressed his knee on the man's back below the arm he had twisted tight, keeping the attacker down in the puddle on the alley floor.

"Cole, you okay?" he shouted. "You're bleeding."

"Yeah, but it's mostly his." Cole said, struggling to his feet. He pushed the man with the pipe to the ground and met no resistance.

"Give me your belt," Denman said. The man beneath him struggled, and Denman applied a little more pressure to the twisted arm. Cole handed Denman his belt. Denman looped it through the man's own pants and then buckled it around his wrists, pulling it tight. He slowly released the pressure from the man's arm and got to his feet.

He took Cole's head in his own hands and looked him over. "You're bleeding behind your right ear. You're going to need stitches. There's blood on your face but I don't see a wound."

"It's his," Cole said, wiping the blood from his eyes and from around his nose and mouth with the sleeve of his jacket.

"What did you do, bite his nose off?"

"No, but it's broken. At least twice."

Denman bent down and pulled the mask off the man, who lay without moving. Denman felt for a pulse. "He's alive." Denman pulled his cell out and dialed 911.

"What are you doing?"

"Calling the cops."

"What if *these* are the cops?"

"Well, then, I guess we're in the animal soup, ain't we?"

"I think we're pretty deep in it one way or another," said Cole, looking around. His vision was still blurry. "We've got to case that room," he said.

"There's nothing there."

"We've got to be sure."

"Police," Denman spoke into the phone. "There's been an assault in the alley between Hastings and Pender, in the one-hundred block. Both perpetrators are immobilized. Yes, I understand." Denman hung up the phone.

"Let's go," he said. He helped Cole to his feet. "You okay? I think we better get you to the hospital."

"I'm okay. Just a scratch. And my ribs. Nothing new. But we case the room first, then we'll see about a hospital."

They reached the room and stepped inside. Cole looked closely at the blackboard, trying to read anything that may have been written there. Denman turned over the garbage bin but it was empty. "They even cleared out their trash."

"They were tipped by the meatball I was following."

"There's nothing here," said Denman. "Let's book."

"What's that smell?" Cole asked.

"Perfume," said Denman, looking out the window at the Lucky Strike. "We've got to get you some help, Cole."

"You take me to the hospital and they will call the cops for sure."

"Juliet."

"Okay. But at my place." They opened the door and stepped onto Pender. Police sirens wailed closer, and the street was lit by the floodlights around the Lucky Strike.

"The cops are raiding the hotel," said Cole.

"What was your first clue, Sherlock?"

Denman pulled his cell from his pocket. "Juliet, it's Denman. Yes, everything is fine. Well, maybe not great. Look, can you hop a cab to Cole's place? Bring your first-aid kit, okay?" He gave Juliet Cole's address.

"I've got to go," said Denman, looking up the street. "There are going to be fifty complaints of excessive force by morning. It will help if I've been on the scene to witness it."

He flagged down a cab. "Get yourself home. Juliet will be there in a few minutes. I'll come by in a couple of hours to check on you."

"Denny," Cole said.

Denman had his cell phone to his ear, waking up his colleagues. "What's up?" he said turning to Cole.

"Thanks."

"All in a day's work."

FIFTEEN

JOHN ANDREWS LOOKED THE WAY a cop should. He was six feet tall, with broad, square shoulders, a flat, trim stomach, and strong legs. He wore his uniform with the crispness one might expect from a senior military officer. Though he could dress in plain clothes if he wanted, Andrews liked the formality of the uniform, especially when dealing with the public, with City Hall, or with reporters.

When he stepped into the briefing room, a flurry of flashes from digital cameras exploded. He kept his expression neutral. He sat down behind the table, the flags of the city, province, and country behind him.

"I have a statement to read," he said, speaking into the two dozen microphones and digital recorders in front of him, "and then I'll take your questions.

"Last evening, members of the Vancouver Police Department's tactical squadron, as well as officers from Division 2's crowd control units, moved to restore public order and protect public safety by disbanding the illegal occupation of the Lucky Strike Hotel. Afterward, Vancouver Police reassembled barricades to prevent access to the hotel, which is a major public safety concern and fire hazard. Our officers escorted members of the End Poverty Now Coalition and other illegal occupants of the hotel from the building. In total, fifty-three arrests were made. Fire officials have confirmed that there were numerous fire code infractions, including open cooking fires, throughout the building. Drug paraphernalia and narcotics were seized. The Lucky Strike Hotel has now been cleared of the illegal occupancy, and the protestors face numerous charges, ranging from possession of narcotics to breach of peace to assaulting a police officer. With this action, VPD and the City of Vancouver are sending a strong statement that this form of illegal protest will not be tolerated in our city."

He stopped and looked up. "I'll take your questions now," he said, pointing to a blond woman sitting in the front row.

"How many officers were involved in the raid?" she asked.

"In total, about one hundred and fifty, including officers stationed outside the building to maintain peace and order."

"There are reports that tear gas was used in the raid. Can you confirm this?" asked the reporter from CTV News.

"Tear gas was used to ensure the safety of our officers when they entered the premises."

"Were their any injuries as a result?"

"Several of the illegal occupants of the hotel required first aid on the scene after they were taken from the premises. None required hospitalization. I should say here that over the course of the last five days, these protesters were given dozens of opportunities to leave the Lucky Strike under their own power, and failed to take the opportunity. Next." He pointed at another reporter.

"Commander, there are complaints surfacing of excessive force. Can you comment?"

"My officers exercised tremendous restraint during this operation. Several officers were hit with paint-filled balloons, and one was hospitalized after being hit with a rock. No protesters were hospitalized during this operation."

"There are reports this morning from Priority Legal," continued the reporter, "that several of the protesters were beaten by police and have not received medical care."

"That's false. Next question." He pointed.

"What sort of signal do you hope this raid sends to protestors, Commander?"

"That the VPD will not tolerate the illegal occupation of private property."

"Even when groups like End Poverty Now feel that their voice isn't being heard any other way?"

"Individuals associated with the End Poverty Now Coalition broke the law. In my mind they are anarchists and hoodlums looking for an excuse to perpetrate violence against any authority figure they can find. For them, it isn't about solving homelessness or ending poverty, as they would have you think. It's about violence and their hatred of the police and of authority."

"That's a strong statement, Commander," another reporter interjected. "The Coalition released a statement this morning saying that VPD had declared war on the homeless with last night's raid. Do you see it that way?"

"No. That's ridiculous. The VPD has an obligation to uphold the law and protect order and civility in this city." The commander seemed to sit up straighter. "We're working with the City to try and address homelessness and poverty. Others are merely trying to get their names in the paper as some kind of ego trip. Next question." He pointed.

"Commander, were any weapons confiscated during last night's raid?"

"The protesters were armed with paint-filled balloons. And as I said, one of my officers was hospitalized after being hit with a rock."

"And what were your officers armed with, Commander? We saw footage last night of officers in riot gear and the tactical team carrying assault weapons. Seems like overkill, doesn't it?"

"I won't comment on our tactical considerations. My responsibility is to ensure the safety of my officers and protect the people of Vancouver."

"You don't think tactical team members are a little over the top for a bunch of protestors, most of whom hadn't eaten in a couple of days?"

"I won't comment on tactics. Next question." He pointed at Nancy Webber.

"Commander," she said, lifting her face from her notes for the first time during the news conference. She flipped her raven black hair over her shoulder. "In the last five weeks two men and two women have gone missing from the Downtown Eastside. They were all homeless. They were all well known to local social service agency personnel. Tell us, please: what is being done to locate these missing persons?"

The man hesitated a moment. This wasn't what the press conference was about, but the media training he'd received over the years dictated that he shouldn't dodge the question. "The Missing Persons Task Force, under the direction of Marcia Lane, is addressing that."

"Can you tell us what steps they are taking?" asked Webber.

"When a missing person report is filed with the VPD, we take a number of steps to quickly resolve the complaint. In the case of persons known to live on the street, we check the welfare rolls and inquire at their last known addresses and with any known family or friends in the area. We inquire at the bus depot and with the ferries and at our sister departments in Victoria and across the Lower Mainland."

"You're describing routine procedure?" asked Nancy.

"That's right. We get half a dozen calls a day. Most are resolved within a few hours."

"Would you say four people going missing from such a concentrated geographic area is routine?"

Andrews paused. "Missing person reports in the Downtown Eastside are common."

"Do you believe that the four disappearances are related?"

"No."

"Do you believe that the four disappearances are linked in any way to the closure of the Lucky Strike Hotel and other SROs?"

"No, I don't," he practically barked.

"All four were known to have stayed at the Lucky Strike at some point."

"Any connection that might be drawn is pure conjecture. There are hundreds of others who stayed at the Lucky Strike and are accounted for." He knew when he said it that it was a mistake.

"Hundreds of others who no longer have a place to stay, you should add," said Nancy.

Andrews leaned forward. "The VPD is working with the City to balance the needs of the homeless with the rights of private citizens to own property and exercise those rights to do with that property what the bylaws and zoning rules of this city allow." Other hands went up, but Nancy pressed on.

"Isn't it true, Commander, that VPD has been aware of these disappearances for some time and that you still haven't officially started an investigation, beyond what you consider to be routine?" she asked.

Above the shouting of other reporters, the commander replied briefly, "As I said, the Missing Persons Task Force is addressing that concern." He stood. "That will be all for now."

He walked from the briefing room, ignoring the flurry of questions that continued. His executive assistant was waiting for him in the hall. As he strode past, he barked, "Get Lane in my office in five minutes!"

"SOUNDS LIKE YOU'RE getting on the good side of Commander Andrews," said Denman.

"I wouldn't say that," said Nancy. She was in her office at the *Vancouver Sun* building, talking with Denman on the phone. "Care to comment?"

"Of the fifty-three people who were arrested last night, twenty-two have filed excessive force complaints against the VPD. The VPD used the kind of force reserved for hostage taking or for armed and dangerous suspects against a bunch of activists armed with water balloons. They seem more intent on flexing their muscle and standing up for condo developers than protecting the rights of Vancouver's citizens and helping the least among us find shelter."

"Anything else?"

"Only that this is just the latest in a string of excessive force complaints to arise since Andrews has taken command."

"You think *he's* responsible for the heavy-handed tactics?"

"I'm not prepared to say," said Denman.

"Then do you think there is a correlation?"

"Excessive force reports with our office and with the police complaints commissioner are up sharply over the last two years. Commander Andrews started his watch over Division 2 two years ago. Your readers can draw what conclusions they will."

"Sounds like you think there's a connection, though."

"Purely circumstantial is all I will say right now."

"So why is Priority Legal defending a bunch of authority-shunning, attention-seeking anarchists?" she changed tack.

"We're defending the citizens' right to peaceful protest. Look, as an old friend of mine once said, no riot police, no riot."

She took a deep breath. "Okay, the interview is over. Can I talk with you off the record? Background only?"

"Sure. Cole once told me there is no such thing as off the record, though."

"Cole's a paranoid malcontent."

"True," said Denman. "What is it, Nancy?"

"Do you think the VPD could be somehow linked to the disappearances?"

"Wow . . . I really don't know. Seems pretty crazy to even contemplate that. I really don't like Andrews, but do I think he's doing something to knock off homeless people?"

"I know, I know, but you should have seen Andrews' eyes when I was asking about the missing people. He was fuming."

"I think he's just got caught with his hand in the cookie jar beating up protesters when there are actual crimes being committed. And that he's overlooking serious crimes."

"Maybe," said Nancy. "But I'm going to dig."

"Nancy, be careful."

"Why?"

"Well, last night, before the raid, Cole and I got into something."

Denman told her what happened. Nancy said, "This is getting stupid. We have four people missing that we know of. You and Cole are playing Dick Tracy. All the while, the cops are breaking down the doors of the Lucky Strike. This city is going crazy."

"Welcome to the Left Coast: get your hair shirt and peace symbol at the Alberta border."

"Is Cole okay?"

"He's fine. Juliet went over to look at him, and I checked in on him after the raid. He's got a bump on his head and needed a couple of sutures, but otherwise he's fine. Physically, that is. Juliet thinks he's suffering from PTSD."

"From what?"

"Post-traumatic stress disorder. She thinks it stems from the time you were both in Lostcoast last spring during the Ravenwing debacle. I know we were all there together in July, but I wonder what happened when it was just the two of you?"

Nancy was silent.

"Nancy, he seems to be taking out his anger on *you*."

"What else is new?"

"Seriously, Nancy," he said, "what happened between you two at Lostcoast last spring?"

SIXTEEN

GEORGE OLIVER SAT ON THE steps of the Lucky Strike Hotel. He had been born into the Squamish First Nation, son of a hereditary chief and destined to be a leader of his people. Born with fetal alcohol spectrum disorder, the disabilities that he developed were minor compared to the effects people suffered from a full-blown fetal alcohol syndrome, but by fifteen it was clear that George would never sit as a chief of the Squamish First Nation.

"We keep picking you up, George," said the officer, his hands on his hips. He looked down at the swaying man. "You know this place is closed. It's off limits."

The rain had finally cleared. George looked up at the slate-gray sky that pressed down on the City of Vancouver. For twenty years he had been wandering Vancouver's streets in search of a comfortable place to sit and rest and watch people pass by.

"Would you stand up, sir?" ordered the second officer. He was young, with close-cropped hair under a dark blue ball cap. He wore a short coat, his service pistol protruding prominently from one side of his utility belt, a collapsible baton clipped to the other side. George blinked as he looked up from the cold, wet steps. He seemed to be having a hard time focusing on the officer.

"Have you been drinking today, George?" asked the first police officer, the senior of the two. He wore a long raincoat and stood with his hands clasped amiably in front of his belt.

George shook his head.

"Do you have any drugs on your person?"

Again George shook his head.

"Can you stand up please, George?" asked the older officer.

George stood.

"Can you open your arms, sir?" the younger officer asked, moving forward, his hands encased in blue latex gloves.

George opened his arms and leaned forward as if to give the officer a hug.

"No hugging today, George," the first officer said, holding back a smile.

George frowned.

"I'm going to search you, sir," said the second officer. George nodded.

"George, where did you sleep last night?" the officer watching asked. "Did you sleep inside?"

George thought a moment. "I don't think so." His clothes felt damp. "I think I slept in the park."

The older officer said, "You know, somebody should do something to keep tabs on people like this." He spoke as if George Oliver wasn't there. "Poor bastard wandering around the streets. All he needs is someone to tell him where to go, and when. Instead he's at the mercy of the streets."

The officer detected a movement behind him and turned slightly. A young man, dressed in jeans and a sweatshirt and a scuffed leather jacket and wearing an overstuffed backpack, walked up behind him.

THE INDIAN WAS like a gift to Sean Livingstone.

He wanted to start over with something completely new, and this one, The Indian, had just stumbled into his path.

Fate could be like that, thought Sean, adjusting the straps on his backpack. Fate could one day just present you with everything that you needed. He was living proof of that. He now had a roof over his head and a brand new opportunity to make arrangements.

The Indian had been sitting on the steps of the Lucky Strike Hotel that morning. Sean arrived in time to see the two uniformed police officers searching him. Sean, dressed in his clean jeans, SFU sweatshirt, and leather coat, had strolled right up and confronted the officers. "What's the problem here, officers?"

"None of your business, son," said the older of the two cops, letting his hands swing down to his sides. He was standing a few feet back from the scene, watching as his partner searched The Indian.

"Okay. It's just that I'm a volunteer with the Carnegie Centre, and I thought that if I could be of any assistance . . ."

The first officer addressed Sean again. "This area is off limits to squatters."

"Maybe I could take our friend back to the Centre and get him something to eat?"

The younger police officer regarded Sean coolly.

The older man said, "Look, George, you need to stay away from here, okay? The Lucky Strike is off limits. You can't come back here." Then he looked at Sean. "You're from the Carnegie Centre?"

"Yup," said Sean affably.

"You must be new."

"First week. I'm still learning the ropes."

"Okay. Well, take good care of George. He's had a tough go of it," said the older cop.

"Don't worry, officer," said Sean. "I will. I'll make all the necessary arrangements."

Sean walked side by side with The Indian down the street. "It's your lucky day," he said.

"Really?" asked The Indian.

"Sure is."

"How do you figure? Them cops come tell me I can't sit there no more. I don't know where else to go. I got problems, you know. Problems with my brain." The Indian tapped his head. "How you figure it's my lucky day?"

"Because you met me. I'm going to make some arrangements. You'll see. Everything is going to be just fine. You're in good hands now."

The Indian stopped in the street, smiling at Sean. "Wow, thank you," he said, and reached over and hugged Sean. Sean let himself be embraced. He felt a wave of nausea as he breathed in The Indian's rank odor—a course mixture of stale beer, body odor, and garbage.

Sean pulled himself away. "Okay, let's get going here." He forced a smile.

"Ain't we going to the Centre? That's what you told them cops."

"No, I've got something even better in mind. You see, I've got a shelter that I'm running in conjunction with the Carnegie folks. It's quiet. It's safe. Nobody is going to try to take your stuff. Nobody screaming all the time. You can have lunch with me, and then you can have a shower and make yourself at home. How does that sound?"

"Too good to be true," said The Indian, stumbling a little as he looked at Sean.

"It's true. You'll see."

"We going to take the bus?"

"Nope, I got a car. Just up ahead."

They stopped next to a Ford Fiesta parked in front of a laundromat. Sean slipped off his pack and rummaged inside. From the jumbled contents of his pack he took a shim that he had lifted from a tow truck the day before. He slipped it in the door and quickly popped the lock.

"You stealing this car?" The Indian asked.

"No, don't be silly," said Sean with a ready smile. "I lost my keys and the dealer is taking their time cutting me another set. Hop in," he said, reaching across to open the passenger door from the inside.

The Indian sat down next to Sean.

Sean fiddled with the wires until the car started.

"You ain't got a second set of keys?"

"Girlfriend flushed them down the toilet," he smirked.

"Wow, that's really sad," said The Indian, his smile fading.

They drove down Cordova to where it dog-legged onto Franklin. Sean almost missed the turn and ran a red light at Hastings.

"Holy cow, be careful, man. You're going to get us killed."

Adrenaline coursed through Sean's body. His heart was racing. He felt hot on the inside, but cool and calm on the outside. He was having a blast.

"This is the place," he said, stopping the car briefly on the road outside of Juliet Rose's house. "The little shelter is around back," he said. "I've got a parking spot up around the corner."

They drove a block up the road. Sean took the corner so fast that The Indian was pressed against the door of the car. Sean drove another block and then nosed down an alley. He parked the car behind a minivan next to a tumbledown garage. "Here we go," he said cheerfully. "Watch your head there," he added as The Indian got out of the tiny car.

"Wow, man, you're quite the driver. Why you gotta park so far from where you live?"

"Just stupid community association rules," Sean quipped.

They walked the two blocks back to Juliet's house, and Sean led the man along the side of the building. "Come on around back, I'll show you." The neighborhood was quiet at midday. A few birds sung in the thick hedge that separated the house from its neighbors.

Sean led The Indian down the concrete stairs that ran along the back of the house. Sean was careful to stay collected.

"Nice place," said The Indian, looking up at the old home. Sean showed him where the steps descended into the concrete bunker.

"Yeah, I've owned it for three or four years now," said Sean as they went down the steps.

"What is this, like, some kind of double basement?"

"Something like that." Sean pulled the key to the new padlock from his pocket and opened the door. He reached in and flicked the ancient switch. The dim forty-watt bulb hanging in the middle of the square bunker came on, pushing the dark shadows back into the corners.

"Seems like a strange place for a shelter."

"Doesn't it, though?" said Sean. "I know this seems kinda weird, but wait till you see where you get to sleep tonight!" Sean closed the door behind them and they passed through the outer room. At the far wall he pushed open a door that lead to another set of stairs. At the bottom a third door led to the inner room. Its fifty-year-old hinges glided smoothly, as if they had been oiled the day before.

Sean fumbled for the light switch. The Indian stayed close to Sean. The lights flickered on; pale, and covered in cobwebs, the three fluorescent bands illuminated a sparse, nearly empty space. Four folding metal chairs lined one wall, and in the center of the gray room a chain hung from a D-ring in the ceiling. A heavy meat hook dangled from the chain. As The Indian stared around him, puzzled, Sean pushed the door closed. Then he pulled on the stained white smock from his pack.

"What the fuck . . . ?" The Indian said, his face ashen, and he turned to try the heavy door.

Sean reached swiftly into his open pack and drew out the come-along, then smoothly swung it in a neat arc toward the man's head, connecting with the skull just below and behind the ear. The Indian took two steps sideways, his eyes glazing over, and then he fell to the floor in a heap. Sean stepped forward, the come-along hanging from one hand. He pushed The Indian with the toe of his shoe. No response. Keeping his weapon at his side, he felt for a pulse at the neck.

"Oh, good," he said flatly. "You're alive. Now, let's see what kind of fun we can have."

WHEN SEAN WAS seven he visited his grandfather in London and found the man's journal of his internment in a Japanese POW camp. He had stolen the journal and read it many times. He learned a great deal from studying it. It proved useful during Sean's second stint in Juvie, when he was locked up for stealing his neighbor's cat and setting it on fire. There he met Paul, a half-witted bully who had nearly beaten a clerk to death for kicking Paul and his friends out of a convenience store for loitering.

Paul was the perfect sidekick for Sean's stay in Juvie. One of their projects had been a boy named Martin Obeg.

"Mind if we join you?" asked Sean congenially, as he and Paul sat down next to the boy in the common room. Martin looked up from his comic book, his pale eyes not registering any strength of feeling. He shrugged.

"Martin, we propose a little experiment. Like a science experiment. We're doing research, see? We're going to see how much pain you can handle without making a sound. Paul here is going to hold onto your arm, and I'm going to pull your fingernails out with these pliers," said Sean calmly, placing a set of pilfered pliers on the table where Martin could see them.

"Your part in this is to keep your mouth shut while we do this. If you don't, Paul here is going to kill you. Does that make sense, Martin?" Martin's gaze moved from Sean to Paul and down to the pliers.

SEAN NEEDED TO wash up before dinner. He locked the door behind him and walked slowly up the stairs into the backyard, glancing over his shoulder to ensure that the door to the bunker looked as it had when he first saw it. Everything seemed in order. His smock and the come-along were tucked safely in his pack.

Juliet had shown him where she hid the spare key, so he made his way into the house and to the bathroom. She had laid out a towel and facecloth for him. First he washed his hands in the sink, the water running red, then clear. He stripped off his clothes and stepped into the shower. He stood there for a long time, letting the hot water rinse the blood from his face and neck and arms and down the drain. As he showered, he considered what he would cook his hosts for dinner that night.

SEVENTEEN

COLE BLACKWATER WOKE ON FRIDAY morning with a headache and a wrench in his neck that felt as though it would hobble him for a month. It had been two days since the attack in the back alley. He turned on the shower, and in a moment the room was filled with steam. He pressed one hand against the wall and felt the water cascade over his back and down his chest and legs. He let his head hang, his hair dripping into his face, eyes closed against the light of day.

He found himself humming as the water poured over him. He mumbled a few tattered lines of a Moby song: "Why does my heart feel so bad? Why does my soul feel so bad?"

Why indeed? Why go on fighting this way? he found himself thinking. He hadn't slept a full night in two months. His nightmares had abated the last two nights, but only because he'd been beaten nearly unconscious in a dark alley. He still had no idea who his masked assailants were.

And if Denman hadn't arrived on the scene when he did, Cole Blackwater would be a troublesome but quickly forgotten memory on God's green earth, he reflected.

Had he really been beaten so badly? Or had he simply given up?

He turned the shower off, took a towel from the rack, and dried himself with slow movements. After he dressed, he picked up the *Vancouver Sun* from his doorstep. He brewed coffee, and in the half light of dawn, opened the paper. On page three was Nancy Webber's scathing indictment of the Vancouver Police Department's handling of both the Lucky Strike raid and the disappearance of two men and two women from the Downtown Eastside.

She had written an opinion piece for the editorial page, which closed with a couple of pointed questions:

> If four people were missing from Point Grey or the West End, would the Vancouver Police Department be taking their disappearances more seriously? If the Lucky Strike Hotel had been occupied by protestors wearing suits, objecting to its conversion from luxury condos

to a single-room-occupancy hotel, would the police have tear-gassed them? The City of Vancouver and the VPD have made clear, with their words and their actions, which of its citizenry it favors.

Cole put the paper down and smiled for the first time in two days.

COLE MET DENMAN on the corner of Hastings and Main. Instead of going straight to the Priority Legal offices, they walked two blocks to Oppenheimer Park.

"What's this all about?" Cole asked as they strolled to the center of the ball diamond.

"Working the kinks out."

"Here?" said Cole, looking around self-consciously.

They stopped. Denman took note of the two dozen homeless men and woman who had slept in the park overnight and were slowly rising with the sun. He said, "You really think some tai chi is going to make you stand out *here*?"

Forty minutes later they continued on their way to the Priority Legal offices, fresh coffees in hand. "We've got to regroup after the Lucky Strike raid," said Cole, rolling his shoulders, feeling them loosen. "We've got the media on our side now. The cops finally stepped over the line. We've got to use this goodwill to build a wave of public support for a comprehensive plan to end homelessness in this city once and for all."

"How are your shoulders?"

Cole stopped his shrugging and looked sideways at Denman. "Okay, so the tai chi is working. And the three homeless dudes who joined in were a nice touch."

THE "USUAL SUSPECTS" is how Cole referred to the conglomeration of activists assembled at Priority Legal when Denman and Cole arrived. Beatta Nowak from the Downtown Eastside Community Advocacy Society was prominent among them, sitting at the end of the boardroom table, a cluster of reports and newspapers around her. Half a dozen other activists from the Advocacy Society occupied the chairs lining the wall behind her.

Francine Lanqois from the Carnegie Centre was in the room, as were representatives from a score of other non-profit organizations serving the homeless in the Downtown Eastside. The room was close and smelled of nervous sweat.

Denman introduced Cole. "We're going to talk strategy and communications for the next hour or so, and I've asked Cole to add his thoughts."

"The End Poverty Now Coalition is talking about retaliation," said Francine. "There's talk of occupying the mayor's or the chief constable's office."

"I'm not going to be able to help them if they do that," said Denman. "There's only so much this office can do. I don't think I can help them out if they take over City Hall."

"I'll pass it on," said Francine.

"It's not a bad strategy . . ." said Nowak.

"The problem is that the cycle never ends," said Denman. "They try to occupy City Hall, or the police chief's office, and VPD then has to use force to put a stop to it, citing concerns over anarchy in the streets. So then what do they do for an encore?"

"But it gets people's attention," said a young man sitting with Beatta.

"Yeah, nothing else seems to!" said a woman to their left.

"Our groups need to find a place, somewhere between the Salvation Army on one side and the End Poverty Now Coalition on the other, where we can push hard for a solution without all ending up in jail," said Denamn. "Cole, what do you think?" Denman turned to Cole.

Cole was staring at Beatta Nowak.

"Ground Control to Major Blackwater?" teased Denman.

Cole cleared his throat and looked around the room. Earnest young eyes on his; solemn battle-weary faces contemplating his dour countenance. "Well." He cleared his throat. "We can't vie for headline space with the Coalition. As crass as it sounds, I think we need to take advantage of the fact that four people have gone missing to highlight the homeless plight, without seeming to be opportunistic—"

Beatta Nowak interrupted. "Make that five." She was holding her Blackberry in her hand, her face ashen. "I just got a message from Juliet. George Oliver is missing. She's over at VPD now filling out the missing person report."

DENMAN AND COLE ran the six blocks to the VPD's Downtown Eastside detachment, where they found Juliet Rose in tears.

"Juliet, what's going on?" Denman asked. The entrance was crowded with people filing complaints.

"It's George. He's missing. It's been almost two days."

"What did the reporting officer say?"

"He said that two days doesn't make someone from the street missing."

"Well, that's a crock. The law says twenty-four hours."

"He was nice about it. He really was. But he said that they get reports from people all the time about friends who are missing and then they show up, hung over or shot full of heroin or whatever, and he said VPD didn't have the manpower."

"Did you talk with Marcia Lane?"

"I asked to see her, but nobody has gone to find her yet."

Denman called her office on his cell phone. "Yes, Marcia Lane, please."

Cole grinned and opened his own cell. "Hi, Mary, it's Cole. We need to do a bit of a media flash mob right away. Can you help us out?"

Denman said, "Ah-huh. Tell her it's Denman Scott calling from Priority Legal. Yes, I can wait, but it's an urgent matter."

Cole walked a few feet away from Denman. "Okay, so let's send out a media advisory. Tell me when you're ready," Cole said to Mary. "Okay, good. Write this: Subject: VPD fiddles while fifth Downtown Eastside resident is reported missing. Vancouver, September 27. Denman Scott, Executive Director of the Priority Legal Aid Society, will make an announcement today—" Cole looked at his watch "—at 11:00 AM inside the reception area of Vancouver Police Department's Main Street detachment about a fifth person who has been reported missing, and will comment on VPD's lack of effective response to the situation. Mr. Scott will discuss the case of a new missing person reported to VPD this morning, and VPD's unacceptable delay of its investigation due to the homeless status of those who have been reported by friends, family, or case workers as disappeared.

"Okay, read that back . . . Can you tighten that up?"

Next to him, Denman said, "Yes, I'm still holding."

"Good, okay, Mary," continued Cole. "Can you fax that to VPD's Main Street switchboard with the name Marcia Lane, and 'urgent' written in bold across the top? Once that has been faxed, get it set up to email to every reporter's Blackberry and wireless in the city. Then just hold on, okay? I'll call you in a couple of minutes and tell you if we need to send it."

Denman said into his phone, "Look, she doesn't need to call me back. I'm standing in your reception area. I'm here with Juliet Rose, who is a street nurse working out of the Carnegie Centre, and we have a fifth missing person to report . . . I know things are busy this morning, Constable, but they are going to get a lot busier. In about—" Denman looked at this watch "—fifteen minutes there are going to be twenty reporters crowding into your reception area while I hold a news conference about this department's lack of response . . . Yes, that is a threat, but not of bodily harm, so calm down and tell Marcia Lane that I'm waiting to see her. Thank you." Denman hung up.

Cole was grinning as he walked toward Denman, who looked at Cole and then back down at Juliet.

"That ought to get their attention," said Cole, standing with his cell phone still open in his hand.

Denman touched Juliet's cheek, brushing a tear from her face. "It's going to be okay. We're going to find him," he said. "He's got to be close by."

Juliet nodded.

"Denny, look," Cole said, still standing at his friend's side, "I think that *did* get their attention." Denman turned to see six uniformed officers come out from behind the Plexiglas and move toward them. Cole hit redial on his cell.

"Mary, hit send."

THEY STOOD ON the sidewalk under the slate gray sky and Denman gave the news conference. Thirty-two reporters arrived within a few minutes of each other, crowding the street with their cars and vans, creating traffic chaos and further raising the ire of the VPD. Cole and Juliet stood some distance away, Cole with his arm around Juliet, her face streaked with tears.

When it was done, they walked to Macy's. Cole called Nancy, who was strangely absent from the news conference, but only got her voice mail.

"Well, there's no turning back now," said Cole, ordering coffee. He bounced on his heels a few times while waiting for his brew.

Denman shook his head. "No, we're in the animal soup now."

Juliet ordered tea and a muffin and they sat down at a table by the window. All three were quiet.

"I can't believe they aren't taking this more seriously," said Juliet finally, picking at her muffin.

"I can," said Cole. "Look, I think it's obvious what's going down here."

Denman looked at him. "What's so obvious about it?"

Cole lowered his voice and spoke in a conspiratorial tone. "I think someone at City Hall has either told VPD to look the other way on this file, or has been setting this whole thing up from the start."

Juliet crinkled her nose. "You *still* think City Hall might be behind these disappearances?"

"Let's play it out here. Vancouver is running out of land for condos. There is enormous pressure for growth in the downtown core and the best place for that is right here. But there's a problem, the SROs. They're everywhere, and they are full of people, but not taxpaying citizens. They are on the fringes of society. An inconvenience to City Hall. An impediment to progress, to growth, to upward mobility. To profit. It's not so far-fetched to think that in the process of setting up plans for developing properties like the Lucky Strike Hotel, someone suggests that it would be so much easier if all the homeless people would just disappear, and that way, the City wouldn't have to find them all a place to squat, or listen to complaints from people like you and Denman."

"You think a city employee got it into their head to bump off all the homeless people in the Downtown Eastside? There are about three thousand of them," said Juliet skeptically.

"Not all. Just enough that everybody else fears for their life, shuts up, or gets out of town. I'm just saying it's a possibility."

"Doesn't seem like the sort of thing a guy in a suit from the planning department at City Hall would have the stomach for," said Juliet.

"Well, first," said Cole, "it might not be someone from the City. My money would be on the cops. Denman has been telling me about the harassment complaints that have been filed. All the excessive force complaints. I think there might be an unofficial policy of harassment in the VPD right now in order to clear the way for condo development. And second, why couldn't a guy in a suit be responsible?"

"Cole's right. If someone has got it in their head to take matters into their own hands, they likely won't look like Charles Manson, all wild-eyed and with a swastika stenciled on their forehead. They're going to look like your neighbor," Denman said to Juliet.

They were silent a moment. "I need more coffee to think that one through," said Cole. He went to the counter for a refill. The bell over the door rang and Cole instinctively turned. A young man in a leather coat wearing a heavy backpack walked toward the coffee counter.

Cole rejoined his friends. He picked up the conversation. "Look, maybe this is a crazy idea, but I still think it's worth exploring. Look at everything that is happening right now. The riot. The Lucky Strike raid. And then there's what went down in the back alley just a block from here a few nights ago." Cole touched his face and neck. "I don't think those goons were after my money. And the hammerheads we were following who led me to that back alley, they were cops, no doubt. How do we find out for sure who they are?"

Denman shrugged. "I don't think we can file a complaint. Maybe Marcia Lane can help us on this?"

Cole continued, "I still don't know about this Marcia Lane person. The trouble is, we're not dealing with someone who has all their bolts tight. I'm just saying that it's possible someone at City Hall, or maybe on the force, got the memo ordering them to use all means to clear the streets around the Lucky Strike and they took it a little too far."

"We've got no proof," said Denman.

"We'll get some."

"How do you propose to do that?"

"Shake the tree."

They looked up when the man with the leather coat and backpack stopped at their table.

"Hi, Denman. Hi, Juliet."

Denman and Juliet looked up at the man. Cole's eyes rested on them a moment before he too turned to look at the young man.

"Hi, Sean," said Denman. "You're looking well."

"I feel good," he said, smiling. His eyes and Juliet's locked a moment. "I'm off the street. Got a place to stay. Maybe even a line on a job." He smiled broadly. Cole looked from Sean to Juliet and back.

"That's great, Sean," she said, shifting uncomfortably. "I'm glad to hear it."

"Yeah, well, I just want to thank you both for your help," he said, warmly. His eyes remained fixed on Juliet's, but Cole couldn't detect any of the emotion that should have accompanied his gratitude. To Cole, it appeared as though Sean was reading the words from a cue card. "I really appreciate everything you've done to help me."

"No problem," said Denman.

"Okay, well, I'm off to a job interview. Wish me luck!"

"Good luck," they all said as he smiled again and left.

"One of your flock?" asked Cole.

"Arrested for taking a piss in an alley the day of the demonstration," said Denman.

"He's been around for a few months," said Juliet. "One of the few people I think can actually be saved."

Cole watched Sean jaywalk across the street.

He slapped the table with the palm of his hand. "I got so distracted by the media conference that I almost forgot," he said urgently.

"What is it, Cole?" asked Denman.

"When we were at Priority Legal. I was preoccupied . . ."

"I'll say. You were making me look bad. People were getting that look, like I had invited you in off the street or something."

"Well, there *was* something. A smell. A fragrance, really. Perfume. I just couldn't figure out where I had smelled it before. It was rosewater."

"Beatta Nowak," said Denman and Juliet together.

"Yeah. I couldn't place it in the room at first. It was subtle, but distinctive. And I'd smelled it somewhere else recently."

"Where?" asked Denman.

"82 Pender."

Denman said, "Where the Lucky Strike Supper Club was meeting."

"You don't think—?" said Juliet, shaking her head. The ringing of Denman's cell phone interrupted her.

"Denman Scott," he said, an apologetic smile on his face.

Cole looked out the window.

Denman listened, then said, "Okay, I'll be right over." He hung up.

"What is it?" asked Juliet.

"This day just gets better and better," he said, standing and grabbing his coat.

"What is it?" Juliet repeated.

Cole looked at Denman. "Nancy Webber. She's in police custody for possession of stolen property. She says she has something called the Lucky Strike Manifesto. The police raided her home and office this morning looking for it."

"Cool," said Cole, and jumped to his feet.

EIGHTEEN

TWENTY-FOUR HOURS EARLIER NANCY STOOD in Frank Pesh's office, looking out at Burrard Inlet.

"It's a fine line between journalist and advocate," said Frank.

"You think I've crossed that line?" asked Nancy.

"Not yet. You kept your story balanced. We'll place your opinion piece tomorrow, just to keep the two separate. I just want to keep in touch with you as you chase down this story. You *are* going to chase it down, aren't you?"

Nancy looked across the inlet at the mountains on the North Shore. "Like a dog after a stick," she said matter-of-factly.

THE COURIER ARRIVED at 4:54 PM. He slipped the package to the receptionist at the front desk of the *Vancouver Sun* and headed back out to his Honda Hybrid and zipped back into traffic. The receptionist dialed Nancy's number.

"I'll grab it on the way out," she said. Since the press conference that morning Nancy had been probing various aspects of the convoluted story of the Lucky Strike Hotel and the disappearances from the Downtown Eastside. Nancy pulled on her overcoat and left in the elevator with more questions than answers.

The elevator chimed and she stepped into the reception area.

"Hi, Nancy, here you go," said the receptionist. Nancy had already forgotten that a package was waiting for her.

"Oh, thanks." She smiled absently and stuffed the package into her briefcase next to her computer.

The week of steady rain had seen Nancy riding the bus home to her West End apartment, but today, though not sunny, was at least dry, so she decided to walk. To amuse herself she watched the progress of a man in a BMW as he crept along beside her. At each light he raced forward, and then at the next red Nancy would catch up to him. It made her think of Cole Blackwater. Two steps forward, two steps back. Three steps back. Two steps forward.

Nancy reached her West End building and took the elevator up to her apartment. She threw her bag on the table that doubled as a work station. Setting a glass of red wine on the counter, she retrieved some leftover Indian takeout from the previous evening. She put it in the microwave, then leaned on the counter sipping her wine, trying to loosen the knots in her neck. The microwave beeped, and she carried her plate and glass, with the bottle, to the living room. She liked to watch the six o'clock news while she ate.

When she was done, Nancy refilled her glass and opened her bag. She took out her computer and the files she had carted home, laying them out on the table in front of her. The corner of an unfamiliar envelope caught her eye.

"What have we here?" she said, vaguely recalling the *Sun* receptionist handing her something on her way out. She tore it open. Inside was a plain brown envelope containing three sheets of paper. She leaned forward in her chair, setting aside her wine glass, and skimmed the pages quickly. Her heart leapt into her throat. "Jesus Christ," she said aloud, reading the three pages again.

NANCY COULDN'T SLEEP. More than a dozen times that night she had picked up the phone, then put it down. She turned the light on and read the three sheets over and over.

Who was she planning on calling? Frank Pesh with breaking news? Denman Scott for reaction? Cole Blackwater for immediate *over* reaction? It seemed almost too wild to be possible, except that the suspected source of the three pages was beyond reproach. Nancy was pretty certain she knew who had slipped her the covert information, even though there was no name to validate that suspicion. Finally, at three o'clock she fell into a restless, wine-clouded sleep. She dreamed fitfully of a cabal of the city's most powerful backroom players conspiring to radically change the Downtown Eastside, changing the face of Vancouver in the process.

WHEN SHE WOKE, it was almost eight. Despite a hangover, Nancy bolted from bed. While her first cup of coffee brewed in the tiny kitchen, she showered and dressed. Without eating breakfast, and forgetting her coffee, she stuffed her files and computer into her bag, along with the three well-thumbed pages, and rode the elevator down to the street. She stopped in at a Quick Printer and made three copies of the three-page document. She mailed one to herself at the *Sun*, one to Denman Scott via Priority Legal, and one to Blackwater Strategies. They would all arrive in the mail in the next day or two, regardless of what happened to the original.

She got to the *Vancouver Sun* office and buzzed Frank Pesh. Five minutes later she was standing in his office, along with the assistant editor of the paper and the *Sun*'s in-house attorney. She had met Veronica White once before, when she was being hired by the *Sun*. White was a plain-spoken, cautious, middle-aged woman who took her job of protecting the *Vancouver Sun* from libel and slander suits seriously.

"You need three sources," said White.

"I'm never going to get any of these people to talk," said Nancy.

"You print those names without them, we'll get our ass sued off."

"What if I track down the source of the leak and get them to talk?"

"So what? What does it prove? Maybe a disgruntled employee. Maybe a lunatic from the End Poverty Now Coalition planting the story. Did you think of that?"

"I haven't discounted that, but I think this came from inside VPD."

"Really?" said Pesh. "What makes you think that?"

"Intuition."

"Intuition isn't going to keep this paper out of court," said White.

"Sometimes you have to take the risk."

"Look, Nancy," said White. "Please don't take this the wrong way. I'm not trying to stomp on journalistic freedom. That's not what I'm doing, really. I have a job to do, and that's to protect you and this paper. I can't do it if you don't listen," she turned to Pesh.

Nancy began to speak, but Pesh cut her off with a wave of his hand.

"I get to decide on this," he said, standing up and looking out over Burrard Inlet. "Does anybody else have this?" he asked.

"I don't think so. If my source is who I think it is, then they sent it to me for a reason. If I'm right, we have it exclusively. I have it—"

"Okay, let's do this," he said, interrupting. "You need to make some calls, Nancy. Veronica is right; this could be a setup. You need to confirm your source and find external collaboration. Find someone who will talk. I can live with one person involved, plus the source," he said, looking at White. "You've got till the end of the day."

BY NOON NANCY had external confirmation, but it wasn't of the sort she had anticipated.

At 9:43 AM she called the office of Beatta Nowak and asked to speak to the executive director of the Downtown Eastside Community Advocacy Society. She was told that Beatta was in a meeting at Priority Legal and wouldn't be back until noon. Next she called City Hall. Again, no luck. At 9:48 she took a deep breath and dialed the Vancouver Police Department. She was transferred to Media Relations Coordinator Beth Moresby.

"Beth, it's Nancy Webber for the *Vancouver Sun*."

"Hi, Nancy. What can I do for you today?"

"Can I speak with John Andrews, please?"

"What's it with regards to?"

"I have a source who is suggesting that Mr. Andrews is part of a group of people calling themselves the Lucky Strike Supper Club. They have authored a document, really just a few bulleted lines on a page, called the Lucky Strike Manifesto. I'm seeking confirmation or denial from Mr. Andrews regarding his participation in this group, and his authorship of this paper."

Nancy could feel her heart racing. There was only a second's silence.

"Can I get back to you? John is in a meeting right now, but I'll ask him to call you as soon as he gets out. Okay?"

"Alright. Sooner the better, Beth. My intention is to make print deadline this afternoon with or without his confirmation," she lied. "I'm holding back on web publication so as not to tip off any other outlets."

"Okay, well, it should be within an hour. Where are you?"

Nancy told her and they hung up.

JUST OVER AN hour later, Nancy was still sitting at her desk when two plainclothes police offers appeared before her.

"Nancy Webber?" one of them asked. She looked up.

"Who wants to know?"

"Detectives Colbert and Vary, VPD, ma'am. We have a warrant to search these premises, and your home," he held out the warrant for her to read.

Nancy picked up the phone. "Frank, call Veronica. We're being raided."

COLE AND DENMAN arrived at the VPD offices for the second time that day, fifteen minutes after Nancy had called. It was another two hours before they could see her.

"We should rent space here," said Cole dryly.

"It's cheap. And the application is pretty simple," added Denman.

"Getting out of the lease is the tricky part," Cole said, grinning.

"This may take a while, Cole. You want to stick around?"

"You kidding? Nancy Webber behind bars is a wet dream come true. Plus, I've got something else that our last conversation reminded me of. I'll be back," he said, and went to cue up at the reporting desk.

Denman dialed his office to check in. Cole rejoined him after an hour in the reporting line. "So the two goons who jumped me in the alley were picked up."

"I got a call about it yesterday. Sorry. I forgot to tell you. It's been a crazy week," said Denman shaking his head.

"The response report says it took twenty-two minutes for a car to arrive on the scene, despite the fact that there were two dozen units a block away at the Lucky Strike."

"Who wants to leave a good old-fashioned tear-gassing to deal with a simple assault?"

"Do you know the guys involved?" asked Cole.

"No, never heard of them."

"Think they might be connected to the VPD?"

Denman shook his head. "I have no idea. Neither of them had a jacket, but that doesn't mean anything."

"How do we find out?"

"Freedom of information request?"

"I don't know what we'd ask for. Badge numbers?" Denman shook his head again.

"What's going on with Nancy?" Cole asked.

"She's being questioned right now."

"She's not alone, is she?"

"Veronica White is with her, the *Sun's* pit bull of a lawyer. Nancy will be fine."

"Better than fine," said Cole. "She's going to be a hero."

IT WAS MID afternoon when Nancy walked through the door with Veronica White at her side. A warm smile lit her face when she saw Cole and Denman. She stopped before she reached them and turned to say a few words to White, then approached the two men while White left the building. Denman, then Cole, reached out and gave her a hug.

"It's good to see you boys," she said, still holding onto Cole's thick frame.

"Good to see you too," said Denman.

Cole and Nancy stepped back from one another, their eyes holding for a moment. Cole took a long, slow, steady breath. He could still smell Nancy's hair. For the first time in months the flood of memories that accompanied her was not unsettling.

"Well, have I got a story to tell." She broke the spell. "We better get at it. I've got to make print deadline," she said, slapping Cole on the arm. "Come on, boys."

THEY WALKED ONTO the street and hailed a cab. As they drove to the *Vancouver Sun* building, Nancy said, "So, first things first. I'm guessing there is a fair chance that we're being followed. The VPD is going ape-shit right now over what has landed on my desk. And the two of you are in the animal soup . . ."

"In more ways than one," said Denman.

"Right. So watch your back. I guess that won't be a problem for Mr. Friendly here," said Nancy, jerking a finger toward Cole. Cole just smirked.

Nancy pulled out her phone and called Frank Pesh. At the *Sun* building, they rode the elevator up to Nancy's office as she continued to talk with Frank. They followed her through the hive of *Sun* reporters, all buzzing with the news of the day, to a small boardroom.

When they were finally seated, Denman said, "So?"

She took a breath. "The Lucky Strike Manifesto is a document penned by a group of influential people from City Hall, the VPD, and the development community."

"Do you know their names?"

"No. But I'm starting to put that together. I know at least one for sure. I can guess at a couple of others."

"Who?"

"John Andrews is one." Denman nodded. "And there is at least one person from City Council. The mayor himself may be party to it. They meet regularly; call themselves the Lucky Strike Supper Club."

"They had been using that Pender Street address, hadn't they?" asked Denman.

"That's my guess. Cole must have just missed them."

"So what is the Manifesto?"

"It's an agreement of sorts, a statement of principles, that this group of people are trying to advance." She dug some notes out of her bag.

"Do you have it?"

"*Had* it. When the VPD raided us this morning, they carted away the three pages I had received by courier. I'll have another copy by tomorrow. So will the two of you. Anyway, I made some notes when I was able; it's really not very complex. The group agreed to pave the way for a massive redevelopment of the Downtown Eastside. Gastown, Chinatown, Oppenheimer, the Hastings Corridor are all included. The goal is to build twenty to thirty new condominium developments in the area in the next five years."

"So fast!" said Cole.

"The agreement also says that these players will work together to elect a city council next year that is dominated by people who will work toward creating a comprehensive new community development plan for the area. The plan will emphasize what they are calling 'urban reunification.' One city. No east side–west side split. Just one Vancouver."

"That's not really news, is it?" asked Denman.

"It's not *what* they are doing, but *how*," said Nancy.

"What do you mean?"

"The Manifesto is a blueprint for what it calls 'interventionist action' by City Hall and the VPD. In essence it says, 'do what needs to be done' to clear the way for aggressive development."

"Hence the rise in complaints of excessive force, and the crackdown at the Lucky Strike."

"The Lucky Strike is just the first of what will be many," said Nancy. "There's more, though. The Manifesto also acknowledges what it calls 'the reality' of the situation. That homeless people have to live somewhere, so it lays out a blueprint for 'resettlement.'"

"Jesus, that sounds ominous," said Denman.

"Yeah. It sounds like a Vancouver version of New York's 'Projects' to me."

"Where?"

"Mostly in Strathcona. Rezoning some areas that are industrial to mixed residential."

"Push the poor and the damaged farther east."

"Till they end up in Burnaby and are someone else's problem," said Nancy, referring to Vancouver's neighboring city.

"Listen," she said, looking at her watch. "I've got to go. We're filing on the raid today, and hopefully by tomorrow I'll have at least one or two independent confirmations for the Manifesto, and Veronica White will let us file on that."

"I think you should add Beatta Nowak to that list," said Cole.

"You're kidding me," said Nancy.

"Nope."

"Listen, Cole, just because someone who wears rosewater perfume was in that room . . ." Denman began.

"It's a hunch, but I think you should call her," said Cole.

"You're not getting paranoid on me, are you, Cole?" asked Nancy.

"*Getting* . . . ?" quipped Denman. "But what does it hurt?" he asked abruptly. "Make the call. Check it out."

"I called her today, but just to ask if she had any suspicions of who might be behind this, not if she was a conspirator," Nancy admitted.

She took a breath. "Between now and then, I wonder if you two might do me a favor?"

"What's that?" asked Cole.

"Try and find out just exactly what the City and VPD are willing to do to get this job done."

"GOT TIME FOR a beer?" asked Cole.

Denman looked at his watch. "Sure. Let me make two calls while we walk."

As Denman opened his phone, Cole's rang and he rummaged around in his crowded pockets for it. "Blackwater."

"Oh, hi, Cole. It's Mary."

"Hey, Mary. Listen, great work today. We kicked butt and took names," he said.

"Glad to be of service," she said. "I have one more piece of information for you that you requested. It took some digging down at the City's department of records, but I found out who the office on Pender Street is leased to."

"Great. Who?"

"A law firm in town called Livingstone, Grey and Barnes. Do you know them?"

"Heard of them. They do a lot of work with the timber and mining sector. Labor dispute resolution, that sort of stuff."

"Well, they've had a lease on that office for about a year."

"Okay, well, that makes sense. I bet our Lucky Strike Supper Club has been meeting there that long."

"Anything else, Cole?"

Cole thought. "Not right now. Thanks, Mary."

They walked to the Cambie Hotel. It wasn't yet five o'clock, and the bar, usually raucous on Fridays, was somber. A hundred years ago the pub had been two separate establishments, and had two separate liquor licenses. Now it was one tavern divided by a chipped white picket fence, with a tiny gate. A sign warned patrons not to carry booze from one side to the other. Enforcing it, Cole had once quipped, would be like asking the pope not to pray.

Cole and Denman took seats at the long, worn counter, close to the pool tables, and ordered pints.

"Juliet will be joining us," said Denman.

Cole was silent. Then he said, "So this law firm, Livingstone, Grey and Barnes . . ."

"You think they're involved in the Manifesto?" asked Denman.

"Yeah. I bet they have a client who's into condos. How do we find out?"

"No way to know, really, unless they've been to court for them."

"Can you check?"

Denman sipped his pint. "Sure."

Cole was silent. He watched the people come and go from the bar.

"What are you thinking?" asked Denman.

"I'm thinking that I should go and brace Livingstone, Grey and Barnes," he said.

"Not a bad idea."

Cole took a long pull on his beer.

"You don't think the City and VPD could be behind the missing people, do you?" Cole finally said.

Denman shook his head. "I just can't see it. Unless they are putting people on the bus . . ."

"You know they're not putting people on the bus. If they are, those people would turn up somewhere. They're not. They're gone."

Juliet arrived and they moved to a table. They caught each other up on the day's events over another pint. Denman and Juliet sat close together, their arms touching. Cole finished his beer and began to get ready to leave.

"I'm going to head 'er," he said, grabbing his jacket.

Denman put his glass down. "Cole, I want to ask you to do something for me."

"Sure, name it."

"Well, you're not going to like it."

"Spit it out."

"I want you to come to therapy," Denman said.

Cole raised one eyebrow and slipped his jacket on.

"No crystals. None of that stuff. I have a friend who is a trauma specialist. He works with the military. He's good, Cole. You'll like him. He's a bit rough around the edges sometimes. Just like you," Denman smiled.

"I'm not going to have to chant or have my chakras recalibrated or any of that mumbo jumbo?"

"Nothing."

Cole took a deep breath. He felt a flash of panic wash over him. For a second his sight went black and he was in the barn. There was blood. As clear as a bell, he heard the blast of a shotgun.

"Cole?" said Juliet, touching his hand.

"When do we go?" he said.

SEAN WASN'T CONCERNED about consequences. Getting caught didn't worry him. The only reason he took precautions at all was because getting caught meant his fun would come to an end, and he had grown dependent on the rush that making each arrangement brought.

He let whimsy carry him up one street and down the other, always keeping the Lucky Strike in view. He passed two patrol officers. Sean's blank eyes roved across them. The officers didn't pay any attention to him.

There seemed to be more cops around, thought Sean. Maybe they were trying to avoid any further dustups with the protesters. Maybe . . .

He spotted a man in a heavy, stained parka walking out of the alley, dragging a duffle bag that seemed to weigh a hundred pounds. Sean crossed the street and approached the ragged-looking man.

"Hey, friend," said Sean congenially. "Need some help?"

"Nope. Don't need no help," said the man as he continued to haul on the sack.

"What you got in there?"

The man looked at Sean, his face darkly tanned and heavily lined, his eyes clear and blue and piercing. "I got metal."

"Metal?"

"Yup. Aluminum, mostly."

Sean smiled at him. "What are you doing with it? Recycling?"

Aluminum Man seemed to look right through Sean. He spoke in a calm, pleasant voice. "Nope. It's for the Mother Ship."

"The Mother Ship?"

"Yup. When they come I give them the aluminum. That way there's always enough on the home world."

"Okay," said Sean. "Maybe I can help you collect some."

NINETEEN

COLE HAD CALLED NANCY FIRST thing on Monday morning. He told her about the law firm Mary had linked to the room used by the Lucky Strike Supper Club.

She phoned the firm's office. "I'd like to speak with the senior partner who is handling the Lucky Strike sale." She was asked to hold a minute.

When the receptionist returned, Nancy was told, "I'm sorry; the firm doesn't have any comment on this file."

"You are handling the sale, are you not?"

"I'm not at liberty to speak about who our clients are."

Nancy couldn't figure out how to get past the receptionist. Cole and Denman tried next.

By the time Cole left his office to meet Denman, they were both armed with copies of the Lucky Strike Manifesto, courtesy of Canada Post. They walked together to the offices of Livingstone, Grey and Barnes.

"What do you think?" asked Denman as they held their copies of the three slender pages in their hands.

"Well, page one is nothing. Whoever leaked the rest of it felt they needed to provide a preface. That's all. Page two and three are the meat and potatoes. Or the tofu and bean sprouts for the West Coast-wise." Cole held the pages in front of him and read as they moved in and out of the crowd.

When he had finished he looked up. "There seems to be a spot for signatures, but of course, there are none."

"So Nancy's source either didn't know who all the signatories were, or didn't want to say."

"My money is on the former. If the source leaked this, then why not the names, if he had them?"

"Or she."

"Right, or she."

"What do you think of it?"

"Well," mused Cole, dodging a man in a suit. "I don't know what to think. I mean, the problem needs to be solved. This so-called Manifesto is one solution. But I really don't know much about this sort of thing. You're the expert."

"To some it would look like a solution, yes. If we printed it in the newspaper, a bunch of folks would say, 'Hey, what are you complaining about? You've got your solution. Shut up already.' But the solution isn't to build a bunch of cardboard and glue apartment blocks and stick all the homeless people, drug dealers, gang bangers, prostitutes, and folks with genuine mental health challenges in together. That just concentrates the problem. New York City and Toronto have both proven that doesn't work."

They turned a corner. "The solution needs to grow from the community up. Tearing the SROs down and moving the people only moves the problem. The solution is more complex than that. Many of the people on the street suffer from a mental illness that can only be managed, not treated. They need stepping stones, what we call graduated housing, starting with community-supported housing. Over time, the folks graduate to independent living. And we need to crack down on the people who are running the drug trade . . ." continued Denman.

"Like our friend Fu?"

"Yeah, him and a dozen others. We need to take away the fuel creating the fire that drives much of the crime and violence in the Downtown Eastside. And we need to create long-term, local, economic solutions that allow people to build their own economy in the area. Real jobs that support people's dreams for themselves."

"Like Macy Terry . . ." interjected Cole.

"Yeah, Macy and other social entrepreneurs."

"I heard she's thinking about running for mayor."

"We've been talking about it."

"Really?" Cole asked with interest.

"The election is still a year and a half away, but this city needs someone with vision in City Hall. Don West just doesn't cut it," said Denman.

"So what you're saying is that the Manifesto is for condo developers and those at City Hall who want to sweep this problem under the carpet," Cole said, returning to the topic at hand.

"It was written from the mentality that if you just crack some heads, you know, tough love sort of thing, then people will respond. Put enough cops on the beat harassing the homeless, they'll all move along . . ."

"Now what?" asked Cole.

"Well, I guess we brace these dudes." Denman looked up at the office tower housing the Livingstone, Grey and Barnes offices. "Find out what we can. See if they are involved. It seems likely they are representing this Captain Condo fellow on the sale of the Lucky Strike. I can't see why they would be worried about us knowing that."

"Unless their involvement somehow reaches beyond just providing legal advice."

"What do you mean?" asked Denman as they stepped into the elevator.

"I don't know. What if it's Frank Ainsworth, the Condo Captain himself, who is behind all these disappearances? What if Ainsworth has hired someone to do some cleaning up around his new property?"

"Why? He's already got what he wants."

"Maybe he doesn't. We know the plan. Twenty buildings in the next five years. Maybe he's hired someone to move the homeless out. Maybe it got out of hand. Maybe someone went too far."

Denman looked at Cole, who was watching the floor numbers appear on the display panel. "Wow, you're really going out on a limb on this, aren't you?"

"Look, I'm just saying that maybe somebody from the Lucky Strike Supper Club is bumping homeless people off. We better start asking the hard questions."

"Let's not go accusing one of the city's most prominent law offices of murder, okay, Cole?"

Cole looked at him, his face serious. "Okay. Not yet."

They approached the reception desk, a broad U-shaped table in a massive lounge filled with overstuffed chairs, teak tables, vases of flowers, soft lighting, and delicate fragrances.

"Do you have an appointment?" asked the dark-haired receptionist.

"No, I'm afraid not," said Denman congenially.

"Who is it you'd like to see?"

"We were hoping to meet with whoever is handling the sale of the Lucky Strike Hotel."

"Oh," she said, suggesting a certain weariness with the whole business. "And who are you?"

"My name is Denman Scott." He produced his card. "With Priority Legal. This is Cole Blackwater."

"I'm sorry, Mr. Scott, Mr. Blackwater. There's nobody here to see you about that."

"Nobody is here, or there is nobody here who will see us?" asked Cole.

"Both," she said.

"We'll wait," said Denman, the receptionist's face registering disappointment.

Denman and Cole found comfortable chairs that provided a good view of the entrance. Cole had looked at the firm's website, so he knew he could recognize Livingstone, Barnes and Grey if they walked in. "We'll just keep a watch out," he said, settling into the chair.

The receptionist picked up her phone and made a call.

"Think she's calling the cops?" asked Cole.

"If she is, I'm calling my lawyer," said Denman.

"Me too," said Cole, fishing out his cell phone. Denman picked up a magazine from the table in front of them and flipped through it.

An hour passed. A few clients came and went, and the receptionist looked at her watch.

"Think we might need reinforcements?" asked Cole.

Denman looked up. "What do you mean?"

"The End Poverty Now Coalition?"

Denman grinned. "I'm not ready to make that call. Not yet."

They waited until eleven o'clock, when a stout man appeared behind the reception desk. "Is this to be an occupation?" he asked.

Denman stood up. "No sir, just hoping for a few minutes of someone's time."

The man stepped forward. He was dressed immaculately in a three-piece suit. "My name is Charles Livingstone," he extended his hand. Denman stepped forward and shook it. Livingstone's grip was firm and dry, the practiced handshake of a man who used his physical presence to his advantage.

"This is Cole Blackwater," said Denman.

"Your wing-man?" asked Livingstone.

"I'm starting to think so," said Cole, and shook the man's hand.

"I'm sorry that you've had to sit out here so long. But I'm really not at liberty to discuss anything about any of the portfolios that we handle for our clients. Surely you, Mr. Scott, should know that."

"We don't want to put you in a position where you're compromising solicitor-client confidentiality, Mr. Livingstone. We were hoping you might help us understand some troubling events taking place that are affecting *my* clients, that's all. Can we take a few minutes of your time? If there's nothing you can speak to, we'll gladly leave."

Livingstone let his gaze rest on first Denman, then Cole. "Very well," he said. "Lucinda, would you ask Elizabeth to join us to take notes?"

"Certainly, Mr. Livingstone."

"Follow me, gentlemen," said the solicitor, and he walked toward a corner office. Denman and Cole followed.

"Please, have a seat," he said, pointing to two leather club chairs facing his mahogany desk. Livingstone seated himself behind it. "Elizabeth will join us shortly."

Cole walked over to the desk, his eyes falling on the framed photographs there.

"Your family?" he asked. The picture showed Livingstone in a sports coat and slacks standing beside a blond woman who was beautiful in a haunted, distant way. Next to her stood a young man, maybe fourteen or fifteen years old. The boy was smiling, but in a manner that made Cole think he'd just been threatened.

"Yes," said Livingstone looking at the picture as if he hadn't seen it in years. "Yes," his voice grew quiet.

Cole was about to ask a question when there was a knock at the door and a young woman entered. Livingstone turned businesslike again. "So, let's get started. What is it that you'd like to know?"

"Well, Mr. Livingstone," Denman began. "Are you representing Frank Ainsworth in the purchase of the Lucky Strike Hotel?"

"I don't think there is any harm in telling you that Mr. Ainsworth is one of this firm's most important clients. We've helped with the purchase of many of the dilapidated hovels that he converts to upscale condominiums. We're proud to be a part of that work."

"And the Lucky Strike?"

"Yes, we provided services. I don't see what the problem is, Mr. Scott. These are routine property purchases. We handle one a week for our various clients."

"Well, the Lucky Strike is anything but routine, Mr. Livingstone."

"Illuminate me."

"Well, it seems that the Lucky Strike is at the center of some—" Denman hesitated, searching for the correct word, "—some . . . malfeasance that involves City Hall and the Vancouver Police Department, at the very least. We think it involves others, possibly from the development community. Police brutality is on the rise in the Downtown Eastside, and we believe the increase is connected to an edict to try and push the city's homeless out of key parts of the region favored by developers, including Mr. Ainsworth. It seems that your client's purchase of the Lucky Strike is at the heart of an escalation of violence and a crackdown by the City and the police that is threatening to get out of control," Denman finished.

Livingstone sat with his hands pressed together, listening intently. He waited a moment after Denman had concluded, then exhaled. "Thank you for bringing these concerns to my attention. My client doesn't want his legal business activities to result in any hardship in the area. I don't see how you can link alleged police brutality to Mr. Ainsworth's purchase of the Lucky Strike." Cole stirred impatiently beside Denman. "You have something you wish to add, Mr. Blackwater?"

Denman looked at Cole. "You know, I think I've had enough lawyer talk this morning," Cole said, pulling the envelope posted by Nancy the day before from his pocket. "This is the Lucky Strike Manifesto. Do you know what that is?"

"Sounds official. City business?" asked Livingstone.

"It's certainly *not* official," said Cole. "It's a pact between people who are intent on razing the low-rent hotels and hostels in the Downtown Eastside and building condominiums, shopping centers, and luxury hotels in their place. It's a plan to sweep the homeless into the equivalent of prisons so that crime, poverty, and destitution will be pushed farther from the city's center so it doesn't get in the way of development."

Livingstone made as if to protest, but Cole pressed on. "And, sir, I believe that it has gotten out of hand. I am willing to bet that someone connected to this agreement has gotten carried away in their enthusiasm for growth, profit, and greed."

"What are you saying, Mr. Blackwater?"

Denman warned Cole with a look. "Nothing. He's saying nothing."

"I believe someone whose name is on this agreement has been part of the disappearance of at least five people from the vicinity of the Lucky Strike Hotel in the last six weeks."

"That's preposterous, Mr. Blackwater."

"I don't think it's preposterous to think that a man like John Andrews or Frank Ainsworth, or even you, Mr. Livingstone, might decide to sanction such action to get what he wants. I've seen it before."

"Mr. Blackwater, that is a most illuminating allegation," said Livingstone.

"Thank you for your time," said Denman, rising.

"No, I want to hear him say that he has no knowledge of these disappearances," said Cole.

"I assure you, Mr. Blackwater, that I don't. Now, if you'll excuse me . . ." Livingstone too stood up, indicating the meeting was over.

"Are you also telling me that when I followed your food delivery to the Pender Street office that *you* rented for the Supper Club, you didn't have a couple of men attack me and nearly beat me to death in the back alley? If it wasn't for this man right here," Cole stood and indicated Denman, "one of them would have slit my throat."

"I'm not going to continue this conversation, Mr. Blackwater. Mr. Scott, I'll ask you and your associate to kindly leave now."

"You were in that room on Pender Street that night, weren't you? You, or maybe John Andrews, got a call from your delivery boy." Cole leaned against Livingstone's desk, his finger now pointed directly at the man. The secretary pressed herself as far from Cole as her chair would allow.

Livingstone reached for the telephone. "I'm going to have to call the police," he said.

"That won't be necessary," said Denman, reaching for Cole's arm. Cole pulled away.

"I'm going to sink the Lucky Strike Supper Club," Cole told

Livingstone. "I'm going to expose the Lucky Strike Manifesto, I'm going to find out how you and your puppets at City Hall and VPD are involved in the disappearance of five people, and I'm going to sink you!"

"Lucinda," Livingstone said into the phone, "would you please call the police and ask them to come to my office? And alert building security."

Cole stepped toward him, but this time Denman slipped a hand around Cole's wrist, and without twisting or turning it, guided his hand away from the desk and walked Cole toward the door. Without a backward glance he led Cole through the reception area and to the elevators. They waited a moment, then Denman said, "We're taking the stairs."

"We're on the twentieth floor."

"Too fucking bad," Denman said.

NANCY SAT IN her office, surveying the stack of newspapers on the table. Frank Pesh had brought them in that morning. "We've been covered by nearly every daily in the country," he said, smiling. "When your paper *is* the news, you must be doing something right."

The *Sun*'s phone had been ringing off the hook all day with Vancouverites voicing their support for the paper. The chief constable also called, but to lambast the *Sun* for what he called one-sided journalism. Pesh asked if he wanted to go on the record, and he declined.

At about ten-thirty, Nancy's cell phone buzzed with a text message.

"Good work," the message read. The texter's ID had been blocked.

She texted back, saying, "Thx," then "Who are U?"

"Friend."

She keyed in, "THE friend?"

"Yes."

"Do U have more?"

"Yes."

"Can we meet?"

Nancy sat watching her cell, waiting for it to buzz. She needed confirmation of who the members of the Lucky Strike Supper Club were and who the signatories to the Manifesto were.

"Victory Square. Noon," the message read. Nancy snapped the cell phone shut and grabbed her coat.

JULIET WALKED UP the front steps of the Carnegie Centre, weaving her way through the crowd. There was safety in numbers. Since George Oliver had gone missing, it seemed like an undercurrent of fear and paranoia had shot through the Downtown Eastside. Up until that point, the disappearances of four people seemed somehow random. But George Oliver was well known in the community, and well loved. She reached her office and took off her coat.

"Have you been waiting long?" she asked her visitor.

"No, just a minute," said Marcia Lane.

"I was at Oppenheimer. I could have come to the detachment. Do you have news about George?"

"I'd rather meet here, and no, nothing new on George," said Marcia. She held her cell phone in her hand.

"What can I do for you?" asked Juliet, sitting down at her desk. "Was there something incomplete in the statement I gave at the detachment?"

"No, everything in your statement was fine." Marcia took a breath. "Listen, you were treated poorly by the reporting constable the other day, and I want to offer my *personal* apology," she said, looking directly at Juliet. "You understand, this isn't the department apologizing. It's me. These disappearances are causing some, well, some serious trouble. Very serious."

"What do you mean?"

"It's complicated."

"Try me."

"After the Pickton situation, there was a shakeup in how we handle missing persons in the Eastside. There was a lot of criticism that VPD doesn't take this sort of thing seriously; that because the missing women in the Pickton case where prostitutes, we didn't put much manpower on it."

"You didn't."

"I *know* we didn't. That was supposed to change. We got a lot of flack from City Hall, and so we created the Missing Persons Task Force. I got promoted to lead it. We've been muddling along with four investigators, and me riding herd, for the last two years. We take it one person at a time, but this is different."

"So you're agreeing that they are all related?"

"The *department* isn't prepared to say that."

"What about you?"

Marcia was silent. She regarded Juliet. The din from the Carnegie Centre's main room was growing as the lunch hour neared. "I have a strong hunch that they are. I've managed to get another dozen patrol officers on the street in the last few days, since your report on Mr. Oliver, but that's a pittance. Most of them are tied up running down the usual red herrings. It's stuff we have to do to eliminate the obvious. First we check in with Welfare to find out the last time anybody collected a check. Veronica and George have only been missing for a few days . . . a week at best, so that doesn't help us much. Bobbie, the fellow who sells umbrellas, he hasn't been on Welfare for more than a year. Jerry and your friend Peaches are both collecting, but neither collected the check—" Marcia looked at her notebook, "—on the fourteenth of this month, but they both collected their payments in August."

Juliet felt a hot fear creeping up her neck and worried that her face was turning red as she listened to Marcia.

"After that it's next of kin. Unfortunately, none of these people had any, at least that we know of. You gave us a name in Saskatoon for an aunt of Peaches, but the RCMP there haven't been able to track her down. They are still trying.

"So that leaves us with a physical search," continued Marcia. "So far, we haven't found anything that's helpful, but as I said, I've only been able to get twelve more people, six units. It's not much for such a huge area, where physical evidence is difficult to distinguish from the trash that just clutters up the streets. Needless to say, if this was happening in the West End, I'd have two hundred officers prowling every alley and doorway and garbage can, looking for leads."

Juliet drew a deep breath. "What about Veronica's coat?"

"We did have some luck there. We found the fellow. He claims to have found the coat in a dumpster. First off, you should know that he was co-operative. He told us where the dumpster was, and we now have the coat in our possession; forensics is looking at it. We're also looking at the area around the dumpster for additional forensic data. The trouble is that traditional methods like spraying the place with Luminal or Bluestar doesn't really help much."

Juliet's face twisted into a question. "What's Luminal and why doesn't it work?"

"Luminal and Bluestar are chemicals—we call them latent blood reagents—that we can use to detect the presence of blood, even in minute amounts."

"And it doesn't work well down here because the place is covered in the stuff," said Juliet.

"That's right. Along with all sorts of other bodily fluids. So we look for blood spatter patterns and try to distinguish between recent deposits and older ones," she explained. "Look, I know what these folks mean to you. I'm prepared to say for the sake of argument that the disappearances are connected. The problem is twofold. First, I don't have any evidence. There's nothing. We don't even have photos of some of these people."

"I have one of George."

"Really?"

"Yeah, he and I were friends. It's right here." Juliet reached over and pulled a photo of a smiling George Oliver from her bulletin board. She handed it to the officer.

"Can I take this? It will really help."

"I'll want it back."

"I'll see to it personally. This is great." Marcia looked at the photo. "The reporting constable should have asked for this. I just assumed he had and that there were no pictures."

"You said there were two things."

"Well, the second one is the question of motive. There's plenty of means and opportunity. In an area as crazy as this, people can easily be taken from the street. The question is, why? I've pretty much eliminated the theory that these people have somehow gotten tangled up in organized crime. There doesn't seem to be any connection. We've shaken down the usual suspects, called in some favors. We've worked some of our low-level informants and we're getting nothing back. All five of these people couldn't have somehow caught onto something that one of the bosses is doing and gotten bumped because of it.

"I know what some people are saying," continued Marcia. "That this is linked to the Lucky Strike, and other SRO closures. What's that guy's name that hangs around with your friend?"

"Cole Blackwater."

"He's on a bit of a warpath right now, saying that somebody at City Hall or one of the developers or even someone in the VPD gave the nod so that these street people can be carted up and shipped out of the area. I'd say that's totally crazy, except that I'm personally getting my ass busted from the boss on this file. Every time I try to get a handle on what's going on, I get knocked off my game by people higher up in the department. But still, I can't believe that anybody in VPD would be aiding in the disappearance of these people. I can't see it. Unnecessary force is one thing: disappearances, that's beyond the pale. That's Venezuela. That's Nicaragua. Not Canada."

"So if not that, then what?"

"Well, we could be facing something else. It could very well be that a very troubled individual, or individuals, are stalking homeless people and killing them."

"My God," sighed Juliet. "Why would somebody do that?"

"Ask Willie Pickton. Ask Clifford Olson. That type of person might be motivated by anything, by money or jealousy or some other emotion. Some of them need no motivation at all. They are psychopaths. They kill or perpetuate other crimes for no reason other than personal gratification. They kill because they *feel like it*, and they operate beyond the societal and personal constraints that regulate most of our behavior. My fear is that maybe there is some . . . entanglement of motivation."

"What do you mean?"

Marcia drew a deep breath. "There's been a lot of interference in this case. I had two of my investigators pulled last week for what turns out to be gopher work for the Big Cheese."

"Andrews?"

Marcia nodded. "And there has been an unofficial policy of pestering."

"I think it's called harassment," said Juliet.

"More like aggressive persuasion. I think it's the wrong way to police a neighborhood like the Downtown Eastside. The reality is that since Andrews took over in Division 2, he's turned a blind eye to some of the rougher elements on the beat. I'm—" She paused for what seemed to Juliet like an eternity. "I'm concerned that maybe someone on the force has stepped over the line. That we have someone who is both a psychopath and operating within some official capacity."

Juliet felt the heat in her neck spreading. "Do you have . . . a suspect in mind?"

"No, this is just a crazy idea. There are lots of crazy things happening right now, and I wanted you to know that I'm covering all the angles on this."

"How do you catch someone like that?"

"If they are on the force, that's one thing. Let's forget that as a possibility for now. And I need to tell you that if I get a call from Nancy Webber from the *Sun* about this, I will deny ever talking about it with you."

Juliet just shook her head.

"If the person is a member of the general public, sometimes we don't catch them because they just stop. They grow older and their behavior changes. Most often, though, they are their own worst enemy. They act on impulse and don't care if they get caught, except that it will spoil their fun. They make a mistake and we get them that way."

"You're saying we might have to wait around for a psychopathic killer, who is targeting the poorest and most disadvantaged in our city, to get old or make a mistake?"

"Manpower would help."

"How can *I* help with that?"

"Well, that's part of what I wanted to talk with you about."

"That and what else?"

"I need to get a feel for these people who went missing. What they did; where they spent their time. The Eastside is a big area, and I've only got limited resources. I need a better feel for where I deploy my officers."

"We have a map."

"Really?"

"Yeah, Cole and Denman have been working on one that might help."

"Can I get a look at it?"

Marcia's cell phone buzzed and she flipped it open. "Just a minute, okay?" she said to Juliet, then keyed in a message and pressed send.

"Organizing a rave?" Juliet joked.

"Something like that," Marcia said. "Can you get Mr. Blackwater or Mr. Scott to bring me that map?"

"It's at Cole's office. He's in the Dominion Building. I can call him."

"I'm going to be in that area at lunch today. I can stop by if that suits him. I'll call him on my way over."

"You said you needed me to do something else?"

"Yeah," said Marcia. "I need some more officers. I can't get the department to budge. I need you to find a way to put some pressure on City Hall to free up more manpower. If my theory is right—that we are dealing with someone who is motivated by personal gratification—then we need to be there when he or she makes a mistake. Can you do that?"

"I can't do it myself," said Juliet. "I work for the Health Authority. I'd get fired. But I will find someone who can."

"Great," said Marcia, looking at her watch. "I've got a meeting over at Victory Square. Got to hoof it." They shook hands and Juliet watched her leave.

TWENTY

COLE'S CELL PHONE RANG WHEN they reached the street. "Blackwater," he said.

"Cole, it's Mary. Listen, I just got a call from someone at City Hall. The caller wouldn't leave her name, but she wanted to give you a heads up."

"Did you give her my cell number?"

"I did, but she said she would just leave a message. She said that tomorrow morning at noon, the mayor would be announcing a 'New Vancouver' campaign. It's his plan to clean up the city. End homelessness, that sort of thing."

"Really? That's amazing timing."

"Yeah, the woman was just giving you a heads up."

"She wouldn't leave her name?"

"Nope. Caller ID was blocked."

"Okay. Thanks, Mary."

Cole snapped the cell phone shut and told Denman the news. They walked across Dunsmuir Street under brooding skies.

"What's your sense of this?" asked Denman.

"I don't know. I'm betting that this announcement is going to be mostly fluff. Lots of Band-Aids. Maybe we'll be surprised."

"Not by Mayor Don West," said Denman. "He's not the surprising kind. And the tip-off . . . ?"

"Yeah, well, we've got friends where we think we have only enemies and enemies where we think we only have friends."

Denman looked at him. "Now Cole Blackwater . . . He's the surprising kind."

"I'm sorry about that."

"We came pretty close to landing in the clink. We may still end up there."

"Whatever."

"You really think that Livingstone is connected to the disappearances?"

"If not him in person, then someone else he knows is in the Lucky Strike Supper Club, and that's collusion, or something."

"It's called conspiracy."

"Well, if neither he nor Frank Ainsworth is behind the disappearances—you know, in conspiracy with someone else—maybe one of the other members of the Supper Club is."

"I don't know, Cole . . ."

"Your problem, Denman, is that you want to give the benefit of the doubt to these people. You want them to play by the rules. But they don't. They aren't."

He stopped walking and faced Denman. His voice was starting to rise. "Denman, I wasn't imagining a knife at my throat the other night. I wasn't imagining getting kicked like a dog in that alley. That wasn't in my head!" Cole pounded a finger at his own temple. "This wasn't just me having a flashback. It wasn't Cole losing his marbles. I was led to that Pender Street office, and I was led into that alley, and if you hadn't shown up, I would be dead!"

A passerby eyed the yelling man warily, giving him a wide berth. "The goons in that alley weren't a manifestation of my addled mind. It wasn't some sort of illusion. That shotgun was meant for me!"

Denman stood listening to him, his expression calm.

"Denman, I'm sorry . . ."

"It's okay, buddy."

"No, I'm—"

"Cole." Denman reached out and put his hand on Cole's shoulder. "Cole, it's going to be alright. I've got someone who can help you. We're going to get you through this."

When Cole's cell phone rang, he jumped, then scrambled to fish it from his pocket. "Blackwater," he said weakly.

"Mr. Blackwater, this is Marcia Lane calling."

"Hi, Marcia. What can I do for you?" he said, composing himself.

"I understand you have a map I might be interested in."

NANCY SAT ON the stone bench beneath the row of flags and waited. Victory Square was an interesting choice of locations for a meeting. On July 2, 2003, activists erected a tent city on this site and maintained it for more than three weeks. At its peak, more than one hundred people made Victory Square their home, living in tents donated by individuals from across the city and eating meals prepared by volunteers. Many protestors—who were mostly homeless people and members of various anti-poverty groups—said that sleeping together in the park, they felt safe for the first time. Some later admitted that as the protest wore on, they became easy targets for drug dealers and pimps. The demonstration lasted until the end of July that year, when squatters moved voluntarily, heeding the request of veterans who felt that the squat at the site of the city's cenotaph was disrespectful.

Nancy looked at her watch. It was 12:02. She waited. Five minutes passed. Then her cell phone buzzed.

"Follow me," the message read. Nancy turned, and just a dozen meters from where she sat saw Marcia Lane walking toward the intersection at Cambie and Hastings. She turned into a parkade and made for the elevator. Nancy followed her from a hundred feet back. When the elevator door opened, Lane held it and Nancy stepped in.

Lane pressed a button and they ascended. "You're taking a big risk," said Nancy.

"So are you," said Lane.

"I take it we don't have much time for chitchat."

"We don't. I'm reasonably convinced that the disappearances are *not* connected to the Lucky Strike Manifesto. I know *you're* not convinced. That's okay, but I want to caution you that following that lead will make you look like an idiot when we do catch whoever is responsible for these missing persons."

"You have proof that they are not connected?"

"No. But I am working up a profile on these disappearances and it doesn't really fit."

Nancy shrugged. "You didn't set this up to tell me that."

"No." Lane reached into her coat and pulled out an envelope that she handed to Nancy. The elevator reached the top of the parkade, and the doors opened. Lane pressed the button for the first floor again.

"What's this?"

"Names."

"How did you get this?"

"I'm a detective."

"Do the people on this list know they have been fingered?"

"Some do, so be careful." The doors opened. "You ride this to the top and then walk back down to Water Street," said Lane. She stepped from the elevator and was gone.

COLE AND DENMAN waited in the reception area of Blackwater Strategies. Mary had gone for lunch. A few minutes later Marcia Lane knocked on the door and Cole let her in.

"Thanks for agreeing to see me," Lane said.

"Thanks for taking this seriously," said Cole.

"Let's have a look, shall we?"

On Mary's tidy desk, Cole rolled out the map he and Denman and Juliet had been working on. "We used Juliet's knowledge of where these folks spent most of their nights in order to come up with this." Denman traced the triangle of marks, his finger resting on the most recent X they had added, where George Oliver had disappeared. "Through the Welfare office, we've confirmed all five people have stayed at the Lucky Strike at some point."

"I've got a photo of Mr. Oliver now. I'll make sure all of the patrol officers have it in the next couple of hours," said Lane, as she looked over the map.

Finally, she said, "I can see why you think this is linked to the Lucky Strike." Cole and Denman looked at her. "As I said to Ms. Rose this morning, I think we're dealing with something else all together."

Cole stepped forward, pointing to the tight cluster of X's surrounding the hotel. "If the disappearances aren't connected to the Lucky Strike, then I don't understand why all five people who disappeared seemed to hang out within a block of the place."

Lane continued to study the map.

"Ms. Lane," said Denman. She looked up at him. "Have you read the arrest report on the two men who assaulted Cole?"

She nodded.

"You don't think that's connected?" asked Denman.

"I didn't say that. I just don't think *this*," she said, pointing to the Lucky Strike Hotel's lot, "is connected to the disappearances."

"Then why are they all in such close proximity?"

Lane put a finger to her lips. "Individual preference would be my guess."

"What do you mean?" asked Cole.

"My hypothesis is that these disappearances are all connected, but I think we're dealing with one individual who is taking people from the street."

"And doing what?" asked Cole.

"I don't know."

"Why just one?" asked Denman.

"A hunch. Look," she said, pointing at the pattern of X's. "All the people who have gone missing are, well, they are all in pretty rough shape. Addicts, a former prostitute, a native man with FASD. These people aren't big, strong men who can defend themselves. Our perp isn't taking out drug dealers or enforcers. He's going after the weakest people on the streets."

"I don't know," said Cole. Denman looked at him. "If we're dealing with one evil dude who is stalking homeless people, why haven't people gone missing from other areas? It's all happening right *here*," he said, tapping the map with his finger.

"You tell me," said Lane, looking at Cole.

Cole held her gaze. "Well, you know my theory."

"It doesn't hold up, Mr. Blackwater."

Cole opened his mouth then closed it. He looked down at the map and crossed his arms. Five X's, all clustered around the Lucky Strike Hotel. "The perp is on foot," Cole finally said. "That's why he's working such a tight geographic area. Because he can't get around."

"If he's on foot, what's he doing, walking his victims somewhere?" asked Denman.

"We don't know. We haven't found any bodies," said Lane.

"Yet," said Cole.

"Hopefully never," said Denman.

"Don't be naive, Denny," said Cole, not too gently.

"I'm afraid statistics are against us on this one, Mr. Scott. Chances are—"

"I'm not willing to give up on these people."

"Nor am I," said Lane. "But—"

Cole interrupted again. "If the perp is on foot, how does he dispose of the bodies? Wouldn't the bodies turn up if he was knocking people off right here in the city? It's not like he could bury them or anything."

"There are lots of places to hide bodies in the city."

"Really? Places that don't get checked at least once a week when the trash gets picked up?"

"I've had my team looking into the obvious places." They all looked at the map.

Cole put a finger on the map. "What about here?" he said, pointing to a patch of green next to Centennial Pier.

"Portside Park?" said Denman.

"Or here," Cole said.

"In Burrard Inlet," said Marcia Lane. She was already reaching for her cell phone.

TWENTY-ONE

WHEN GEORGE OLIVER WAS TWELVE, his brother and some of his friends tied him up with a skipping rope and left him to sit in the sun for most of the afternoon. Eventually George had worked himself free, dislocating his shoulder in the process. The injury had never been attended to by a doctor, and to this day, George could pop his shoulder out of joint by simply pressing it against a door jamb.

He waited in the darkness. The pain was bearable. He'd endured worse.

The hardest part was not being able to free the other two men who were in the stinking cell with him. In the total darkness of the room, George couldn't even see them, though he was aware of their presence. He had seen the man with the flat eyes who called himself Sean come in with each of them. Each had been unconscious when Sean had dragged them down the stairs and into the concrete bunker. Through the light of the open door, and then by the dim glow of the dust-caked florescent tube, George had watched Sean beat them with that strange metal object on their backs, legs, chest, arms, and neck.

George closed his eyes. The sick fuck had tied him to a chair with rope, his hands behind his back, his fingers free. He taped George's mouth shut with thick strands of duct tape. Then he pulled his fingernails out one at a time.

George had passed out after the fourth nail.

The one Sean had called Aluminum Man hadn't lasted past the second nail. He had pissed himself, the dark stain emerging through his already filthy pants, then his head slumped forward onto his chest, a thin stream of vomit leaking from the corner of his mouth to congeal in his ragged beard.

The third man Sean had brought down just that morning. He had "introduced" him as Pigeon Boy. He had managed to thrash in the chair while Sean worked on his fingers and flipped over backward, cracking his head on the concrete floor of the bunker, knocking himself unconscious.

George thought that was lucky for Pigeon Boy. Sean had stopped working on his fingers, and instead wiped his hands on an oily rag to clean off Pigeon Boy's blood. The white coat he wore was covered in blood.

Pigeon Boy hadn't moved since, and George wasn't certain now if he was unconscious or dead.

Now George hunched in the darkness where he thought the door to the shelter must be. He had rocked his chair until it fell over. Then he was able to wiggle out from under the rope. His hands were still bound, but by dislocating his shoulder, he had been able to slip his hands under his feet and get them in front of him. If he was wrong about where the door was, Sean would come into the bunker too far away for George to knock him down and get away. Or Sean might knock George over as he came through the door to the concrete room. But if he was right, he might have just enough time to bowl Sean over and reach the road, and safety.

He huddled in the reeking darkness for what seemed like an hour, then fell asleep.

He woke suddenly to the sound of the outer door to the fallout shelter being pushed open.

JULIET SAT IN her office for an hour after Marcia Lane had left, thinking about their conversation: a psychopath, on the loose in the Downtown Eastside. Now, faced with the very real possibility that there was one prowling the streets killing homeless people just for kicks—or for some other bizarre motivation only the psychopath knew—Juliet felt overwhelmed. She sat at her desk and looked at the bulletin board on the wall. Dozens of grainy black and white photos were thumb-tacked to the cork, each the image of a man or woman Juliet had come to know and care for in her eight years working on the street. She felt hot tears staining her face, and pushed them aside with her knuckles.

"Time to get back in the game," she said to herself.

THE NEWS WAS about to break all at once.

Nancy reached Water Street and hailed a cab. On her way to the *Vancouver Sun* office, she tore open the envelope and read the missing names—the signatories to the Lucky Strike Manifesto.

"Oh, no . . ." she said, as her eyes fell on one of the familiar names. She grabbed her cell phone from her pocket. "Pesh, it's Nancy. I've got the rest of the names."

"Where are you?"

"I'm two minutes out. I need some help on this, and I've got to call a couple of people. This needs to all happen at once."

"I'll have two senior writers in your office in five minutes."

Nancy paid the five-dollar fare and ran through the *Sun*'s lobby, catching the elevator just as it was closing. When she stepped out, Pesh was there. She handed him the list as they walked through the corridor to her office. He read as he walked.

"Well, that one's no surprise," he said, pointing to a name. "But that one . . . Ah shit, this isn't going to be pretty."

"Frank, we're not going to be able to get these people to talk."

"I know."

"What about Veronica?"

"She'll have to live with it. She works for *me*. You got your source face to face. That's going to have to be good enough."

Nancy reached her office. Two of the *Sun*'s senior City Desk writers were already standing there. "Okay," she said. "Here's the plan."

They began to prepare material to post on the web, and after making several phone calls, Nancy joined them. As she was writing, her cell phone rang.

"Nancy, it's Cole."

"Can't talk now," she said. "I just got the missing names."

"Can you tell me?" Cole asked.

Nancy looked around the room. "No. I'll call you when I'm posting to the web. I'm afraid you won't be surprised."

"Well, I'm calling with a heads up. Mary took a call from a female caller at City Hall, leaking the news that the mayor is making an announcement tomorrow on a new project called 'A New Vancouver.' You heard about this?"

"Just what he told me last week when I interviewed him after the riot," Nancy said, typing. "It's supposed to be his response to homelessness, poverty, crime, etc."

"Details?"

"I got none." She cradled the phone in her shoulder as she typed. "What time will it be?"

"Eleven. City Hall."

"I guess I'll see you there," said Nancy.

"I'll try to be there. Hey, Nancy . . ."

"Yeah."

"Well, Denman and I braced Charles Livingstone this morning."

"Really?" She stopped typing.

"I guess I went a little overboard."

"Surprise, surprise."

"Funny. We almost got our butts thrown in the cooler. He's tied up in this. His client is Frank 'Captain Condo' Ainsworth."

"Cole, Charles Livingstone's name is on my list. So is Frank Ainsworth's."

NANCY POSTED A teaser story on the web at 4:15. By 4:45 Livingstone, Grey and Barnes had called the *Sun* demanding an explanation and threatening a lawsuit. Veronica White, grinning, encouraged them to file. Calls came in from City Hall, the VPD, and other media seeking confirmation of the information before they posted or aired it over the radio and TV.

Nancy sat in her office and looked at the names. Her cell phone rang again and again. She checked the call display and ignored most of the calls. She picked up at Cole's number.

"Sorry, I forgot to call."

"It's okay, busy afternoon. Wow. You're right. I had my suspicions."

"Yeah, it's still going to hurt."

"There's something else. Denman and I met with Marcia Lane this afternoon . . ." Nancy smiled and was about to say something, then thought better of it. "I showed her the map. We got to hypothesizing. You know, where have these missing people gone? If they weren't put on a bus, why haven't they shown up somewhere? A dumpster? In a dark alley? Lane says she's got a dozen uniforms prowling for this sort of thing. We were sitting there looking at the map, and thinking about who might have done this, what kind of person. I'm not giving up that this is connected to the Manifesto, you know? But Lane thinks differently, and I'll admit, she made a few good points."

Nancy felt suddenly weary. "Cole, what are you getting at?"

"Bodies, Nancy. Where are the bodies? These missing people, they haven't turned up. No bodies. So I looked at the map. Only a few blocks from where all of the missing people were last known to hang out is a place called Portside Park. It's right on Burrard Inlet. I think Lane dispatched divers there this afternoon."

"Jesus, you're kidding me!"

Nancy hung up the phone and ran from her office to Frank Pesh's door.

"Frank, I need a photographer, now!"

SEAN LIVINGSTONE SAT in the backyard of Juliet Rose's Salisbury Street home, listening to the sound of birds in the trees and watching the momentary band of sun that had pushed its way through the opaque gray sky. He studied the clouds and thought that by midnight there would likely be rain again.

He looked around the yard and up at the house where he had been a guest for a week. It was a great setup, he thought.

Sean took a moment to appreciate how his plans were coming together. Though he had known for a long time what his end game would be, he hadn't figured out *how* he would get there until one evening two years ago. His father had a couple of business associates over for dinner and afterward they retired to his study to talk, smoke fancy cigars, and drink port. Sean had made himself scarce, but when he heard the men enter his father's den, he crouched outside the door, his heart racing. He simply couldn't help but eavesdrop.

"We're running out of room, Frank," he heard his father say.

"In the West End, Charles. But there's always more land."

"We're running out of room in the West End, in Kits, in Yaletown, and even on the North Shore," said his father.

The man his father addressed as Frank said, "It's simply a matter of waiting for the economics to be right. Burnaby is already attractive. So is Mount Pleasant. Who would have imagined *that* ten years ago?"

"Yes, but you're spending as much to build there and only getting two-thirds the price per unit, and half the height."

"You worry too much, Charles," said Frank.

"That's what you pay me for."

"What do you think?" Sean heard Frank say.

The third man in the room had been silent through the exchange so far. "I think this is damn fine port," he said, with only a hint of a Chinese accent. "And I think that the two of you are overlooking the best development opportunity this city has to offer."

"Where's that?" asked Sean's father.

"Chinatown."

His father laughed quietly.

"Laugh if you like. It's already started. Tinseltown is done, and it's attracting more people every day. New condos around the SkyTrain station are going up quickly. Smaller units next to the American and Cobalt hotels are proving to be a good investment. Mr. Ainsworth here already owns one across from the Central Pacific Station. Why is that so funny?"

"It's not," said Frank Ainsworth.

"I'm not laughing at the idea. It's just that the obstacles are enormous. Yes, you call it Chinatown, but the rest of the city calls it the Downtown Eastside. It used to be called Skid Row until twenty years ago. And while you might have pretty street lamps and ornate buildings in a few areas, the rest of the place is a shithole, pardon my French."

"You see only the problems. I see a solution," said the third man.

"Here's what I see," said Sean's father. "I see a massive swath of this city that is overridden with drugs, violence, organized crime, poverty, and homelessness. What are there, a thousand people on the streets?"

"Closer to three thousand."

"My case in point, and it's an open-air drug market. The place is run by people like Hoi Fu, who don't want condominiums, because that brings an additional police presence, and pushes the drug market upscale. Cocaine, rather than crack. Hash, rather than meth."

"Hoi Fu won't be a barrier. He's a businessman, as am I."

"What are you saying?" asked Ainsworth.

"Only that Hoi Fu knows that to succeed in *his* businesses, he must walk the tightrope between two worlds. In one, violence and intimidation get you what you want. In the other, influence does."

"Don West will be elected but he will be a lame duck mayor. The whole city knows that Fu supported him in the last election. West will get one term but then he is on the way out," said Sean's father.

"But I am on the way up."

"Mayor Ben Chow," said Ainsworth. "It's got a nice ring to it."

"Hoi Fu understands this. He understands that the next mayor of this city will have to solve the problem of the Downtown Eastside. Don West will be a place holder while we work behind the scenes. We are an international city, with international visitors, and they don't want to be tripping over drunks. They don't want to stub their toes on HIV-infected needles or to have their kids solicited by whores."

"So what do we do?" asked Ainsworth.

"We make a plan."

"A plan for what?" asked his father.

"For the redevelopment of the Eastside. Twenty years from now, Oppenheimer will be the new West End. Chinatown will be as trendy as Kits was in the '80s."

"And what do we do about the homeless?"

"Move them out," said Chow.

"Where?"

"Anywhere. We'll think of something. We'll get some of the liberal poverty people on board. Give them their say. Make sure they are a part of this, but not *too* much a part."

"It's an opportunity for you to become mayor," said his father.

"Oh, yes. And for you, gentlemen, to become very, very rich."

"Who else needs to be a part of this?" said Ainsworth.

"We need someone in the bureaucracy who can smooth the way inside the system. I know a few people I can speak with discreetly," said Chow. "And we need the cops. Without them, we're going to be running into trouble, left, right, and center."

"You think the cops are going to sit down with the likes of Hoi Fu?"

"They already do. The VPD also knows that men like Hoi Fu keep order, such as it is, in the drug trade and in the gang rivalries. Without him and others of his ilk, the Downtown Eastside would resemble Afghanistan. The VPD won't mind knowing that Fu is in the background. We, like they, need him, if only in the shadows."

"I don't know," said Sean's father. "My job here is to keep Frank's business safe from harm. Having Fu involved—"

"Having Fu involved is the only way we're going to make things happen, and happen fast."

"Who else?" asked Ainsworth.

"Someone from the bleeding hearts club," said his father.

"That lawyer, Denman Scott?" asked Ainsworth.

"Too much of a hard-ass," Chow stated. "He'd never go for it."

"No, we need someone who is tired. Who's anxious for a solution? Whose ego is big enough that we can pander to it?" asked his father.

"Beatta Nowak," offered Chow.

"From the Community Advocacy group?" asked Ainsworth.

"That's the one," said Chow.

"Isn't she a bit of a raging bull?"

"It will probably seem like that for the first few meetings," Chow replied. "She'll come around and she can control things. It will be perfect." Sean could almost see him rubbing his hands together. "Nowak can run interference for us, keep the End Poverty Now people from getting on top of this."

"She can't know about Fu. That would never wash," said Ainsworth.

"She won't," assured Chow.

"What's in it for her?" asked Ainsworth.

"We build some low-cost housing."

"Where?"

"We throw some in the mix, but we build the bulk of it out of the main economic zone. We rezone and work with the Burnaby Council."

The room was silent. Sean thought that maybe they were done and he began to slowly back down the hall, and then he heard his father speak.

"Okay, how do we get started?"

"Let's invite some folks to supper."

"Not here," said his father.

"No, let's get a space in the Eastside. I know a place on Pender Street that's perfect," Chow laughed. "We'll get takeout from the Golden Dragon. Fu will love it!"

"It's got to be quiet. We can't afford to attract attention to this," said his father. "If we attract attention to ourselves before all the pieces are in place, then this won't work. We're sunk."

Sean couldn't help but smile, listening outside the door.

"We'll need to slow down the rest of the development community," said Ainsworth. "We're not the only ones waking up to the fact that the last place to build in Vancouver is the Downtown Eastside."

Chow laughed. "I will take care of that. I'll introduce a motion at council at just the right moment to put a freeze on conversion of SROs to condos. That will allow us to put our pieces in place, and then when we're ready, I can repeal and we can move forward."

"So where do we start, property-wise?" asked Ainsworth.

"The Lucky Strike," said Chow.

"It's not on the market," said his father.

"Not now."

"Who owns it? We looked into that last year, didn't we, Charles?" asked Ainsworth. "It's a numbered company."

"The property, dear friends," said Chow, "belongs to Mr. Hoi Fu. I imagine he'd be willing to take a reasonable offer."

SEAN SAT IN the sun and listened to the birds. That was two years ago, he mused.

For the last two years his father's life had been wrapped up in the pursuit of a hotel, many hotels in fact, but one hotel in particular. For almost as long, Sean had been thinking of ways to make his father pay for what he had done. The Lucky Strike had become Ground Zero in the old man's life, and now Sean had made it the epicenter of his own arrangements.

He stood up from the chair and stretched. It was time to check in on his guests.

TWENTY-TWO

COLE SAT SILENTLY IN THE back of a cab, Denman next to him. It was Monday evening.

"I still think—a few beers and this whole problem would disappear." Cole looked out the window as they crossed the Burrard bridge.

"Yeah, for you. For me, it would just amp up."

"Well, then it's you who needs the treatment," Cole said, turning to his friend, his mouth drawn back in a half grin.

"You don't have to be nervous, Cole. The guy we're going to see, well, *you're* going to see is a straight up Doctor of Psychology."

"Didn't you say something about wiggly eye treatment?"

"It's called Eye Movement Desensitization and Reprocessing."

"You read about that somewhere on the internet, didn't you?"

"Yeah, but it's a common treatment these days for post-traumatic stress disorder."

"That's what I've got?"

"The doc will make that assessment."

Denman paid the cabbie and they both got out and walked around the side of the house, following signs to the office portion of the home. They mounted a set of stairs and knocked. A compact man in his forties answered the door. His salt and pepper hair gave him a look of maturity, while his face, tanned and finely lined around the eyes, gave him a youthful air.

"I'm Greg Brady," said the man, inviting them in. "You must be Cole," Brady said, extending his hand. Cole introduced himself.

"This is Denman Scott, my cheerleader," said Cole. Brady shook his hand.

"Slip your shoes off here and follow me upstairs." They followed the man as he mounted the stairs to a small room containing several chairs.

"You can have a seat here, Denman. If you would like tea or coffee or water, help yourself." He motioned to a small serving tray with a kettle and the fixings for hot drinks. "Cole, would you like anything?"

"Have you got Kick Ass Lager?"

"Afraid not," smiled Brady.

"Just a glass of water then."

Cole waved to Denman, like a child leaving his parents on the first day of school, and followed Brady into his office. "Have a seat," said Brady, motioning to two leather club chairs by the large windows.

"No couch?"

"I'm not a Freudian."

"Good, 'cause I'd likely just fall asleep."

"Denman tells me he believes you're suffering from post-traumatic stress disorder."

"That sounds serious," said Cole.

"It can be," said Brady. "It's a common issue. We first started diagnosing it in war veterans. We now know that many people who have been exposed to a terrifying event, something that threatened them with physical violence, or actually resulted in them being subjected to it, suffer from PTSD."

"That sounds about right. I got the hell beaten out of me as a kid." They spoke for a while longer about Cole's childhood. Then Brady asked, "Is there a single event that is haunting you?"

"Yeah." Cole took a deep breath, then began to tell the whole story. Half an hour later Cole was exhausted. He leaned forward with his face in his hands. "I guess this is pretty much hopeless," he said, looking up and rubbing his face with his hands.

Brady smiled. "On the contrary," he said. "What we're going to do, Cole, is take away the anxiety that you feel when you think about that event." Brady shifted in his chair. "PTSD often means that things that you associate with that event now bring you great discomfort. When you are in a situation that reminds you of the event, you become anxious. You startle easily. You can't sleep. You have flashbacks. Maybe you feel depressed, or even suicidal. You avoid contact with places or people that you associate with that event. Maybe you're moody . . ."

Cole grinned.

"Sound familiar?"

"It's just that I've been moody all my life."

Brady smiled again. "Well, we can work on personality issues some other time. Tonight, we're going to do something that will help your brain process the stress it is feeling about the traumatic event that has occurred in your life, and make it so that you don't keep reliving it over and over again. We're going to do something that will mean you don't associate people or places with that event."

Cole nodded. "Wiggly eye."

"Right. You've heard of EMDR."

"Wikipedia."

"Hmm, not sure if that's the best source. Eye Movement Desensitization and Reprocessing was first developed by a Doctor Shapiro in the late 1980s. She happened to notice some troubling thoughts were resolved when her eyes followed the waving leaves during a walk in a neighborhood park. She developed a clinical model for this."

Cole interrupted. "Doc, I've been walking in parks all my life. Big parks. Jasper, Banff, Pukaskwa. Looking at lots of leaves blowing in the wind. Still feel like shit."

Brady laughed. "Cole, the idea is really very simple. Our brains process thousands of thoughts and emotions every second. Sometimes when something really traumatic occurs to us, our brains can't process it, so it keeps spinning around and around. Sometimes seemingly unrelated events can become associated with this trauma. What EMDR does is help your brain reprocess the information around the traumatic event, so that you don't feel anxiety or depression when you think of it. Does that make sense?"

Cole nodded.

"So the first thing we're going to do is get you to focus on the traumatic image. Cole, it's really important for you to be honest with yourself during this. If it helps you to close your eyes to recall this traumatic image, then do so. It's not necessary, but if you like, you can say out loud what the image is."

Cole closed his eyes.

The barn door swung open and he walked into the darkened space.

"Looking for me, son?" The shotgun in his father's hand.

Cole's blood boiling. The years of abuse in the ring, the same ring where his father stood now, holding the gun loosely in his hand. The confusion. "Wait!" A son trying to rescue his father. The barrel raised, and then the startling blast, the dark spray of blood across the canvas; the explosion of thousands of tiny pellets, each one like a knife. The explosion of pigeons over head.

Cole kept his eyes squeezed shut.

The dock at Port Lostcoast. Nancy. Nancy, dragging the information out of him. Unearthing the emotions Cole had buried for four years.

"Cole, tell me what you feel about yourself seeing this image in your head."

Cole took a breath. His voice came weakly from his throat. "I can't . . ."

"Cole?"

"I couldn't save him: he was my father. I can't save anything."

"Go on."

"Helpless. Inadequate. Not worthy. Not good enough."

"What else?"

Cole sat a moment. "Anger. Hatred."

"Cole, tell me where you feel this."

His eyes were still shut tightly and he pressed his fingers into his stomach.

"Okay, Cole. Now, tell me on a scale of one to eleven, with one being mild, and eleven being severe, how you would rate your anxiety related to this feeling?"

Cole grinned. "Why not one to ten? Is this a Spinal Tap spoof?"

"Good question, Cole. I don't know. It's just the scale we came up with. One to eleven, Cole."

"Ten."

"Okay, now. I want you to think about the emotions that you'd like to experience when you recall the traumatic event. Positive emotions. They don't need to be happy sunshine thoughts, Cole. But they need to be positive."

Cole sat with his eyes closed. "I want to feel like I *can* save something. I don't want to feel powerless."

"So, empowered?"

"Yes."

"What else?"

"I want to feel self-worth."

"You want to feel as though you are adequate."

"More than that. Not just adequate. I want to feel worthy."

"Good. How would you rather feel than angry?" Cole breathed deeply. He could feel the knot of rage in his belly. "I want to feel calm. I want to feel at peace."

"Cole, can you give me a statement about yourself that explains how you feel now that you've replaced these negative emotions with positive ones?"

Cole grimaced. "I don't know that . . ." He stopped. "I feel free. I feel free from the anger and rage that has held me in its grip since my father . . ." He stopped again.

"Do you want to finish that statement, Cole?"

"Since my father killed himself in front of me."

"Cole, on a scale of one to seven, how much do you believe that statement, one being not at all, and seven—"

"One," Cole interrupted.

"Okay, one," said Brady calmly. "Now, what we're going to do next is what you refer to as the wiggly eye part. I'm going to ask you first to visualize the memory that has been troubling you, Cole. At the same time, I want you to rehearse, in your head, the negative feelings you have about yourself when you recall the trauma. I want you to feel the physical sensations associated with it. Right here." Brady pointed to his own flat stomach to mirror Cole's indication. "And while you're doing this, I want you to watch my finger very carefully." Brady held up his right index finger. Cole's eyes roved around the room a moment and then settled on the man's finger. "Okay?"

Cole nodded.

"Let's start with recalling that event, and rehearsing the things you feel about yourself when you do. Feel them in your gut. Okay now, I want you to follow my finger." Brady began to move his finger laterally back and forth, back and forth, Cole's eyes locked on it. Brady moved his finger back and forth twenty-four times, then stopped.

"Okay, Cole. I want you to take a deep breath and blank the memory of the trauma from your mind."

Cole pushed the blackness from his mind and exhaled. He focused on the man's finger. After a moment, Brady said, "Now, I want you to recall the trauma. One a scale of one to eleven, how would you rate your distress?"

Cole closed his eyes. A long moment passed: "Seven."

"Good," said Brady. "Very good. Now, again."

IT HAD BEEN a long day for Juliet and it was only Monday. It was growing dark when she stepped off the bus and made her way toward her quiet home. She felt a moment of anxiety when she remembered that Sean was still there. He had been for a week. She tried to count the days in her head but lost track. She had to admit he was a courteous and thoughtful guest. Even her roommate, who had seldom warmed to any of Juliet's overnight projects, thought that having Sean around was delightful.

"He cooks *and* does the dishes," Becky had said the day before. "He can stay a few more days."

Juliet walked up her steps and unlocked the door. The house was dark. She remembered that her roommate was traveling for work this week. Lucky. Montreal, New York, Philadelphia. Juliet's work took her to Hastings and Main. She took a deep breath as she walked in the door. The house was quiet. "Sean?" she called.

Nothing. She flipped on some lights, dumped her backpack by the stairs and made her way to the kitchen to put a kettle on the stove. She opened the fridge and looked for the leftovers from last night's meal. Her fridge had never been so clean and well organized. She smiled. If Sean wasn't careful, she might hire him.

She pulled out a casserole dish with one hand and a head of lettuce with the other. When the fridge door closed, Sean stood a few feet from her in the open back door. Her heart jumped and she screamed, dropping the casserole dish. It exploded, shards of glass and ceramic scattering across the floor. He stepped into the light. He was covered in blood.

"Sean, holy shit . . ." She started toward him, then stopped. He walked into the kitchen, his feet crunching the broken pieces on the floor. He looked vacantly at her. "Sean, what happened?"

His nose appeared to have been broken. Blood still leaked down from it over his mouth. He had a gash under his left eye that was also bleeding. His eye was partially closed. His hands were covered in blood, almost up to his elbows, yet he seemed completely calm.

"Got in a fight." He stepped over the pasta on the floor and sat down.

Juliet watched him as he took a seat at the small kitchen table and put one hand there, his blood stained palm pressed lightly on the Arborite surface. He was in shock, she knew, and would need medical attention.

"Stay here," she said, and went to the front entrance to retrieve her pack. When she returned to the kitchen, he was smiling at her through the smear of blood on his face.

She pulled on gloves from her first-aid kit and said, "I'm going to examine your face, Sean. Is that okay?" He kept smiling and nodded. She put her hand on his jaw and moved his head around gently. She touched the bridge of his nose with her fingers.

"Your nose is broken pretty badly, Sean," she said. She found a large gauze pad and used it to mop up some of the blood. "I need you to hold this right here." He put a bloody hand on the pad. "Okay, now let's look at that laceration." She pressed another gauze dressing on the cut under his eye, and then gently pulled it away. "You're going to need stitches." She checked the rest of his head and neck for injuries.

"You mean in the hospital?"

"Yes."

"Can't you do them here?"

"Sean, you've got some serious injuries. I think you might also have a concussion. I can't treat you here."

She looked at his hands. His right hand was still on the table. "Can you move your fingers?"

He wiggled them and winced.

"You're going to need an X-ray. You may have broken some bones. I'm going to call a cab. We'll get you over to Vancouver General."

Sean said, "I need my backpack."

"Where is it?"

He thought about it. He had been wearing it when he had gone into the bomb shelter.

HE HAD DESCENDED the stairs to his own personal shelter, thinking how well his arrangements were working out.

Then The Indian had tackled him.

"What the fuck—!" Sean managed to exclaim before his head hit the concrete floor with a loud whack. The Indian came down on top of him, his bound hands before him, scrambling for the door. Sean brought his knee up and connected with the man's groin and watched as his expression changed from rage to agony. The Indian drove his head down into Sean's face and mashed his nose. He did it again, cutting Sean's cheek below his left eye. Sean drove his hand up into The Indian's belly and then into his ribs again and again as they rolled on the floor. When The Indian was on top again, he drove his head down for a third time and Sean's world went dark.

GEORGE OLIVER PULLED himself up, his breathing coming hard, his lungs unable to take in enough air after Sean's repeated blows. He dragged himself across the floor toward the open door. He felt his way across the dirt-covered concrete to the outer door of the root cellar. He felt numb. His forehead was cut where he had smashed Sean's nose and cheek, and he could taste the salty brine of blood. George saw the slanting gray light of day on the stairs, dust motes dancing on the breeze, and sensed the open space beyond. He felt the cool rush of autumn air on his bleeding face.

Now. Up the stairs. Last step. The small, quiet yard beckoned. That's when he heard the low, guttural sound behind him, and he turned to see the come-along swung hard, connecting with his legs, breaking bone, knocking him to the grass. George instinctively rolled into a ball to protect his stomach, but with his hands bound, he was unable to protect his head. Sean's next blow made a low crack as it connected with his skull. A small spot of blood spilled onto the lawn as George's semi-conscious body was dragged down the steps and back into the darkness.

HE HAD LEFT his bag in the bomb shelter. "I don't know," he said.

"Sean, I think you've got a concussion. We should go."

The taxi appeared on the street. Juliet took Sean buy the arm and gently guided him down the steps and out to the waiting car.

"Thank you," he said, as she helped him into the cab.

They sped off for Vancouver General.

NANCY WEBBER LEFT her office and took a cab to the Downtown Eastside Community Advocacy Society.

When she had left Portside Park at six-thirty that evening, two VPD dive teams were still scouring the sprawling park and adjacent pier. Nothing had turned up yet, but Lane had told Nancy, on the record, that the search was only beginning. When asked what led her to believe that bodies might be discovered there, Lane had just shrugged and said that policing was mostly guesswork.

Nancy didn't find that reassuring.

She had cabbed it back to the *Sun* building and made another round of phone calls, hoping to elicit a comment from one of the Manifesto signatories despite the late hour.

"Beatta Nowak, please."

"Who's calling?" the voice on the phone was rough and unpracticed.

"Nancy Webber, *Vancouver Sun.*"

A moment passed. Nancy could hear voices in the background. Though she'd never been to the offices of the Downtown Eastside Community Advocacy Society, she imagined they were staffed with a mixture of professional activists and volunteers recruited from the street population that the Society served.

Beatta Nowak's voice was a combination of exhaustion and anger. "What makes you think I want to talk with you about your baseless allegations, Ms. Webber?"

Nancy took a breath. "Ms. Nowak, are you telling me that you're not familiar with a document called the Lucky Strike Manifesto?"

The line was silent a moment, then, "No. I've never heard of it."

"It's a document penned by a group of people calling themselves The Lucky Strike Supper Club . . ."

Nowak cut her off. "I've read your story online. You know I'm trying to save people's lives?"

Nancy continued, "They meet at an old office building on Pender. The document has some very noble intentions: clean up the Downtown Eastside, get the homeless into housing. It's also a developer's dream— replace SROs with hotels, condos, shopping malls, etcetera. But I believe a lot of Vancouverites will find the content of the document troubling.

The signatories to the document state that extreme measures must be taken to get people off the street. Their solution is a homeless ghetto in West Strathcona and another in Burnaby." She paused.

"Ms. Nowak, I now have a copy of the names associated with the document." Nancy could hear the woman breathing over the phone line. "Ms. Nowak, your name is among them. Councilor Ben Chow. VPD Divisional Commander John Andrews. Frank Ainsworth and his attorney Charles Livingstone. Trish Perry, the deputy planning commissioner, and you. Care to comment?"

"Can you come to my office? I don't want to do this over the phone."

"Of course," said Nancy. "I'll be there in fifteen minutes." She hung up and yelled down the hall, "Frank, I've got a live one!"

TEN MINUTES LATER she walked through the doors of the Community Advocacy's building. The slate gray sky hung low over the city, and Nancy guessed that by midnight it would be raining again. Beatta met her at the door and ushered her into her office and closed the door behind them.

"You must have a good source," she said to Nancy when they were seated.

"I do. High up in the VPD. It's solid. As you know, we've posted a teaser on the internet. We're going to run the full story tomorrow."

"I wish you wouldn't. You have to understand, we're trying to do something no one has tried before."

"Why don't you tell me about it?" Nancy took out a small digital recorder and put it on the desk. Nowak looked at it. "I need to tape this interview so that you and I don't face each other in court someday." Nowak nodded.

"Listen, you can either be one line in the story as a conspirator to this so-called Manifesto, or you can tell your side of the story and set the record straight. It's up to you."

Nowak let out a deep breath. "You have to understand the history of this place to understand why I've done this. This used to be the heart of the city. Things went sour for the east end over time. Someone made a decision to limit street car access, and so shoppers began to migrate toward Granville Street. That was a long time ago. It's little things like that that made a big difference." She looked out the window.

"With fewer people walking the sidewalks and window shopping, stores began to close," Nowak continued. "That had a domino effect. City Hall moved. Rent in the east side of the city was lower than elsewhere in the city, so we had a real mix of people. Lots of immigrants found homes in Strathcona. The low rents and the conversion of tourist hotels into SROs also attracted more and more people who lived below the poverty line. People started calling the area Skid Row. The name stuck. Woodwards, the department store, closed in the early 1980s. That was the nail in our coffin. A bunch of us decided that if we were going to salvage this area, we had better shake off the Skid Row moniker, so we called the area the Downtown Eastside. It's funny how *that* name is now synonymous with poverty, too." She turned back to Nancy.

"Well, that's the history. It's been getting steadily worse since Woodwards. Then along comes Gordon Campbell and his so-called Liberal government. Liberal my ass. The government raised the welfare cut-off, and suddenly we have a few thousand more people living rough. They also cut care for thousands of people living with mental illness. Add the gangs and the increasing availability of drugs . . . I tell you, I've been doing this for more than twenty-five years, and I have never seen it worse than it is right now. People are dying. They are killing themselves, and they are killing each other."

"So you decided to take extreme measures?"

"It didn't seem like that at first. A few of us decided to get together to talk. That's all. Have supper. We called ourselves a Supper Club. That was two years ago now. We were finding some common ground. It was a good idea."

"You still think it is?"

Nowak shrugged. "Well, I guess others are going to decide that now. Our intent was to come up with a solution that we could implement ourselves, instead of waiting for the province and the federal governments to come to our rescue. We wanted to solve the problem with our own resources."

"And what resources are those?"

"Ingenuity, creativity."

"Haven't you always advocated for integrating the homeless into society?"

"I have, and I still do. But you take what you can get. I know there will be critics. I know people will call me a sellout. I know that. You think

I don't? Try sitting and negotiating with these people sometime and see how it goes. To get a thousand units of social housing is something. It's really something."

Nancy took a breath. "Tell me about the Lucky Strike."

"Sometimes you have to give things up to get something. I've given up my entire life for these things. And maybe things have gotten out of hand, but something had to be done. Someone had to try."

"I have one or two more questions, and then I have to file. Do you think there is any connection between the Lucky Strike Manifesto and the disappearance of five homeless people from the Downtown Eastside in recent weeks?"

"I don't see how there could be."

"Would you know if there was?"

Nowak was quiet a moment. "No," she said. "No, I wouldn't."

Nancy watched her. "Tell me," she said carefully, "about the relationship between Hoi Fu and the Lucky Strike Manifesto."

The silence that hung in the room was as thick and heavy as the sky that pressed down on Vancouver like a dark hand.

NANCY HEADED OUT into the street and rang for a cab. It was almost eight, and the street quiet. The cab wouldn't arrive for twenty minutes, so she decided to walk.

She called Frank Pesh. "I've got what I need, Frank. I'll be at the office in about twenty minutes. Can you hold the print deadline?" When he had confirmed that he would, she picked up her pace and began to pen the story in her head. It wasn't as cut and dried as she would have liked. Nothing ever was. And there was one very significant unanswered question.

Nancy was so focused on shaping the story in her mind that she didn't notice two men on foot slip from the shadows and begin following her.

TWENTY-THREE

DENMAN AND COLE SAT IN Cole's living room, sipping beer and listening to music.

"It's funny," said Cole. "I haven't listened to music in, like, two months. I missed it." Cole turned the volume up a little—an old album by The Guess Who. Cole crooned, his bottle of beer held loosely in his hands.

Denman closed his eyes as the music fill the room.

"Denny," said Cole when the song had stopped. "Thanks again."

Denman smiled. "That's two you owe me, Junior," he said, trying to sound like Harrison Ford in *The Empire Strikes Back*. Cole just laughed. He felt as though he hadn't laughed in a year.

Denman's cell phone rang and he groaned. It was 10:00 PM. "Denman Scott."

"Denman, it's Juliet. I'm at the hospital."

"You're not hurt, are you?" he said, sitting up.

"I'm fine. Someone staying with me got hurt, and I took him here. I don't suppose you'd be able to come to Vancouver General and talk to him. He got beat up pretty badly. He says it was the cops. I think you might want to see him. I know it's late and all . . ."

"I don't mind. I'm at Cole's place. Just around the corner. I'll be there in twenty minutes, okay?"

"Okay. And Denman, just so you know, well, you know this guy. You represented him a couple of weeks ago. A young guy named Sean. You'll recognize him. I'll tell you all about it when you get here."

"I'll be right there."

"Thanks."

Denman snapped his phone shut and looked at Cole. "Duty calls, partner."

"What's up?"

"It appears that Juliet has a thing for taking people in off the street. This guy that's been at her place, a guy named Sean—you met him at Macy's, remember?"

"Oh yeah, that smooth-talking kid. I remember him," said Cole, sipping his beer.

"Anyway, he says the cops beat him up."

"This seems to have gone too far, don't you think?"

"Well, I want to talk with him and see what happened. See if he got a badge number."

"Hey, Denny . . ."

"What is it?" he asked as he pulled on his jacket.

"You don't think . . ."

"Come on, Cole, spit it out."

"Well, you don't think that this kid staying at Juliet's place, that he might be connected to the Manifesto, do you? That maybe those dudes that jumped me in the alley, or maybe those meatballs we were following, beat this kid up, and are trying to send us a message. Like, a 'we know where you all live' sort of message."

"You make this sound like a B-rated movie, Cole."

Cole grimaced. "I just mean, well, keep your eyes open, okay? Do you want me to come along?" Cole started to get up, but Denman pressed a finger to Cole's chest and he sank back into the couch.

"You think this is just a work thing? I don't need to be chaperoned," said Denman, walking to the door.

"Okay, but call me if you need me. And watch your back, Denny,"

"Will do," said Denman, taking the outside walkway to the yard. He set off at a jog toward the Vancouver General Hospital, two dozen blocks away.

Cole sank back into the couch. He finished his beer and closed his eyes. He felt sleep coming. He didn't feel afraid.

He had been out for maybe ten minutes when his cell buzzed in his pocket. "Yeah," he said, holding it to his face. "This is Cole."

"It's Nancy. I think someone followed me home." He snapped awake.

"What time is it?"

"It's almost eleven."

"Are your doors locked?"

"Yes. And I've got the deadbolt and chain on."

"Can you see them now? Out the window?"

"Hold on." He heard the rustle of blinds. She came back to the phone, her breathing quick. "Yes. I see someone across the street, just standing under a lamp."

"Under a lamp? Not trying to hide in the shadows?" Cole pulled on his coat and found his keys.

"No, he's just standing there, looking up at my apartment."

"You sure he's not just a dealer?"

"Pretty sure. I can see him pretty good. He's clean-cut, mid-thirties. A big guy. Mustache."

"He sounds familiar, Nancy. I think it might be one of the dudes that Denman and I followed."

"Should I call the cops?"

"No. I think he *is* the cops."

"Fuck."

"I'll be there as soon as I can. Don't answer the door. I'll call. If anybody comes to the door, don't open it. Dial 911 and let them sort this out between themselves. Got it?"

"Yeah."

"Call again in five minutes. Clear?"

"Okay. Thanks, Cole." She hung up.

Cole dialed for a cab. He hit the steps at a run, ignoring the lingering discomfort in his side.

DENMAN ARRIVED AT Vancouver General Hospital and found Juliet on the fourth floor, sitting in a metal chair in the hall outside a room with eight patients in it.

Denman walked down the hall toward her. Juliet got up and they held each other for a moment, then she pulled back and looked at him. "Aren't you a sight for sore eyes? How was the thing with Cole?"

"Good," he smiled. "Really good. That EMDR really works. Cole's going to go back next week for some follow-up, but he was like a new man when I left him. I think he was going to fall asleep and dream of nubile nymphs tonight, not his bastard of an old man."

Juliet grinned and hit him on the arm. "You men are all the same."

"Cole being more 'the same' than most," said Denman. "How are you?"

"I'm fine, but Sean is pretty busted up."

"Can I talk to him?"

"I think so. Let's go in and see." They started toward the door, and Juliet caught him by the arm. "Denny. I'm sorry I didn't tell you he was staying at my place."

"As long as he's okay. Let's go check on him, alright?"

They entered the room and walked past the patients poorly concealed by the thin drapes hanging from the ceiling. They found Sean watching TV from his bed. His right hand was in a sling and his face was bandaged.

"Hi, Sean," said Juliet as she approached. He smiled broadly despite the bandages. "I hope you don't mind, I contacted Denman after you told me what happened."

"Oh," he said, and his smile faded a little.

"Don't look so down," Denman said. "I'm a lawyer, but I'm one of the good guys. You might remember me—I took your statement at the police station after the Lucky Strike riot. Can you tell me what happened?"

"Well," said Sean, clearly distracted by the TV. "I was, well, you know, just minding my own business, hanging out. I was actually picking up a few things to cook for dinner, you know? And these cops came into the shop and just started busting me up!"

"Tell me exactly what happened."

"I was getting some vegetables. I was going to make stir-fry. I'm a good cook, ask Juliet. And these two cops just walked right up to me and one of them grabbed me by the throat—" Sean motioned to his neck, "—and the other grabbed my hand and smashed it on the counter. Then the first guy held me by the throat and smashed my face into the counter. He just kept hitting me," said Sean, closing his eyes.

"Sean, were these police officers wearing uniforms?"

"Yeah."

"Did you happen to see badge numbers?"

"No, it all happened so fast."

"What about witnesses? There must have been witnesses."

"Maybe."

"The shop owner?"

"Yeah, maybe him."

"What shop was it?"

"Some place on Gore."

"Can you remember which one?"

"No, I can't. My head hurts," said Sean, closing his eyes.

"Sean, I'm only asking to establish the facts. Had you stolen anything?"

"What does that matter?"

"It doesn't really. I'm just trying to understand what prompted this action by the cops."

"No, I didn't take nothing. I've never stolen anything in my life." Denman looked at Juliet.

"Okay, Sean, you get some rest, and we'll talk more in the morning."

"You going to get those fuckers?" he asked, and Denman was surprised by the venom in his voice.

"We'll talk about it in the morning."

Denman and Juliet stood in the hall together. Denman looked back into the room to determine if they were being observed.

"What do you think?" Juliet asked.

"I don't know," said Denman. "Something's funny about Sean's story. It just doesn't wash."

Juliet looked at him, her eyes dark with fatigue. She felt a wave of panic. She wondered if maybe this time her judgment has been clouded by her past and she had invited the wrong person into her home.

"What? What doesn't wash?"

"It's just that it seems so entirely unprovoked. I'm going to have to track down the grocery he was in and ask around. I'll check with the cops. Look, you had better get some sleep," he said. "You look exhausted."

"Thanks. You're a sweet-talker," Juliet said, but she smiled.

"I'll call you a cab."

"Thanks." Juliet added, "Why don't you ride it back to my place with me? We can talk this through."

COLE HAD THE cab stop four or five blocks from Nancy's apartment. He paid the fare and stepped out into the cool night. He looked up and down the quiet residential block. The street was lined with the typical six- and eight-story apartment buildings bunched together around the north side of English Bay. There was no one on the street. Cole peered west toward Nancy's building and couldn't see a soul. He took a deep breath and walked in that direction.

It occurred to him that he'd never been to her apartment in the months she'd been living in Vancouver. Good God, he thought, he'd been so damned wrapped up in his own shit. According to Dr. Brady, he had never processed the memory of his father's suicide, and the trauma that it brought, which had sent him into a spiral of depression, anxiety, anger, and even suicidal thoughts. He knew he had come to associate Nancy with that trauma.

He walked beneath the canopy of trees. Cole's plan was to appear as if he was out for an evening stroll so he could surprise whoever was watching Nancy. He spotted the silhouette of a man leaning against a lamp pole in the verge of the empty road. The man seemed to be looking up at Nancy's building. Cole slowed and wondered if *he* had been seen. There was no place to circle around and sneak up on the observer, so he just put his hands in his pockets, pulled up the collar of his leather coat, and walked on, as if returning home from an evening downtown.

Three street lamps separated them. Then two. Cole walked slowly but purposefully, keeping his eyes low, as if absorbed in his own thoughts.

One lamp. His breathing slowed; his focus narrowed. He could feel the familiar rush of adrenaline through his body, but instead of it controlling him, he was determined to control *it*.

"Nice night," he said as he strolled past the watcher. The man said nothing. Cole could not see his face.

Cole stopped. "I said, nice night."

"Yeah, it's nice," said the man, not turning around.

"Watcha doing?"

Cole could see the man's shoulders rise and fall. "Waiting for a friend," he said.

"Your friend live in that building?" Cole asked.

"Piss off, pal," the man said. He was big enough to be one of the men that Cole and Denman had followed, but the voice wasn't familiar.

"Well, it's just that this is a Crime Watch community," said Cole congenially. "We look out for one another so, I'm going to ask again where your friend lives."

"Maybe you didn't hear me the first time. I told you to fuck off."

Cole took a step toward the man. "No, no, I heard you. Heard you just fine. And I asked you—"

The man turned on him, but Cole was ready, his hands out and hanging loosely at this sides. The man had a blackjack in his right hand, a small club with a steel core under a rubber outer layer. He swung it at Cole's head. Cole blocked the blow easily and landed two quick right jabs in the man's face, knocking him back on his heels. The man tripped on the curb and fell into the street.

"Who are you?" said Cole, stepping toward him, hands balled into fists.

The man scrambled to get to his feet and came at Cole quickly, low and hard. Cole stood his ground, and as the man met him, he brought his knee up into the man's chest, winding him. Cole stumbled backward against his attacker's forward rush. Cole managed to stay on his feet. He brought his hands down together on the man's back, sending him to his knees. Cole stepped back.

"Who are you working for? Andrews?"

The man got up and came at Cole again, this time catching him in the stomach with a low punch that Cole couldn't block, and then swung at his head with the blackjack. Cole blocked it easily and swung hard and high for the man's face, splitting open the skin under the left eye, blood spraying across the glow of the street light.

Cole only had a second to react to the sound of footsteps coming at him from the side. He pivoted in time to see a second man, bigger than the first, emerge from the shadow of the shrubs. Cole set himself and hooked the man as he came close, but the man's momentum carried him into Cole and they both ended up on the ground. Cole grimaced at the violent jar to his ribs. The big man was on top of him, but Cole brought his knee up into the man's groin. The man winced in pain, and Cole was able to roll the man off him and stagger to his feet.

"Okay, cowboy," Cole heard the first man say. "That's about fucking enough." He looked up to see the man holding a compact automatic pistol, the metal on the gun gleaming under the streetlamp. The second man got to his feet.

"Looks like you win. So now what?" asked Cole. "I'm not leaving, and you've got the drop on me. Are you planning on shooting me here on this nice quiet street?"

The first man lowered his aim a little. "The next time the three of us get together, Blackwater, you won't hear us coming. This is the only warning you're ever going to get." The men backed away, disappearing between two apartment buildings.

Cole straightened and sucked air into his lungs. He glanced up at the apartment building in which Nancy lived. He pulled out his cell phone and hit redial. Nancy answered.

"I'm here," he said.

"I know," she answered.

TWENTY-FOUR

MARCIA LANE SAT IN HER office at the VPD's Downtown Eastside detachment. It was nine-fifteen on Monday night. She had spent the entire day on the move. At the end of it, she had left the teams to clean up for the night and caught a ride with a patrol car back to the detachment. She was exhausted, and she was a long, long way from being able to sleep.

There were five people known to be missing now. As team leader for the Missing Persons Task Force, she not only had to direct the operations, but she had to file most of the reports. She turned on her computer and sat back in her office chair, pressing her knuckles into her eyes. She should get a cup of coffee to keep her awake through the next few tedious hours of paperwork, but she knew if she did, there would be no getting to sleep before three or four in the morning. And she had to be back at the pier by first light to supervise the ongoing search.

While she waited for her computer to slowly fire up, she contemplated the decisions she had made over the last few days. If she was caught, she might receive "official" commendation, but unofficially her career in the VPD would be through. She might keep her job as head of the Task Force, but that would be the end of her advancement. She was pretty sure that John Andrews' days as Divisional Commander were done, but the likelihood of him being fired was minimal. He'd be disciplined, a letter would be put in his file, and he'd get transferred to another assignment for a while. In a year or two he would be back climbing the ladder. And Lane would probably never know if his participation in the Lucky Strike Supper Club was linked to some of the egregious actions taken by the VPD over the last few months.

It didn't even seem as though Andrews cared if he was caught, she thought. He had used a detective from her squad to run errands for the Lucky Strike Supper Club. It was going to get back to her. She thought this was part of Andrews' plan, to test the loyalty of his team leaders. Her first loyalty was to her duty as a cop; the chain of command was a distant second.

She opened her email account to check if anything interesting had happened since she had left the office at eleven that morning. Nothing much had. She was about to start filling out reports when her cell phone rang.

"Lane, MPTF."

"Sergeant, it's Frank Dicks from the dive team. I've got news."

"What is it? I thought we'd shut down."

"Yeah, me too. An hour ago we were pulling in our lines and gear and we got tangled in something. I sent Sorensen and Munroe down with lights to free the lines. They came back with a stiff in a shopping cart. We found another one two dozen meters away. Bodies were wrapped in tarps. We've got them out of the water. You better get down here."

"Be there in five minutes."

Lane snapped her cell shut and grabbed her coat. She ran from her office, leaving her computer on, and started toward the garage. She swung by the staff sergeant's post.

"Is Andrews still here?"

"Yeah, he's burning the midnight oil." Lane half walked, half ran down the hall to the executive offices of the detachment. Andrews was sitting at his desk, a stack of papers in front of him. He looked up over his bifocal reading glasses as she entered the room. His face registered nothing.

"Commander, sorry to disturb you, but we've got two bodies at the pier. I just got the call. I'm heading there now."

"Okay," he said, taking off his glasses and putting them on the desk.

"Do you want to ride along?"

"No, I'm going to stay here."

"Do you want me to call the Media Relations department?"

Andrews was silent a moment, then said, "That will be fine, Sergeant."

"You want to brief?"

"No, it's all yours. Is that a problem?"

"No, sir."

"Anything else?"

"No, sir." She turned and left. Biggest missing persons case since Pickton and not even a "Good work, Lane."

ANDREWS WATCHED LANE walk down the hall. He waited a moment after she was gone. This might be a good break, he thought. It was too bad about Lane. She was a good cop, a good investigator and team leader. Now that all seemed irrelevant to him. He picked up the phone and dialed a familiar number. The phone rang four times and he was preparing to leave a message when a woman answered.

"Beatta?" he asked.

"Yes." She sounded flat, gray.

"It's John."

"Hi, John. Funny, I guess I was expecting your call."

"What's up?"

"You first."

"Marcia Lane just came by my office. They've found two bodies at Centennial Pier. I think they'll be two of the homeless people who are missing."

"That's some good news, I guess . . . I was just going to call you. Phone tree. Remember that? Two years ago, I think. I couldn't remember who I was supposed to call."

"Shit, now what?"

"The press has all the names. All of them. Me, you, everybody."

"Who? Which reporter?"

"Webber, at the *Sun*."

"Did you talk with her?"

"She was all over me, John. I had to. I'm trying to save my organization."

"Fuck," he said.

"It's over, isn't it?"

"Goddamned right it is. Fuck. What does she know?"

"She had all of our names. She had the document before, but somehow she's come up with all the names. I don't know how she got them."

"I think I do."

"Is it too late? Can we do anything?"

"No. I don't think so. The cat's out of the bag now."

"I'm sorry, John."

"It's okay. We knew we were taking a chance. I think it's good that it's you she reached. Maybe the press will go easy. The public will understand. We're just trying to clean up this fucking city, is all."

"Do you remember who you were supposed to call?"

"Yeah. Trish. I'll call right now."

"Good night, John."

"Goodbye, Beatta."

TRISH PERRY HEARD the phone ring from inside the shower. It rang four times and then went quiet. Then it rang again. She stepped from the shower and grabbed a towel, catching the bedroom extension on the fourth ring.

"This is Trish," she said, holding the towel around her.

"Trish, it's John."

She felt her heart sink. She looked at her watch. "It's all out, isn't it?"

"Yeah," he said.

"Okay, who's got it?"

"Nancy Webber at the *Sun*."

"Anything that can be done?"

"Nope."

"Did anybody talk?"

"Beatta."

"Figures."

"Yeah, that was a mistake."

"How much did she say?"

"I don't know . . . I don't know."

"Someone isn't going to be very happy."

"I know. At least I don't have to make *that* call." Andrews cut the line. Still in her towel, Trish dialed the phone.

CHARLES LIVINGSTONE WAS just finishing his second glass of port when the phone rang. He looked at his watch. He snatched it up, not wanting to wake Martha, who was sleeping, though only fitfully.

"Yes?"

"It's Trish."

"Okay."

"The *Sun* has it all."

"I know. Anybody go public?"

"Nowak."

"What did she tell?"

"Don't know."

"Fine." He hung up the phone.

He finished his port and put the glass down. Charles Livingstone was beyond caring what happened with the Lucky Strike Manifesto and the pathetic cabal of people who for the last two years had met in that grimy room and eaten rotten Korean and Chinese food. He could care less. He reached for the bottle of port. There was nobody left around him whose opinion he gave a damn about. Martha had been mostly absent for the better part of a decade, and his miserable son had disappeared months ago, stopping by only to con Adelaide, their housekeeper, into letting him pilfer the family home for money to do God knows what with. He had fired her when he discovered Sean had been in the house.

It was just him now. He really didn't care.

He picked up the phone and hit "1" on the speed dial.

"This better be good," said Frank Ainsworth. Livingstone could hear music and voices in the background.

"The *Sun* has all of our names. It will be out tomorrow."

The sound of disembodied voices and a distant tenor sax solo filled the long silence.

"Okay. How much do they know?"

"We've got to assume everything."

"I hope they don't know *everything*. That would be upsetting."

"They got to Beatta."

"But she didn't know. We kept her apart from that . . . delicate matter."

"For reasons that are obvious now," said Livingstone.

"Are we doing anything?" asked Ainsworth.

"I'm guessing Andrews has got someone on it. But I think it's too late."

"What about Chow?"

"That's your call."

"Okay. Well, bottoms up."

BEN CHOW SAT on the low bench, his back against the rattan curtain. The dining room was filled with the sound of barbecue food sizzling on conical grills, many Asian languages and dialects, and much laughter. Chow wasn't laughing. Things were coming undone. First the media had gotten wind that the Lucky Strike Manifesto existed, and they had an approximation of what it said. It would only be a matter of time before whoever Nancy Webber's source was would dig up names. It was only a matter of time.

Now, Don West, the bumbling, incompetent mayor of this fair city, would be rolling out his "New Vancouver" program in the morning. It wasn't that Chow was against the program. In fact, he was all for it. He had written most of it, but city politics being what they were, West had insisted that if it was to be a city program, then he as mayor should announce it. Chow would be given second billing at the news conference.

The good news was that some of the connections were intact. While everybody in the Supper Club believed that the Manifesto was about development and ridding the Downtown Eastside of the homeless, Chow alone knew its more clandestine purpose. He was immersed in that thought when his cell phone chimed and he jumped. Several of his friends made comments but he just answered the phone.

"Ben, it's Frank."

Chow knew what the call was for. "When?"

"Tomorrow morning's paper. The *Sun*."

"Who?"

"We don't know the leak, but Beatta talked."

"Too bad."

"Yeah. Okay, well, so long."

Chow hung up without saying goodbye. He slipped his phone in his pocket.

He addressed his friends and told them that he had to use the facilities. He slipped through the busy restaurant and found his way to the back stairs where a big man stood with his arms crossed. Chow just nodded to the man and went up the stairs. He walked down the long hall and came to the portal where two men stood.

"Please tell Mr. Fu that I would like to speak with him," he said to the men.

One of the men went inside, then came back out and nodded. Chow walked between them. Chow said, "Mr. Fu, we have a little problem."

TWENTY-FIVE

"I'VE GOT TO GET HOME," Cole said, standing in Nancy's kitchen. She was making coffee. "I can't show up for work wearing the same clothing that I had on yeasterday. Mary will be suspicious."

"Mary basically runs Blackwater Strategy, doesn't she?"

"Pretty much. At least its one relationship with a woman I don't have to cower from."

"Are you and your ex still at each other's throats after all this time?"

"No, it's not as bad as that. I'm just kidding around. I mean, it's not peaches and cream, but we're okay. She still hates my guts, but so do most people, so that doesn't really bother me."

Nancy poured a cup of coffee for Cole and one for herself. She took cream from the fridge for Cole. "I still hate your guts, too," she said, tasting her coffee.

"Really?" he said, raising his own cup.

"Oh, yeah."

Cole shrugged. "Maybe there's a club somewhere you could join. I think there's a Facebook page."

"I could be the club's mascot," said Nancy.

Cole leaned toward her.

"I have coffee breath."

"So do I," he said, and he let his lips touch hers. She pressed herself into him, her mouth opening.

They drew apart and she looked into his eyes. "Thanks for coming to my rescue last night," she said.

"I'm a rescuing-the-damsel-in-distress kind of guy. I think you should come and stay at my place tonight," said Cole. "Just to be on the safe side, you know . . . ?"

"Just for safety's sake," she said, smiling.

"Just to be safe," he said, kissing her again.

DENMAN WALKED FROM Juliet's home as the first shops were opening for the morning. Though he had slept little, he had a bounce in his step.

They had sat up drinking red wine, talking. "So you took him in. Hard to find fault with that."

"Some would. Like my boss at the Health Authority, as well as the director of the Carnegie Centre."

"Besides *them*," smiled Denman, relaxing in a chair at Juliet's kitchen table. He had helped her clean up the mess when they had first arrived at her home.

"I felt that he might come around. I still do. People get trapped into a cycle on the street. They sometimes need a helping hand to get out of that crazy vortex."

"Shelters?"

"No, you know that a guy like Sean wouldn't last there. The hard cases would pick over his bones. A month and he'd be in the pen. He'd be smoking crack and doing petty theft to feed his addiction. He's, well, malleable. He's vulnerable. He's been through a lot."

"You know that he's been in and out of jail?"

"I didn't . . ."

"Yeah. He's done some time. Most recently he was charged with assault."

"Sean? This Sean?" she said, pointing to the kitchen as if he were there.

"His name is Sean Livingstone."

"Yeah, I think I knew that."

"Did he ever tell you his last name?"

"Well, no." Juliet looked down at her wine. Her face was red, but not from the drink.

"So he's not a model citizen."

"Yes, that's clear. He's on the street."

"But before that."

"Well, his parents died. Their will is being contested. That will mess up your life."

"I didn't get into his personal history. Still . . ."

"What is it?"

"Well, if I'm going to look into his allegation that he was assaulted by the police, I'm going to look into his life, too. I want to make sure everything checks out."

Juliet sipped her wine. "I've grown fond of him. He's been so great to have around here. He cooks, cleans, picks up after himself, even after me. I was thinking about trying to get him work at the Carnegie Centre. He really seems to have a lot of compassion for people on the street now that he's had to live among them for a while. You think I should?"

"Let me do some digging first, okay?"

"Alright . . ."

"Can we stop talking about Sean?" Denman said. "I mean, it's one o'clock in the morning. I think it's time we punched the clock, don't you?"

Juliet laughed. "Slacker," she said. "Lawyers always book off early. I guess you're going to bill me for this little chat, and for your research time, aren't you?"

"I don't know," Denman said. "Can you pay?"

Juliet smiled. "Hmm," she mused. "I might be able to think of some way of making it up to you."

DENMAN TALKED WITH the greengrocers who might have seen Sean. Nobody witnessed a man being assaulted by police the night before. None of the shops had reported anything more serious than a shoplifting that night.

Denman then walked toward the VPD detachment at Hastings. He stopped to buy a newspaper when he read the headline in the *Vancouver Sun*: "Lucky Strike Manifesto Revealed. Influential Developer, Lawyer, Homeless Advocate, Top Cop and City Councilor Linked to Conspiracy to Bulldoze Chinatown." He saw Nancy Webber's byline.

When he folded open the paper he saw a secondary story with a different reporter's name attached: "Two Bodies Found near Centennial Pier. Missing Homeless Man and Woman Believed to Have Been Recovered." Denman grabbed his cell phone and hit speed dial.

TWENTY-SIX

MARCIA LANE WOKE TO A knock at her door. She had folded her coat into a ball and put her head down on her desk for a few minutes around three that morning, after returning from the Centennial Pier, just to catch a little shut-eye. She looked at her watch. It was six forty-five.

"Come," she said, not caring that her hair was mussed and her face drawn and pale.

"I'm Constable Winters, Sergeant."

"What is it, Constable?"

"I saw this in the squad room." He held up a photocopy of the photo that Juliet Rose had given her the day before.

"Do you recognize him?"

"Yeah, of course. His name is George Oliver. He's a regular. My partner and I talked to him the other day."

"When?"

"Let's see, it's Tuesday today, so that would have been, like, Thursday?"

"Where were you?"

"We were at the Lucky Strike. We were on Andrews' detail. You know, doing cleanup around the hotel. Oliver has stayed there on and off for years. He was just sitting on the steps. We were chatting with him, you know, maybe giving him a bit of a hard time. Nothing serious. Anyway, somebody from the Carnegie Centre came by and offered to take him there for a hot meal. We let him go. Oliver never caused much trouble. Bit of a problem with the bottle and some petty theft, but that's it."

"Man or woman?"

"It was a man. Young guy. Backpack. Leather jacket." Winters closed his eyes, remembering. "About five ten, one hundred and fifty pounds. Nothing remarkable. Blackish hair. No scars. His eyes were—" he hesitated, "—were gray."

"I'll need you with me this morning, and your partner. I want to see if we can find this guy at the Carnegie Centre. If that doesn't work, we'll do a sketch. Circulate it around." Lane stood up and stretched. "It was Winters, right?" she said, looking at him.

"Yes, ma'am."

"I don't suppose you'd find a girl a cup of coffee, would you?"

SOMETHING WASN'T RIGHT, thought Cole. He sat in the back of the cab, heading toward his downtown office, having showered and changed at his home. It was going to be a big day. Mayor Don West was making an announcement at eleven that morning about his plan for the Downtown Eastside. It was being sold to the media, and a weary public, as a celebration. Cole guessed that the End Poverty Now Coalition would be out in full force, and so would the riot police.

And Denman had called with the news that Marcia Lane's Task Force had found two bodies in Burrard Inlet, off the end of the Centennial Pier. He had read the piece in the paper to Cole over their cells. The victims were wrapped in tarps and folded inside shopping carts.

Coming on the same day as news of the bodies and Nancy Webber's front page story about the Lucky Strike Manifesto, and its signatories, the mayor's announcement would be anything but a celebration.

But it wasn't these things that were vexing Cole. An image was lodged in his head that he couldn't shake. Something he had seen—something just in passing—that was now gnawing at him. He watched the city roll past as the cab wove its way downtown. He closed his eyes to try and recall the image that was tickling the corners of his mind. It was a photograph or a still image of some sort, but he couldn't quite see the faces.

JULIET ATE HER breakfast in a quiet house. Denman had left early to talk with the merchants along Gore Street before their memory of any assault the night before faded. Sean was in the hospital. She toasted a bagel and poured a cup of coffee, then sat on the back steps of the home listening to the birds. She took a bite of her bagel and heard the radio announcer say that the news was up next. It was already nine. Time to get her day underway. She stood to turn the radio up to listen when the phone on the wall next to the back door jangled. She picked it up.

"Juliet, it's Denman."

"Couldn't stand to not hear my voice for even a couple of hours? How sweet . . ."

He cut her off. "It's not that. Look, I'm so sorry. They've found two bodies. I'm on my way to the VPD right now."

THE MORNING WAS gray, a light rain pattering against the window of the hospital room where Sean lay. His bed was next to the window. Being able to watch as the morning dawned was a relief. He hadn't slept at all that night. With seven others in the room, Sean was constantly being awakened as his roommates tossed and turned, coughed, moaned, talked in their sleep, or were woken by nurses making their rounds. All he wanted to do was check himself out of the hospital and get back to his routine.

Things were working out pretty well, he mused. Though the tussle with The Indian had been unexpected, at least it was a thrill. It had given him a jolt of excitement despite the pain of his injuries. He had liked it so much that he might try to incorporate that into his arrangements from time to time. Set one of his guests free to run, or to fight back, so he could try and recreate that adrenaline rush.

He touched the bandages on his face and forehead, and felt the stiffness in his back and shoulders. Before any new arrangements could be made, he'd have to finish up with his ongoing commitments. The shelter beneath the woman's house was getting full, and he'd have to make some room there before he could welcome a new guest to his own special sanctuary for the homeless. If he wasn't already dead, The Indian would have to be taken care of before Sean could bring anybody else in out of the cold.

He sat up and rubbed his hands and arms. That lawyer would want to talk with him again. Sean didn't really want to see him. He thought it would be best if he was gone before the lawyer returned.

He sat on the edge of the bed and waited. The rain began to fall harder against the clear pane.

"SAY THAT AGAIN?" asked Pesh on the phone.

"There were two men. I only saw one of them at first. He was just standing across the street from my apartment. He wasn't trying to hide. When Cole talked to him, he attacked Cole, and then a second man joined in."

"What a fucking circus this is turning into. Is Cole alright?"

"He's fine. He cleaned their clocks."

"Did you call the cops?"

"For all I know, these two guys *were* the cops. That's what Cole said. The VPD is mixed up in this. We've exposed a senior member of the force in a conspiracy theory so big that I'd be surprised if half of City Hall and VPD still have jobs by the end of the day."

"Okay, well, what's next?"

"Tell Murray to keep on the bodies story. I'm going to brace the mayor at his little pep rally today. Have you been in touch with his office? Is he still going ahead with it?"

"I called but couldn't get through. I haven't seen anything that says otherwise."

"Fucking ballsy."

"Or stupid."

"Either way, I'm going to be there."

COLE HUNG UP his office phone. He and Denman had just spoken for the fourth time that morning. Everybody was in a panic about the mayor's planned announcement. Cole sat back in his chair, stretched his arms above his head and groaned. He couldn't shake the feeling that something important had been right in front of him and he just couldn't see it. He closed his eyes to try and conjure the image. Other images came into his head. The empty room on Pender, the sweet aroma of Korean food clinging to the air, the sense that people had only just been there moments before. The smell of perfume: of Beatta Nowak's perfume. Those people now had names and faces. And now there were two bodies. While they hadn't been identified yet, Cole couldn't help but connect the dots.

Cole pressed his knuckles into his eyes and blew out a breath. The stream of air rustled the papers on his desk and a few pages fluttered to the floor. He reached for them and instead knocked a small pile of files over, sending them cascading into the blue recycling bin on the floor. Maybe that was just as well. Why did he still have so much paper now that everything was electronic? He reached for the tottering remains of the stack of papers, his eyes lingering on the framed picture of Sarah behind them.

Wow, Cole thought, that photo is really old. Need to get a new one. He reached for it, intending to wipe off the layer of dust, when his hand stopped in mid-air. His fingers began to tremble as a number of missing pieces suddenly fell together.

BEFORE HEADING FOR the Carnegie Centre, Marcia Lane stopped at the pier. She stepped from the unmarked patrol car and stood in the pouring rain, watching two separate VPD dive teams descend into the gunmetal waters of Burrard Inlet. The pier had been cordoned off with sawhorses and yellow police tape. A bank of television cameras was contained behind a chain-link fence fifty feet from where Lane stood. She felt the ache settle into her body.

A plainclothes detective approached. "Good morning, Sergeant."

"Detective, anything this morning?"

"Nothing yet. The boys are only on their second tank and there's a kilometer of docks and piers to search."

"Can we get another crew in?"

"We're trying to get North Vancouver to lend us some of their SAR team. I'll have something by noon."

"I'd like to have another body by noon," said Lane, turning to look at the cameras. "This thing has been fucked up right from the start. If I had another body to announce right before His Worship goes on TV to say that he's going to solve homelessness, I wouldn't be too disappointed."

The detective nodded, rain dripping from his nose.

A cell phone chimed and both Lane and the detective reached into their coat pockets.

"It's me," smiled Lane. She flipped her phone open. "Lane here."

"Sergeant, I've got something for you."

"Related?"

"Maybe."

"I'm a little busy with this—"

"Sergeant, it's a missing person report that just came in."

". . . Homeless?"

"The office manager at the Downtown Eastside Community Advocacy Society just called. Beatta Nowak didn't show up for an eight o'clock meeting. Someone went by her house and she's not there. Her car was found by the mounted patrol in Stanley Park, near Lion's Gate Bridge."

"I'm heading over to the Carnegie Centre shortly to talk with one of their volunteers. Keep me informed." She snapped the cell phone shut. It was time to find out who exactly the two patrol officers had handed George Oliver over to.

JULIET PUT THE phone back in its cradle. Two bodies. There would be more. Juliet felt numb. Her intent had been to go into the office, but now she just wandered around the house. Finally, she took a shower and got dressed and returned to her breakfast. She cut a fresh bagel and put it in the toaster and waited for it to pop. She stood by the back door, looking at the yard as the rain began to pound harder. She felt tears track across her face once more as she absent-mindedly stepped into the yard and felt the cool drumming of the rain. She walked into the center of the yard, her clothes becoming soaked through, the rain tickling her neck and back.

She nearly tripped over the backpack. She looked down at it, immediately recognizing it as Sean's. Juliet bent to pick it up and then saw the torn sleeve of a shirt on the lawn ten feet away.

TWENTY-SEVEN

BY ELEVEN, THE RAIN DROVE sideways into the placards and banners strung between the Gore-Tex-clad arms of protesters. Their heads were bent against the wet, faces mistily reflected in the steadily growing pool covering the paving stones. Seventy-five souls stood in the courtyard of Vancouver City Hall, held back by wooden sawhorses and police officers in riot gear and black helmets that glistened in the rain, masks of implacability.

The crowd, which had started to assemble shortly after nine, was growing agitated, anxious for anything to provide relief from the chill of the rain and the boredom. Mayor West wasn't scheduled to make his announcement until noon. A man in a hooded black sweatshirt and dark sunglasses despite the driving rain elbowed his way to the front of the crowd. Five or six others dressed in similar fashion soon found their way alongside him. They clenched their fists and shouted at the police, taunting then, challenging them. The police maintained their implacable front.

Behind them half a dozen members of the End Poverty Now Coalition sang an appropriated union song, making it clear to everybody that they were there to stay.

TRISH PERRY SAT in her office overlooking the courtyard of City Hall. The mayor's office had instructed the switchboard to redirect all media calls to the communications department. She had spoken to her mother, who lived in West Van, and to her lawyer. Now she sat and waited. She knew two calls would be coming. She just didn't know which would be first.

She started at the sound of a crack from the courtyard. She half stood to look down on the spectacle of protestors and police and saw a pale plume of blue smoke—someone had let off a firecracker. The police line shuffled. She gave West five minutes, if that. The weather meant the announcement would be moved inside, but some of the protesters would infiltrate. She figured he'd last five minutes, maybe less, before all hell broke loose. She was settling herself back into her chair when her phone rang and she jumped again. She looked at it, trying to see, through the beige plastic handle, which of the two calls she expected had come first.

On the third ring she took up the receiver. "Planning, Perry."

"Trish, it's Henry calling from the mayor's office." Henry Hogan was Chief of Staff. She felt almost relieved.

"Don can't make this call himself, Henry?"

"He's a little tied up today, Trish. I guess you understand."

"Hummm . . ." she said, distracted by more jostling in the courtyard below.

"Listen, Trish, can you come and see me in the mayor's office, please?"

"I'll have to check my schedule, Henry. I've got a pretty tight afternoon."

"Trish, let's not play coy."

"Henry, just cut the crap. I know I'm fired."

SEAN LIVINGSTONE COULD hear the pop of fireworks. Somewhere someone was having a party, he thought. He stood at the corner and waited for the light, his hair matted against his forehead in the driving rain. He wore only a sweatshirt and jeans, which were now soaked through. The bandages on his face pressed tightly against his pale skin, the dark sutures beneath them showing through the fabric of the dressings. When the light changed, Sean walked purposefully toward the bus stop across the street from City Hall.

He stood waiting for the bus that would take him back to Juliet's place, absorbed in his own thoughts. He didn't notice the young man across the street reach into his backpack and take out a paint-filled balloon and lob it at the line of riot police. He did look up when the crowd roared as the balloon burst against the helmet of an officer, the red paint spraying across his armor, obscuring his vision. The officer buckled from the blow and grabbed at his helmet, trying to clear his visor. The officer next to him watched the spray of red paint drip from his mask and mistook it for blood. He raised his whistle to his lips and blew. The police drew their batons and began to close the gap between them and the youths at the front of the crowd.

Sean saw more protestors hurl paint balloons and then watched the riot police rush into the group of young men, swinging their truncheons.

Several protestors fell to the ground, covering their heads, being trampled as their mates rushed to escape the black-clad riot police.

The bus arrived and Sean stepped through the open doors.

MARCIA LANE STEPPED through the double doors of the Carnegie Centre for the second time in two days. The presence of the two uniformed police officers accompanying her, their visors dripping with rain, their heavy coats sodden, turned a few heads. Lane stepped to the information counter just inside the doors and cleared her throat.

"Good morning," she said, trying not to drip on the desk. The volunteer looked up at her. "I'm Marcia Lane, VPD." She reached into her coat pocket for her identification card. "I'd like to speak with whoever manages your volunteers."

"That would be Ted. He's on the third floor," said the volunteer. "Want me to give him a call?"

"No," said Lane. "We'll just drop by."

She climbed the aging circular steps to the third floor, Winters and his young partner Jason French following behind. Lane inquired after Ted, and when he appeared she was pleased to see that he was a clean-cut, middle-aged man wearing a pressed button-down shirt and clean, tan docker pants. She introduced herself.

"Sorry to trouble you like this, but it's important. Do you know if this man is a volunteer for you here?" she asked, showing Ted the sketch of the man who had approached George Oliver.

Ted took a pair of glasses from his breast pocket and hung them on his nose. "He looks familiar. I'm sure I've seen this face. But that doesn't mean anything." He took his glasses off. "I see so many faces. Can I show this around the office?"

"Sure," said Lane, handing him the sketch. She turned to the young constable. "Go and canvass the cafeteria downstairs."

Ted returned a few moments later. "I still think he's familiar, but I don't remember him volunteering here. Without a name it's hard to say. Sometimes folks just come for a few shifts, or a week, and I forget them as soon as they're gone. I do keep all their names, just as I would a personnel file, you know?"

"This would have been recently. Within the last month," said Lane.

Ted was shaking his head. "I don't remember this person volunteering here," he said.

"Would it be possible for a volunteer from the Centre to intercept a homeless man somewhere in the area and escort him back here for a meal? Is that likely?"

"Someone might. It's not a normal thing our volunteers do, but I suppose if one of them came across someone in need, they might bring them here for a meal."

"Hold onto the sketch," she said. "If anything comes to mind, give me a call, would you?" Lane handed him her card. He nodded, and Lane and the older constable turned back to the door and then started down the stairs. They met French coming up.

"Anything?" she said.

He nodded, a smile on his face. "The guy eats here nearly every day. He's not a volunteer," he said, a little out of breath with excitement. "He's a . . . well, a client, I guess they call them."

DENMAN HAD BEEN waiting for nearly two hours when the staff sergeant finally called him over. "Listen, Mr. Scott, I really am sorry to keep you waiting this morning. It's been nutty around here today." The staff sergeant was a squat, powerfully built man in his mid-fifties. "Now, you're asking about an arrest on Gore Street last evening?"

"Yeah, I've got a client who says that he was shopping in one of the Chinese grocery stores when two uniforms busted him up."

"I don't like the sounds of that."

"The kid is pretty messed up. Bunch of stitches in the forehead. Black and blue. Broken nose. A real mess."

"Let's see if we have any arrests on Gore last night," said the staff sergeant as he punched in some keys on his computer screen. "I don't have even a complaint filed on Gore last night. Are you sure it wasn't Main Street, or Pender?"

"No, the kid said Gore."

"What was his name? Let me run it that way."

"Livingstone, first name Sean."

More keys. "Well, I have this fellow in our files alright," said the staff sergeant, looking up. "There's nothing yesterday. Last time we saw young Mr. Livingstone was a couple of weeks ago."

Denman held up his hand. "Look, between you and me, I think our boy is crying wolf. I'm actually a little worried about this kid. I think . . . well, I think he's not entirely stable. I ran the trap line along Gore and Main this morning. Nobody saw anything go down last night. Can you ask around and let me know if anything did? If so, I'm going to file a complaint, but it's going to be light on the superlatives. If it didn't, I'd really like to know. Okay?"

The cop took a breath. "You got a card? I'll give you a call."

Denman handed the staff sergeant his card and thanked the man for his time. He headed for the door. He felt his heart beating and wasn't sure why. He reached for his cell, but before he could dial, it rang in his hand. "Scott."

"It's Cole. You know that meeting we had when we talked with Livingstone?"

"Yeah, his name was all over the paper this morning. Part of *your* Lucky Strike Manifesto."

"It's not *mine*, it's Nancy's. Anyway, something has been bothering me, and it jarred loose this morning. It was a photo he had on his desk, a family picture. The kid in the picture was at Macy's when you, Juliet, and I were there on Friday. You talked with him. That kid is Charles Livingstone's son."

"Fuck," said Denman, looking around in a mild panic. "I can't believe I missed that."

"What is the son of a rich lawyer who is working for the biggest developer in Vancouver doing bumming on the streets of the Downtown Eastside?" asked Cole.

"I don't know," said Denman, breaking into a run, "but I'm about to find out."

NANCY ARRIVED IN a taxi and raced through the rain into City Hall. She held her cell phone to her ear and had to yell over the din of the traffic and hiss of the rain. "Say that again?"

Cole repeated, "Charles Livingstone's son is a street kid. Both Denman and Juliet have dealt with him." He explained how he knew. "Denny didn't make the connection. Lots of Livingstones, I guess."

"Is this kid connected to the Manifesto?"

"We'll find out soon enough," said Cole.

"What do you mean?" Nancy stepped into the mezzanine and handed a security guard her ID card.

"I'm in a cab. I'm heading to Juliet Rose's place right now. Denny says that she has been letting this Livingstone kid sleep on her couch the last couple weeks."

"Holy moly."

"Yeah, I know. It's crazy. I guess she takes her work home with her. I'll call you if anything turns up."

"Right. By the way, I guess you ought to know there's a riot outside City Hall right now."

"Seen one riot, seen 'em all. Just another day on the West Coast," said Cole, and hung up.

Nancy snapped her phone shut and found a seat. She looked at her watch. It was two minutes before noon.

ANDREWS SAT IN his office. Sometimes he wondered if he shouldn't have just stayed a beat cop. Maybe he could have done so much more good that way. Instead, he had climbed the ladder, moving quickly through the ranks, from constable to sergeant to staff sergeant and now divisional commander. But for how long? He had been waiting for the phone call all morning. He knew it would come. When this whole Lucky Strike affair had started, he hadn't intended for things to get to this point.

He had agreed to get involved because he thought he could control the process. He had looked around the room and believed he could out-flank anybody there. While some of them had money, and others had courage, he had the power of the police force at his disposal. He had been wrong. He had been wrong because he had forgotten one of the most elemental rules of warfare: know thy enemy. He hadn't known who his enemy was. Then five weeks ago, people had started to disappear.

People going missing hadn't been part of the plan. Andrews couldn't be certain, but he guessed that someone had gone too far. Someone had gotten overly enthusiastic. As people began to disappear, the press began to ask questions, and people began to poke their noses into his business. He knew that he had made a mistake when he pulled in officers from the Investigation unit. Someone on Vice or Missing Persons or Homicide had started knocking street people around. But dumping the bodies off Centennial Pier? That didn't jive. He scratched his head and watched the rain fall in sheets on the gunmetal roadway.

He wondered what Marcia Lane was saying to the media. He simply couldn't face the press. Not with her. He knew that she was the leak. But what could he do about it? If he still had a job at the end of the day, it would be a miracle. If he fired her for insubordination, she'd end up a hero. There was no way for him to win.

Andrews had been correct about one thing right from the start. He had guessed it would be Beatta who would come undone first. That was no surprise to him. She was, after all, a bleeding heart first and foremost. That reporter had known exactly who to call. He had told the others that during their first conversation. They insisted that when the Lucky Strike Manifesto finally became public—something that wasn't supposed to happen for another year, long after resettlement had begun—they would need her for legitimacy. Now Beatta had joined the missing.

The phone rang on his desk. Andrews calmly picked it up to receive the news he had been expecting all morning.

He said "Okay" into the phone and hung up. He stood and pulled his badge from his wallet. He placed it on the desk. Then he put on his coat and stepped from his office, closing the door behind him.

JULIET BENT TO pick up the rain-drenched, torn sleeve. She looked around her yard, suddenly very cold, her back involuntarily quivering and her shoulders hunching up toward her ears as a chill drove through her body. She unzipped the backpack that lay in a puddle and looked inside. Balled into a plastic shopping bag was a white smock and a box of plastic gloves. Juliet carefully opened the bundled-up smock. It was soaked with blood.

She dropped the shopping bag.

Beneath the smock, near the bottom of the pack, nestled a number of items. She put her hand to her mouth. She recognized the kits that she handed out to people on the street to help with the prevention and spread of disease, along with various personal items, including those for at least one woman: articles of clothing, a hair brush, a pair of fingerless gloves, a sun visor, a small make-up compact with the word "Peaches" scrawled on it in childlike writing, a wallet with a faded and worn driver's license belonging to George Oliver.

Juliet's mind began to race. Sean was in the hospital but she hadn't been in touch with him that morning. The gravity of her misjudgment suddenly bore down on her and she felt a wave of nausea wash over her. She doubled over to vomit on the sodden lawn. She wiped her mouth with the sleeve of her soaked sweatshirt and tried to focus her eyes.

She turned again in the yard, trying to corral her stampeding thoughts. The stairs heading down the side of the house caught her eye.

Juliet moved toward the concrete steps that descended to the root cellar, and the fallout shelter beyond. She halted on the second step. A long, oddly shaped tool sat in the pooling water there. She stooped to pick it up. It was heavy. She lifted it closer. Caught in the chain that wound tightly around a pulley on one end was matted hair and what looked like human skin. She dropped the tool.

Juliet looked around her, her eyes wild with panic. She reached into her pocket for her cell phone, but it wasn't there. She hadn't left the house yet that morning and hadn't completed her morning ritual. The cordless phone by her bed seemed so far away.

She could see that the door at the bottom of the stairs was closed. She put her foot on the next step down.

SEAN TRANSFERRED BUSES. He felt a wave of euphoria wash over him as he relished the task at hand. He would go home, get cleaned up, maybe take a hot shower, fix a late lunch, and then attend to his guests. It was going to be a great day.

DENMAN RAN HARD into the rain toward Juliet's house. He had his cell phone in his hand and hit redial again. He listened—his hand a few inches from his ear—to her voice mail click in for the tenth time. Fuck it, he thought, better to be safe than sorry. He punched in 911 as he ran.

BY THE TIME Don West walked from his office and into the mezzanine that doubled as a press gallery, the unrest in the courtyard outside had been quelled. As he took the podium, the five members of City Council from his right-of-center party filed behind him, Ben Chow among them. The reporters leapt to their feet and fired questions at the mayor and at Councilor Chow.

"Please," he said into the bank of microphones. "Please, take your seats. I have an announcement, and then I'll take questions."

But the reporters were not satisfied. Someone yelled, "Are you asking Councilor Chow to step down?"

"Has John Andrews been fired?" called another.

"Please," continued West. "I'm here to tell you about 'The New Vancouver,' and then I'll take your questions about this exciting initiative."

The press would have none of it.

"Councilor Chow," shouted a woman from CTV News standing behind Nancy. "Are you going to step down?"

"Today," West said loudly, "I'm here to announce 'The New Vancouver.'" He spoke over the questions of reporters and one by one they sat and became quiet.

"We live in a great city. We live at an exciting time. We have a prosperous future. But we have challenges that we must face if we are to meet our own lofty expectations," said West, looking down at his text. "Crime in our city is still too high. We have too many people who live on our streets without food and shelter. 'The New Vancouver' is a four-year program that will attack crime in this city and cut it off at the base. We're going to attack the drug trade in this city, get the dealers off the streets, and put their bosses behind bars. We're going to ensure that every member of our society has the opportunity to have a good life with a roof over their heads and food on their plates. There will be no free lunch in this city. People will have to work for their living but we'll make sure that there are opportunities for all."

West looked up at the crowd of reporters, blinking, and forced a smile. He was sweating under the glare of the lights.

"You're a fucking moron!" came a shout from the back of the room. The reporters turned to see a man standing along the back wall, just behind the television cameras. "You don't care about the homeless! You don't care about people who live in poverty. All you want to do is push the poor and the homeless out of the way so all the people who want to can buy condos. You're a fucking Nazi!" yelled the man, reaching into his coat.

In the seconds that passed during the rant, Nancy watched as West's face turned ashen, then bright red. His hands gripped the podium and his eyes looked wildly about, first for the source of the angry voice, and then for the police who were supposed to have kept protestors out of the media event. Nancy shifted her focus from West to Chow, who stood serenely behind him. She could swear a faint smile came to his face, and she watched as his eyes calmly moved from the mayor to the protester, and then to two well-built men with mustaches standing next to the entrance to the media room.

The men seemed to straighten when Chow looked their way. Then they reached for the protester, as if to escort him from the room, but the man saw them coming. His right hand emerged from his coat holding a balloon.

The lights of the TV cameras fell across the protester's face, and the flash strobes of digital cameras raked him. The protester threw his balloon between the two approaching men. The balloon exploded on the corner of the podium and thick red paint sprayed out, roping Don West with cords of rouge. Someone screamed. The two men managed to grab the protester and slam him into the floor. His face made contact and his nose exploded.

The media in the room erupted in a frenzy, while the mayor shouted for restraint. Nancy watched as Ben Chow faded into the shadows of the room and slipped through the double doors into the Council Chamber.

THE DOOR WAS locked. A heavy new padlock dangled from a rusty clasp. Juliet rattled the door in futility. She pressed her palms against it and looked around her. She was at the bottom of a dead-end staircase, flanked by concrete walls on either side. Storm clouds pressed down overhead, and the rain fell mercilessly on the fair, dark city of Vancouver.

SEAN WALKED SWIFTLY through the rain. He could see the neat, yellow home just a few doors up the street. He grinned. He felt great. Maybe he would skip the shower and get straight down to business.

THE CAB ROUNDED the corner too quickly, its tires squealing on the wet surface. Cole leaned forward from the back seat.

"There, that one. That's it!" he said, digging into his pocket and jamming a twenty into the driver's hand. Without waiting for change he jumped from the cab and rushed into the rain. He ran up the walkway to the house and banged on the door. He could hear nothing from inside the house. He pressed his ear to the door. Denman's last call had sounded desperate. Cole pounded on the door again and tried the knob. It was locked. He jumped the railing of the porch and hit the walkway running, racing around to the back of the house.

SEAN PAUSED ACROSS the street as a cab pulled up outside the yellow house. The cab door opened and a man in a black coat raced up the walk. Sean watched him pound maniacally on the door. Sean felt his fists tighten and his vision narrow as the man leapt over the railing. He started to cross the street when he heard a shout from very close and turned to see someone barreling toward him.

JULIET RATTLED THE heavy door again and pounded on it vainly with her fists. She looked around again, then ran back up the stairs. She had just reached the top when a burly man in a black leather coat tore around the side of the house. She screamed.

"Jesus Christ, Cole, you scared the piss out of me," she cursed angrily, but her face reflected relief more than fear.

Cole was breathing hard. He put his hands on her arms. "Are you okay? Is *he* here?"

"No. I don't know where he is."

"Where's Denman?"

"I don't know. Cole . . . Down there . . ." She pointed to the door that led to the shelter.

"It's locked," she called as Cole headed down.

Cole got to the bottom of the stairs, stood back, and with a booted foot kicked the door in, the old wood exploding in splinters. Juliet followed quickly behind him.

The room beyond the door was in darkness. "Is there a light?" Cole asked.

"I don't know. I've never been down here. The owner said it was just storage." Cole felt the wall beside him for a light switch. He found one and flicked it on. A bank of fluorescent lights illuminated the room. Juliet pointed to a dark, wet stain that snaked across the floor. Cole stepped into the chamber. It smelled like mothballs and mold and something else. Something dank and putrid. Juliet took Cole's arm and they walked across the room.

Juliet's eyes followed the stain. "The blood ends at that wall."

Cole pressed his hand against the wall as if feeling for a pulse. He pushed on the wooden shelves and they moved.

"House of secrets," he said. The shelves opened onto a second set of stairs that descended farther into darkness.

"Got a flashlight?" he asked.

"In the house. Do you want me to get it?"

"Not alone. We don't know where Sean is. Stay with me."

Cole dug into the mess in his pockets. He pulled a out keychain with a small penlight that Sarah had given him for his birthday. "That's handy," said Juliet.

"I'm full of tricks," said Cole, twisting the light on. It cast a small, narrow beam, but it was enough to see by. They descended into the gloom, the stench growing ever stronger.

DENMAN SAW THE cab pull up and Cole jump out and run for the house. He could also make out the figure of a man standing on the other side of the street, about to walk across, and knew for certain it was Sean.

Though he had been running for nearly twenty blocks, he pushed himself even faster. When Denman was only ten meters away, he shouted and Sean suddenly turned toward him. Denman half expected Sean to register fear, to react somehow to the sight of him running full speed toward him, but the young man's face remained implacable.

Sean seemed to buckle the moment before Denman hit him. They skidded through the sheet of water that had collected in the grass and came to a rest with Denman still clutching Sean around the chest.

Sean drove his forehead forward, connecting with Denman's left check and eye. The cacophony of the storm drowned out the crack of bone against bone. Denman momentarily blacked out, long enough for Sean to push himself away. As he rolled free he kicked his right leg toward Denman's groin, but Denman saw it coming and pivoted on the ground to block the kick with his own leg.

Denman threw two quick jabs with his right toward Sean's face, connecting both times, stunning Sean and giving himself time to rise to his feet. Then Sean was on him again, grabbing him around the knees and pushing Denman back toward a row of parked cars. The two men crashed into a car, setting off an alarm, and both fell into the garden along the edge of the street. Sean held Denman in a vice-like grip around his knees, while Denman punched at Sean's neck and ears, trying to break the man's grip. Sean bit Denman just above the right knee, sinking his teeth into the muscle of Denman's leg. Denman kicked at Sean and the two men broke free.

Sean rushed at Denman, his head low, but Denman easily flipped him. Sean crashed to the lawn, sending a spray of water into the air. Before Denman could lock Sean's arms behind him and hold him, Sean grabbed a stone the size of a grapefruit from the garden and swung for Denman's ankle. The rock connected with a loud crack, and Denman groaned. Sean lunged at him, the rock in his right hand swinging wildly for Denman's head. Denman blocked the blows, stumbling backward.

Denman could see Sean's face clearly. There was no emotion. Just emptiness. Denman backed toward a house, Sean raining blows at his head. Denman twisted painfully on his right foot and looped Sean's arm through the air, throwing him heavily toward the front stairs of the house. Sean landed at the foot of them, but quickly scrambled up and mounted the steps. He crashed into the front door, which exploded in splinters.

Denman ran up the stairs, his ankle throbbing. He could hear sirens now over the blare of the car alarm.

He reached the hall entrance of the house in time to hear Sean crash through the back door, into the yard behind. By the time Denman limped to the back of the house, Sean was gone.

THE HEAVY STEEL door at the bottom of the second set of stairs was not locked, but barred from the outside with a metal rod. Cole removed the rod and pushed the door open. The smell was putrid, and Cole felt bile rising in his throat. He swung the light around the room and gagged.

Juliet pushed past him into the darkness. "Cole, here, on the floor," she said. Cole pointed the light toward her. On the floor lay a body in a pool of blood. Juliet knelt beside the man and put her fingers on his neck to feel for a pulse. "It's George Oliver. He's barely alive."

Cole swung the light around the room.

"Oh my God," he said. There was a man tied to a metal chair, his head lolling forward. Another man hung from a hook in the ceiling, his arms above him, his face gaunt and pale. Cole knew without checking that he'd been dead for several days. The room reeked of bile and vomit, urine and feces and decay.

"Cole, help me get this man untied, and call for an ambulance."

They heard feet on the stairs and Cole looked up sharply, his body tensing for action. The feet were accompanied by a flood of lights.

"VPD—we're coming in!"

"We're here!" shouted Juliet. She was laying a second man down on the floor as half a dozen members of the tactical team burst into the room, pistols and shotguns held at the ready, lights on their weapons sweeping the room for danger.

"This room is clear," said one of the men into his headset. "We need an EMT team in here, and hurry."

Cole helped lower the man from the chair to the floor. "You okay, partner?"

The man looked up at him, his eyes glistening in the darkness, reflecting the glare of the police lights.

"I've seen better days," said the man.

"I bet you have," said Cole, his hand resting on the man's arm. "I bet you have."

TWENTY-EIGHT

NANCY STOOD IN THE MEZZANINE of City Hall with a clutch of other reporters when her phone rang.

"Webber."

"It's Marcia Lane."

Nancy looked around her. "Are you talking on the record today?"

"This is just an information call."

"Okay, go ahead. I'm just standing here at City Hall waiting to see if there are any more riots."

Nancy thought she heard Lane laugh a little, then grow somber. "I've got two things. First, my divers have recovered two more bodies. Same scenario as before. Shopping carts. Tarps; in one case, burlap sacking. They were farther west along the pier. The heavy traffic in Burrard Inlet kicks up a lot of sediment, so these two bodies already had a coating on them. We haven't got a positive ID yet. It may take some time."

"You said there were two things."

"Yeah, we just got a 911 call from a house on Salisbury Street. I'm pretty certain we're going to find the other missing people there. I'm heading that way right now. We've got a dozen units there, including tactical. Nancy, I'm pretty sure the call came in from your friend Denman."

"Jesus Christ. Juliet Rose lives on Salisbury Street."

"I haven't got a situation report from the tact team yet, Nancy. But I'm pretty sure the guy we're looking for has been passing himself off as a volunteer at the Carnegie Centre."

Nancy walked as calmly as she could from the gaggle of reporters and stepped into the rain, then broke into a run. It took her five minutes to hail a cab, all the while her heart beating furiously. She hit speed dial on her phone and tried to reach Cole, but he wasn't answering his cell. She then tried Denman, to no avail.

As she got in the cab she called her editor and asked him to send a photographer to the address. "Is everything okay, Nancy?"

"I don't know. I can't reach anybody."

"I'm sure everything is fine," said Pesh.

"It's just that Cole has a habit of, well, getting in too deep."

"Listen, Nancy, there is something else."

"God, what?"

"Well, you're not going to like it."

"Just spit it out, for Christ's sake, Frank."

"Beatta Nowak didn't show up for a meeting this morning."

"Fuck."

"Her car was spotted by a VPD mounted patrol unit in Stanley Park just after nine this morning. Look, it's only been half a day. She could be out for a walk . . ."

"In the rain?"

"It's Vancouver."

"Possible, but not likely."

"Nancy, these things happen."

"I know, Frank. I've been at this a while. I don't take responsibility for what happens after I report a story."

"Okay. Well, I thought you'd want to know."

"Thanks."

"Call me when you get there?"

"I will." She hung up without saying goodbye. The streets near the Salisbury house were choked with emergency vehicles. She handed the cabbie his fare and walked up the rest of the way. Three ambulances waited in the road, their crews wheeling stretchers toward waiting doors. She could see groups of men standing around in body armor and carrying automatic rifles and shotguns. A uniformed officer stopped her.

"Are you a resident?" he asked.

"Press," she said.

"Crime scene perimeter is right here." He pointed to the sidewalk beneath their feet.

"What happened?"

"Found three people in a bomb shelter beneath that house there," the officer pointed to the yellow house.

"Alive?" asked Nancy.

"Don't know."

"Anybody else involved?"

"The woman who rented the place found them," said the officer

"And the perp?" asked Nancy.

"On the run," said the cop.

"You're kidding me." Through the rain she made out Cole's dark, hulking form. "Cole!" she yelled over the hiss of rain and the wail of sirens. "Cole!"

She saw him peer over the railing of the porch and then rush down the stairs and run along the sidewalk, another uniformed officer following him.

When he reached her, they held on to each other, the two cops looking on. "What happened? Is everybody okay?"

"Juliet and Denny are fine. Juliet is in shock, but she'll be okay. Denman is in the back of that ambulance. Broken ankle."

"What happened?"

He told her. "Denman tackled the freak, but he got away. The kid, Sean, he's the one, the killer. The police are setting up a perimeter. I think they might be too late," said Cole, looking at the officer who had followed him. "I think the freak has given us the slip. He's crazy, and he's still out there."

TWENTY-NINE

"IS THIS AN OFFICIAL VISIT?" asked Charles Livingstone. He was seated in his plush office, his fingers pressed together in a tent in front of his chest, his body slouching slightly in his huge leather chair.

"Constable Winters and I are really here for information. And, I suppose, to give you something of a warning, really," Marcia Lane acknowledged.

Livingstone leaned farther back in his chair. "A warning? That sounds ominous." He smiled thinly. "It's already been a difficult day, you understand."

"I do understand. This isn't related to the newspaper stories, at least not directly. Not that I can see. It's about Sean."

Livingstone's body seemed to deflate at the mention of his son's name. "What about him?"

"When was the last time you saw him, sir?"

Livingstone pressed his fingers more tightly together so that the tips became white. "It's been some time. A year, maybe?"

"Do you know where he is right now?"

"Well, he should be in school. He *was* attending college here in the city."

"He isn't living at home while he attends school?"

"No."

"Why not?"

"That's a personal matter, Sergeant."

"Humor me."

Livingstone contemplated this for a moment. "My son has a problem with authority. He doesn't accept mine, or anybody else's. I won't tolerate that in my home. It's just too disruptive. Too disruptive. To me. To my wife. To my home."

"So you kicked him out?"

"I wouldn't say that. He left; I made it clear that he wasn't welcome back. He's well provided for, I assure you. He's an adult, twenty-four years old, for God's sake."

"Have you ever heard from him?"

"The last time I heard from him he'd been kicked out of Simon Fraser. He had decided on a new career path, and was enrolling in the community college. He was looking for more money, as usual."

"No phone calls?"

"No."

"He never drops by the house for a visit?"

"Sergeant, where is this going? I'm being interrogated without counsel present. I'd like you to explain to me what this is all about."

"You're not being interrogated, Mr. Livingstone. I assure you, if you were, you'd know it. I am trying to establish what I can about the patterns in your son's life. He has quite a record, doesn't he?"

"Surely you can't blame that on me. My wife and I have done everything we can for Sean. It's not our fault that he's a rebel. Without a cause, I might add," he said, shaking his head.

"I'm not blaming you, Mr. Livingstone. Lord knows children develop their own propensities, regardless of our parenting. Did you know he committed assault in September? He broke the nose of a classmate right in front of his whole class, and then walked out and was never seen by the school again."

Livingstone leaned forward. "Nothing about Sean surprises me, Sergeant. Now, if you wouldn't mind cutting to the chase, it's getting on in the day, and I really should be heading home. My wife is not well."

"What troubles her?"

"That's a private matter, Sergeant."

Lane nodded. "Sean isn't at your home now, is he?"

"I've already told you, I haven't seen him in a year! Just exactly what is this all about?"

"Mr. Livingstone, your son is wanted in connection with the murder of five people, and the kidnapping and attempted murder of two more."

The blood drained from Livingstone's face.

"About thirty minutes ago our officers found three people tied up in a fallout shelter under an address in the east end of the city. One of the men was dead, the other two are now in critical condition at Vancouver General. For at least one of them, the next couple of hours will be the deciding moments in his life. Sean also assaulted a well-known community activist who confronted him before our tactical team arrived, and your son is currently the subject of a city-wide manhunt. If you should hear from your son, we'd like to know about it immediately. If you see him, consider him extremely dangerous and call 911 immediately. Do you understand, sir?"

Livingstone simply nodded, his blue eyes inscrutable.

"FRANK, IT'S CHARLES."

"How are you today, Charles?"

"Fine. You?"

"I'm doing okay, all things considered."

"Backlash?"

"Some. To be expected."

"Listen, Frank. I feel I haven't served you very well in this matter. I had a meeting with the partners this morning, and we agreed that I should recuse myself from this file. The other partners have agreed that if you still want the firm to represent you, one of them will step forward. We also want to give you the opportunity to back out of your contract with us all together."

"Let me think about that a little."

"We wouldn't blame you if you wanted to seek counsel elsewhere, Frank."

"Well, it may be a necessity, but if I do, it's not because you haven't served me. We stepped into this mess together, Charles. We both thought this was what was best. I still do, by the way. I'm still planning on moving ahead with much of what our little Manifesto stated."

"Well, I think that's probably the right thing to do, Frank. But I'd suggest laying low on some of the more controversial stuff for a while. Let the Lucky Strike sit for a time. Hell, Woodwards sat for fifteen years. I don't see any reason to rush into things at this point. If the people of this city think it's so terrible for a businessman to do what the law entitles him to do, then let them live with the alternative: a cesspool of crime and disease and filth full of people who live like animals."

"Okay, Charles, I get what you're telling me. Like I said, I've got to think this over."

"What is the Board of Trade saying?"

"It's ironic that I've got to present to them this coming week, don't you think?"

"Did they ask you to not talk to them?"

"They would never do that to me, Charles. I *own* the Board of Trade. I did get a call from the chairman today. He asked me to avoid the subject. Let it all blow over. There will be more than the normal level of media interest this coming week. He suggested talking about the West End projects."

"Fucking cowards. You should talk about the projects just to spit in their eye."

"Are you okay, Charles? You sound like you're taking all of this personally. It's just the cost of doing business in Lotusland. Can't help but piss off the bleeding hearts."

"Yeah, I'm okay . . . It's just a family thing."

"Is Martha okay?"

"Well, not really, but it's not that, it's just . . ."

"What?"

"It's nothing. Anyway, I'm sorry this has turned out so badly."

"It's not so bad, Charles."

"We don't know that yet."

"Have you heard from *him*?"

"No. You?"

"No."

"If there are any threats, call the police, Frank."

"I'm okay. I'm fine. He might control the east side of the city, Charles. But I control the west. And I'm not entirely without recourse to the tools that he employs."

"Frank, if there are any threats, just call the police."

"Okay, Charles, okay. You sound like my mother."

"I'm sure she was a smart woman. You'll get back to me about the representation, right?"

"Next week. We'll have lunch. Let's just see how this plays out."

"Okay. Listen, I'm just heading into the car park, where the signal . . . spotting . . . lose you, we'll . . ."

"You're breaking up a little, Charles. I'll talk with you next week."

THE CELL PHONE lay on the concrete next to the tire of his black Jaguar. The tiny voice could still be heard coming from the earpiece.

"Charles? Okay, well I guess you've cut out." Then the line went dead.

Charles Livingstone's hand was still curled, the fingers grasping at air. He lay prone between his car and a BMW, his dark suit rumpled.

"Hi, Dad. It's good to see you," said his son, his left hand curled around a tire iron.

THIRTY

"I'VE GOT TO WRAP SOME things up at my office. Why don't you head over to my place, have a bath, and make yourself at home?" Cole fished into his pocket for his keys and handed them to Nancy. They were sitting in the boardroom of Priority Legal.

"You think Juliet is going to be okay?"

"She's fine. Denman will take her to his place tonight."

"I doubt she'll ever go back to *her* place again."

"Hard to blame her after what that freak did."

"What did you think of what that shrink from UBC said?" Nancy asked, looking intently at Cole.

"Hargrove? Well, it makes sense. Sean is a psychopath."

"I'm glad Denman called him to talk with us. What Hargrove said, about these people being able to burrow into your life, it's pretty scary. I really feel for Juliet. She must be feeling horrible right now," Nancy said, shaking her head, her raven black hair floating across her shoulders. "I mean, how are we to know? How is anybody to know? The guy knew all the right things to say. Knew exactly how to get into her life. It was like he could read her mind, knew all the weaknesses there. And then just played her like a fiddle."

"I found it particularly interesting what he said about the music. That people like Sean know all the words but not the music."

"Yeah, I found that interesting too."

"I mean, I met the guy. I'm a good judge of people, I think. I didn't see anything wrong with him, except that he seemed, well, flat, was all."

"I'm glad that Denman brought him in," said Nancy again. "I think it will help Juliet."

Cole stood up. "So I'll see you at my place?"

"Don't be long," said Nancy. She stood and touched his hand. "You're taking a cab, right?"

"You call me when you're at my place."

"Cole?"

He turned to her at the door. "Yeah?"

"I, well . . ."

"I know, Nancy. I'll be home soon."

Cole walked toward the back of the law offices. Before he turned into Denman's tiny cubicle office, he knocked. "Can I come in?" he asked.

"Come on in, buddy," said Denman.

"How are you guys doing?"

Juliet sat in the only chair in his crowded office, while Denman leaned on the edge of his desk. His left foot was in a cast; a pair of crutches leaned against the wall.

"We're okay," said Juliet.

"Thanks to you," said Denman. "You showed up just in the nick of time."

"Juliet, how are you feeling?" asked Cole.

"Sick," she said, looking down at her hands.

"He hoodwinked you, girl. Denman, too, and everybody else who came and went in his life."

"I should have seen it. I'm a health-care professional."

"Most doctors can't diagnose psychopathy," said Cole. "You heard what the professor said."

"I see mental illness every day."

"This is different."

"Maybe . . ." Juliet's voice trailed off. "It's just that I can't get those people out of my head. Peaches, George. They were all good people."

"Is George going to be okay?"

"I don't know about okay. He'll live."

"Any word from Marcia Lane about Sean?" Cole asked, looking at Denman.

"I just talked to her. She talked to Charles Livingstone an hour ago. Officers are staking out the family home, as well as all of our places, in case he decides to surface. She thinks if he doesn't show in the next twenty-four hours, he's likely given them the slip. She says she's got two hundred officers mobilized, checking traffic on the highways, the airport, the bus terminal, the train depot, and the ferries."

"Impressive. Too bad she didn't have two hundred officers on the case when people were getting whacked." Cole saw the look on Juliet's face and said, "Sorry, I'm just pissed."

"Me too."

"Me three," said Denman, "but Lane is on our side."

"So you say."

"Well, she's not on Andrews' side. I'm pretty sure she is Nancy's source."

"Did Nancy tell you that?"

"No, she never would, would she? But I've got a hunch."

"What about Beatta?" asked Juliet.

"Nothing new. Her car was found this morning in Stanley Park, and that's all we know. The search and rescue team has been combing the park all day. It's really not that big a place. If she's there, they'll find her."

"What are you thinking, Cole?" asked Juliet.

"Bad thoughts," said Cole.

"You don't think . . . I mean, you don't believe that Beatta was, well—"

"Killed? I don't know, but her name is all over the story about the Lucky Strike Manifesto," said Cole. "Nancy got her to talk. The other conspirators can't be too happy. At least one of those guys had a couple of thugs outside Nancy's place last night, and maybe even had those two dudes jump me in the Pender alley."

Juliet shook her head.

"Cole, where you heading?" asked Denman.

"My office. I've got to deal with about a month's worth of messages from paying clients before I can call it quits. Why?"

"I'm going to take Juliet to my place."

"Alright."

"You going to the Cambie after?" said Denman, looking at his watch.

Cole grinned. "You know, I think I might let Dusty and Martin enjoy each other's company tonight. I've got a much better offer."

COLE STEPPED ONTO East Hastings. He looked up and down the street for a cab, then decided to walk. It wasn't more than twenty-five minutes to his office, and after this day, a brisk walk in the cool night air would provide just the break his mind needed to unwind. He needed to try make sense of the insanity that had been visited on him, his friends, and his city in the last twenty-four hours.

He hadn't been walking for more than five minutes when his cell phone chimed. He expected it to be Nancy telling him she was home.

"Mr. Blackwater, it's Marcia Lane."

"Long day for you, Sergeant."

"Indeed. You too."

"What's up?"

"Some bad news."

"Nancy . . . ?" He felt his heart jump.

"No. No. It's Charles Livingstone. He didn't get home from work tonight."

"Jesus Christ." Cole gave up on not swearing for the day.

"My sentiments exactly."

"Where was he last seen?"

"His office. I was actually at his desk at about four this afternoon. His secretary said he left shortly after. His wife just called and said he hasn't come home yet. No answer on his cell. Normally we wouldn't worry, you know, out for a drink with the boys . . ."

"I understand. Why are you telling me, Sergeant?"

"We've got some smart people on the force, but there are some smart people on the outside. You and your friend Mr. Scott got the fix on Sean before we did. I just thought I'd put this out there, in case something clicks."

"So Sean didn't show up at the old man's place?"

"We've got four units in the area watching the house. If he was there, we'd know."

"What about the car? Livingstone's?"

"In the parking garage. We have a forensics team on site."

"Stolen vehicles in the garage, in the area?"

"Nothing reported."

"The pier?"

"Our cleanup teams are still there. They've been alerted."

"Okay, well, that's all I've got," said Cole.

"Call me if you think of anything."

"I will." Cole hung up. Doctor Hargrove had told them that psychopaths often operate without any motive whatsoever except self-satisfaction. They act on whims, on impulse. He also said psychopaths were capable of holding grudges that could color their actions for a very long time. He had offered it as a warning to all four of them to not let their guards down until Sean was safely behind bars.

Cole's cell phone rang. "Blackwater."

"It's Nancy. I'm safe and sound."

"Good. Lock the door, okay?"

"You bet. Don't you have anything besides kid food here?"

"I like kid food," he said.

"Where are you?"

"Hastings and Carrall."

"Nice 'hood. Sean's old stomping grounds."

"Well, he's not around here now. Lane just called and said his old man was missing."

"You're kidding me!"

"Sean seems to have had a busy night."

"I'm going to have to make some calls," said Nancy.

"Can you do it from my place?"

"Yeah. I can."

"Good. I want you where I can keep an eye on you."

"Two eyes would be my preference."

Cole smiled. "Two it is. Listen, it's a little dicey here. I should keep focused."

"Being careful?"

"Nope. I got a roll of twenties hanging out in my pants."

"Is that what you call it?"

"Funny."

"'Cause it seemed more like fives to me."

"Put a cork in it, Webber."

"See you soon?"

"About an hour or so." Cole snapped the phone shut and stuffed it into his pocket. He passed the corner of Carrall and Hastings. A gang of thugs eyed him suspiciously, but he ignored them and walked on. A "new Vancouver" my ass, he thought. Same old Vancouver was more like it, at least in these troubled parts.

Cole made his way between the prostitutes who crowded near Pigeon

Park. He looked south toward Shanghai Alley, and at the dark hulk of the Lucky Strike Hotel rising against the pale underbelly of leaking clouds. Sean's old stomping grounds.

Cole stopped in the street. A hooker approached him, thinking his abrupt halt was to inquire after her wares.

He waved her off, and continued to stare south.

"You need somethin', man?" a wiry Hispanic man asked him.

Cole ignored him.

"I'm talking to you, man. You got somethin' in your ears?"

Cole looked down at him. A flash of rage passed over his face and the pimp took a half step back.

Cole turned and dashed across Hastings Street between traffic. He could hear the pimp shout, "You better run, motherfucker," behind him, but his mind was already a block south, in the catacombs of the Lucky Strike Hotel.

THIRTY-ONE

THROUGH THE BROKEN GLASS OF the windows, Charles Livingstone
could smell the rain. If he closed his eyes and focused, he could push
the rancid smell of urine, vomit, and feces from his senses, and allow
the dark coolness of the evening to penetrate the stench of the room.
He recalled a night, many years before, when he and Martha had sat on
the porch of their home and watched as a rare electrical storm pulsed
across the Lower Mainland. Sean hadn't been born yet, and Martha
hadn't descended into the living hell of bipolar disorder—the fancy new
terminology for manic depression—and all was still well with the world.
They had sat hand in hand on the swing they had hung from the porch
roof of their new home.

A harsh spray of rain blew through the broken glass and snapped him
back to reality. He opened his eyes. The room was eerily lit by city lights
reflecting off the clouds pressing down against the bleakness. He lay face-
down, his body surrounded by broken glass and garbage. Used syringes
dotted the bare wooden boards of the uneven floor. A pool of rainwater
and God knows what else collected under the window.

Some of the liquid is your own blood, thought Charles, and he felt a
wave of panic. He struggled to rise and free himself.

"Lay still, Dad," said Sean's voice from across the tiny room. "You're
not going anywhere."

Charles turned to find the boy's voice. How long had he been back in
the room? He had left, hadn't he? He had said that he was hungry, and
that he was going out for food, and that he'd be back. How long ago was
that? Half an hour?

"Sean, untie me."

"Fuck you."

"Sean, please. No matter what you've done, I can help."

"Fuck you, Dad."

"Please son, I can help. You know I can. I can get you off. Plead out
insanity. Serve a few years in a hospital. You can come home with your
mother and me."

"I don't think so, Dad. Not this time."

"You'll see. We can do it."

"You should know that there are cops everywhere," Sean said, distracted. "I couldn't find a goddamned thing to eat out there. I couldn't get more than a block without running into a fucking pig. But they didn't see me."

"Sean, listen, we could go home. Adelaide could fix us something . . ." Charles lied.

"Not this time." Sean got up and walked across the room to where his father lay on the floor. He nudged him with the toe of his shoe.

"Please, Sean, your mother is sick. She needs me. She needs us."

"You blame me, I know you do."

"I don't."

"It's okay. I know you do. I do. I know it. But it's not true. She was fucking batty before I came in the picture. I know she was. You're just too stupid to see it. She's better without us, Dad. Don't sweat it. There's lots of cash. She won't even notice you're gone."

"That's not true. She needs—"

Sean's foot connected with Charles' face. "Shut the fuck up, Dad. Shut up." The old man spit blood. "That's all you ever do, talk, talk, talk. You're going to listen to me this one time. I'm the one making the *arrangements* now. You got it?"

Charles nodded, his eyes glazed over.

"You think you're such a big man in town. Making things happen. Making things work out just fine. Well, how'd things work out this time around? Not so good, huh?"

Charles didn't say a thing.

"I asked you a fucking question!" Sean kicked the man again, this time in the stomach. Charles vomited on the floor.

"No," he managed, when he had spit the last of the vomit onto the floor. "No, not so good."

"You had it all going on, had the whole thing figured out, didn't you? You and your cronies. But you didn't count on me finding out, did you? Did you? You would have gotten away with your little plans if I hadn't got involved."

"You got us, Sean. You got us."

"Taking care of those stupid fucking bums got the whole city looking *this* way. Everybody started snooping around; asking questions. This place became Ground Zero." Sean paced back and forth in front of his father's body, hands gesturing wildly. Charles watched the tire iron in his son's hand. "And now look at you. Big man. So smart. So connected. Pathetic piece of shit, laying on the floor in your own blood and puke. Look at you now, big man."

Sean stopped. "Dad, I'm going to show you a little something I learned one of the times that you let me rot in Juvie. It's going to hurt like hell." Sean bent over and took one of his father's hands in his and pulled a pair of pliers out of this back pocket.

"Did you know that fingernails come off?" he whispered to his father. "They do. Here, let me show you."

Sean heard a cell phone chime from somewhere beyond the room, in the darkness of the corridor. He stopped and turned his face into the bleak room, listening. The ringing was cut short. Sean stood and ran toward the door.

COLE LOOKED ACROSS the street at the Lucky Strike Hotel. There were few people out, and next to no cars. He crossed to the front of the hotel. Two police cars drove past, their lights raking the building, and then were gone. Cole ran to the front steps, his leather coat pulled tightly against him in the gale. The double doors were crossed by tattered yellow police tape that swirled in the wind. He pushed his hand against the doors, but they were locked. Now what? Go to the office? Have a drink? Get back to the apartment where a beautiful woman waited for him? Call 911 and who knows what you're going to get, he thought. Let's have a look, and if you find anything, you can ring Marcia Lane directly.

He stepped around the corner of the Lucky Strike, a gust of wind driving rain into his face and battering his coat, in time to see a figure move through the shadows toward the rear of the hotel. Cole's instinct that had led him here also told him the shadow slipping into the Lucky Strike was Sean.

Cole looked quickly around and set off at a jog toward the back of the building. He slowed when he reached the end of the side wall and peered around. A gray service entrance door was flanked by garbage bins he could smell from the corner.

Cole darted for the door and eased it open. He carefully leaned into the darkness in time to see Sean walking down a long hall. The only light in the corridor came from a broken exit sign, its few remaining bulbs throwing a sickly red light down the otherwise unlit hall. Cole closed the door gently behind him and stepped into the passageway. He slipped his cell phone from his pocket and was about to hit redial when he decided he had better follow Sean and find out where he was holding his father, and then retrace his steps and call for help.

Cole followed Sean as he disappeared at the end of the hall. His heart in his throat and his left hand gripping his phone, Cole held out his right arm in the dark, ready to fend off a blow or brace himself if he tripped and fell. In a moment he reached a stairwell without a door and stopped to listen. Despite the wind he could hear above him Sean's footfalls against the bare wooden boards. Sean was humming softly to himself. From somewhere higher above a narrow shaft of pale light entered the stairwell. Sean's figure cast a shadow every time he ascended the set of stairs on the eastern wall.

Cole began to climb quietly, pausing to listen for any change in Sean's pace, trying to keep track of how many times the long shadow loomed. After what seemed like an eternity, Sean's footsteps on the stairs stopped, and Cole guessed that he was on the sixth floor. Cole hurried up the last three flights, trying to quiet his heavy breathing in the cold, damp air. Faintly, Cole could hear the sound of voices, of shuffling or a heavy blow.

Maybe his plan hadn't been the wisest. Maybe in delaying he had given Sean time to do damage. He flipped open his phone, scrolled down the list of recent calls, and hit Send.

"Lane," came a tired voice.

"It's Cole Blackwater," whispered Cole.

"Mr. Blackwater? I can hardly hear you."

"I've found Sean."

"What?"

"I've found Sean. I had a hunch. I found him."

"Where are you?"

"I'm at the Lucky Strike Hotel. Sixth floor."

"Hold the line. If I lose you I'll call you right back."

Cole was about to say *no, don't,* but Marcia Lane had already put him on hold.

Cole heard a heavy sound come from a room down the hall. The phone at his ear went dead. Leaving it on to avoid the shutting-down chime, he snapped it shut and put it on the floor. He edged out of the stairwell, and crouching low, made his way toward the sounds.

He heard someone yell, then Sean's voice. "You would have got away with your little plans if I hadn't got involved. You would have gotten away with it."

Cole reached the door and crouched down, his hands balled into fists. It would take at least five minutes for the first cops to arrive and make it to the sixth floor, and by then Charles Livingstone might be dead. The best chance was to take Sean by surprise. Cole closed his eyes a moment to visualize what he had to do. Wait until the sound of Sean's voice revealed that his back was to the door and then rush him; take him out with a heavy blow to the back of the neck. Try not to kill him, Cole thought to himself, but if he did . . .

Cole counted in his head. One . . . Two . . .

And then his cell phone in the stairwell rang.

Cole froze. He knew it was Marcia Lane, but he had hoped he would get to Sean before she called back.

Sean came barreling out of the room, his right hand gripping a tire iron. Cole didn't hesitate. He charged into the man, his head connecting with his sternum, and drove him back fifteen feet until they both collapsed on the floor of the hall. Cole pressed his advantage, driving his right fist into Sean's startled face with two quick jabs, mashing his already broken nose and blackening his eye. Sean recovered quickly from the surprise, staying cool, and drove his knee up into Cole's tailbone. Cole winced in pain. He tried to adjust himself to protect his groin, and Sean swung at him with the tire iron. Cole blocked most of the blow with his left shoulder. Sean swung again and Cole was forced to roll away, using the momentum to stand.

Cole stepped back, sensing the wall behind him in the darkness of the corridor. Though Sean was less than ten feet away, Cole could barely see him in the gloom. He drew a deep breath and let it out slowly, focusing on the man before him. Sean had a stream of blood running down his face, over his mouth and onto his clothes. He wiped at it with the back of his hand and Cole thought he saw the flash of a smile.

"Why don't we talk this through?" Sean said, stepping toward Cole, glass breaking under his feet. "See . . ." he said, spitting a thick rope of blood onto the floor, "my old man there is the lawyer to a big developer. You and me, we're on the same side. We should be working him over together, not scrapping with each other. What do you say?" He took another step closer, the tire iron dangling at his side.

Cole could see his eyes now, dark and flat.

"Come on, man, you and me, and maybe that other lawyer friend of yours, we should be partners. We could work together, put a stop to the builders, put them in their place. What do you say?" Sean asked, and as he did he lunged for Cole, swinging the tire iron in a neat arc at Blackwater's head. Cole pivoted to sidestep the blow, and as Sean's arm cut through the air, Cole grabbed it a few inches above the wrist. Cole drove his open left palm into Sean's elbow. The joint broke with an audible snap. Sean's right arm went limp, and the tire iron clattered to the ground. Cole balled his hand into a fist and drove it into the soft flesh of Sean's ear. He stepped back as Sean fell to the ground.

Sean writhed amid the broken glass and garbage. Cole stepped over him into the room. He bent over the man who lay tied on the floor.

"Cavalry's here," said Cole.

Livingstone looked up. "You a cop?"

"Nope, I'm a—" What was he? Cole began untying the man's hands. "We met at your office. Cole Blackwater."

"I remember now," said Livingstone.

Cole finished with the man's hands and started on Livingstone's feet. Livingstone put his hands under him and began to sit up. He yelled suddenly, "Watch out!" and Sean rushed into the room, his right arm dangling, the tire iron raised in his left hand.

The first blow caught Cole in the left shoulder, the second clipped his ear. Sean had lost much of his strength and he swung the tire iron wildly. Cole kicked out Sean's feet and Sean stumbled over his father. Cole stepped across Sean's father to move in close to Sean, landing two quick jabs at Sean's face.

The tire iron clattered to the floor. Sean struggled as Cole pushed him down. Cole, knowing the boy's strength was gone, held him down, keeping his own knees together to protect himself.

"Do you know what this this was all about?" Cole asked the father, gritting his teeth with exertion. "About stopping the building of a condo?"

Sean spit a thick stream of blood and phlegm into Cole's face. Cole had a vision of driving his forehead down into Sean's visage, mashing his nose. It might kill the boy. But he drew a deep breath instead.

"It wasn't about that," said the boy's father. "It wasn't about *anything* like that." He pulled his feet up and tried to undo the knots with shaking hands. "He's crazy. He's just crazy."

Cole could just make out Sean's face in the light from the broken window. His face, bloody and bruised, seemed serene. For a moment Cole looked into Sean's eyes.

There was nothing there.

THIRTY-TWO

MARCIA LANE ANSWERED THE PHONE on the second ring. It was Friday morning, and three days had passed since the discovery of three people in the bomb shelter in the Salisbury Street home, and four bodies in Burrard Inlet. She was still finishing up the paperwork.

"Lane, Missing Persons." She listened a moment and then said, "I'll be there in twenty minutes."

When she arrived in Stanley Park, along a remote section of the sea wall, there were two dozen police and paramedics on scene. She was met by a constable who patrolled the park on horseback.

"What have we got?" she asked.

"Jogger found the body."

"Have we got an ID?"

"Nothing. No purse, no wallet. But we've got a woman, middle-aged. Heavy set."

"Show me."

They walked to where the sea wall dropped off into the rough waters below. Lane noticed a man in running clothes sitting on a rock while two uniformed officers spoke with him. The constable led her down a rocky embankment to a mound covered by a black tarp. Several officers and two paramedics stood near by.

"Looks like she's been dead for four or five days. The coroner is on his way," said one of the paramedics.

"Let's have a look."

The paramedic carefully pulled back the tarp.

"That's Beatta Nowak," said Lane. She had the woman's photo on her bulletin board from the missing person's file. "We'll have to get someone in to do a positive ID, but that's her."

"We don't have a bullet wound, not that we can see. But the coroner will look for other signs of a struggle," said the paramedic.

Lane let her gaze rove from the morbid scene before her to the span of the Lion's Gate bridge to her right, its arch hundreds of feet above the choppy waters of the Inlet.

THIRTY-THREE

BY THE FIRST DAYS OF December, winter had descended on Vancouver and its inhabitants. Rain fell steadily for a full week.

The emergency shelters in the Downtown Eastside were filled to overflowing. Denman Scott stopped to drop a few coins in a man's hat, to say a few words, and to touch the man's arm. Cole paused with him.

"That's what they need the most, connection," said Denman, limping along with the help of a wooden cane. "It may have been half a lifetime since someone touched them in a way that made them feel *human*. We don't look them in the eyes for fear of what we might see there. We don't even see them. These people are on the vanishing track right before our very eyes."

"How do you do it? How does Juliet?"

"We've gone a little crazy, a long time back. We passed through it. Now we're on the other side of crazy, and we can allow ourselves to feel love for these people as kin, and not be overwhelmed by the hopelessness that some people feel. Because there is hope. This problem is a human construct, and we can solve it."

"Not with paper tigers, like Don West's 'New Vancouver,'" spat Cole.

"Don West didn't really want to solve homelessness. He wanted to *sound* like he was going to solve homelessness. He was a stuffed shirt. Always was. Always will be."

"I hear he's going to bow out," said Cole.

"That's what I'm hearing too," said Denman.

"You think Ben Chow will run?"

"I absolutely do."

"Even after being tarred with the Lucky Strike Manifesto?"

"People have short memories. Plus, the people he needs to win the nomination for his party loved that document. They held their nose for the unpleasant talk about resettlement and applauded wildly when they read about rezoning the Downtown Eastside and sweeping the streets clean of crime. For some, homelessness still falls into that category. A crime."

"If Chow becomes mayor, we're going to be in a heap of trouble."

"Can you keep a secret?" Denman asked.

"Depends on how good it is." Cole smiled.

"It's pretty good," said Denman. "Macy Terry is going to run."

"Really?"

"Yup."

"That is *great* news."

"Will you help us?"

Cole didn't miss a beat. "Damn right."

They walked a block in silence.

"Hey," said Cole. "It seems like Juliet is doing fine. We really liked seeing her the other night at dinner."

"She *is* great," said Denman, smiling.

"So she's not going back to that Salisbury Street place?"

"She's pretty happy bunking with me, actually. She was back on the street after a few days' rest, and has really been showing her stripes as a leader on the homeless issue. The attention that came with this whole Sean thing, as tragic as it has been, has forced all levels of government to get together. She's really stepped up."

"Which is more than can be said for others."

"You mean Andrews? Well, I'm sure he's going to just love being on the Kelowna Police Force," quipped Denman. He stopped.

"So about this lunch thing . . ."

"Yeah?"

"You are up for this?"

"Oh, sure. You know me . . ."

They walked another half block and stopped outside a familiar landmark, the Golden Dragon. "After you," said Denman.

The room was nearly empty. It wasn't yet eleven in the morning. A few wait staff hustled about, preparing the spacious room for the lunch rush. One of them came to the two men and explained they weren't open until eleven-thirty, and to please come back.

"We're here to see Mr. Fu," said Denman in Mandarin.

The waiter nodded and disappeared into the back. A moment later one of Fu's bodyguards appeared and escorted them up the stairs, Denman putting his weight on his cane.

Cole looked around, searching for possible exits and trouble.

"Relax, Cole. We're not going to get rubbed out today. Not here," said Denman with a smile.

Cole said nothing. They reached the end of the hall and the bodyguard opened a set of curtains and nodded them into the room beyond.

Hoi Fu rose from a low bench. He bowed slightly to each of the men. Denman nodded in response. Cole tilted his head awkwardly. Fu stepped forward and shook their hands.

"Good of you to come, Denman. Thank you. And this must be Cole Blackwater. You're developing quite the reputation, Mr. Blackwater. I hope only half of what I have read about you is true."

"Almost none of it is," grinned Denman. "Cole uses a stunt double."

They sat and Fu looked at them. "The last time we spoke, we addressed your concerns that maybe the people who were disappearing from the Downtown Eastside had run afoul of the drug trade. As your friend Mr. Blackwater discovered, that was not the case. I am happy such a nasty piece of business was put to bed."

"Three men and two women died, Mr. Fu," said Cole, looking straight into the man's eyes. "Two more narrowly escaped death. They suffered torture at the hands of a psychopath."

"This is most unfortunate. But as you know, it had nothing to do with my legitimate business interests in the area."

Cole shrugged.

"You seem to doubt the veracity of my claims, Mr. Blackwater. Please, tell me what's on your mind."

Cole was about to speak when the bodyguard reappeared with a tea service. Fu turned to him and said in English, "Just leave it. I will honor my guests by pouring for them." Fu poured each of them a cup of tea.

Cole began, "No doubt, the guy was a psychopath. There is no direct link between his crimes and your—what did you call them? Legitimate business interests?"

Fu nodded.

"Sean has been very forthcoming about his reasons for what he did. As insane as he was, he targeted homeless people who lived in or around the Lucky Strike as some kind of attention-getting behavior. The attention he wanted, he says—as sick as it sounds—was not for him. He wanted people to look at his father's business interests in the Lucky Strike and the Downtown Eastside."

"He told you this."

"He told Nancy Webber."

"Your journalist friend."

"Yes," said Cole. "Sean said that he came up with the idea when he overheard a conversation between his father, a man named Frank Ainsworth, and a third man whose name he can't remember. What I came here to ask you is this: we don't know who the third man in the room was. It stands to reason that he was involved with the Lucky Strike Manifesto." He stopped and held Fu's eye. "Do you know if Ben Chow was in that room with Livingstone and Ainsworth?"

Fu was silent for a long while. "What difference would it make? The past is in the past. The Manifesto is over and done. The social housing it would have built is off the table. People have been shamed. The City is no further ahead than it was six months ago."

Denman spoke up. "It matters because Ben Chow is still on City Council, and he is positioning himself to challenge Don West for his party's nomination for mayor. If Chow becomes mayor after orchestrating something as underhanded as the Lucky Strike Manifesto, it will be disastrous for this city."

Fu smiled. "You are a principled man. I honor that. I do not know if Ben Chow was in that meeting. I had nothing to do whatsoever with this so-called Manifesto. I run restaurants. A grocery store. Some laundromats. That is all. Nothing more. But hear me on this: Ben Chow *is* going to be the next mayor of Vancouver. He will announce he is challenging Don West very soon. Don West is a buffoon. A grave disappointment. He will step down when Ben Chow steps forward."

"You're going to back Chow?"

"I will vote for him."

"Donate? Organize?"

"Gentlemen, please," Fu said, opening his hands. "We are having tea. This is not an inquisition, is it?"

"Let me get one thing straight," said Cole. "You can sit there and protest all you like that you are a legitimate business man, but everybody on the east side of the city knows you're dirty." Cole stood up, his hands flexing. "You're backing Ben Chow? That tells me that Chow will have to be defeated. You're looking at the guy who is going to take him down."

Fu shook his head slowly. "So sad," he said softly, "So sad. I thought that you had learned to control your temper, Mr. Blackwater. I do hope that you will come again for tea. I would very much like to continue this conversation when you have calmed down."

"I'm perfectly calm, Mr. Fu. Understand this: you back Ben Chow and I find out about it, you'll be reading about it on the front page of the *Vancouver Sun* the next day."

Cole left the room without shaking hands. Denman bowed slightly to Fu, who started to speak, but Denman shook his head and left after Cole. He caught up with him on the street.

They stood silently outside the Golden Dragon for a minute. Then Denman asked, "You okay?"

Cole exhaled a long breath. "Fine, just fine."

"You've got a way with people," said Denman. Cole looked toward the downtown office buildings, cloaked in mist.

"He had Beatta Nowak killed," said Cole. "No doubt about it. Chow was his puppet and Andrews was Chow's. I know it. He had her killed, and he used those two goons I beat up outside Nancy's place to do it. I know that, too."

"So what do you want to do about it?" Denman asked.

"We get proof. We take those goons down. We take Ben Chow down. We take Hoi Fu down."

"And just who is going to do all this taking down?" Denman asked, smiling.

"Well . . . you and me, of course. And Nancy, Juliet, Macy Terry, and a hundred others. A thousand others. But we'll start with just you and me."

EPILOGUE

JOHN DAVID EDMONDS SAT ON the park bench and surveyed the buses unloading the morning's commuters. He had been one of those once. John was the sixth of ten children. He had been born in Moncton, New Brunswick, in 1952. His father had to work two full-time jobs: six days a week, sixteen hours a day, and on Sunday he dressed in the same suit he had owned for two decades and took his burgeoning family to church. Afterward the old man would change, cut the lawn, and then disappear into the tool shed for the afternoon, where he listened to baseball on the radio and dreamed about what might have been.

Even at a young age John David knew that his father drank during those long afternoons in the shed. The term alcoholic wasn't widely accepted during the 1950s, unlike today. He was a functional drunk. The children all learned in time to avoid the shed, but sometimes trouble found them regardless of where they hid.

John David left home when he was fourteen and hitchhiked to Saint John where he sold newspapers and lied about his age. He lived in a hostel. By the time he was sixteen he'd been to jail twice and had twice been returned to his family home, where he received tremendous beatings from his father and faced the pitiful tears of his helpless mother.

After leaving home for the last time at sixteen, he never spoke with his father again. He didn't correspond with his mother for years, and then only once a year at Christmas, the first letter coming to announce that his father had died at his own hand the previous fall.

John David's big break came when he was eighteen. He had been hanging around the newsroom in the evening, bringing the reporters coffee, when a cub reporter who wrote filler for the entertainment section was hit by a car on his way into the office. The man wasn't seriously injured, but twelve column inches needed completing that night, and no one was around to fill the space. The entertainment editor knew that John David liked movies, so he asked him to write the copy on whatever film he had most recently seen. A year later the paper was helping John David through college and in 1973 he had a regular column for the entertainment section. And like his father, he was a functional drunk.

In 1978 he was offered a position with the Victoria *Times Colonist*. He and his young family moved across the country where he became the editor of the paper's entertainment section. He had big dreams, but bigger obstacles.

In 1980 he moved again, to Saskatoon, and then to Winnipeg. And Calgary.

By 1984 the pattern had become clear. The young man from Moncton, with the quick wit and the biting commentary on movies and culture of the day, performed well for the first year or two at each paper, but he soon began to disappear and would be found sleeping off a week of binge-drinking on the couch of a stranger. John David's wife left in 1989, taking their three children with her, proclaiming they deserved better. And he knew they did.

In 2001 he attended his first Alcoholics Anonymous meeting. He stayed for fifteen minutes and then walked two blocks down Eighth Avenue in Calgary and drank himself unconscious. He spent the night in the drunk tank and the next thirty days in a detox program. Then he found a job with *Fast Forward* magazine.

He flew to Toronto for his daughter's graduation from a good MBA program. She didn't know he was in the room. After the ceremony John David found a bar a few blocks away and had his first drink in two years. He woke up in the Toronto General Hospital.

His family never learned he was in the city, and when he checked out of the detox program, he caught the Greyhound and rode it straight back to Calgary. There he learned he'd been fired, and that his meager posses-sions had been sold at auction by his landlord to cover his unpaid rent.

He got back on the bus and with the last of his money rode it as far as Vancouver.

Years passed. He watched movies, ate candy and popcorn he found on the seats when the other patrons left, and twice a day attended Alcohol Anonymous meetings.

Sitting on the park bench that morning, his fifty-eighth birthday, his cell phone rang.

"Hello," he answered, his throat dry.

"John David, is that you?"

"It is. Who's this?"

"It's Deborah." His wife.

He was silent.

"John . . ."

"Is everything alright? The kids?"

"They are fine," said Deborah, in a weary tone.

"What then?"

"Your sister just called. Last week. Your mother passed away. Nobody could find you."

"Thanks . . ." he said, distracted. His eyes filled with tears as he hung up.

He caught the SkyTrain. The afternoon was dark, the sky crowded with ominous clouds that threatened rain. He found an AA meeting in the basement of the Pennsylvania Hotel. After it ended, he sat in the chair for half an hour. The man who ran the meetings asked if he was okay and John David said he was and got up and left.

It was dark and raining when he reached the street. He didn't have an umbrella so he turned up the collar on his coat and dashed down the block. It was a Friday night and light spilled from the Cambie Hotel into the rain-slick streets like a beacon. John David followed it like a moth to the flame.

He woke up without his coat or wallet behind a dumpster in Trounce Alley. He tried to stand but couldn't. He begged for money to buy food but bought a cheap bottle of vodka instead. A week passed. He slept in the alley. One night he woke from a dream about his wife and children. A gentle rain was falling on his bare head.

Somebody was softly nudging his arm. He tried to turn over and go back to sleep. His head was resting against the rough brick of a building and his movement jarred him awake. He tried to blink but his eyes felt as if they were on fire.

A tender hand rested on his arm. He blinked again and his eyes came into focus. A young woman was hunched down beside him. An orange backpack sat next to her.

"What is it?" he said.

"I'm Juliet," she said. "I'm a nurse. I work for the Health Authority. Do you need help?"

He blinked again, tears pooling in the corners of his eyes. His face felt like sandpaper had been scraped across it. "I'm an alcoholic," he said, a tear trickling down his face.

"It's okay," the woman said. "It's going to be okay. We can get you help."

WITH GRATITUDE

WRITING A NOVEL IS AN act of faith and perseverance. Many people expressed their confidence in me during the writing of *The Vanishing Track*, but none more than my wife, Jennifer. For her love and unwavering belief in me, I am deeply grateful.

My best friend, Josh Slatkoff, has been a constant support in the development of the Cole Blackwater series, and never more so than in the penning of this novel. I will never forget the day in 2006 when, running over the rocky dome of Victoria's Mount Doug, Josh and I first discussed the character of Sean Livingstone.

Frances Thorsen of Chronicles of Crime in Victoria, BC, has become so much more than just a favorite bookseller. She is a champion for my work, and I am humbled by her support. As my story editor, she has provided firm, steady guidance for the refinement of this novel, and I am grateful.

Without the support of so many other booksellers across Canada, the Cole Blackwater series would not be possible. I am grateful to all those stores that have stocked my books and continue to promote them.

My gratitude to the team at TouchWood Editions, and especially Ruth Linka. Working with a publisher who shares your vision is a deeply satisfying experience, one I wish every author could have.

In particular, my thanks goes to Lenore Hietkamp, who was the copy editor for *The Vanishing Track*. You have my gratitude, and my sympathy.

There are many people working in the Downtown Eastside of Vancouver who are doing the hard work of making the lives of the homeless better, and they have taught me much over the last six years. John Richardson, formerly of Pivot Legal Society, David Ebby of the BC Civil Liberties Association, and Judy Graves, the City of Vancouver's advocate for the homeless, stand out among them. My gratitude also to VPD Constable Jodyn Keller who provided me with the essential perspective of the on-the-ground effort of the Vancouver City Police to address the issue of homelessness.

And to Jennifer, Chris, David, Richard and Sharon: They are just a few of the many people I have met in Vancouver and Victoria whose lives have not turned out as they might have expected, who are living on the streets, who are suffering, and who have taught me so much.

STEPHEN LEGAULT IS AN AUTHOR, consultant, conservationist, and photographer who lives in Canmore, Alberta. He is the author of four other books, including the first two installments in the Cole Blackwater Mystery series, *The Cardinal Divide* and *The Darkening Archipelago*, as well as *The End of the Line*, the first book in the Durrant Wallace Mystery series. Please visit Stephen online at stephenlegault.com or follow him on Twitter at @stephenlegault.

Other books by Stephen Legault

Carry Tiger to Mountain: The Tao of Activism and Leadership (2006)

THE COLE BLACKWATER SERIES
The Cardinal Divide (2008)
The Darkening Archipelago (2010)
The Vanishing Track (2012)

THE DURRANT WALLACE SERIES
The End of the Line (2011)

For information on new books in the Cole Blackwater series, the Durrant Wallace series, or other books by Stephen Legault, visit stephenlegault.com/writing.